SENSUOUSLY

Elise almost gasped. She had never seen such crystal blue eyes. She moved forward silently as the music rose in crescendo and her heart pounded so hard she was sure he could see it beating against the thin silk of her gown.

"Elise, this is Christopher Mann," said her friend Jesse. "He's from New York and here on business with your father."

"How do you do, Miss Kendall. I'm very pleased to meet such a lovely young woman after so many dreary weeks in Mobile."

Like velvet, like liquid velvet, thought Elise. The sound of his voice excited her beyond all comprehension. It was sensuous and it filled her with desire.

Suddenly Elise felt a lump in her throat. She could feel her breasts swell as her nipples rubbed against the soft fabric of her gown and she felt her body begin to tremble. She forced herself to tear her gaze away . . .

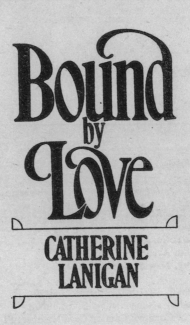

Bound by Love

CATHERINE LANIGAN

AVON
PUBLISHERS OF BARD, CAMELOT, DISCUS AND FLARE BOOKS

BOUND BY LOVE is an original publication of Avon Books. This work has never before appeared in book form.

AVON BOOKS
A division of
The Hearst Corporation
959 Eighth Avenue
New York, New York 10019

First Avon Printing, December, 1981

AVON TRADEMARK REG. U.S. PAT. OFF. AND IN OTHER COUNTRIES, MARCA REGISTRADA, HECHO EN U.S.A.

Printed in the U.S.A.

WFH 10 9 8 7 6 5 4 3 2 1

For Jan—for being there, always and ever my friend
and
For you, wherever you are. . . .

One

THE city of Mobile had begun to awaken as the sun pulled itself up from its temporary hiding place. The leaves of the oak trees that spread over St. Anne Street groaned under the weight of the heavy dew. A humid breeze moved over the city's inhabitants as they began their daily chores. The fish and vegetable peddlers had already filled their carts with garden and sea delights. During the night, banana boats had sailed into Mobile Bay and docked beside the tall steel columns that lined the piers. With aching backs, workers filled the large carriers with the tropical fruit. From the depths of the hold, the carriers rose up to the waiting wagons. The bananas were packed in boxes of straw against their long journey across the continent. Many hands of bananas had broken off, and the peddlers were quick to buy these to fill their carts. Leaving the waterfront, one banana peddler headed up Government Street to sell his wares.

Government Street was the most prestigious residential area in Mobile. It boasted the oldest mansions and the finest families. Many of these residences had been erected before the Civil War, and it was on warm days like this that their owners rejoiced in their good fortune at being in such close proximity to the bay and the cooling breezes of the gulf.

The Justin Kendall family resided in one such structure. The eldest daughter, Elise, sat on the veranda drinking steaming coffee from a fragile china cup as she contemplated the bustling activity of the household staff. She could see two laundresses in the large bricked-in area beyond the gardens behind the house, where the wash shed was located. The black women were dressed in white cotton aprons that reflected the sun's brilliant rays. There were two zinc washtubs and a large black iron kettle. The smaller of the two women was boiling the family's white cottons. After building an intense coke fire in a round charcoal burner that sat on the brick paving, she placed the kettles over it and filled them with an enormous number of table linens. Presently she erected the clothesline and poles and began to heat the flatirons. Elise knew there would be more than the usual daily assortment of linens at this time next week. The Kendalls intended to celebrate her father's birthday with a most elaborate dinner party. Elise could hear the sounds of her mother's voice as she issued orders to the maids, the cook, the gardeners, and even Elise's two sisters.

She placed her coffee cup upon the wicker table and walked into the back foyer hallway. Her riding boots clicked on the marble floor. She was just about to exit through the front door when she was approached by her mother.

"Elise, where on earth do you think you are going now?" Dorothea Kendall inquired. There was a strained and frustrated edge to her voice.

"I thought I'd ride down to the waterfront and paint for a while. I heard a stableboy say that ships from Venezuela were due in today, and I love to hear the foreigners speak. It's so exotic!" she exclaimed, as she closed her eyes and let her mind wander to that mysterious land. The sound of her mama's scolding snapped her out of her reverie.

"Not today you won't, young lady. Elise, there is too much to be done and no one in this family will be excused." Handing her daughter a small slip of paper, Dorothea said, "Take this list and please do your best to fill this order." Dorothea started to walk away, halted, and turned to face Elise.

"Oh," she said with a soft smile, "don't forget that you girls are invited to Jesse's house this afternoon for lawn tennis. I wouldn't want you to think I am turning into a general, Elise, although it must seem that way. I suppose I've been brusque in issuing so many orders to everyone."

2

"Oh, no you haven't, Mama! We all understand." Elise kissed her mother's cheek.

The walk to the poultry shops on Dauphin Street was only a few blocks, but Elise felt uneasy; a sense of foreboding replaced her earlier gay mood. The air was already oppressive, but there was something more. Elise endeavored to translate her feelings into logic, but only found herself more confused than ever.

She realized she was drawing closer to the business district, for the stench of the poultry shops suddenly pervaded the humid air. Bile rose in her throat, but she choked it down and continued with her errands. She selected a half a dozen plump hens, and while the vendor plucked them for her, she checked to make sure the order for the quail had been properly filled. Despite the heat, the streets were crammed with shoppers. Elise gazed at the stacks of crates along the sidewalk, marveling at the many varieties of poultry to be had in Mobile. She gave a little Negro boy her address and, as she pressed a small coin into his palm, asked him to deliver the chickens.

As Elise walked away, she was thankful to be rid of the noxious odors of the poultry vendor. It would take three washings with castile shampoo to rid her hair of its awful smells, for it clung to her skin like sticky tar and made her stomach churn. As the day grew warmer, her steps began to falter. When she approached the Lyric Theatre in Government Street, she paused for a moment to rest. Farther up the street she passed Barton Academy. She had graduated just last year, and now her sisters were enrolled at the academy, as were all the young ladies from the finest Mobilian families. It had an impeccable reputation now, in 1914, just as it had before the Civil War when it had been established. Luckily, it would not be far to her home now.

Within thirty minutes Elise had changed into her tennis clothes and was sitting in a white wicker rocker on her front veranda. "Lord, but it's hot," she said as she put her reed fan down on the table. "That's doing more harm than good," she mumbled to herself. "What could be keeping Jesse? She's always so slow. Probably still primping." She sighed in disgust as she drummed her fingers on the table.

She fidgeted in the chair and nervously smoothed the

3

white cotton of her tennis ensemble. Sweat formed on her upper lip, and tiny beads trickled down her back and between her breasts. She looked up into the sky. Even the trees seemed to slump in the heat, as if they could not bear to raise their limbs. Unconsciously she straightened herself in the chair.

"Sit up, Elise. Stand tall, Elise." If she had heard Mama's words once, she had heard them a million times. Elise was taller than all her friends, and Papa was convinced that since she was almost twenty and had not yet received a single proposal, she was doomed to be an old maid. The simple fact was that Elise was so preoccupied with her studies, she could not care less.

Elise had always focused most of her energies upon her studies. She couldn't remember a time when there was not an open book lying on her night table; she was an avid reader. As a child, Papa had encouraged her by purchasing her expensively bound volumes of poetry and other literature. She supposed, with a sly smile upon her face, that at the time, Papa had believed if he could keep her entertained with those books, she might spend less time climbing trees and riding horses with the young boys in the area.

Elise laughed to herself when she remembered what a tomboy she had been. And why not? She had always been taller than all the boys her age. Reckless and fearless, she fit into their daredevil games quite easily. Very often she thought that her antics would please her papa. He had no sons, and Elise knew, although he never would say, that he regretted it. She wondered now whether she had wanted to be that son for him; she knew she had made quite a poor showing as a daughter.

Many times, Papa would fly into a rage over some of her escapades, especially as she became older. By the time she was thirteen or fourteen, she finally gave in to his threats and tried to abandon her free-spirited ways. But even now there were so many times when she missed those egalitarian days of childhood. There had been no division of the sexes. It had all been so simple then. Why was everything so complicated now? None of the boys were forced by convention to change their ways. They were able to come and go as they pleased; they were al-

4

lowed to go swimming, crabbing, and fishing at the bay without their parents thinking less of them. They could be as free as the wind.

Elise stomped her foot when she thought of the injustice of it all. Why was it her misfortune to be born a woman? Men had everything they wanted! It just wasn't fair! She was just as accomplished as any of the boys she knew. In fact, she could ride better than anyone in the county. It riled her that it was expected that the girl should let the boy win any competition. It was positively degrading! No wonder she hated the prospect of marriage. It was bad enough that she couldn't play a simple card game to win—but to have one's life dominated by a man was ludicrous!

Elise wanted desperately to please both her parents. But the task was almost impossible. Mama wanted her to be a perfect young lady and, someday, a good wife to the right man. And Mama had never disguised her aims in the least! Papa, on the other hand, had recognized her high level of intelligence. Of course, he felt she had inherited that from him; Elise assumed it was true. What she could not understand was why, when she did pursue the subjects that interested her, he balked. How could she be both things to both parents? It was a doomed struggle that Elise had fought all her young life. Many times, the encumbrances of that battle weighed heavily upon her and, inevitably, she found herself on the defensive with one parent or the other. Somewhere, someplace inside her, she would find the answers, but now they seemed lost to her.

Elise smoothed the worried frown on her brow with her fingertips. Although Mama often praised her for her artistic talent, Elise knew that Mama would have been happier had she been more like Violet. Every family had its beauty, and it seemed that Violet had inherited all of Mama's traits. All the girls were adept at entertaining and knowledgeable in the daily household routines and responsiblities, but Violet excelled in them. Violet was extremely close to Mama and desired only to be the perfect wife and mother. Often Elise wondered just why she herself couldn't be happy with a similar dream. Violet loved parties and clothes, even though she needed Mama's guidance in their selection. And, of course, Violet loved the

5

attention her beauty brought to her. There were many gentlemen callers at the Kendall household, but Violet had revealed no particular preference for any one suitor. That fact had caused Papa a great deal of consternation, and he had made his feelings known to everyone in the household. It seemed to Elise that lately, if Papa was not enraged with her for something she had done, he was furious with Violet for not encouraging one of her suiters. Papa had said just a few days ago that if Violet did not show some interest soon, there would soon be no callers. So Violet had her problems too.

"But," Elise said aloud, "who has time for men? There are so many more important things to do." Lately, she seemed to be unduly restless; she found it increasingly difficult to concentrate on her Shakespeare and her archeology. And once again Papa had thrown a fit! She had wanted to enroll in private archeology classes. He said it wasn't practical, not to mention that he disliked the tutor immensely. Elise had thought it would be intriguing to discover the ancient ruins, the pyramids and the Sphinx. She admitted that the subject matter was a bit out of the ordinary, but for Elise that only increased its appeal. She conjured up visions of the cool green Nile. She imagined that she was Cleopatra, dressed in her finest silks with gold chains looped about her throat, arms, and waist. She was lying on a lush divan, drinking a glass of sweet wine and anxiously awaiting the arrival of Marc Antony. He would come to her, kiss her, hold her, caressing her shoulders, her breasts, and . . . Elise shook her head.

"What is wrong with me?" She rose and walked over to the balustrade, sat down again and leaned against a post.

She loved this house. It wasn't the grandest home in Mobile, but it was one of the loveliest; Mama had seen to that. It was a rambling white Victorian structure complete with turrets and catwalks. Almost all the windows were of leaded or etched glass. There was certainly enough room for the family of three girls, her parents, the cook, two housemaids, and, of course, Crystal.

Crystal had been born at her grandfather's mansion outside New York City. She had always taken care of Mama, and when Mama married Justin Kendall, she came along to Mobile. Neither could bear separation, for they had been together for so long. Crystal always claimed she had been the best part of Mama's dowry, and Elise did not doubt it one bit. It just wouldn't be home without Crystal's warm smile. She was just about the biggest woman Elise had ever laid eyes on, and her heart was even larger than her circumference.

Jesse and Andrew came chugging up Government Street in Andrew's new motorcar. Elise still was not too sure about these automobiles. She much preferred to ride Sandy, her mare. Papa had scolded her on numerous occasions for riding Sandy and not having the chauffeur drive her to town for her shopping. He felt it was inappropriate, considering their "place in the community." So now, she would ride only when she wanted to go to the bay and paint. As Sandy galloped the sand, Elise could feel her long red-brown hair streaming like a veil behind her. It was the only time she felt really free and in command of her own fate. Prudence made Elise keep her rides a secret, and she dutifully took the motorcar to classes.

"Elise, come on!" Jesse shouted. "Everyone is waiting for us. Andrew was late, and my daddy is going to have kittens if we don't hurry."

Elise laughed as she picked up her scarf and ran down the front steps. Jesse was always late, but she always thought it was someone else's fault. Andrew jumped out of the car to open the door for her. Andrew was a school chum of Elise's and Jesse's. He had had a mad crush on Elise two years ago around Christmastime, when Elise was growing up and Jesse was growing out.

Jessie was Elise's dearest friend. She was a year younger than Elise, petite, and now quite voluptuous. She had honey-gold hair, and her eyes were the color of sea turquoise. Elise could have been terribly jealous of Jesse, for Jesse was everything Elise wanted so desperately to be, but Elise loved Jesse too much to bicker over a boy. Andrew was nice enough, very good looking and from a fine Mobile family, but Jesse seemed more interested in him—and in boys in general—than Elise had ever been, or ever intended to be. His father was tremendously rich and had been elected for his second term to the state senate. His father's cousin, Emmett O'Neal, was the incumbent governor. Jesse's father was currently campaigning for

7

election to the United States Congress. Jesse and Andrew had a lot in common and had been inseparable since work had begun on the campaign last fall. Elise had a feeling, however, that Andrew was the persistent one.

"Mama told me to thank your parents for having this outing for us all today, Jesse," Elise said. "She just detests having us all around when she is busy with her party preparations. The chaos is too much for me, but she thrives on it and it pleases Papa, especially since it's for his birthday party. The cook has been screaming for two days about the menu, the liquor, deliveries, the ice. It's ridiculous at times. Mama is more worried about the floral arrangements and the placement of the orchestra than anything else," Elise explained.

"Is your papa still upset with you for not having an escort for the party?" Jesse asked.

"He most certainly is! When he found out from my big-mouthed sister, Violet, that I had turned down Jack Beauvais' offer, he flew into a rage. But I just don't care to marry that scoundrel, or any other man in Mobile, for that matter!" Elise found herself getting angry. But this was not something to be discussed in public, so she looked out the window, pretending to be absorbed in the countryside. She tried to put the matter from her mind, but she kept remembering that day last week when Papa had summoned her to the library.

She had been at the dressmaker's to have her final fitting of her gown for the birthday party. Madame Renaud had surveyed the seamstress's work and exploded. "It is wrong, wrong, wrong! This is not how it should be. You look like the broomstick! It will not do. The sleeves should be larger and the neckline of the underdress must be lower. And the organza should cover the entire bodice and gather into a beautiful ruffle at the throat. Ah! Such a long, lovely neck . . . much like the swan. Vraiment, you should be proud! And a French-blue ribbon tied at the midpoint of the throat. Like so!" Then she adjusted the ruffle and flounced out the leg-o'-mutton sleeves that were made of the sheerest white organza Elise had seen. As she turned to regard herself in the mirror, she blinked a few times to focus upon the reflection that met her eyes. The gown was magnificent. The underdress was pure white silk that had been cut straight across the tops of her breasts; it fit so snugly to her ribs and waist that she felt if she were to take a deep breath, the fragile fabric would split open. Two layers of silk formed a skirt that cascaded over her hips and down to the floor. An outer layer of the organza was appliquéd with lace flowers across the bottom border and the bodice. Her waist was tied in a French-blue taffeta sash that matched the ribbon around the neck ruffle. The sleeves were fitted tightly at the wrist and fastened with tiny pearl buttons. There were more of the same buttons down the back of the dress from neck to waist. She knew she was entirely encased in fabric, and yet she had never seen so much of herself revealed before.

"Why, this can't be me! Has my waist really gotten this small? And these hips and breasts, where did they come from?" she asked, dumbfounded. Madame Renaud beamed at her. "Truly it is you, child; but you are no longer the child, eh? You are a woman now, and all shall see that it is so!"

"But Madame, I am nineteen years old! Surely I would have noticed all this before now. Why, all of a sudden did this happen? I don't understand."

"It is the late bloomer that you are. Sometimes, it is not for us to question the ways of nature. It is important that it did happen, oui?" Madame Renaud said.

Elise smiled and agreed. Perhaps this was why she had felt so strange of late. There had to be some reason why she hadn't been able to eat or sleep. Lord! She couldn't remember the last good night's sleep she'd had. She had started walking in the gardens at night to cool off. Mama had said she was as fidgety as a two-year-old. Sometimes, as she lay awake in her bed, she felt as though her blood were aflame.

Madame's clucking at the seamstress roused Elise from her daydreams. She quickly stepped out of her ballgown and decided it was time to get back home.

Elise bounded up the front steps. "Hardly the picture of decorum Mama wants me to be!" she giggled to herself. As she rushed into the reception area, she tried to slow her steps before she flung back the heavy oak doors that lead to the library. She loved this room, with its scent of leather and Papa's tobacco. There were hundreds of leather-bound books in the cases that filled the walls.

Justin Kendall had his back to his eldest daughter as she entered the room. He had a grip on the mantel as he stared into the fireplace below it. He had been annoyed with Elise for months over her reluctance to entertain any serious suitors. Her rejection of Jack Beauvais was the last straw! Even his friends at the club were starting to poke fun at Justin and his wallflower daughters. True, Violet was pretty, and he couldn't understand her reluctance to accept the suitors that came to call. Sometimes he wondered if Violet merely hung back in social deference to her older sister. Once Elise was spoken for, perhaps then Violet would take a more agreeable view toward the matter. And Sadie! God! There was absolutely no hope in the world for her! The girl was far more outspoken than Elise, if that were possible. But Sadie was very young, and he had plenty of time to straighten the child out. Sadie had always been different, somehow. They were all "different." And therein lay the crux of the problem. Perhaps his preoccupation with the other two girls and their futures had occupied so much of his time that he had neglected Sadie. Maybe all she needed now was some firm guidance.

More than anything else, he wanted his daughters to marry well. A match between Jack Beauvais and Elise would be to his liking. The Beauvaises were an old Mobilian family, as were the Kendalls, and Antoine Beauvais had managed to increase the family holdings substantially. Young Beauvais was a likable person and ambitious. He would provide well for Elise.

Get a grip on yourself, Justin, he said to himself. The boy only asked to be Elise's escort, not her husband. And yet, he thought angrily, he had spoken to Elise on numerous occasions about her seeming indifference to the young gallants of the city. Well, he had had enough of her defiance. She was the eldest, and it was imperative that she marry soon. She was no raving beauty, what with those freckles and that height, but she was not unpleasant to look upon.

If she would get out of the sun and quit gallivanting around Mobile Bay on that damned horse of hers!

10

The more Justin thought about it, the more upset he became. He was barely in control of himself when Elise entered the room.

"Papa, you said you had something to discuss with me?" Elise asked quietly.

"You're damn right I do. Sit down, young woman," he raged. "Both your mother and I are tired of making excuses for you. You are nearly twenty years old, and quite frankly, your mother and I had hoped that this birthday party—on which your mother has spent so much time, energy and expense—would also celebrate a proposal for your hand. Your attitude seems quite flippant to me, young woman. And quite irresponsible! We have a good name to uphold in this community, and I for one intend for it to remain that way. If all it takes at this point is a marriage between you and Jack Beauvais, so be it," he stormed.

"But Papa, I don't love Jack, nor he me. We're just friends. I think you're making too much of this, Papa. He doesn't want to marry me. He only wanted to be my escort. I'm not romantically interested in anyone. Papa, please! I have my studies and my painting to pursue. I am only nineteen!" Elise pleaded.

"Only nineteen! My God, Elise, your mother and I had been married for two and a half years when she was nineteen and you were a year old. And not only that, she was carrying Violet at the time. It's high time we did something about this—this—situation. Two years ago you were told what lay in your future, and you have dilly-dallied long enough. From now on, you have nothing to say about the matter. This is the last conversation we shall have on the subject." With that, Justin Kendall stormed out of the library and slammed the oak doors.

Elise stood in the center of the room in shock. "He can't possibly mean that! No one can dictate to a woman who she should love. It's absurd! Do you hear me, Papa?" But she was screaming at closed doors. Willing herself not to cry, she balled her trembling hands into white-knuckled fists at her sides.

"It's so very wrong for me. . . ." Her pleas ended in a whimper that was rendered all but inaudible by the ticking of the mahogany grandfather clock.

"Elise! Are you there?"

Jesse's laughing voice brought Elise out of her unhappy reverie. No point in getting all agitated now, she thought.

"Yes, Jesse, I'm here. Just daydreaming. Let's play tennis!"

Two

As he stood gazing at the imposing white mansion before him, he lit a cigarette and leaned against a two-hundred-year-old oak tree whose branches arched half-way across Government Street. He was watching the young girl sitting with her back against a porch column.

How in the hell can she sit there and look so cool on such a hot day? he thought. She looks rather a prim sort; prim, pure, and cold. She was definitely the old-fashioned type, and not very pretty. Ordinarily, he wouldn't even look at her. He peered around the massive tree trunk, but still could not get a good look as she came down the steps and was greeted by her friends.

He stared at the blond girl in the car. Now there's a girl and more to my liking, he thought as he noted her voluptuous curves in her tight white and blue striped silk shirt and white cotton skirt. He turned back toward the house as the motorcar sped down the street.

So, this is Justin Kendall's home, he mused. Well, old man, whatever it takes to bind our "investments" and expedite matters, so be it. If it means marriage to your eldest daughter, then that is what I will have to do. It would certainly help my social status here in the South. And even in New York, the correct wife is always an asset.

Christopher had heard at the gaming tables and social clubs in town that Justin Kendall was putting most of his energies into marrying off his three eligible daughters, and without much success. Consequently, he had slowed many of his business ventures to a dead halt in order to devote time to family affairs. But now time was running

13

out and Christopher Mann needed Justin to devote his attention to the business investments at hand. Word was that if Justin could marry off his eldest daughter, Elise, he would breathe easier and get back to his cronies in the political arena.

This party tonight couldn't have been more perfectly planned if I had done it myself, Christopher thought. He knew Justin was looking forward to showing him just how hospitable the lovely city of Mobile could be.

Christopher Flynn Mann crushed out his cigarette with his highly polished black boot, pushed back his damp black hair, and sighed. God! His New York friends would never believe his thoughts at this moment were he to tell any of them of his plans. At the age of thirty-three he had established himself as a genius in the New York investment and banking houses. He had a natural instinct for the stock market. But this deal with Kendall had the highest stakes he had ever contemplated, and Christopher was playing every card he had to come out the winner. He didn't relish the idea of marriage to anyone, let alone Justin's daughter.

Christopher loved his free and easy life. He never lacked companionship, especially the female variety. There had been numerous women in his life. He particularly preferred diminutive blondes with pretty faces and plenty of what he referred to as "God's graces." The honey blonde in that red motorcar was just his style. He hoped she would appear at the evening's festivities and save it from being a total disaster.

Putting his white linen jacket over the back seat of his car, he took one last look at 1500 Government Street, started his engine, and headed out toward the bay to the little summer house that he had rented. These small southern towns had a charm all their own. They even smelled different from the towns and cities up north, he thought; perhaps it was the breezes off the bay that made the difference. Despite this loveliness, he preferred the noisy hustle of New York. Christopher pulled up in front of the little white cottage and stopped the car. He went inside and, upon viewing the gentle waves of the bay, decided to go for a swim before it was time to dress for the party that evening.

Anticipating an invigorating plunge into cold water, he

ran out the door and into the rolling waves. He immediately stood up in the shallow water. "Damn!" he muttered. "Even the bay is hot." With that he dove in again and swam out about a quarter of a mile before heading back for shore. Hauling himself out of the warm water, he lay on the sand and breathed deeply, enjoying the beauty of his surroundings. He looked along the shoreline at some of the lovely homes facing the bay and noticed a group of young people playing tennis on a lawn. He squinted his eyes to see if he recognized anyone, but it was too far away. He could make out only forms and colors. Suddenly, he saw flashes of blond hair. There were two young men and two girls. That taller one, that must be Elise. "Oh God!" he muttered. "What am I doing? I must be completely mad." As he lay back, a black scowl crossed his face and distorted his otherwise handsome features.

Three

DOROTHEA Kendall had put her all into the preparations for this party. She was aware she was known as Mobile's finest hostess, and wanted this to be the grandest, most elaborate party she had ever given. Unfortunately, the raison d'être for all the show had been pulled right out from under her: Antoine Beauvais had led Justin and herself to believe a proposal was forthcoming from Jack, and they all had assumed Jack would wait for the birthday party to ask for Elise's hands; but Elise had definitely stated that she and Jack had no such plans. Since the party was ostensibly to celebrate Justin's fiftieth birthday, they would not be embarrassed in front of their friends.

As she walked through the dining room, she thought that in the past year her daughters' unmarried status had become a topic of conversation at more and more social affairs. All her friends were discussing their own daughters' many proposals, engagements, parties, showers, and wedding plans. It did not help one bit that Violet was the only decidedly pretty child they had produced. And even so, many times it seemed that Violet did her utmost to subdue her looks. She could not understand Violet's actions, nor her unenthusiastic attitude toward the boys who came to call.

Dorothea's brows knit together when she remembered something that she had never shared with Justin. And she knew it had a lot to do with Elise's attitude toward men. As Dorothea peered into the silvered glass of a huge gilt mirror, her mind traveled back to that day eight years ago when Elise had arrived home from school quite late. Dor-

16

othea had just entered the house from the gardens with a basketful of spring flowers. Upon hearing the door open, she had spun around to see eleven-year-old Elise standing before her, her face a mass of bloody cuts and bruises. She was breathless from running and was sobbing hysterically. It took Dorothea over thirty minutes to elicit the truth from the tall, chubby girl.

"Mama! Mama! Why did they do this to me?" Elise sputtered.

"Do what, Elise? You must tell me who it was and what they did to you . . . exactly." Dorothea said, fearing the worst.

"It was . . . those boys . . . you know. I told you they always make fun of me!"

"Elise," Dorothea said, trying to calm her daughter as she wiped away the blood from a deep gash near her eye. "Please, dear. Did they beat you? Or . . . ?"

"No . . ."

"But these cuts! And your arms are all bruised!"

"They . . . they threw stones at me . . . big ones," she sobbed, and choked on her words.

"They stoned you? What in the name of God for?"

"They hate me! They all hate me because I'm so ugly and fat. They said I was lower than dirt! Mama . . ." she cried.

Dorothea took Elise into her arms and comforted her. She then led her upstairs and made her strip her clothes off so that her wounds might be bathed. As the girl stood clad only in her cotton chemise, Dorothea's rage grew until she trembled visibly: Elise's back and rib cage were marked with tiny bruises.

Dorothea spent that night caring for her child. She found herself glad that Justin was in New York on business. Not that he wouldn't have been concerned about Elise, but he might blame what had happened on her tomboyishness. He was always saying that her unfeminine behavior was going to have dire results. And now it had.

They shared dinner in Elise's room, and Dorothea read poetry to her daughter. Just as Elise climbed into bed, Dorothea leaned down to kiss her good night—and stopped abruptly as she saw the strange, determined look on the girl's face.

"What . . . what is it, Elise?" Dorothea asked.

17

"Mama," she responded intently, "never, never again will anyone ever do this to me. I'll never let anyone call me names like that. I'm not afraid, not after this. I'll show them, Mama. I swear to you, I will. I'll be the best at whatever it is I am to do with my life. But, never, never again . . ."

"Yes. Yes, dear . . ." her voice trailed. Dorothea thought it best to leave the child alone with her thoughts. She kissed Elise's cheek and quietly left her.

Dorothea blinked her eyes and came back to reality. To this day Elise had a slight scar just below her right eyebrow. But it was the invisible scars that concerned Dorothea. From that day on, there had indeed been a change in Elise. She grew up that day, but in ways that often caused her mother much concern. That incident was the well of her daughter's strength and determination, but it also was the source of her apparent apathy toward men. Still, Dorothea was enough of a romantic to hope that if the right man came along . . .

She thought of her other girls, and all she could do was throw up her hands! Lord! Neither of them even dressed with any style! Dorothea couldn't understand it. All three girls were intelligent and talented, but these were hardly feminine attributes.

She looked deeper into the gilt mirror and regarded herself. She was thirty-seven and was still referred to as "an enchanting beauty." Her hair was still a lustrous chestnut brown, and there was not a wrinkle on her face.

As for her figure, she was ample in just the right places, and even after three children, her waist was only an inch larger than it had been the day she had met Justin in New York.

Justin Kendall was the most exciting human being Dorothea Barnett had ever encountered. He was over six feet tall and had the deepest brown eyes she had ever seen. His nose was aquiline, and he had a strong jaw. But it was his full, sensuous lips that made her heart beat faster; she had actually fainted the first time he kissed her.

Although she was only sixteen when they met, she had been to Europe three times with her family and favorite friends; in England she had even been presented at court.

18

Her life in New York on Park Avenue was a full and busy one. Everyone in the Barnett family rose early in the day to meet their social and charitable obligations.

Justin had been visiting with her father to confer about some railroad business when Dorothea had burst into his law offices unannounced. As she rushed in, dressed in gray velvet trimmed with silver fox to match her hat and muff, she could only gape at him. He took one look at her clear silver-gray eyes and fell in love with her. After six months of proper courtship, he asked for her hand. Although the Kendall family was genteelly impoverished, its social position was impeccable, and Dorothea's father accepted the ambitious and personable young southerner into their family. Their lavish wedding was followed by a fairytale honeymoon in Venice.

Waking from her reverie, Dorothea found her gray eyes staring back at her from the mirror. She frowned at the reflection.

What is the matter with Elise? she thought. She can be so awkward. I hope Crystal can do something with her by tonight. Dorothea shook her head and decided it was time to return to supervising the circus this party had become. She had only a few hours to tend to the finishing touches.

The front parlor had been transformed into a ballroom. The thick India rugs had been rolled up, and the dark oak floor polished to a high mirror gleam. Over the mantel the gilt sconces held the finest pink beeswax candles. The gilt-and-crystal chandelier in the center of the room was electric. Justin had sent it to New Orleans to be specially wired and outfitted. He had not wanted to take any chances with a chandelier that had once hung at Versailles. Justin always wanted the newest and the best of everything. All other lighting in the room would be romantic candlelight. The orchestra was to set up its instruments next to the French doors that led to the terrace and gardens behind the house.

The florist had just left, and in his wake lay a beautiful assortment of white and pink roses. The ligustrum topiary trees were spaced around the ballroom; in between each pair of them were rose silk brocade Louis XVI occasional chairs, intended for the older guests who wished to watch the dancing. God forbid one of her daughters should sit even one dance on those chairs! More ligustrum topiary trees had been arranged in the dining room and on the terrace. On either side of the French doors, Dorothea had filled enormous sterling silver elevated buckets with fresh greens, baby's breath, and gardenias. The aroma was marvelous. When the appointments met with her approval, she went to the dining room to supervise the last of the floral arrangements. The enormous Louis XVI dining table had been replaced by a dozen round tables that would seat eight. Each table was skirted in watered moiré of pastel pink. Covering this skirt was a square of pure-white linen. Gold ropes swagged the lower edge of the cloth and were caught with tiny nosegays of pink roses with streamers of white piqué ribbon. Each napkin was appliquéd in Belgium lace and rested inside a Waterford crystal napkin ring. The sterling silver flatware was highly polished, as were the Waterford crystal goblets, two wineglasses and port glasses. The pink and white Haviland china glowed in the light of the setting sun. Dorothea saw that as the sun struck the prisms of the two enormous crystal chandeliers, a rainbow of color was reflected in each of the four tall gilt mirrors. It was as if she were standing amid the aurora borealis! She instructed the maids to place a silver bowl of pink and white roses on each table between the crystal candlesticks.

"On my word," she gasped as she looked out over the terrace. "No one has put the lanterns in the gardens." She ran for the door, then checked her unladylike pace. If only Elise could learn to do that, she thought.

Justin had finished checking the wines, champagnes and port; and he started up the stairs to dress. Eyeing Crystal in the reception area, he asked, "Just where have the girls been all day, Crystal?"

"Why, Mr. Justin, they been at Miss Jesse's playing tennis. Then they had to go to the dressmaker's and then they been takin' their naps. Miss Violet and Miss Sadie is already bathed. I was just about to see to their hair, right this minute, Mr. Justin. Don't worry, 'cause everythin' is goin' to be fine."

"And where, pray tell, is Elise?"

"Right here, Papa!" Elise said breathlessly as she ran in the front door.

"God almighty," he stormed. "Just look at yourself. Crystal, for the love of heaven, *do* something with her, please! And, Elise, for once in your life, walk, don't run. Do you think you can manage that?" He scowled at her and went up the stairs, shaking his head. At the top of the stairs he turned and said: "Don't forget it *is* my birthday today. See if you can please this old man this once, Elise."

Elise looked pleadingly at Crystal.

"Your papa's right, chile. Now git on up them stairs 'fore I turn y'all over my knee," she said, grinning.

Elise smiled back, hugged Crystal, and slowly, decorously mounted the staircase.

While Crystal went to see to her sisters, Elise opened her French doors to let in the evening breeze. As she peeled off her damp tennis attire, she remembered her father's words. "Lord!" she exclaimed as she flung her shoes on the floor. "He gets so upset at trivial things. He has no idea what I really want."

She gazed around her beautiful lavender and blue bedroom. She and Mama had spent months choosing the perfect damask for the walls. Across from the cream silk draperies that were tied back from the French doors were two matching French armoires. They had gold grille doors and were backed with fabric that matched the blue and cream damask of the walls. There were two bergère chairs in soft lavender velvet, and her large canopy bed was draped in a soft lavender moiré that matched the chairs. The pillows and linens were snow white, and lovely eyelet ruffles decorated the pillows that were piled on the bed.

"Well, time to get into a nice hot bath," Elise said wearily. She took a pink satin wrapper from one of the armoires and walked into the bathroom that she shared with Violet. From the room's disarray, she knew her sister had long finished her toilette.

A footed white marble tub with gold faucets stood against the south wall underneath a brilliant stained glass window. The faucets had been a real indulgence of Mama's. She had not been able to resist the impulse when she saw them in a shop on Royale Street in New Orleans.

Elise filled the tub with hot water and added half a container of lavender-scented bath salts. She went back to her room and plucked a white gardenia from the lush bouquet in the silver bowl and floated it in the bath water.

She slowly sank down into the scented water and felt all her muscles relax. As she luxuriated in the silky, hot ripples of the bath water, Elise began to sense some strange tingling in her breasts as they were buoyed in the water. She felt flushed, and her heart was pounding. She was overcome with dizziness. Quickly she sat erect and began to scrub her skin with the coarse sponge. As she rubbled her arms and legs, that same feverish excitement grew in her again.

"What is happening to me? I must be sick, I feel so hot." She splashed water all over her body and rinsed off the sweet-smelling suds. She stepped out of the tub and dried herself briskly with a fluffy towel that Crystal had left on the small stool beside the cheval mirror.

She padded over to the mirror, dropped the towel, and objectively assessed the reflection that met her eyes. Tears welled up in her eyes. Nothing about her was the fashion. Her legs were very long, even a trifle muscular. She was slim-hipped, but at least her hips were somewhat rounded in back. Her waist was small, but her friends at the academy possessed smaller ones. And worst of all, her breasts were not voluptuous like Jesse's. They were high, round, and firm. Nature had shortchanged her on many things.

She snatched up the towel and flung it at the mirror. "No wonder nobody wants me! *I* don't like me!" She was surprised at her own words, for she had been adamant about not being interested in men. She covered herself with the wrapper and peered into the mirror.

It doesn't matter! she thought. There are so many more important things in my life. Poetry. Art. Yes, my painting! Tomorrow I shall go down to the bay and paint. I have to improve my sketches of the cotton warehouses and the ships. I cannot let Papa's plans upset me. He can't manipulate my future. No one can!

When she entered her room, night had drifted over the city. From downstairs the sound of laughing voices reached her ears.

"Heavens! I haven't even dried my hair yet, and the guests are arriving!" she exclaimed.

The armoire had been opened, and her freshly pressed gown hung before her. It was even more beautiful than she had remembered. Crystal laid out her blue kid slippers, silk stockings, and underthings. Just then Violet burst into the room.

"What on earth? Why, you aren't even dressed yet! Papa is going to be even more angry with you," she said, aghast at Elise's indifference to their father's rage. Violet was dressed in a flurry of pink silk, and her brown hair was plaited and caught in a knot at the back of the neck. Even with her hair worn this severely, Violet's features were lovely, but Elise had seen Violet when she had looked more beautiful. She wondered why her sister had not put forth more effort for tonight's party.

Wearing her usual scowl, Sadie came rushing in behind Violet. She looked a younger version of Violet, but she had Mama's gray eyes. She was dressed in pale yellow, which only served to make her freckles stand out and her eyes seem dull. Elise thought of her own freckles and chided herself for being so unkind. She hoped that the lemon juice she had been putting on her face had faded them somewhat.

"Well, if you will both please leave, I promise that I will dress quickly and pray that Papa doesn't notice how late I am," she said while trying to dry her hair. "This is going to be just dreadful. The guests are arriving and I'm dripping wet!"

Crystal was a miracle worker with the curling irons and combs. She followed a picture Mme. Renaud had given Elise and created a wonderful coif with Grecian curls entwined with French-blue ribbons. Her coppery hair was her best feature, Elise mused. It was ridiculous! She had never taken such pains with her appearance before tonight. Even as late as this morning it had not seemed important. And now she was worrying over every curl. All day long she had felt as if someone were watching her; as if something momentous was going to happen. And that was impossible! She splashed herself with lavender water before Crystal helped her into her gown. As Crystal fastened the pearl buttons, Elise slid her feet into the soft kid slippers and reveled in their touch against her skin.

23

Suddenly the night felt cool, but once again Elise sensed a foreboding in the atmosphere. In an effort to shake her trepidation, she turned to check her gown in the mirror. Her breath caught in the throat when she regarded herself. Even her face seemed transformed. Everything was changing so fast. Her hair glowed in the lamplight, and her lips and cheeks were flushed a delicate pink. The greatest change had occurred in her eyes. They had seemed unremarkable before, but now they were luminous and soft. They were an indescribable blue, almost the same French blue as her hair ribbons.

"Crystal, why do my eyes look so different tonight?"

"Chile, they no different, they always looked like that. You got the same beautiful blue eyes you always had. You just finally decided to look good and hard at what's there."

"I still say something has changed, and drastically at that," she sighed.

"It shore has, honey, and if y'all don't know what it is, you shore is stupid." Crystal laughed as she shuffled her weight out of the room.

"Stupid, am I?" Elise was more confused than ever as she left the room in a soft flurry of rustling silk.

Four

ELISE ran to the staircase railing, then stopped dead in her tracks. No, she wouldn't hurry this night. She wanted desperately to make peace with Papa. She still felt that strange anticipation; she knew something portentous was about to happen.

Slowly she began her descent down the massive oak staircase. The waltz that was being played by the orchestra seemed to envelop her. She caught the warm scent of the May roses and gardenias. Mama had spared no expense this time, and even the reception area was banked with flowers. It was magnificent.

It was then that Elise saw him. He was standing at the end of the reception line, smiling at an entranced Jesse. He was very tall, even taller than Papa. He had the widest shoulders she had ever seen, and his black tuxedo fit him beautifully. She could see the muscles in his arms right through the fabric of the jacket. And she had never seen a man's trousers fit like that—every time he shifted his weight, she could see each muscle in his thighs and flanks. He was obviously enchanted with Jesse and she with him.

Jesse wore a gown with a full skirt and a neckline low enough to display her "charms" most advantageously. The fabric appeared to be spun gold, and it beautifully enhanced her golden hair. Her turquoise eyes shone with excitement. Elise had never seen Jesse look so breathtakingly beautiful, and the raven-haired stranger was taking it all in.

"Elise! Finally!" Jesse exclaimed. "I was about to come

25

see if you were all right. . . . Why, Elise, how lovely you look."

Elise smiled at Jesse without taking her eyes from the stranger. She came to the landing and stopped. He slowly turned and looked at her.

Elise almost gasped. She had never seen such crystal-blue eyes. They were liquid and shining and seemed to surround her, pulling her into them. She moved forward silently as the music rose in crescendo and her heart pounded so hard she was sure Jesse could see it beating against the thin silk of her gown. Never did she divert her gaze from those blue eyes. She could see the sunsets and sunrises of all eternity there. He held all her yesterdays and all her tomorrows captive within their depths. Then suddenly, a steel door fell over his eyes and seemed to shut off their blueness. They were a cold grey and his face was cold.

"Elise, this is Christopher Mann, who is here on business with your father. He's from New York, Elise. Isn't that exciting? Elise?" Jesse stared at her friend, wondering if she had taken ill.

"How do you do. I'm Elise Kendall."

"How do you do, Miss Kendall. I'm very pleased to meet such a lovely young woman after so many dreary weeks here in Mobile."

Like velvet, like liquid velvet, thought Elise. His voice was the most soothing sound she had ever heard. It cascaded over her, engulfing her entire being. She felt as if she had been caressed lovingly by knowing hands. In just those few words, the sound of his voice excited her beyond all comprehension and simultaneously calmed and comforted her. It was sensuous, and it filled her with desire.

He surely must talk to the angels. He could calm the seas or still the winds whenever he spoke, she thought to herself. Suddenly Elise felt a lump in her throat; her palms became clammy and that now familiar feeling deep in her stomach had returned. She could feel her breasts swell as her nipples rubbed against the soft fabric of her gown, and she felt her body begin to tremble. She forced herself to tear her gaze from his now cold eyes. She wondered how they could change so quickly. She longed to look into the sky-blue color once more, but above all she wanted to hear him speak to her. Elise glanced around and saw that her parents were beckoning to her.

"I'm sorry, I must tend to some family duties. Please be so kind as to excuse me. I hope that I'll see you later, Jesse. And you too, Mr. Mann." As she turned to walk away, she breathed a sigh of relief. She had to get control of herself. But, oh, it was so exciting to be in his presence!

Well, well, thought Christopher. She was rather insipid, and far too icy and polite for his taste. However, she wasn't as bad as his friends at the club had told him. He looked after Elise and thought that she hadn't seemed so tall to him. And he had been told that she was downright homely. This girl was not plain at all. Still, he wished it were Jesse's hand he would have to ask for and not that of Elise Kendall.

I guess my little charade of a courtship had better begin immediately or no one will believe me, he told himself. If he didn't move away from the beautiful Jesse quickly, he would have to excuse himself or it would be apparent to everyone just exactly what was on his mind. He was just beginning to leave when the call to dinner came.

The guests slowly meandered into the dining room. There were gasps of delight from everyone upon viewing the tables and arrangements of roses and gardenias. Dorothea had decided to mingle her guests a little more than usual. Everyone was wandering around the room searching for his name card. It was like a treasure hunt, thought Jesse. No husband sat at the same table with his wife, no escort with his lady.

How intriguing, and what a novel idea! The conversations this evening will be quite lively, Jesse mused.

She found herself seated next to a young man she had not met before, a Wilhelm Schmidt. He informed Jesse that he was here in the United States on a very important business matter with Mr. Kendall. Until this moment, Jesse had been enthralled with Christopher Mann. Scanning the room with her turquoise eyes, she saw Christopher assist Elise with her chair and then sit down next to her best friend.

Disappointed that she was not at Mr. Mann's table, she turned her attention to this young man who was rattling on in hesitant, somewhat accented English about his first

27

voyage to this country. Appearing to be listening, she took her napkin and placed it on her lap; then she absent-mindedly looked up into the face of Wilhelm Schmidt and was struck dumb.

Why, he could be my twin! she thought. He has the same blond hair and the same turquoise eyes. But he must be every bit of thirty-five!

He had wide shoulders that tapered to a very narrow waist. He had a square jawline, an almost too large nose, and a double row of thick, pale lashes. His eyebrows were bushy, and he wore his hair a little longer than was the mode of the day. The fact that he was tanned golden brown by the sun puzzled Jesse. He had mentioned that he was in the business of investments, as was Mr. Kendall. She wondered how he acquired such a beautiful golden skin if he worked indoors.

His narrow lips spread in a very pleasing smile, and all thoughts of Christopher Mann were banished from Jesse's mind. And for once she tossed her coquetry aside. This man was different; extremely different. She smiled warmly at him, knowing this would be an interesting evening.

Christopher settled himself in his chair and introduced himself to the others at the table. There was a Dr. Harding Kent; Mrs. Amelia Mason, the elderly grande dame of Mobile society; Antoine Beauvais and Michael Rawlings, both of whom Christopher had met at the Kendall offices; and a young matron, Mrs. Clarissa Greene. Pleasantries were exchanged as the champagne was poured, and then the birthday toasts began.

Elise sat enraptured as Christopher expounded on his travels both in America and abroad. Her eyes were glued to his face, although he barely glanced at her. She did not laugh at his jokes, but merely smiled, for she was afraid she might miss a word.

Dorothea's choice of menu was impeccable. The escargots en bouchées were followed by tomato soup with herbs. For the fish course, coulibiac of salmon was served, accompanied by Riesling d'Alsace. The main course was braised quail served with wild rice pilaf, spinach timbales, and an orange and onion salad. With this course Justin had chosen Château Ducru-Beaucaillou. For dessert there was more champagne, double chocolate

28

napoleons and espresso rum bombe. For those that so desired, an after-dinner port was served with the coffee.

Elise found she could only push the food around her plate trying to concentrate on the conversations around the table. Her entire mind was much too full of the sight and sound of Christopher for her to let anything else distract her. Suddenly, she realized that Christopher had asked her a question.

"Pardon me, sir, I'm sorry. What did you ask me?"

"I said, 'Would you be so kind as to tell me which of your sisters is which.' I went through the receiving line so quickly that I didn't catch their names," he stated. Probably because they all look alike, he thought.

"Well, at the far end of the room is Sadie, she is the youngest. She's seventeen. The boy next to her is Andrew McKinney. He's been almost a part of the family since we were children. He had no brothers or sisters and has always spent a lot of time here. I suppose that's because there are so many of us and we always have a houseful of guests and friends. Sadie is very involved in politics and is quite free-minded. I'm afraid that Sadie has listened to me on too many occasions when I may have said something I shouldn't have."

"What do you mean by that?" Christopher asked.

"Just that if I'm angry at Papa, I do have a tendency to rattle on . . ." Elise responded.

"I see," he chuckled.

"Anyway," Elise sighed and continued, "Sadie has always been idealistic. And she's very impressionable. Perhaps that's why she loves politics so much. She loves to go to fund-raising parties, and she does seem to spend a great deal of time conversing with the candidates."

"Perhaps she just likes the stimulating conversation that such occasions afford her. Intelligent people always enhance our thinking and our lives."

"I agree." Elise said, looking Christopher full in the face.

She cleared her throat and continued. "Then there is Violet, over there," she said, indicating the center of the room. "She is sitting next to Jack Beauvais."

Hearing his son's name, Antoine Beauvais cast his eyes in his direction. "My God!" he exclaimed under his breath. As he watched the girl, he saw that Violet Kendall's face shone with a rosy glow and she appeared to be breathless with excitement. He also noticed that Jack had squeezed her hand a little too long.

No, it couldn't be! But it is! he thought to himself. It was love he saw in the girl's face. Antoine vowed that he must speak to Jack quite soon, and, shaking his head, he lifted his champagne to his lips.

Christopher turned his gaze on Elise, and once again she saw that clouded look in his eyes. It was as if he were keeping something hidden. What dark secrets could he possibly have? The sound of his voice broke her thoughts.

"Miss Kendall, please may I call you Elise? Good! Elise, I was rather hoping you would honor me with a dance later this evening. Would that be possible?" Christopher asked as he realized that she was falling under his spell. His plan was working.

"Quite possible, Mr. Mann."

"Call me Christopher. I have some business to discuss with your father this evening. I know that this is a purely social gathering, but sometimes these things can't be helped. However, I intend to spend every other moment with you. You do understand, don't you?" he said, smiling at her.

"I do, yes, Christopher," she stammered, and then asked herself, What am I going to do? I can't even say his name without falling all over my tongue. It feels like a lump of cement in my mouth. She grasped the edges of her chair in order to still her trembling hands.

Justin Kendall rose and said: "Please, everyone, I would now like to invite you all to come and enjoy the music. The gardens and terrace have been opened for your pleasure. I toast you, my dear friends, for your part in making this a most delightful day for me." Justin raised his crystal glass and sipped the French champagne. Moving toward Dorothea, he took her hand and led her into the ballroom.

Christopher and Elise followed the guests to the dance floor. He took her into his strong arms and swirled her gracefully around the room. The music seemed to heighten the trance that she felt she was in. Christopher's eyes never left her face, and his muscular arms held her securely but gently. She could do nothing but gaze up at him and smile demurely. She said nothing, but she was seized by a rush of emotions and sensations.

The room was filled with a myriad of brilliant hues. The colorful gowns of the ladies were reflected in the gilt mirrors, and Elise only glimpsed rushes of pinks, sapphires, emerald greens, lilacs, and daffodils that surrounded her vision. She felt as if she were floating in the sky encircled by iridescent rainbows and whirling pinwheels. In their midst she stood with Christopher. He supported her weight against his body and would not allow her to plummet to the earth below. The air in the ballroom grew sultry, and Elise felt the silk of her gown begin to cling to her skin. Gradually, Christopher eased her toward the French doors and then waltzed her onto the veranda. Though the air was pleasantly cooler here, Elise had difficulty overcoming the feverish heat within her.

Christopher scanned the ebony skies. The stars seemed so close tonight, more like the tiny glowworms he had captured in his hands as a child when his family spent the summer at Cape Cod. He wanted to reach out now for these stars and for that long-ago place where he could become a child again.

In one movement, Christopher brought his head down and pressed his cool lips to Elise's. It was a brief kiss. He looked at her, pulled her closer to him, and brought his lips down on hers again. He pulled her so close to him that she could feel the entire length of him against her body. Her breasts were crushed to his chest, and the buttons of his jacket bit into her skin. His lips parted hers and his tongue probed her mouth. Elise could not decipher the emotions she was experiencing. Every muscle in her body had turned to jelly. Her arms were leaden. She couldn't lift them to hold him even closer, as she wanted. Her legs would surely give way in a matter of seconds. She felt the earth begin to quake beneath her feet as the heady scent of roses wafted up to fill her nostrils. Elise was breathless with ecstasy. She breathed deeper and deeper. Her breasts were heaving against his massive chest, and she wished he would hold her closer still, if that were possible.

Suddenly Christopher pulled away, gave her a black scowl, and stalked off. Elise grasped the balustrade in an effort to steady herself. The stars spun about her head, and she prayed she would not faint.

Why had he left so abruptly? What could be wrong? Nothing could be more perfect! And yet so very strange!

Her body was throbbing with a sensation she had never experienced. Had the pit of her stomach fallen away? One thing she knew for certain: No one would ever kiss her as Christopher had. If this was love's first kiss, would it always be like this?

But why isn't he here with me? What could have made him so angry?

Christopher couldn't believe it. *Good God almighty! That girl is an iceberg! She didn't move a muscle!* he exclaimed to himself as he strode through the ballroom to the punch table. He poured himself a glass of champagne and stood watching the dancers. What a prim little maiden. Certainly she had been kissed before! She *was* nineteen. God! And this was the girl he was going to marry. It was going to be worse than he had thought. But he might as well bite the bullet and make his move now. He was on a tight schedule, and there was no time for a lengthy engagement.

"Justin, I'd like to speak to you in private, if I may," Christopher said.

Five

JUSTIN led the way to the library. "Please, sit down. Would you care for some brandy? I have a fine Napoleon here, and some Havana cigars," Justin said as he offered Christopher a chair.

"Why, yes to both, thank you. You always have the finest taste in everything. Now, Justin, we have had business dealings before, but the matter I wish to discuss is entirely personal if you wouldn't consider it an intrusion at this time. I understand, with the party and your guests—"

"Certainly, Christopher," Justin cut in. "I admire you a great deal. You know that you should feel free to discuss anything with me. We have known each other long enough to dispense with any formalities. Please, go on."

"Justin, I have spent some time with your daughter this evening. I realize this may sound hasty on my part, but I am a man of quick decisions. Quite frankly, I have become enchanted."

Justin, who had his back to Christopher, spilled the brandy on the parquet table. He couldn't be serious! He must not have heard Christopher correctly. Turning, he said, "Perhaps you had better elaborate, Christopher. I don't seem to follow you."

"To put it bluntly, Justin, I would like to ask for Elise's hand in marriage. I want her to be my wife," he said.

Justin almost choked on his cigar.

"I would prefer to be merely asking for the opportunity to court her. But, Justin, as you well know I must leave for New York in a week, and then in a month I depart

33

for Europe. I don't know why I'm telling you all this, you know the details better than I. It would be a rather hurried ceremony, I'm afraid. However, I must point out that I feel most strongly about Elise and cannot possibly wait until my return from Europe, which may not be until the end of next year.

Justin was grinning widely. Last week he had about given up hope. He was not about to make Christopher wait a year. A sought-after young man like Christopher Mann didn't appear every day, and he might get to Europe and find its attractions more compelling than a commitment to his daughter. Still, Dorothea wouldn't like this at all. Only a week to prepare for a wedding. . . . Oh, he could hear her recriminations already. But he wasn't about to let Christopher get away. He knew what business Christopher had in Europe.

"What has Elise said to your proposal?" Justin asked.

"Frankly, I came to you first. I didn't want to get into any hot water about all this. I thought it best to get your approval."

"Well done, my boy, and I'll speak to Elise shortly. We can announce the engagement at midnight. How does that sound?" Justin asked the smiling Christopher.

"Fine; marvelous in fact," Christopher said. "I'll let you handle the entire matter then," Christopher said. He downed his brandy, shook Justin Kendall's hand, and left the room.

Justin felt like clapping his hands. It didn't matter whether Elise wanted this arrangement or not. He was determined that she be married. He sent word for Elise to join him in the library.

Presently he heard her soft knock at the oak doors. As he opened them to his eldest daughter, he saw she was beaming. Why, this couldn't be Elise! No wonder Christopher had asked for her hand! He was stunned by the transformation. She was radiant with an almost ethereal glow. Elise smiled at her father and kissed him on the cheek.

"You wished to see me, Papa?"

"Yes, my dear. I have something of the utmost importance to discuss with you, and it very much concerns your future. Elise, I have just spoken with Mr. Mann. Please, sit down here next to me," he said, patting the sofa beside him. "Elise, Christopher has informed me that he wishes

34

to be wed to you." He paused and awaited her reaction. Her expression revealed nothing.

"Naturally, I gave my consent. I think you will agree with me that it's a fine match. He is wealthy and influential and can care for your needs quite well. It goes without saying that he will make you a fine husband. I like him, Elise. I gave him my assurance that there will be no problem. I shall announce your engagement to him at midnight while our guests are present."

He hesitated briefly, then plunged ahead. "The only problem is that he must return to New York at the end of the week. Upon conclusion of business matters there, he will sail for Europe. Events necessitate that he remain on the Continent for almost a year." He drew in a deep breath and proceeded immediately.

"So, you see, Elise, the wedding must be next Saturday. This may appear a trifle rushed to your mind, but it's for your own benefit."

Elise was in shock. She didn't know what to say first.

"You both decided all this, without so much as consulting me? Papa, he doesn't love me! I hardly know him. I have no idea how he feels about anything. How could you so blatantly disregard my feelings? Papa! What are you trying to do to me?" As Elise's voice rose, tears welled up in her eyes and burned tiny paths down her flushed cheeks. She was confused, unsure of everything. Her world had been overturned once again by forces she couldn't control. Here was her own father evicting her from her home. She knew he had been upset with her lately, but *this* punishment was drastic. How could they conspire against her like this?

"Christopher hasn't even proposed to me, Papa! And I've always wanted a church wedding with all our friends in attendance. What about all that? The parties I'll miss! I won't even have time to have a gown made. Papa! *He doesn't love me!*" Elise was now hysterical. Her nerves had been strung like a fine wire all week. Was this what she had feared would happen? Or did she want it to happen?

"Elise, for God's sake, get ahold of yourself! I'm not sending you to the guillotine. I warned you I would take matters into my own hands. If this had been left up to you, Christopher Mann would sail for Europe without

35

you, and after a year you would maybe, just maybe, get around to thinking about him again. Well, I won't have it, do you hear? You aren't letting *this* one escape. Now go pull yourself together and make yourself presentable. In fifteen minutes I want you both in the ballroom so I can announce this marriage."

Elise ran from the room and up the stairs, and slammed the door to her room with such force that the guests below heard the noise. She sank down in the middle of the carpet and sobbed.

"You don't know what I want!" she screamed at the walls. "You don't know who I am or what I need! You are not my judge and jury, Papa!"

At this moment she herself didn't know what she really wanted, she thought. Violently, she wiped the hot tears from her cheeks.

"Why has everything changed so much in just a few short hours?"

Yet even in her misery, as she conjured up a vision of Christopher, she knew she was hopelessly drawn to him.

"I do want him! But on *my* terms, and in my own time! Why can't things slow down for me?" Her shoulders slumped with the weight of her depression.

They were to have no courtship at all. No moonlight walks or quiet suppers or even picnics by the bay. There would never be any quiet times to discover each other. The thought of the power of his kisses made her heart beat thunderously against her breast, and she believed the room was echoing the sound.

Christopher! He was waiting for her downstairs, as was Papa. She must compose herself. Above all, she didn't want anyone to think she was upset. *Upset* was hardly the word for the rage she felt at her father's robbery of her right to choose her own husband. This was 1914! It wasn't the Middle Ages! She thought things like this happened only in the novels she read. They surely didn't happen in real life.

But Christopher was real. He was handsome and strong. For the first time it dawned on her! Why would a man like Christopher, who was so wordly and sophisticated, choose her above all others after only knowing her for a few hours?

A dark web of suspicion wove its way through her mind. She felt she was the victim of some plot.

"For heaven's sake, Elise Kendall, that is absurd!" she chided herself.

She stood up, went to the mirror and pinched her cheeks to put some color back into her drained face. She opened the door and saw Christopher waiting for her at the foot of the stairs. Her destiny was sealed. He took her arm and gently led her to the ballroom. Suddenly, he stopped.

"Elise, has your father told you?" He smiled down at her. "Just to make it official, will you be my wife?" he asked.

She tilted her head back and looked into his eyes. She felt herself melting all over again. Leaning close to him she said, "Yes, Christopher, I will be your wife."

Oh, God! If only he felt the same way I do. If only he truly loved me, she thought. Maybe I do love him already. She vowed to herself she would make him happy. She would make him feel the same way she did now. He leaned over and kissed her cheek. It was just a slight brush against her skin. She trembled in his presence and began to feel that heat once again.

Justin had instructed the waiters to serve everyone a last glass of champagne. The orchestra ceased playing. With the unknowing Dorothea at his side, he addressed the room;

"My dear friends, tonight has been the fulfillment of my fondest hopes. I am most proud and happy to announce to you all the engagement of our dear daughter, Elise, to Mr. Christopher Mann of New York. A toast to the betrothed couple."

Gasps of surprise filled the air, but the guests all raised their glasses and drank to the happiness of the young couple. Justin could see that Dorothea's face had gone ashen.

"Just don't faint," he whispered to her.

She was making every effort to form a smile. The guests closest to her realized she was just as surprised as they. Dorothea gulped her champagne and stared at Elise. The musicians resumed playing, and Justin led Dorothea in a waltz. One by one, they were joined by other couples.

When the room was full once again, Dorothea looked questioningly at Justin.

"Not only that, dear wife, but the wedding will have to take place next Saturday," he said.

"Oh stop, Justin. Don't even make such a joke," Dorothea said. "I can't possibly arrange a wedding in such a short period of time. Why on earth must it be done like this? It's impossible!"

"It can and will be done. You have no choice and neither does Elise," he replied. "Christopher leaves for New York on Sunday afternoon, and the trip can't be delayed. He has business to conduct for me."

"Business! What has business to do with your daughter's wedding? Why, there is the trousseau, and the gown to be made. And flowers, music, a church, and the guests. I can think of a hundred details," she exclaimed.

"It will be a small ceremony in this room for just the family. Perhaps we could have a few friends, if you must. But that's all. I will not hear any more of it. You do the best you can in the time allowed. Now . . . I, for one, will see to the departure of our guests this evening," Justin said, and stalked off.

Dorothea stared, unblinking, after him. She turned and watched Elise with Christopher. The girl had a look of rapture on her face. Perhaps Justin was right after all. There was nothing she could do but her best to make the day as special and memorable as possible. Elise looked beautiful tonight. She still couldn't believe that just this morning she was lamenting that all her girls were wallflowers. Obviously, she had been quite mistaken.

Six

ELISE awoke to a room filled with brilliant sunshine. She yawned and stretched her arms over her head, then brushed a long lock of hair away from her face. She had been dreaming the most delicious dreams. A pair of crystal blue eyes gazed out at her from the most handsome face she had ever seen. They held her spellbound; she could speak no words. She could think of nothing save the feeling that she was sinking in their depths. Down, down she descended into his soul; and there she was held, loved and cherished. All around her were the deep melodious strains of his voice.

"Elise," he called to her. "Elise, I'm here waiting for you. Come to me, Elise." She floated foward to his outstretched arms and he held her so close, so very close; and she looked into his eyes again, and then she saw a steel door come crashing down inside them.

Elise sat up in bed. What was he hiding? Why did his eyes turn to stone? Maybe she had imagined the whole thing. But all night when she was with him, his eyes had not reassumed the clarity she had seen when she had descended the stairs. She must not have seen him correctly; it must have been a trick that her eyes had played.

She lay back again and reveled in the cool white linen of her bed. She was still tired, and the bed soothed her aching muscles. She stretched again, and thought of Christopher and the way he had held her. She ran her hand over the sheet next to her and wondered what it would be like to have him lie beside her.

She imagined her body pressed against his. Not just

her breasts, but her stomach and thighs and legs. She stirred and gave a soft moan. She remembered his kisses, and again she felt the stirring in her loins.

"Oh, my God, I don't know if I can wait a whole week. I need to see him now, this minute!

Elise edged over to the side of the bed, put her feet into her slippers, and pulled on her satin wrapper. As she began her toilette, she thought of all the details that needed her attention. She had no clothes for New York, much less for Europe. How could she ever get it all accomplished? This was not a day to dawdle. She dressed quickly and went downstairs.

The breakfast room was a large, nearly circular room. Floor to ceiling, etched panes created the effect of an enormous bay window. The room overlooked the gardens, which were resplendent with summer blooms. Elise crossed to the huntboard and served herself eggs and sausages from the covered silver casserole. There were fresh rolls and creamy butter that she was unable to resist. She put her china plate on the parquet dining table and was filling a cup with hot coffee from the small server when Dorothea entered the room.

"Elise, dear, I'm so glad you're up already. We must be at the dressmakers in less than an hour. Then we need to see the caterer, the florist—"

"Mama, please! I haven't recovered from last night! I had no idea you had so many plans. Besides, it's Sunday. How can we discuss all these things when the tradesmen are at Sunday services? And where is everyone this morning? Why is it so quiet here?"

"First, I've already phoned Madame Renaud. She was kind enough to give us this special appointment. She had informed me that she cannot create a suitable wedding gown for you on such short notice, but she has graciously consented to alter my gown for you. It's twenty years old, but it will have to do. Then there are a few basic items you'll absolutely have to purchase. Madame has promised she can garner some things you will need for your trousseau. The rest will have to be purchased in New York after your arrival. It may work out better that way, because then you'll have plenty of time to study the new fashions and order just the right things. In the meantime, Madame needs your measurements." Dorothea pulled her daughter's hand. "I hope all this meets with your approval," she said, obviously pleased with her progress this morning.

"Quite, Mama," Elise mumbled as she began buttering a second cinnamon roll.

"Elise! This is *not* the time to stuff yourself with food. I'm praying you can be squeezed into my gown. You don't need a larger waistline," Dorothea scolded.

"Yes, Mama," Elise replied, reluctantly putting the roll back on her plate. "Now what about the other appointments?"

"We have to place our orders for some simple arrangements from Mr. Randolf. Since it's to be a small affair, that shouldn't be anything too difficult, even with such short notice. And the same with the caterer, except for the cake. Justin has said we'll have a small supper on the lawn with cake and champagne for dessert. It was most difficult procuring the octet I had last night. I felt fortunate to have them. Musicians are in such demand this season. I hope you didn't have your heart set on music."

"Mama! I had my 'heart set' on a lot of things it seems I am to be denied by my papa!" Elise stormed.

"Now stop it this moment! I won't listen to it, and I won't allow you to say such things. Everyone's nerves will be strained this next week, and it won't do for you to create any more scenes than we need. Do you understand me, young lady?" Dorothea demanded.

"Yes, I do. I'm sorry Mama. You're right. It's just that so much has happened so fast. I can't comprehend everything," Elise said.

"The girls went to early services with their papa so that we could try to accomplish something here. The Beauvaises have invited us all for supper this evening. So we have all day to work on your wedding. Perhaps we can make time for you to take Sandy for a ride along the bay. That should soothe your nerves." Dorothea smiled knowingly.

"Mama! How did you know? I thought I had kept my secret well. Papa doesn't know that I still ride, does he?" Elise asked.

"I'm not sure, but I don't think he knows. I know how much the freedom means to you—perhaps you need to have that feeling today. Now, help me get these things

41

out of the way so you may have some time to yourself."

Hours later, Dorothea had finished her long list of errands and finalized all the necessary orders. And all this on a Sunday! Elise was impressed that her mother wielded so much influence with the retailers and tradespeople.

Elise sat in her lavender bergère chair and wondered if she had the strength to change into her riding habit.

"Where does Mama get all that energy? I could never keep up with her!" Elise crossed the room, opened the armoire doors, and drew out her white linen riding habit. After she dressed, she reached under her bed and withdrew her sketch pad and an assortment of watercolors, brushes, and charcoals. She placed all these items in her art satchel.

Her heels made a hollow clicking noise as she crossed the dining room floor. She stopped when she reached the French doors, then spun around to look at the spot where Papa had announced her engagement. Fury rose within her. She was incensed, not so much at Papa, but at the whole world. A world where, because she was a "mere" woman, her freedom and independence could be taken from her by the utterance of a few words from a man's lips.

She wasn't in charge of her life anymore, if ever she had been. Life's most important decisions were being made for her. At what point would she be able to to think and, most importantly, to do for herself? How many other women were in these circumstances? Would women always remain chattel?

She prayed she could live to see the change Sadie insisted would come. Perhaps her sister was right after all. How could an individual woman be happy until society recognized such inequities?

A heavy weight descended upon her as she ran past the sheds and farther on to the stable, where Sandy was kept. She couldn't wait to get to the beach. She pulled her long tresses back and tied them with a scarf. With a gentle pressure of her thighs, she urged Sandy on over the hills and onto the dirt road that eventually led her to the beach and the blue waters of Mobile Bay.

She sat straight and proud in the saddle and used only her leg muscles to direct Sandy. He sensed her every command. They had galloped down the beach for about two miles when she slowed her horse and contemplated the water.

"Just look at those colors, Sandy! Such greens and blues!"

She dismounted and took out her satchel. She sat on a large piece of driftwood and began to mix some colors. After an hour she had created perfect jades, turquoises, and indigos. Now the sky had filled with clouds and the sun was beginning to reach for the deep blue of the horizon she had just painted.

"Good Lord!" she exclaimed to herself. "I'm to be at the Beauvaises for supper! And what will Christopher say when he sees me looking such a mess!"

Her hair fell wildly about her face, and her linen riding habit was smeared with waterpaints. She tried without much success to brush off the sand that clung to the back of her skirt. When would she ever grow up? Whenever she started painting, she forgot the world and escaped to a place where no one could reach her or hurt her. She wasn't sure she had any talent, but she loved what she was doing. At least this was all hers, and these moments couldn't be stolen from her. She gathered up her things, mounted Sandy, and galloped toward the setting sun.

Christopher walked out onto the porch of his summer house and stared at the girl in white riding down the beach. He only saw her back and her magnificent long hair. He was fascinated. At first glance her tresses were black. But as the setting sun became infused with pink, lilac, and gold, her hair radiated red-gold highlights. Or was it deep auburn with brown streaks? She moved her head with grace and dignity. Each time she did so, he noted another color change. She rode regally toward the sun, and now there was a copper halo about her head. He never saw her face, but he vowed to find her.

Christopher watched her until he couldn't see anything but the sun and the clouds. He rose and went inside. Luckily, he had sent a message to the Kendall residence and wouldn't have to show himself until the wedding day itself. If there was anything Justin Kendall understood, it was the obligations of business.

The girl didn't matter. She would be busy enough with

all the wedding plans that women invariably managed to dream up. He was happy it would be a small ceremony and he wouldn't be put through the hell of a long, drawn-out affair. And after all, he needed time to contact his associates in New York. And there was this meeting tonight he must attend. He hoped his detectives would have some information for him.

Christopher crossed to the server and poured a deep bourbon and added some branch water. God! What some men would do for money! It never ceased to amaze him. He had heard that every man had his price, and he had yet to see anything to refute that.

Elise sat open-mouthed in amazement. Violet was making a spectacle of herself over Jack. Thank God there was only the family here tonight. Everyone was so busy discussing the upcoming wedding that no one paid much attention to Violet. She had her back up against a huge oak tree, and Jack was leaning over her, supporting himself with his outstretched arm against the massive trunk. He was smiling at Violet, and she was gazing at him look of rapture. Jack whispered something in her ear. Then Elise saw him place his mouth upon her sister's lips. It seemed an eternity before they parted. They must have felt they were hidden from view—or, worse, they just didn't care.

Elise looked around and realized that no one else had witnessed the indiscretion. She glanced back only to find that the couple had disappeared. Didn't Violet know of Jack's reputation? Why, he was practically notorious with the young ladies of Mobile.

Elise worried more about Violet as she thought about it. They had been gone for over half an hour. Elise was just about to go look for them, no matter how embarrassing a situation she found them in, when they came strolling toward her through the garden.

Now she had the second shock of the day. She had observed Jack Beauvais' tactics for years, but the look on his face and the way he tended to Violet—as if she were the master and he the slave—meant only one thing. Jack was truly in love with Violet. How could she have missed it before this?

Jack took Violet's arm, and they strolled over to where

Justin and Dorothea were seated. Jack said something to Justin, who jumped up abruptly and kissed Violet soundly on the cheek and began to shake Jack's hand. Dorothea was obviously beside herself with happiness, for she was crying and smiling at the same time.

It finally dawned on Elise that now she was not the only one in the Kendall household who was engaged. She rose to go to Violet and offer her congratulations. She wished with all her heart that Christopher were with her now. *Business!* How she had grown to hate the word!

Crystal shuffled into Elise's bedroom and quietly tied back the silk draperies. Crystal thought that this should have been a sunny day, a glorious day. Instead it was gray and dreary. She looked at Elise's sleeping form.

"Poor child. That man of hers ain't hardly showed his face all week!" she muttered.

Christopher had neglected Elise during this period, which should have been festive and gay for the bride-to-be. The Kendalls had declined all invitations for dinner parties, and Elise had attended only afternoon luncheons given in her honor by her mother's closest friends, since Christopher's presence would not be required at such affairs.

She had not complained to anyone about his obvious absence, but Crystal had noticed her sad eyes and her restlessness. She hadn't eaten a thing for days, and Crystal was frankly surprised to find the girl asleep now.

Crystal went to the bed and softly nudged Elise. "Wake up, Sugar. It's your big day. Come on, now. I brought you some fine breakfast. There's hot coffee and rolls my baby loves so much. Miss Elise, wake up."

"Good morning, Crystal. I'm awake. What time is it?"

"Why, it's almost ten o'clock! You must be plumb weary. I heard all that pacin' you was doin' last night. I saw you in the garden 'bout midnight. And I didn't see no shawl on you, neither. What you want to catch your death o' cold for?"

"I'm all right, Crystal. Don't worry. I just couldn't sleep. That's been happening a lot lately. I guess I've got prewedding jitters," Elise lied.

She wasn't jittery. She was terrified! In a very few hours she would marry a man she had been with for only

45

six hours. She must surely be insane! But then none of this had been her decision. It was Papa who had made the choices for her. And Christopher would guide her destiny. She felt as if she were a pawn for the both of them. At the moment, she saw no escape. She felt like a trapped animal. How good it must be to be the master of one's own fate!

Crystal went into the bathroom to draw Elise's bath water. Elise sat down to her favorite breakfast, but found she couldn't swallow the buttery croissants. The lump in her throat wouldn't allow it. She did drink the steaming, sweet café au lait. Crystal had obviously asked the cook to prepare the coffee in the New Orleans fashion. It was thick and blended with chicory, and Elise loved it. She was the only one in the household who preferred her coffee this way. Elise appreciated the thought that went into Crystal's gesture.

The scent of lavender bath salts filled both the bedroom and bathroom. Elise padded across the carpet to look at her wedding gown in her armoire. Madame Renaud must have spent some late hours getting it ready. It was simple in style and of heavy white satin. Elise lifted a slender sleeve and realized this was a winter gown. She would suffocate in the heat, humidity, and heavy satin!

The veil consisted of yards of French silk illusion fastened to a small cap of satin that was encrusted with seed pearls. The gown was so stark that the only parts of her anatomy that wouldn't be covered by the white material would be her face and hands! She didn't have time to examine it further, for Crystal was scolding her again.

"Git in here this minute, Miss Elise, or I'll bat your bottom," she said.

"I'm coming," Elise sighed. She sank into the hot, lavender-scented water. Giggling, she ducked her head under the water and splashed around as if she were a child. Laughter always seemed to ease her tension. She shampooed her hair, and Crystal rinsed it for her. After soaking for a few minutes and scrubbing her skin until it was rosy and tingling, Elise rose from the tub, dried off, and put on her wrapper. She sat at her dressing table and began to towel-dry her hair. Crystal combed and brushed it until it was dry and shone with coppery highlights.

As Crystal was curling Elise's hair, Dorothea swished

46

into the room with a note for her daughter. Dorothea kissed her on the cheek and sat in one of the bergère chairs.

"It's from Mr. Mann, isn't it, dear?"

"Yes, Mama." Elise opened the note. It merely stated that their train was scheduled to depart at noon on Sunday. At the bottom were Christopher's initials.

Elise glared at her reflection in the mirror, and the rage built within her. How cruel he could be! He had abandoned her all week; and now, when she hoped to receive an apology from him, or at least a few kind words, he had sent this.

"It's our departure schedule, Mama," Elise sighed, and quickly changed the subject. "Now, how are the preparations coming?"

"My dear, I'm amazed. I guess it is because so much that we used last Saturday can be utilized again for the wedding. We can't set up tables on the lawn and terrace because of the weather. We'll have to serve buffet, which will be much easier. Most of the greenery is still fresh, and the florist has added new white roses. The fireplace has been banked with palms and calla lilies. Oh! I almost forgot! Violet will bring up the lilies for you to carry. I came to give you the blue handkerchief I carried on my wedding day, dear, and here's a new penny for your shoe. This is from your papa," she said as she handed Elise a large square box. "It is to be the 'something new' you need to complete the tradition," Dorothea said.

Elise opened the box and peered at a necklace of the most beautiful blue stones she had ever seen.

"What are they, Mama?"

"Blue diamonds, dear. Aren't they lovely?"

There was a gold chain with five large stones placed symmetrically at the base of the thin chain. The two largest stones in the box were for her ears. They were beautiful in their simple settings and flashed blue color from every direction.

"Papa wanted a stone to match your eyes, Elise. On such short notice, this was all the jeweler could find. I hope they please you," Dorothea replied.

"Of course they do, Mama. But why didn't Papa give them to me himself?"

"Your father had to meet with Christopher on business.

47

With so many preparations and the wedding in three hours, he just didn't have the time." Dorothea was well aware of her daughter's disappointment, and knew no explanation of hers could ease the pain of his oversight.

"I understand fully about business!" Elise almost spit the words out as Dorothea rose.

"I must get dressed myself," Dorothea responded. "Your father will be here to walk you to the altar at three o'clock. Your sisters are receiving their baskets of flowers and petals now from the florist. I think everything is moving along fine in spite of the rain. Crystal and I have been up since five this morning."

"Oh, Mama! I'm so sorry! I haven't thanked you for all you've done. You have worked so hard and I've been selfish and uncooperative. I should have done more to help. Mama, please forgive me," Elise pleaded.

"There's nothing to forgive. You've handled yourself like the sophisticated young woman I knew you would grow to be. I thought you were marvelous at the homes of our friends without your fiancé's support. You've had a lot on your mind, too. My problems were nothing in comparison to yours. I pray that you will be happy, Elise." Dorothea hugged her daughter and fled the room, her eyes filled with tears.

The rain beat violently against the glass panes of the French doors. Elise could barely make out the forms of the wedding guests as they rushed into the house to escape the torrents of rain. She could hear the musicians playing softly downstairs. And she had been so sure there would not be any music for her wedding. She should never have doubted Mama's capabilities.

She walked over to Crystal, who was ready to help her dress. It took both women over a quarter of an hour to button the pearl buttons that ran up the front of the gown from the tiny mandarin collar to the floor.

The gown fit her form very snugly. It made her waist look small, but enhanced little else. The fabric stretched tightly across the shoulders and didn't fit properly over her breasts or hips. She had to kneel so that Crystal could attach the combs and pins that would secure her cap and veil. She pulled the shortest layer of illusion over her face. Crystal handed her the calla lilies, which were tied with long taffeta streamers reaching almost to her knees.

Violet and Sadie, all giggles and smiles, entered the room.

"You look lovely, Elise," Sadie said.

"I look a sight, Sadie, and you know it. Surely Mama was beautiful on her wedding day, but I am far from it. I guess there is nothing to be done about it now," Elise said dejectedly.

Justin Kendall tapped on the door and peeked in.

"Girls, it's time. The guests are seated and Reverend Preston has arrived."

Sadie, followed by Violet, started the procession down the stairs. Violet was dressed in a beautiful gown of palest apricot organza and silk. Now that her engagement had been announced, Violet was like a summer rose awakening to its full beauty. It was as though she had been playacting. She and Jack had gone to great lengths to create the illusion of the wallflower and the rogue. How could she have fooled her family for so long? Elise then realized how truly loving her sister had been. Violet had purposefully not taken the initiative in regard to her own marital plans, because she had wanted Elise's future to be secure before she made any commitments of her own.

It appeared to Elise that everyone in the family had their own secrets and interests. Sometimes she thought that the only interaction they had was at supper every night. She often went all day without laying eyes on Violet or Sadie.

Sadie! What secrets was she keeping? Elise knew that Sadie's ideals were based on her own beliefs, but she worried that Sadie had embraced them a bit too intently, fearing the girl could be hurt someday when reality inevitably would invade her romantic notions of justice and equality for women.

Sadie looked so young and innocent in her aqua gown. Elise realized that she knew her sisters hardly at all. They had all changed. Elise had always thought of her sisters as children. But those days were blown away on the winds of time. They could never return, no matter how much she wanted them to.

At the base of the stairs each girl began strewing white rose petals on the white marble floor. The main salon had been transformed into a small chapel. The guests were

49

seated on the rose Louis XVI chairs. Garlands of greenery created an aisle effect along the rows of chairs, and tall candelabra stood at the end of each row. Flickering white candles dispelled some of the gloom created by the rainstorm. Outside it was black as night, and an ominous feeling pervaded the room.

Justin and Elise descended the stairs arm in arm, and they too entered the "chapel."

"It's so beautiful," Elise whispered to her papa. "I don't mind at all that I couldn't have my wedding in a church."

Justin smiled and moved ahead with the music. At the fireplace Reverend Preston stood with Christopher.

"Why, he is more breathtaking than the bride!" she thought ruefully.

She left her father's side and stood next to Christopher. Once she had uttered each of the words she spoke over the next twenty minutes, Elise could remember barely any of them. At one point, Christopher placed a band of diamonds on her finger. More phrases were intoned by Reverend Preston. She said "I will," and Christopher said something similar. She was truly conscious only of Christopher's presence. When her arm brushed his, her skin began to tingle.

"You may kiss your bride," Reverend Preston said.

Christopher turned to her, lifted her veil, and placed a soft, swift kiss on her cheek. They turned and walked out of the "chapel" to stand in the reception area at the base of the staircase.

Was that it? It was all so quick! Elise wondered if it were legal! And he hadn't even kissed her lips. All week she had anticipated his kiss. She felt cheated.

Elise stood next to Christopher and greeted their guests. There were only a hundred people, but by the time they all passed through the line, she felt there could have been a thousand. Her face ached from smiling. She had no *reason* to smile; she wanted only to run and hide. No, she wanted to scream at her Papa; but mostly, she wanted to beat her fists against Christopher's chest. She wanted to hurt everyone who had ever hurt her.

The photographer took pictures of the wedding couple. Then the cake had to be cut and the gifts opened, since they were leaving for New York in the morning. All these traditional trivialities were giving Elise a headache.

The buffet supper was simple, but elegant. Mama had chosen oysters on the half shell, crabmeat mornay and consommé royale for the fish course and appetizers. There was canard à l'orange, boeuf en croûte, and a pheasant. There were several vegetables and, of course, ample champagne for all. For dessert everyone would share the wedding cake, and a small piece of cake in a tiny velvet-lined basket would be presented to each female guest as she departed.

As the guests formed the buffet line, Justin pulled Christopher aside.

"Well, I just wanted to offer my congratulations, my boy. You have made me a most happy man. Yes, indeed. This has indeed been a landmark week for the Kendalls," Justin said almost gleefully. For a moment Christopher thought his mood indicated an overindulgence in champagne.

"What do you mean 'a landmark week'?" Christopher asked him.

"You must be joking. Elise has married you, and young Jack Beauvais asked our permission to marry Violet. I don't mind telling you, that one really surprised me. Seems the two of them have been enamored of each other for some time now, but Violet refused to marry until Elise was spoken for. They intend to marry in September before Jack leaves for Harvard. Dorothea says she can't believe the difference in Violet. She's been pensive and secretive for so many years. Ha! Now we all know the reason, eh?" Justin chuckled

"I can hardly believe it myself, Justin," Christopher replied. "As you said, 'a landmark week.' "

Justin had almost started to go when he said: "By the way, I didn't think you'd mind if I stepped up the tempo of some of our business matters. I think things can be expedited now. I've wired a quarter of a million dollars to my associates in New York. The rest of the investors will have sent equal amounts. Does this meet with your approval?" he asked.

"Yes, yes of course" Christopher said as Justin walked away. He couldn't believe it! He had not needed to marry her after all. Just look at her! She couldn't even fill out the dress she was wearing, and that veil was absurd. Her hair was pulled away from her face so he could barely even make out its color.

Elise was speaking to Jesse. God! She served to remind him of all the womanly delights he had just closed the door upon. Or had he? Certainly he could not approach Jesse; that avenue was closed forever. And witnessing the manner in which Jesse clung to the arm of Wilhelm Schmidt, Jesse probably wouldn't have been interested anyway. Jesse seemed spellbound by the good-looking German.

Once Christopher was in New York, there would be plenty of women who would happily ignore the fact that he had acquired a wife. The more he thought about his situation, the better he felt about it. Perhaps he should thank Elise. Now he wouldn't be hounded by New York matrons trying to marry off their ugly daughters. By God! He could have the best of both worlds.

He walked back to the bridal table and sat down next to Elise. She had her head turned and was talking to her sister Violet. A scowl crossed his face. After seeing her again, he felt sick. No matter how he tried to rationalize the entire matter, what he was doing was wrong—wrong for both of them. A loveless marriage was never right. Thinking of the long night ahead of him, Christopher decided he needed more than a single glass of champagne.

Seven

ELISE turned the brass handle on the door to her bedroom for what might be the last time, and her eyes misted with tears. Wearily she made her way to the bergère chair and slumped into it. After a few minutes, she lifted her hand to her neck and began to unbutton her sweat-soaked gown. Her fingers were aching by the time she was able to peel it away from her body.

After stripping off her silk stockings and undergarments, she walked to the bathroom to fill the tub. The sound of the rushing water drowned out the strains of the sobs she could no longer stifle. Elise sat in the tub until the water had turned cold.

Although her body felt refreshed, her soul was still weighted with despair. She dried herself with a large soft towel as she walked to the mirror. Her face was swollen from tears, so she splashed it with cold water.

She thought of Christopher and his attitude toward her. He hadn't even looked at her all afternoon, and during the supper he had conversed almost solely with Papa. She couldn't remember him smiling once. Elise had been frightened by the anger and frustration she had sensed in him. What had Papa said to him to make Christopher so furious?

"Papa, oh, Papa! How could you do this to me?" she sighed.

If Christopher had been oblivious of her presence all day, Papa had been more so. In her worst nightmares she had never dreamed that Papa could be so distant. He had no loving words for her. It was as if he were eager for her to leave his home. She had always thought that the father of the bride would have wanted to set aside a special time for himself and his daughter to speak of memorable times. She had wanted Papa to hold her and tell her she would always be his little girl. Wasn't that what was supposed to happen?

Damn him! she thought. He even sent Mama with my wedding jewels.

Every childhood dream of her wedding day was now shattered. Nothing was as it should have been. Mama had done her utmost, but Elise was not blind. She hadn't been a beautiful bride; she had appeared dull and ordinary in her mother's ill-fitting gown. The only good thing she could say about her ensemble was that the veil covered her entire face exquisitely. By the time supper had been served, she was so hurt by Christopher's moodiness that she herself hadn't smiled or in any way resembled the "happy bride" the guests had expected.

She looked in the mirror and saw that her eyes were no longer red, only slightly puffy.

"That will just have to do! I don't care about anything!" she muttered.

It didn't matter, because no one would see her anyway. When she opened her armoire she saw four beautiful gowns and peignoirs. They were incredibly delicate—turquoise crepe de chine, cream-colored lace, a French-blue chiffon, and pale salmon silk.

"Why, this must be my trousseau! Mama said that Madame Renaud had sent some things for me!" she exclaimed elatedly.

Glancing at the bed, Elise was surprised to see an exquisite lavender negligee on the coverlet. She picked it up and caressed the soft, sheer silk. She wondered if it were not a little too sheer, as she could see her hand through the four layers of silk. She could hardly imagine herself in such a daring creation.

The sleeveless gown was cut straight across the breasts and had tiny braided gold straps. As Elise slipped it over her head, she marveled at the sensuous touch. She adored it. The matching peignoir fit more like a cape than a robe. It had no buttons and was completely open in the front, leaving only one layer of sheer silk across her breasts. Elise wondered where Madame had found such a gown.

Then, she noticed a small white card resting on the pillow. It read:

Elise, dear, Madame Renaud regrets she had no white negligee and peignoir for your wedding night. This was the finest of her French lingerie. I hope that you are not too terribly disappointed. Because it was your favorite color, I did not think you would mind.

Lovingly,
Mama

Elise didn't mind at all. It was the finest thing she had ever owned. She pulled the pins from the tight bun that held her hair in a knot at the back of her head and let it cascade down her back. As she began to brush it vigorously, she thought of how wasted the effort was. Christopher was too busy talking business with Papa to see her at all.

Christopher! Would he come to her tonight? He didn't mention anything about his spending the night in the Kendall home. In fact her wedding night hadn't entered her own thoughts until this moment. She had been so hurt by Papa's and Christopher's abandonment of her all week that she hadn't consciously thought of Christopher taking his "conjugal rights," as they called it.

"God! Even lovemaking sounds like vassalage!" she cried. "I can't stand it! I'm too tired now even to care."

She turned out the light and opened the doors to let in the fresh air she hoped would clear her mind. Perhaps she could sleep better then. She stayed in the doorway, absentmindedly continuing to brush her hair as she enjoyed the silky night air caressing her soft skin.

Christopher reluctantly mounted the stairs, desperately hoping to think of some excuse he could give Elise. He could say he still had some packing to do.

"No, that wouldn't work either. Much too flimsy. She could see through that one for sure," he said to himself with his thickened tongue. "Too much brandy, old man," he chided himself.

The last thing he wanted was to spend the night with this frigid, awkward girl. He stopped midway up the stairs and turned to go back. All he wanted was to flee

55

from this house and this asinine situation he had placed himself in. He was a fool! If he had only waited instead of plunging into this farce of a marriage. But now, Justin was sure to push forward with his business plans. There was a renewed forcefulness to Justin's statements this evening. On second thought, Christopher guessed it was for the best. And there was no way out of it.

"Oh, hell!" he said when he remembered Justin's hints to him that he had better see to his bride. He could only hope she was asleep by now; she had appeared bone weary to him when her mother had sent her upstairs hours ago.

Christopher reached the door and gently turned the knob. He peered in, and his breath caught in his throat. He shook his head in an effort to clear his brain and focus his eyes. He must have had more to drink than he remembered.

The room was aglow with the green-silver light of the moon. She was standing at the open French doors with the night breezes washing over her body. The gown she wore fluttered, and created an aura of lavender about her. Through the sheer fabric he could see the most incredibly beautiful legs he had ever laid eyes on. They were quite long, and perfectly formed. Her stomach was flat and her waist was almost small enough to be encircled with his hands. Gently, she raised her delicate arm to smooth her long tresses away from her face.

Her hair! It shimmered red and gold and brown in the bright moonlight. He was right.

It's her! he thought as he choked down the lump in his throat. I've found you.

But that was impossible! This was Elise's room, wasn't it? Maybe he had come to the wrong room and this was one of the wedding guests. Whoever this was, he was sure it was the girl he had seen on the beach earlier that week. Yes, he was certain of it. Her proud body and that gorgeous hair proved it.

She tensed, sensing his presence in the room. She turned toward him silently, and he came to her. Her eyes were wet with tears. He gazed into their unfathomable depths. Her high cheekbones began to color, and her soft, moist lips trembled. He took her face in his hands and gently covered her mouth with his. Before the illusion vanished, he wanted to taste its sweetness. He encircled his arms about her to the small of her back and pulled her body close into him. He slipped the peignoir from her shoulders and moved his mouth down the length of her throat onto her shoulders. His hands grasped her waist tightly as she let her head fall back. His hands moved upward to her breasts and cupped them gently. The straps of her gown slipped to her shoulders, and suddenly the gown lay at her feet.

He gasped at her beauty. The blood in his veins pulsated, and he felt his manhood straining against the fabric of his trousers. He could feel her heart beating against his chest. She wanted him as desperately as he wanted her. He lifted her off the floor and carried her in his strong arms to the bed. Gently he laid her upon it, and her eyes seemed to smolder with desire and need.

Quickly, he removed his clothes. Lying next to her, he ran his hands over her marvelous legs. Her skin was smooth as velvet. Elise quivered beneath his practiced touch. Her nipples began to harden as he caressed her stomach, and he heard her gasp as he reached her silky mound. Ultimately, he found the essence of her being, and she moaned softly into his ear. He brought his lips to her breast and reveled in the honey taste. He continued to caress and tease her until he could no longer withstand the wait. Gently, he parted her thighs and moved over her. Cautiously, he entered her and began slow, measured thrusts. Stroking her with himself, he met the barrier of her maidenhead and gave a quick thrust. He smothered her soft cry of pain with his mouth.

"It will be better now, I promise you. I will make you mad with pleasure," he whispered into her ear.

His thrusts quickened their pace now, and she began to move beneath him. Her hips tilted to meet him, and he drove ever deeper into her softness. His heart pounded in his chest, and his breath came quickly. Both their bodies were soaked with sweat. He was reaching the pinnacle, and as she moaned softly, he could no longer control himself. He felt as though he were being whirled into the outer reaches of the galaxy.

He felt his muscles relax, and he kissed her lips tenderly. He rolled over onto his side. He stared down into the limpid pools of her eyes. Her beautiful hair was damp around her cheeks, and he brushed the locks away with his fingertips. He kissed her eyelids, her ears; he moved his lips to hers. His tongue found hers, and he felt himself begin to stir again. He would never get enough of her.

But she had barely responded to him. Not once had she reached up her arms to clutch at his hair or to grasp his arms. She had never really held him. He would give anything to excite her as much as she had thrilled him. The brandy had finally cleared the haze from his brain. As he focused on her face, he realized just what he had done.

"My God! Elise, it's you!" he mumbled almost silently in shock. He had not consciously or clearly put the two women together. How could the mousy prude he had married be one and the same as this beautiful and sensuous woman from the beach? But they *were* the same. It was incredible! He knew what he was seeing and still he couldn't believe it. Elise was a mystery.

"What were you saying, Christopher? I didn't hear you," she said faintly.

"Nothing, Elise. I . . . I didn't hurt you, did I? It wasn't too painful for you?" he asked tenderly.

"No, it's all right, Christopher," she said and she rolled on her side and began to weep silently. He quickly fell asleep. His breath became measured and deep.

Elise stared into the black space surrounding her. She was still on fire; she was afraid to move. All these past weeks her body was responding to nature's intent for her as a woman, and she hadn't known what was in store for her. In her wildest imaginings she never thought anything could be so deliriously wonderful. She chided herself for not reaching out for him, but the fact was that she just couldn't. She had never experienced such physical pleasure or an emotion so intense and exquisite.

She had been afraid that if she moved, she might break the spell and make the feeling disappear. Every nerve in her body was experiencing the ultimate in pleasure. Her body had felt like lead one minute, and then she had begun to float through the air. But it was at the moment he spoke into her ear that she had utterly lost control. Even his voice made love to her. As before, it excited her body and made it burn with passion and longing. But it was more than that—something more significant. It entered her soul and held it captive. No other man in the world would make love to both her body and soul as Christopher had.

Thinking of that moment once again, she could see the white lights behind her eyelids. She had best stop! She couldn't stop, though; she never could.

Her mood changed as she wondered if she had pleased him. Her insecurities rose to the surface once again as she realized how horribly inexperienced she was. She had no knowledge of love's workings, and she believed she was ugly and inadequate in his eyes. She would never be enough for a worldly man like Christopher.

Oh, God! Make him love me. Someday, I vow, Christopher will love me. I must make him need me as much as I need him. I'll do everything to make you happy, Christopher. I'll love you and cherish you. These are my wedding vows to you. Is this the way it is for all true lovers? Is it always this painful and yet still wonderful at the same time?

Elise wept bittersweet tears throughout the night as she lay beside the slumbering man.

Eight

ELISE awoke to find that the space beside her was cold and unoccupied. Christopher must have been gone for quite some time.

"Why would he leave?" she wondered aloud, fearing she had displeased him in some way. At the tapping on the door, Elise sat up in bed.

"Yes, who is it?"

"It's me, Miss Elise. I came to get you ready for the trip," Crystal replied through the door.

"Come in, Crystal," Elise said as she got out of bed. Surprised to find herself naked, she quickly slipped her peignoir over her body.

"I'll start my bath myself if you'll lay out my suit and pack the last of my things. Oh! Crystal, did Mr. Mann have his breakfast yet?" she asked, still wondering when he had left her side.

"Shore did, Miss, Elise. Hours ago. He said he had things that needed tendin'," Crystal chuckled. "He shore is a purty one, Miss Elise. And real nice, too. You got a fine husband, child."

"Yes, a fine husband," Elise sighed. But will he ever be a real husband to me? she whispered to herself.

After bathing and dressing her hair, Elise spied the suit hanging in the armoire. Here was her honeymoon suit! She hadn't even asked Christopher if they were to have a real honeymoon. She assumed they would consider his business trip to Europe as one. But now perhaps he would want to leave her in New York.

Looking back at the suit, she felt a sadness and empti-

60

ness at leaving. This was her home. Everything she had ever known was here, her family and friends. . . . She looked around her. Her room! This had been her refuge when she had felt lonely, angry, and, on occasion, happy. These walls had known her every thought and all her dreams.

And she was leaving Mobile, too.

And there was the bay! All the painting she had done there. And Sandy! She thought of her late-night rides along the beach. She was leaving her girlhood, and she felt as if she were sliding into a deep black hole. Tears streamed down her cheeks, and deep sobs caught in her throat.

She was leaving with a man who didn't love her or need her. She didn't know why he had married her. She didn't know where she was going or if she would ever see her home again.

Her trembling hand pulled the light-blue linen skirt over her head. She fastened the gold buttons of the blue silk blouse and tied a bow under her chin with the matching scarf. The short linen bolero had gold braid around the neckline, the lapels, hem, and cuffs. It was very smart, and she wished she could hold Mama and thank her.

"Oh, God! Make this pain go away!" she prayed.

Elise entered the empty breakfast room and decided she couldn't eat anyway. She decided to search out her parents and bid them good-bye. Just then, Dorothea rushed into the room.

"Oh! Elise. There you are, dear. My! Doesn't that suit look lovely on you. It certainly enhances your figure more than my moth-eaten wedding gown, doesn't it?" Dorothea said in a strained voice. She saw the stricken look on Elise's face. "I'm sorry, dear. I didn't mean to sound cruel. It's just that you look so pretty in your new suit. Now, Elise, you must come and make sure that Crystal and I have packed all your things. I have a note here for you from Madame Renaud, and some notes from your friends. Put them in your purse and read them on the train." Dorothea looked fondly at Elise.

"Oh, Mama! I can't leave!" Elise cried as she burst into tears again.

Dorothea thought her heart would break at bidding her firstborn child good-bye for God only knew how long.

61

No mention had been made of their ultimate destination, nor had Christopher said where they would set up permanent residence. Her sense of loss was excruciating. She ran to her child and embraced her.

"Elise, you must be calm. We'll go together to the veranda, where everyone is waiting to say good-bye. I'll miss you, but your life is with your husband now. You must always remember that."

"I know, Mama, I know," Elise sobbed, and wiped away her tears.

"Your trunk and suitcases have been sent ahead. We are running late. Say your good-byes, Elise," Christopher said.

Elise looked at him standing next to the running car. He was a tower of self-assurance. And he was impatient for her to get this all over with. She reluctantly kissed her father, and then hugged Violet and Sadie. When she reached for Crystal, the large woman grabbed her and held her to her enormous bosom.

"Be happy, chile," Crystal sobbed.

Elise looked at Dorothea and merely said: "I love you, Mama."

Christopher watched Elise bid her family farewell. Damn! How he hated himself for what he was doing. She looked so vulnerable and sad. Could he ever make it up to her? He was wrenching her away from the only world she had ever known and had offered her nothing in return. She didn't know how much he wanted and desired her, and he vowed she never would. The hand had been dealt. Eventually, she would be the one to be hurt; he knew it. All he could do was soften the blow.

Right now, all he wanted was to protect her from those cruelties she would endure at his hands. The most difficult part was to protect her from himself. Luckily, she wasn't in love with him. After what he would be forced to do, the misery he would cause her would only be amplified if she loved him. He must keep her at arm's length, for her own sake, if not for his own.

God, but that would be torture for him. Even now as he helped her into the motorcar, he wanted to take her in his arms and make her want him.

Elise and Christopher drove away, each silently immersed in despair.

The train trip to Atlanta had been hot and dry. And worst of all, it had been uneventful. Elise was left alone in their compartment a good deal of the time. In fact, she saw Christopher only when he came to take her to the dining car, and he always brought her back straightaway. No matter how late she stayed awake waiting for him to come to her, he never did until she was fast asleep. By the time she awoke in the morning, he was dressed and gone.

She didn't know where he went or what he did all day, but she was hurt at his avoidance of her. She had busied herself with the wedding thank-you notes she had to write to friends. She read the notes from Jesse and Madame Renaud. The latter had some relatives in France, and Madame was certain' that should Elise ever get to that country, they would welcome her. She opened her art satchel and placed the two notes inside for safekeeping.

Elise felt wretched at leaving her family, but, more than this, she felt utterly rejected by Christopher. He acted as if he could not be bothered with her. Had she so greatly disappointed him that he couldn't stand to be with her for a few moments? Their meals were partaken in total silence. He barely looked at her. He simply stared out the window at the countryside that seemed to pass by them like colored streamers.

Well, why should he want to be with me, she thought as she threw the satchel on the floor. All he's seen is an ugly bride in' an old remade white gown. Then, if that wasn't bad enough, I've been crying since I said "I do." What a mess I've made of everything. Why should he want me if all I do is sit in sad silence all day?

But, Elise thought, she had every right to her depression. Everything she had ever known was now only memory. Elise doubted her ability to cope with the loss of so much so soon. She wondered if anything, even the death of a loved one, could create a sense of mournful lamentation any worse than what she now experienced.

She had never been "out in the world." She had known nothing except the physical and emotional shelter her parents had given her. Surely, she would not find the world as cold as so many people had said it was. But, as she reflected on her relationship with Christopher, she realized that this man who was the closest to her heart, could possibly strike her with life's cruelest blows.

Banishing the painful thought, she decided to change into her beige linen suit to leave the train in Atlanta. She realized she had failed to ask him why they were departing here and not simply traveling on to New York.

By this time she knew she had married a man of many secrets and stormy silences. She simply didn't have the courage to question him. She wished he would just come and talk to her. It wouldn't have to be about anything important. Just to be with him again and hear his voice. . . . She wondered if he ever thought of her, and if he did, just what was it that he thought?

"Need I even ask myself?" she said aloud. "He thinks I am an ugly, undesirable girl! But then, why did he marry me?" she puzzled.

It didn't make any sense. The night of the party she had looked her best, and she had been stupid enough to think he had been entranced with her beauty. And then there was his kiss! But now, as she looked back on the entire affair, she put some facts together. She remembered all those important business meetings with Papa. And there was her father's rage at her a few weeks ago. He had made some reference to being unable to attend to his business matters while worrying about family problems and obligations.

"Oh, dear God! It can't be true! It just can't be!" she cried.

But it was all too true, she realized. It made sense now. Everything that had happened was a business arrangement. She might as well be an investment portfolio; she meant no more to Christopher than that.

Her mind raced over the past days, and she knew it was true. She had been betrayed by her father.

Papa said he loved me! Is this love? Selling me to the highest bidder? Was I just an obligation to him and just another pressure he felt? If this is love, then I want no part of the variety that Papa dishes out, she thought angrily.

The rage built to a peak inside her as she thought of

64

Christopher. No wonder he wasn't here now! But even in her anger, she had only to think of his face, remember his voice and his lovemaking; she was deeply wounded.

"What can I do? What is there for me? I'm in love with a man who despises me, and my own family has been the thrust behind the pain I feel. Where do I get the strength to go on?"

"Atlanta, next stop, Atlanta," the porter cried as he walked through the companionway.

In a few minutes Christopher came to fetch her.

"Elise, we'll have a short ride from here, and then I'll give you an experience you'll remember all your life. It'll be marvelous," he said as he beamed at her. God! How devastated she looked, as if she had just lost everything she had in the world. She must still be upset about leaving her family, he thought. Knowing that he had contributed to her pain, he felt guilty. He hoped his surprise would be just the thing to ease her melancholy.

They went from the train to a chauffeur-driven motorcar. They drove out into the country to an area that was flat and barren. Elise tried to make out the structure in the distance, and as they drew closer, she couldn't believe her eyes.

"Christopher, you aren't serious? You can't be! I can't go up in that . . . that contraption!"

"You can and you will," he said as he grasped her hand and squeezed it. "It'll be fine, Elise. You'll love it," he replied.

"But it only has room for two people. Who will fly it?"

"Your husband, my dear. I assure you, I'm a very capable pilot. You'll be amazed at how quickly we can fly to New York. Now don't look so skeptical. Wait till you're in the clouds! It's total freedom. You'll see the world from a whole new perspective. It's one of my weaknesses. When I'm soaring up into the heavens, I forget everything except the marvelous sights I see. I hope you'll love it as much as I."

"I'm afraid. I don't even like to go fast in a motorcar," she said.

He looked impatient. "You've been very sheltered, Elise. I intend to change all that." Then he smiled that smile. "Here, put on these goggles and cap. And this

65

overcoat. It's a lot cooler up there than it is down here among mortals."

Christopher climbed into the cockpit after helping Elise into the plane. With assistance from the chauffeur, who started the propeller spinning, Christopher revved up the engine, turned the airplane around toward the long narrow dirt road and they sped down the road till the front wheel lifted off the ground and they were airborne.

Elise experienced nausea, delight, terror, and excitement all at once. After fifteen minutes or so, she relaxed enough to loosen her grip on the sides of the plane. The wind that the plane created was extremely forceful, and she was glad she had the cap and goggles.

She explored the skies about her. No wonder Christopher loved this. It *was* wonderful! She looked below her, fascinated by the little squares of brown, green and tan that she saw. Farmland! That's what it was! She viewed lakes, rivers, towns, and forests. For what seemed like hours they flew, and she could not tear her eyes from the marvelous spectacle below her. She loved the floating sensation and sense of timelessness. Presently they headed downward, and Elise could see an area that looked like the one they had left. Had they come full circle? No, there was a lake near by, and the trees were greener here. As Christopher steered the plane toward the land, Elise squeezed her eyes shut and braced for the crash they must surely have upon impact with the earth. But they only bumped a good deal, slowed, and stopped. Elise sat glued to her seat.

"Elise, you can open your eyes now, you are safe," he said, chuckling at her.

"Where are we? Why did we stop?" Her eyes were full of the excitement.

"Just a short refueling stop. It won't take too long. Why don't you get out and walk around for a while?"

Christopher helped her out of the plane and onto solid ground. He hesitated a moment, letting his hands linger at her waist. Feeling the surge of his warmth against her skin, she looked up at him questioningly. For a brief moment her hopes rose as she saw a tender look in his eyes.

Suddenly he turned and walked over to instruct the two men who were running toward him. She couldn't hear their conversation, but Christopher pointed to the plane, and the men nodded in unison. One scurried off and returned with the necessary fuel.

Soon they were airborne once again. This time Christopher had given Elise a map of their charted route. They were scheduled to land just south of Roanoke, Virginia, that night.

Elise spent the remainder of the flight studying the map, calculating their exact position as they flew over the mountains. She was fascinated by the blue-green of the foliage below. As evening descended and the air cooled on the ground, a silvery mist settled itself inside the deep valleys. The setting sun warmed the left side of her face, and as they passed through a cluster of clouds, she was relieved from the blinding rays.

Not much before their landing, the sun had disappeared, and Elise feared that Christopher would find it difficult to ease the biplane into contact with the ground. However, just as before, he displayed his technical skills, and she found she had unnecessarily braced her body for a jolting impact.

This time they were met by a youth who approached them carrying a kerosene lantern to light the way back to his horse-drawn wagon. Elise guessed the boy to be about fourteen years old. He had sandy hair, and she thought how unfortunate it was that his otherwise handsome face was marred by pockmarks. His manner with her was quite uncertain, but he appeared to know Christopher quite well.

The trio rode in the wagon toward the city.

"You will go back and check on the plane, won't you, Billy?"

"Don't you worry about that, Mr. Mann. My pa said he'd take care of everything for you. Said he'd sleep in the damn thing if necessary." Billy blushed when he remembered Elise's presence. " 'Scuse me, ma'am. Didn't mean to swear in front of a lady."

"Billy, this is my wife. Elise, this is Billy Walters. His father and I have a mutual passion for airplanes. Since I have been conducting so much business in the South, it's given me a chance to see them more often than usual."

"That's right, Mrs. Mann. Pa arranged for you to stay

at the hotel in town tonight. It isn't real fancy, but you should be comfortable. It's even got indoor plumbing!"

"I'm glad about that!" Elise laughed.

Christopher gave her a curious look, and then focused his eyes straight ahead as they entered the main section of town.

They stopped in front of a weathered brown frame structure that stood two stories high. Elise quickly closed her gaping mouth as she thought of Billy's understatement about the hotel. It took every ounce of restraint she possessed not to look at Christopher. For some reason, she had the feeling that he knew very well what the hotel was like. She wondered if he was playing some kind of game with her. She decided not to let him have the upper hand.

They ascended the unsteady wooden steps, crossed the porch, and entered the lobby. Although it was stark, Elise was astonished at the homey atmosphere. The lace curtains at the sparkling windows were bleached to a snowy white. The red patterned rug underfoot was clean, and the woodwork smelled of verbena wax. An abundance of lush green plants filled those corners that were devoid of furnishings. The electric lamps were lit, and a warm amber glow escaped through the glass shades.

Elise was involved in her inspection of the immaculately kept lobby while Christopher signed the register. After a moment he came up from behind her, took her arm, and escorted her to the staircase.

"You take the key and go up to the room. It's the third door on the right. I'm going back to the plane with Billy to check on things. I'll be back in an hour or two."

"Christopher? What about dinner? Aren't you at least going to take me somewhere to eat?"

"I'm not hungry, Elise. The desk clerk said the restaurant next door has good home cooking. You go ahead." He turned away from her.

"But I don't . . . " Her voice faded as she watched him disappear through the door.

Elise was stunned by his instructions and abrupt departure. Her eyes narrowed into slits as her fury mounted. She wished she could throw something at him.

"I'll show you, Christopher! I'll be just fine by myself!"

With that she stomped her foot and pranced down the stairs and through the lobby.

Elise was astonished at the unsuitablility of the restaurant, and upon viewing the long narrow tables covered by worn cotton cloths, she wondered if the food would be edible. She was approached by a stocky young woman who gave her a contemptuous look as she blantantly assessed her patron.

"I assume that it's not too late to be served." Elise said carefully, for the girl's stare was so filled with loathing that Elise didn't want to upset her further.

"No, you aren't late," she replied sharply. "Follow me, please." She turned and led Elise to the rear of the room next to the kitchen doors. She put a tattered menu on the table and left.

Elise was astonished by the girl's rude behavior and wondered what she had done to deserve it.

Elise's anger toward Christopher was replaced by confusion at this encounter. She looked over the top of the single-page menu to see the girl watching her intently. Elise glanced at the entrée choices and placed the paper on the table, folding her hands on top of it. She looked at the girl, who knew full well that Elise was prepared to order. Elise waited for the girl to return, but it was obvious she intended to refuse Elise service. For over twenty minutes the silent confrontation continued until, prodded by her employer, the girl approached Elise.

"I'd like baked chicken, broccoli, and strawberries for dessert," Elise said with as much dignity as she could summon.

The girl snatched away the menu and stalked off.

Elise shook her head and wondered if her dinner would ever arrive.

Within fifteen minutes, the girl came scurrying forward with a steaming plate of delectable-looking food.

"If there's anything else you need, just ask," she said, and hurried away.

Elise tasted the juicy chicken and found it beyond reproach. The broccoli was tender, yet crisp. She finished her meal in silence. After the girl brought the berries, Elise remembered something that Jesse had told her, which was that when someone reacted violently to a person it most usually indicated jealousy. Elise swallowed the last strawberry and wondered what there might be about herself that could cause jealousy in another woman.

Christopher prodded the sleeping Elise with a gentle nudge, but got no response. He tenderly smoothed the dark mass of hair away from her face. Her long eyelashes cast tiny shadows over her cheeks.

"You have the fairest skin, Elise," he whispered as he allowed his fingertips to move over her shoulder and down her arm. She twitched in her sleep, then rolled onto her side, snuggling closer to him. His hand continued its path down her side, to her waist and onto the curve of her hip. His hand increased its pressure as he pulled her body into his. He felt himself drift into the passion that threatened to overpower him. His conscious thoughts fled as he buried his lips into her neck. He felt himself melt into her. His tongue seared the skin on her throat, and when he reached her ear, she awakened and moaned his name over and over until his mind came back to him.

He pulled his head back and blinked several times, then let his arms relax. He started to speak, found he couldn't, and cleared his throat.

"It's . . . it's time we got started . . . a long flight," he muttered.

"What . . ." she sighed sleepily.

He rolled away and sat with his back to her on the edge of the bed.

"It's time we leave. I'll see to the readiness of the plane after breakfast. Billy said he'd be here at seven this morning." He got up and began to dress.

Elise focused her sleep-filled eyes, but found the effort too much for her. Just as she had almost retreated back into unconsciousness, she heard his sharp voice again.

"Get up, Elise! I'll order breakfast while you dress. I'll meet you at the restaurant." He finished buttoning his shirt and placed his hand on the doorknob.

Elise stretched her arms over her head, and as he turned to leave, he was most aware of her sensuous movement and the wanton look that filled her eyes.

She came more fully awake at the sound of the door closing behind him. She rubbed her sleep-filled eyelids with her palm and stared at the vacant room. She touched her growling stomach, then threw the bed linens aside and sprang from the edge of the bed. She dressed hurriedly, and within minutes had dashed out the door, headed for the restaurant.

As Elise swallowed the last of her coffee, wondering just where Christopher was, he appeared beside her.

"I don't have time for breakfast. Billy is here now, so if you are finished—"

"I am. Are you sure you don't want something to eat?"

"We'll have several stops between here and New York. I'm anxious to get started." He paid the bill and then firmly ushered her outside.

Billy smiled at them both and held the reins steady as Christopher and Elise seated themselves.

The morning air was warm and pleasant as they drove to the site where the biplane had landed. Billy halted the wagon next to the airplane, and Christopher helped Elise with her goggles and helmet. As she settled herself into her seat, she once again unfolded the chart and prepared herself for the takeoff.

Christopher adjusted his goggles and flipped his white scarf around his neck. He ignited the engine while Billy spun the propeller. Elise kept her eyes open during the ascent and leaned over the side to see the earth sweep past her vision.

Although the plane could fly as fast as eighty miles an hour, they still had over four hundred miles to travel.

The second day of flight seemed an uncoordinated mélange of stops, refueling tanks, unfamiliar faces on the ground, and swirling clouds in the sky. When Christopher pulled on the rudder stick, Elise was tossed from side to side. He barrel-rolled the biplane only once. Thank God! Elise thought to herself. Her stomach would never be the same! By the day's end she was exhausted and hungry. When Christopher landed the plane for the last time, she wasn't sure exactly where they were. Christopher bounded out of his seat and helped her from the plane. She viewed the lush green landscape about them.

"It's beautiful here! Where are we?" she asked.

"Welcome to New York, Elise! Come, we have a business dinner to attend this evening." He turned and walked toward a black sedan that awaited them just beyond a group of maple trees.

Elise was incensed at his announcement as she watched him stroll away from her.

"He can't be serious! A social engagement tonight?" she exclaimed. "I'll never make it through without falling asleep!" Reluctantly, she followed him to the motorcar.

Nine

THE motorcar pulled up in front of the large brown-stone mansion. Surrounding the great home was an iron fence; inside the ornate gate were beautifully laid gardens and walkways. The structure sat fairly close to the street, and it was strange to see so many plants and trees in such a small yard. Elise was used to the rolling lawns of her Mobile home.

Christopher was giving orders to the chauffeur and to the butler, whom he referred to as Bailey. Their luggage hadn't arrived, and someone was discharged to go to the railway station to procure the trunks and suitcases that Christopher and Elise had sent ahead. Christopher took Elise's arm and led her up the stone steps to the heavily leaded glass double doors.

Stepping inside, Elise was overwhelmed by the grandeur of the reception area. The floor was composed of large squares of black and white marble blocks that were heavily veined in gold. It created a fascinating checker-board effect. At the far end of the room was a beautiful oak staircase that rose to the second floor. Even though the room was paneled in hand-carved oak, it was not dark or dreary. On the far right side of the room was a massive white marble fireplace. Elise was sure she could stand to her full height in its arched opening. Two Chippendale settees faced each other in front of the fireplace. They were covered in a white-on-white silk damask. Underfoot was a lovely plush rose, cream, and gold Aubusson carpet. In the very center of the room hung a twelve-branch Waterford crystal chandelier. Directly beneath the chandelier stood a pink marble table. Ruberum lilies arranged in an enormous clear glass bowl rested upon it. At various intimate corners of the room were fauteuil chairs upholstered in a white petit point brocade with tiny pink fleur-de-lis embroidered into the fabric. Elise was surprised that Christopher had such exquisite taste; either that or he had procured some sophisticated help in choosing the decor. The room definitely had a woman's touch. It was not long before Elise was to discover just who that help was.

At the sound of the knocker, Bailey opened the front door to the visitor. She entered the room with grace and self-confidence. She was slightly older than Elise, three years or so. She was the most beautiful blonde she had ever seen, except for Jesse, perhaps. But this woman had an unmistakable cosmopolitan air. Her hair was the color of moonbeams and not the honey-gold of Jesse's hair. Her eyes were deep brown and were rimmed with thick black lashes. Her cheeks and lips were rosy pink, and her skin was impeccable.

"Why, she doesn't have a single freckle or blemish anywhere!" Elise whispered to herself. Her breathtaking figure was dramatically displayed in a soft rose silk evening gown. Its neckline was cut to reveal most of her pearly breasts. There were pink feathers at the shoulders and a cluster of the same feathers at the side of her tiny waist. She floated across the room, smiling with perfect white teeth at Christopher. She flung her arms around his neck, pressed her breasts against his strong chest, and crushed her lips to his as if she had not seen him in years.

Elise stood aghast at the spectacle the young woman was making of herself. The disturbing fact was that Christopher did not seem to mind the affectionate display. In fact he acted as if he both expected it and enjoyed it.

The woman reluctantly pulled away from Christopher's embrace as he cleared his throat and said: "Ah, hem, Elise, I'd like you to meet a . . . ah . . . friend of mine, Deanna Worthington. Deanna, may I present my, uh . . . wife, Elise," he stammered, finding the words difficult to speak.

"Your wife!" Deanna exclaimed as she glared at Elise. "My, but aren't you full of surprises, Chris, darling. You should have let us know so that we could have been better prepared to give your wife a more proper welcome," she said condescendingly.

Christopher had his arm around Deanna's waist and made no effort to release her. Deanna seemed to revel in his attention.

"Elise, Deanna is an accomplished woman and a good friend. She has been kind enough to help me during the past months while I had my home refurbished. And I must say I am grateful for her expertise. I don't know what I would have done without her."

Deanna beamed at her, radiating sensuality as she did so. "You have the good taste, just not the time it requires to do all this, Chris, dear."

"Deanna, would you be so kind as to show Elise around while I make some phone calls? Tonight will be a busy evening for us, and I have some long-neglected affairs to attend."

"Of course, darling, I'd love to. She turned to Elise. "Shall we see the bedroom now or later?" she asked hatefully.

Elise was too stunned to answer and merely blushed as she mumbled, "Not quite yet, thank you." She lowered her eyes to avoid the jealous rage she saw in Deanna's face.

"Well, come along and I'll show you the main salon and rooms on this floor. Hannah, the housekeeper, can take you to your rooms." Deanna stormed off through the vestibule doorway. Elise sheepishly followed her, berating herself for having fallen victim to this torment.

Presently she entered a large parlor. Beautiful casement windows faced south and east, and the sunlight streamed into the room even at this late afternoon hour. Elise noted the fine antiques that appointed the room. A pair of large Queen Anne wing chairs with delicate cabriole legs and spoon feet were covered in the same pastel blue damask that graced the Chippendale sofa opposite them. Above the sofa hung an ancient Chinese silk screen. The dark-stained parquet floor was covered with an Oriental rug of richest blues, yellows, and creams. The walls were painted a delicate daffodil color, and the draperies were white watered moiré taffeta that had been tied back to reveal the gardens outside. A delicate china teapot, cups, and saucers had been placed on the tea table, and Deanna sat on the sofa to pour tea.

"Lemon or cream?" she asked a little too sweetly.

"Just a little lemon and some sugar," Elise said as she sat down in the wing chair opposite the beautiful young woman.

"You must forgive my bad manners. This has been such a surprise to us all here. The servants are all in a dither. Hannah assured me that your room will be readied presently. I hope it will be to your liking. Tell me, Elsie—I'm sorry, I mean *Elise*. Just how did you ever land such a catch as New York's most notorious bachelor? You must have some magic spell that bewitched him. New York's most beautiful ladies from the finest families have been trying to make their way into his bed for years, much less get a marriage proposal out of him. You must have something unique, mustn't you, dear?" Deanna asked coldly.

"I can honestly say I don't know what you are talking about," Elise said, putting her teacup down on the table. "If you will excuse me, I've had a very tiring trip and I do need to bathe and dress for our dinner engangement." Elise rose and, with all the dignity she could muster, slowly glided out of the room.

"That was the best acting I've ever done!" she said to herself. What she had wanted was to fling her teacup at that hussy and flee back to Mobile. Instead, she started up the stairs. Upon reaching the landing, she saw a small round woman in her forties who wore her gray-and-black hair in a tight bun on top of her head. She smiled brightly at Elise. Elise felt her heart lighten at the welcome she saw in the woman's eyes.

"I am Hannah, and I've drawn your bath for you, Mrs. Mann. Follow me and I'll show you to your rooms."

The upper hallway was wide, and all along the north side of the house were numerous casement windows that overlooked a beautiful terrace and well-tended gardens.

"Will you be interviewing for a personal maid, Mrs. Mann? I know that Mr. Christopher would not think of such things. Men never do."

"Hannah, I don't really see that its necessary. We will be here for such a short time. I merely assumed there would be someone already under employ. With three girls in our family . . . well, I guess you understand," she laughed.

"Yes, ma'am. But you see . . . Mr. Christopher never needed a lady's maid before." And Hannah joined in her laughter.

"However, if you happen to know of someone who would be interested in the position even though it would be of short duration, I'd be most willing to speak to her." Elise replied.

"I'll see what I can do."

"Thank you."

Elise then entered the bedroom. It was spacious, with a great row of floor-to-ceiling windows along the south wall, facing the street below. Elise favored such an exposure, since it admitted every ray of sunshine to this place she was to share with Christopher. The walls were painted white to reflect even more light. The walnut planked floor was covered with an enormous thick Oriental rug of China blue and white.

Two China-blue velvet Chippendale wing chairs with matching ottomans sat facing each other near the windows. The heavy velvet draperies matched the upholstery of the chairs. Flanking an oversized Chinese Chippendale mirror were identical cherry bureaus with filigreed brass pulls on each drawer. A walnut testor bed with China-blue bed hangings and bedspread overpowered everything else in the room. Elise felt there was an uneasiness about the room. It was all too perfect.

While Hannah prepared her bath, she decided to explore what lay beyond the heavy Christian door at the end of the room. Turning the knob, she gently pushed it open. Then she wished she had left it alone, for it confirmed her worst suspicions.

The room that lay behind the door was decorated completely in soft rose—the same soft rose that Deanna wore. Everything was extremely feminine. Yards of rose cotton trimmed in white eyelet covered the windows, the bed, and the chaise. She felt a sinking feeling in the pit of her stomach as she realized that Deanna was a live-in mistress! Or at least she spent a great deal of time here— enough time that Christopher saw fit to renovate a room entirely for her. In her wildest dreams, Elise had never thought about the other women in Christopher's life.

Vaguely, the idea must have crossed her mind, but finding herself staring at the living proof of his liaison was quite a shock to her.

You were a fool, Elise, she said to herself. He'll never belong to you.

Hannah walked up behind her. "Oh, my heavens! When did Miss Worthington do all this?" she exclaimed in shock.

Elise looked at Hannah.

"Truly, Mrs. Mann. None of us knew about . . . about this room at all. She was instructed to furnish it as an adjacent study for Mr. Christopher."

"It's all right, Hannah. I'll just take my bath now. Thank you."

"Yes, ma'am." Hannah hung her head, turned, and left the rose-colored room.

Elise knew Hannah was just making excuses. She knew she would have to do something, but she was at a loss. Deanna was a formidable foe and though married to Christopher, Elise knew she didn't hold his heart. She needed not so much to do battle with Deanna as to win Christopher for herself. She didn't know how, but she believed she would find a way. At this moment she needed to leave this awful room. Her stomach churned at the sight of the room itself, and at the thought of its implications.

She rushed back into her bedroom and slammed the door behind her. Wishing it was just as easy to slam the knowledge about its presence out of her brain, Elise sank down in one of the wing chairs. Staring out the window she absentmindedly unbuttoned her light jacket, contemplating the day's experiences. First the flight here; her new home; the confrontation with Deanna—and now this.

"God, how much am I to endure? How much pain must I suffer? Now, just stop that, Elise," she scolded herself aloud. "You've got more courage and brains than to become undone by some hussy. Time to move forward!"

Good heavens! She was to be dressing for their dinner party, and Christopher had been adamant about her looking her best for her first New York party. She was to be introduced to some of Christopher's closest business associates. At least she wouldn't be around Deanna all night; she would have Christopher all to herself.

In a lighter mood, she undressed and took a beige wrapper from her small suitcase and slipped it over her exhausted body. Hopefully the trunks would be sent up before too long. She would need to instruct the maid to press her gown.

Elise walked to the two walnut sliding doors and rolled them back. She was hardly prepared for the splendor that greeted her. She was sure it must be the most modern and opulent bath in existence. The white marble flooring was so heavily veined in gold that it appeared iridescent. The walls were tiled in cobalt blue, and each one was edged with a thick band of gold. The fixtures were gleaming white marble with gold faucets in the shape of swans. Four large brass mirrors hung behind the tub, virtually covering the wall. In the center of the room hung an enormous crystal chandelier. It gave off a tremendous amount of light, and the mirrors reflected it a thousand-fold.

She filled the tub with hot water and eased her tired body into the soothing warmth of the water. She took an oversized natural sponge from a footed gold dish and created a thick lather with a bar of jasmine-scented soap. She sighed, and felt better in just a few moments. She could forget every trouble she had when she was able to luxuriate in the bath like this. She thought she would even treat herself to a short nap. After rinsing and drying off, she glided back to the bedroom and, without benefit of gown or wrapper, crawled in between the cool satin sheets, totally naked. The feel of the slick material against her freshly cleansed skin was delicious. She fell asleep almost in an instant.

Christopher had finished his business calls and had given orders to the servants regarding their luggage and the readying of their dinner attire for that evening. He crossed the large reception area and entered the salon where Deanna sat sipping her tea, gazing out the window at the street activity. He noted Elise's absence from the room.

"Ah, Deanna! Where is Elise? And did you show her

79

the house?" Christopher asked, accepting a cup of tea from Deanna's dainty hand.

"First she has gone to bathe. She said something about being travel weary. Did you wear the poor thing out already, darling? Sorry, that wasn't kind of me. And no, I didn't show her the house yet. She seemed to prefer the retreat upstairs. Pardon me for saying this, but I'm a little incensed about all this, Chris. The least you could have done was to wire ahead. None of us were ready for this shock. Perhaps *shock* isn't a strong enough word. *Catastrophe* is more like it! Just what the hell is going on?"

"My, my, listen to the little guttersnipe. I'd like to ask what the hell you were doing here today anyway."

"Don't yell at me, Christopher Mann! I want to know who that girl is and why you keep calling her your wife. Where did she come from? My God, Chris, she's an amazon! And her clothes are despicable. From first glance anyone can tell she doesn't have any taste or style! Who is she?" Deanna demanded furiously.

"I call her my wife because she *is* my wife. We were married Saturday afternoon in Mobile. She is Elise Kendall," Christopher said.

"Not Justin Kendall's daughter? Oh, Chris, darling! You didn't! You didn't marry her for your blasted business, did you? Or was it for her prestige and family?" She looked into his face and exclaimed: "It's both! My God! What have you done to yourself and that poor girl? A marriage like this will be worse than the tortures of hell for you both. You don't love her. You love me, I know you do. If you had only waited, we could have reasoned with my parents. They would have relented sooner or later," Deanna cried.

"Probably later. Most likely it would have been never. Deanna, you choose not to hear these words whenever I say them, but I am not in love with you. I don't love anyone. You're fun to be with, you would be an asset socially, and I do like making love to you. But even if your parents don't think I'm good enough for you, it doesn't make any difference. I still would never have married you. You, my dear, are a wildcat, and I don't like to tangle with wildcats every day of the week. And I'm still not forgetting my earlier question. What *are* you doing here?"

"Well, I had planned a surprise for you. But seeing

80

the foul mood you're in, I don't think I should tell you. And I worked so hard on my project, I thought it would please you," she purred at him.

"And what project is this?"

Becoming quite animated, Deanna said: "Well, you know that stuffy room next to you that you wanted me to redecorate as a study for you?"

"Yes," he answered.

"The carpenters came and put in a doorway into your room, hung a door, and now you can pass through to the room more easily," she said.

"The study is finished? Great!" Christopher said, quite pleased.

"Not exactly, darling. I had it made into a bedroom for me."

"A *what!*" he exclaimed. "You did what? Oh my God! How can you be so presumptuous. God! I wonder why I ever put up with you at all. I think perhaps you had better gather your things. Why do you always have to be so damned obvious? Get out of here, Deanna. Now!"

Christopher was so angry his knuckles were white. Deanna was such a predatory creature. He was glad Elise was here now; maybe Deanna would quit hounding him.

Deanna swished out the front door when Christopher's mind flashed. Elise! She was upstairs in his room! What if she had seen that new room?

"Damn and blast all to hell!" he cursed as he bounded up the stairs two at a time. Coming to the door of the old study, he flung it open. When he saw what Deanna had done, he felt sick. She really could be a bitch. To do all this without so much as a word to him!

He hoped Elise hadn't seen this. He didn't know if he could explain this one. Should he tell her the truth? But then, Elise was merely a business arrangement, and he had promised himself to keep her at arm's length. God! But Deanna could be cruel! She really must have delighted in taunting Elise.

He walked into the room and looked at all the pink and white. He couldn't lie and say that he had arranged this all for Elise. There hadn't been enough time. As he glanced down at the floor, wondering how he would handle the situation, he spied one of Elise's gloves. He bent down and picked it up.

"So she had been here!"

He immediately opened the door to his own room and saw her lying in his huge testor bed. The spread had been pulled down to the foot of the bed and folded neatly. She lay on her stomach, sprawled across the width of the bed. The white stain sheet had been twisted, and it covered only her derriere. Her long silky legs were exposed to his gaze. The setting sun sent shafts of glinting rays across her body, but her hair seemed to radiate a haze of amber all its own. He stood mesmerized by the lights dancing in its depths.

He moved slowly to the bed, not wanting to break the spell. How he wanted her now! With a feather-light touch he stroked her leg. He didn't want to awaken her, not just yet. He had never felt such a need to protect anyone. The sun had begun to fade, but before it did he touched her hair, wondering if he could catch the sunbeams held within it. As she did, the magic vanished before his eyes, and he sensed a feeling of loss, as if he had profaned a sacred moment. She stirred and moaned softly in her reverie, and he gently tried to awaken her.

"Elise, we need to get dressed for dinner. Elise, wake up," he whispered into her ear.

Her long thick lashes fluttered against her pale cheek as she tried to float back to the world of consciousness. She turned her face toward him and slowly pushed away the curls that hid him from her view. Upon seeing his face, she smiled expectantly at him.

"What a lovely way to wake up," she said.

Fearing that he saw love in her velvet blue eyes, he abruptly stood erect, whacked her on her bottom, and said, "From now on, put some night clothes on when you take your afternoon naps, madame! The servants are in and out constantly, and I don't want anyone viewing such a spectacle!" He stormed into the bathroom and shut the door. It was for her own good, he thought. He just wished he knew what was good for him besides the ice-cold bath he would have to take to cool his ardor.

Tears spilled from Elise's eyes as she witnessed her husband's rage at her nakedness.

"He can't stand to see my body. Will it always be like this?"

Every time she saw him she loved him more, even though he treated her with indifference and, sometimes, even cruelty. She thought again of Deanna and her pink room and felt nauseated. Her husband had the beautiful and provocative Deanna at his disposal. Elise felt desolate, and there was no one she could talk to in this city. She wished she were home again and with Jesse.

"Oh, Jesse! I need you now. I feel so alone!" she lamented, but the walls were silent to her grief.

Ten

THIS dinner will be tedious for Elise, Christopher thought. He would have to leave her alone a good deal of the time. But she would be under the watchful eye of New York society's matrons. He stood in the library, smoking a cigarette and watching the grandfather clock slowly move its longest hand around its gold face.

Christopher was steadily growing uneasy at the thought of tonight's task. He restlessly paced the red Oriental rug and tried to calm himself. He went to one of the book-cases and scanned the rows of books in front of him. He pulled out *Othello*. Upon hearing her footsteps in the hall, he returned the book to the shelf and crushed out his cigarette. He picked up a stack of files from the massive walnut desk and placed them in a small valise. From the back of the wing chair, he took up Elise's black evening cape. It was not cold now, but out on Long Island it did get chilly at night. He was amazed as the thought crossed his mind. Why was he so concerned about the damn weather? Was it Elise he truly cared about? He dismissed the thought as nonsense.

He walked up the two shallow steps to the reception area and saw her standing there. God! He did have to agree with Deanna: this girl didn't have any style at all. The few gowns she owned had been badly crushed in the trunks, but at least she didn't look as deplorable as she had on their wedding day. He could not understand why the Kendall girls dressed so horridly. Perhaps Justin had cut off their clothing allowances.

"Elise, tomorrow I want you to make an appointment

84

with Deanna's dressmaker and have her make some suitable things for the parties we'll be attending. Your attire was acceptable in Mobile, but New York is more sophisticated. Now come, the chauffeur is here," Christopher said as he turned away from her.

Elise was so mad she could spit! How dare he say such things? She had never known anyone so callous. Well, if that's how he wanted to play the game, so be it. But she would die before she'd go to Deanna's dressmaker. She would find the most expensive designer she could and present Christopher with a bill he would never forget.

The more she thought of it, the more delicious she found the idea of revenge. She wouldn't stop at the dressmaker's, either. She would go to the milliner, the bootery, Tiffany's for some jewels. And she would need some imported perfumes. On the ride to the Winston's home, she planned her glorious shopping spree. After all, she was doing it all to make sure she would be the proper ornament that he obviously desired. She laughed aloud.

"What's so funny?" asked Christopher, disturbed by her strange laughter.

"Oh, nothing. Just something funny Hannah told me."

He didn't like the mischievous look in her eye, but dismissed it, for he had more important things on his mind. It wouldn't be long now; he should be able to finalize all the arrangements tonight.

The car drove up a wide circular driveway and stopped in front of a white-columned covered portico. The butler opened the door for them and helped Elise alight. Christopher took her arm and guided her through the large white door.

The brick Georgian mansion was ablaze with electric lights. There were twenty-four guests for supper. Christopher had told her that these were some of the most influential people in New York. Judging from the attire of the men and the richly begowned women, she fully believed him. Now she was horridly depressed. No wonder Christopher had been displeased with her. Why had he chosen this night to present her to his friends? She wished that she had something finer than this unsuitable gown. She had purchased it without having any alterations, and it fit no better than her wedding gown had.

Luckily, the color was a pastel blue that brought out the deeper blue of her eyes, and her hair appeared darker. She suddenly felt bold. She would rise above the gown. She would conduct herself so that no one would even look at the pitiful thing. If they would remember anything of Elise Mann that night, it would be her eyes, her hair, her carriage, and her conversation. She held her head high and glided into the main salon on Christopher's arm, smiling radiantly at everyone she met. She loved the champagne, and it helped to lighten her spirits.

By the time the guests were called to supper, Elise had won everyone's admiration. They were fascinated with her lively manner and her soft Southern speech. Christopher watched her out of the corner of his eye as he conversed with a senator and two manufacturers. What an enigma he had married! He had believed that after his reprimand earlier, she would have retreated to a corner somewhere and he wouldn't have to worry about her all evening. Instead, even in that ugly dress, she had stolen the hearts of all the matrons and won the respect of his colleagues. He was more confused than ever. One moment she was a terrified mouse; the next moment she was sensuous, beautiful, and sensitive to everyone around her. God! He felt even more protective of her tonight than he had even a few short hours ago.

The dining room was long and narrow, and both the chair rail and crown molding were executed in cherry wood. Above the chair rail was a gold-on-cream wallpaper with a chrysanthemum pattern. The wall below was painted cream. Above the Georgian double-pedestal table hung a twelve-branch brass Williamsburg chandelier. Elise did not know how many leaves had been used, but all twenty-four guests were seated in matching Duncan Phyfe chairs with seats of cream moiré. Upon snowy Belgian linens, white bone china thickly banded in gold sparkled in the low light. The tableware was gold vermeil, and the thin crystal goblets and wineglasses were also banded in gold. Six large golden bowls brimming with white roses were perfectly spaced down the length of the table.

The dinner itself was quite light. Chilled artichoke soup was served in fine white china soup lugs with golden handles. This was followed by the main course of sole and shrimp en papillote, and flowerettes of cauliflower were topped with buttered bread crumbs. There was a water-cress, pear, and grape salad with chrysanthemum petals scattered on top. For dessert a chocolate mousse subtly flavored with orange was served. Elise found the wines delectable, and she was thoroughly enjoying herself until she saw Christopher looking at her with a dark frown. Would he always be displeased with her? If it wasn't her clothes, it was because she didn't have anything on at all. She was becoming impatient with his authoritarian atti-tude toward her.

Presently the men rose to leave. The time for their meeting had arrived. Accordingly, the ladies retired to the main salon, where they were to be entertained by a so-prano soloist. A very buxom matron stood next to the grand piano; she wore a gown of deep plum crepe de chine that did nothing for her coloring or her yellowed gray hair. But when she began to sing, no one noticed the dress or anything else save the melodious strains of her voice.

Christopher lit a cigar and cautiously eyed the other men. He wanted to garner as much information as possi-ble before he spoke. He needed more facts and figures. For now he would play a waiting game.

Mr. Winston spoke as soon as everyone was settled. "We have much to accomplish tonight. Unfortunately, this is the first and last time we will be assembled under one roof. After tonight, there will be no further communica-tion among us. If anyone has information to transmit, it is to be sent to a special post office box number I shall give each of you tonight. Everything that is discussed here is highly confidential. If there are no questions, I'll pro-ceed."

No one stirred.

Winston continued. "As we all know, we are about to set into action a chain of events that will create havoc throughout most of the industrialized world. The plans for these events were drawn up many years ago, some by our own fathers. In 1870, after the Franco-Prussian War, my father was present when Germany seized Alsace and parts of Lorraine. He was in many ways responsible for its seizure. Many disruptive acts have followed this first step, and there are many displaced peoples in Europe.

The national desires of these people have not been met, and therefore we have been able to aid the instigation of many the little wars in the Balkans. We have also organized war cults, which have met with a small success. The members of these groups work to create dissension. We have spread sensational stories in the German newspapers. Our propaganda has inflamed many. This is according to plan also. The German ambassador has warned France: 'Peace remains at the mercy of an accident.' Gentlemen, we are prepared to give the world that accident. . . . Mann will now give us his report on our domestic operations."

Christopher rose. "Gentlemen, let me assure you that everything is very much under control. Wilhelm Schmidt is handling all our operations splendidly. I spent a great deal of time with Justin Kendall, and after inspecting the munitions factories in Birmingham, I am happy to report productivity is up. We have gone to full production of the machine gun. The new heavy machine gun will fire five hundred rounds a minute. Because it is so devastating, we feel it will sell well. We have many new orders, but our market penetration is not what it could be. For this reason and others, I intend to establish and direct our international divisions. We also have found that we must elevate our shipping tempo. For this, we'll need more men of high caliber—and, gentlemen, it will cost money for their loyalty. We will need approximately three small boats for night operations, and our base in Cuba will need to be enlarged to accommodate two larger seagoing vessels. I have leased a cargo ship to handle the Atlantic end of the delivery. I have submitted a report tonight, with a copy for each of you, indicating what our expenditures have been and my request for more operating funds. If there are no further questions, Mr. Winston will continue."

"May I say on behalf of us all, Mann, we appreciate your thoroughness of detail," Winston responded. "Now, gentlemen, in your presence I want to issue to Christopher his instructions for the next month. In less than two weeks, he will sail to Rome. I have changed a few details in order to have everything appear as it should on the surface. We are at the peak of our endeavors, and there can be no security leaks. Since Christopher has just been married, it would seem natural if his wife accompanied him on this trip. It will be the perfect honeymoon. I have informed Christopher of this slight change, and he has agreed to the plan. He and I do not feel she will be any threat to us, because of the propitious circumstances of her birth. Since Justin Kendall is one of our most valued colleagues, we feel she may even be a valuable asset. After their arrival in Rome, they will fly to Sarajevo, where we have financed a society known as the Black Hand. We have word that a small group of Bosnian revolutionaries have completed their training program and are prepared to proceed with the assassination. We have sent out instructions to the Black Hand society for relay to the assassins. Christopher will conduct the financial aspects of the negotiations. When he sails, he will carry the two million dollars needed to pay the Black Hand. Our last communiqué from Bosnia stated that Archduke Francis Ferdinand had scheduled his visit for the end of this month. All is ready." Mr. Winston looked sternly into the faces of the men seated about the room as he finished.

Christopher nodded seriously as each man received financial statements. After everyone read these and the other papers, all the copies and files Christopher had brought with him were burned in the fireplace. As the flames flickered and died, each of the twelve men took a filled crystal brandy balloon from the French parquet console and drank a toast to their continued success.

Eleven

ELISE was surprised at how cool it was for early June. She was glad that Christopher had thought to bring her cape. Even in the motorcar, she needed its warmth. She thought of her experiences that night. When she had been at home, her family had never been involved in such business dinners as this. She had nothing in common with any of these people, and yet she knew it was necessary for her to always say the proper things at just the right time. She had found herself smiling all night and making the most banal conversation. Since she had never expounded on any of her beliefs or feelings, everyone had thought her the model wife. She had made a favorable impression, just as she had set out to do, but the thought of how easily it had been accomplished disgusted her.

At this point, all she could think about was the pure torture it would be for her to live her life in such a manner. Only the food and music had interested her. The women were overly concerned with their husbands' careers and their children's accomplishments. No one spoke of art or literature.

They were all nothing more than extensions of their husbands' wills. If she had said that she believed women should command their own destiny, the shock waves would have been astounding! Somehow she had hoped that the sophisticated world of New York would be more interesting than this.

All she heard discussed were products, deliveries, investments, and something about how they would all be benefiting in large profits quite soon. She did wonder about all that. What had they invested in so heavily, and what were they anticipating would happen?

Mostly, she could not stand the condescending attitude of the men toward her simply because she was Christopher's wife. Were all their dinners going to be conducted in such a manner? She dreaded the two weeks of parties that lay ahead of her.

When she had attended parties at home with her friends, she always enjoyed herself. Again she realized how much she missed Jesse. She mused about the times the two of them would sit over tea in Mama's salon and talk about anything and everything for hours; they never tired of each other's company. She and Jesse truly cared for one another; as Elise said, they had always been kindred spirits. They were so different physically, and yet so much alike. Jesse could lift her spirits at any time. Jesse was much the more beautiful, but Elise never envied Jesse or disliked her because of it.

Elise's eyes misted with lonely tears as she thought of how far Jesse was from her now. She wished she could tell her how much she missed and needed her.

Elise locked away all her fondest thoughts for her best friend. She visualized her house on Government Street and what everyone would be doing on a night like this. Papa would be reading, and Mama would be working on the embroidered linens that always seemed to be in her busy hands. Perhaps Andrew would be there, sipping lemonade and listening to Sadie lecture on women's rights.

Elise gave a slight chuckle. Lord! She could just imagine how Sadie would have reacted to her ordeal this evening. She would have reprimanded Elise without mercy about her complacency during the evening. Sadie would have reacted much differently; but then Sadie was stronger and more independent. She was persuasive and forceful; she usually won her arguments. Perhaps that was because Sadie's ideals and politics were based on the grandest and most humane of all ideals: "Do unto others as you would have them do unto you." But how could this apply while women were not considered the equals of men?

She looked at her husband as he sat next to her. He was no different from other men. Perhaps it was not his fault at all. Maybe men were just as much the victims of society's rules and caste system as women. Was it just as

91

difficult to be the master as it was to be the slave? Did he have pressures that he could not bear? Did he ever feel, as she did, that he wanted to stand in the middle of a room and scream till his lungs burned with the pain of the injustice of it all? What did he feel about *anything?*

Suddenly, Elise was engulfed with fear. She wanted to know the answers to her questions, and all she ever found were more questions and more insecurities. She could never please Christopher if she didn't know what he needed or wanted. At least she had come to realize that she had definitely been a business transaction between her Papa and Christopher. What she didn't know was whether she had been the trophy or the bribe; she feared it was the latter. Christopher had probably said he would take her off Papa's hands if Papa would transact certain business matters with him. She could see them standing in Papa's library discussing her future as if she were a crate of chickens like the ones sold on Dauphin Street. By the time the motorcar had stopped at their home, Elise was seething with hate, frustration, and rage. She could not wait to get away from him.

"I'm going to have a brandy before retiring. Would you care for one?" asked Christopher as he took her cape from her soft shoulders.

She spun around, glared up into his cold eyes and almost hissed at him.

"No thank you. I have a violent headache!"

With that she raced up the stairs and slammed the door to their bedroom. Elise stripped the dress from her body, crossed to the cherry bureau, took out a pair of scissors and cut the hideous dress into tiny pieces. All the frustration that welled up within her, she took out on that awful blue dress. She wanted nothing to remind her of her initiation into the sisterhood of corporate ornaments. She threw the scissors on top of the pile of rags she had created and stalked off to the bathroom. She took off her chemise and sat in the cold marble tub. Turning the handle, she let hot water from the mouth of the golden swan pour over her trembling body as she wept.

Christopher half-filled a lead crystal brandy snifter and warmed it over a candle. He drank deeply, contemplating the auspiciousness of the evening's events. Perhaps never before in the course of human history had such a small group of men been able to dictate such irrevocable disaster. The fuse had been lit tonight, and no one could stop it—that much he knew. If he were not the impetus behind this assassination, they would only find another messenger to take the money to Europe. It was better in the long run that it be him, and not someone else. That thought gave him an uneasy comfort. He might be an integral part of the destruction of the western world, and he was trying to ease his guilt. That was one thing he just could not do; yet the time for guilt feelings had long passed.

He saw Elise resting in one of the wing chairs. She wore a soft apricot wrapper and was staring out the window with her feet propped up on one of the ottomans. Her feet were bare, and the wrapper had fallen down the sides of the chair, revealing her long legs. She was turned in the chair so that he could only see her freshly brushed hair against her beautiful profile. The moonlight streamed over her, illuminating her high cheekbones. Her eyes had the same appeal for him that he had felt on their wedding night. He realized that once again she had been crying. Damnit! Why the hell was she always crying? Was it because she was afraid of him? Did she detest his lovemaking so much? Both times he had come to her, she was crying. Damn her! Damn the whole world.

Before he fell prey to his irrational anger, he took a deep breath. It wasn't Elise's fault that he felt such guilt. It would be unfair to take it out on her. Above all, he longed for the comfort she could give him. Even though he had vowed to be aloof from her, he wondered how long he could resist.

"Elise, it's time to get some rest."

"Yes . . . I know," she replied. Without looking at him, she got into the bed.

He tenderly kissed away the wet, salty tears from her velvety cheeks. His lips moved softly to her ears. As he buried his face amid the abundant glory of her hair, he whispered:

"Don't cry, Elise. I won't hurt you."

He kissed the back of her neck and her shoulders, and groaned with rising passion.

"Oh my God, Elise, I do want you so desperately."

She moaned with pleasure at the sound of his voice. She felt her skin tingle, and she wanted him close to her; she could never have him close enough to her. His lips burned against her cool skin. As he gently nipped at her breasts, she felt her entire body begin to glow with a warmth she hadn't known before. The intensity of the warmth grew to become a flame of desire. His hands were everywhere. And as before, the ecstasy was overwhelming and she couldn't move. Every nerve in her body was electrified. She wanted her arms to encircle him and feel the muscles of his back, but even the thought vanished quickly as she felt her pulse heighten and her breath quicken when he entered her. He filled her with the love she so desperately wanted and needed. Only he could give her that love, and it saddened her that he didn't want to. He grasped her hips and brought her forcefully to him, delving deeper and deeper until she reached the pinnacle of bliss. Behind her eyelids she saw a kaleidoscope of white and blue lights. Waves of desire transported her to a joy she wished were eternal.

He groaned suddenly, and she felt him quiver and shudder. The leaden weight of his spent body pressed her farther into the soft bed beneath her. At last he moved away from her, then pulled her close again and pressed the length of her long lithe body against his. Now she placed her hands on his back and felt his smooth skin with her fingertips. It was as soft as a baby's skin, and she traced the underlying muscles and was stirred once again. She realized his breath was measured and deep.

She lay there until dawn broke; and if she had not completely lost her heart to him before, she did so now. She let her eyes delight in his sleeping form. She could never love any man this way again. He had given her his name. Why, oh why, couldn't he give her his love?

"Oh, Christopher, love me. Please, don't allow Deanna to hold your heart. Let me be the one that fills your thoughts the way you fill mine. I want you all to myself, for all time." She gazed at him with profound sadness.

She thought of his voice and wanted him again. Her body flamed, and she placed his head on her breast and held his sleeping body as tightly as she dared. Never would she let him go. Just to hold him close to her was all she needed to wash away the loneliness and frustration she had felt earlier. This was the moment she would always cherish. He couldn't scold her, and she could pre-

94

tend that he truly loved her. She kissed his black wavy hair and let her fingers explore the terrain of his face; his lips and eyes and ears. God! How she loved him!

As the rosy light of early morning washed over their entwined bodies, Christopher stirred. Elise moved her arms down to her sides lest he awaken too soon. She closed her eyes and feigned slumber.

He awoke and gazed at her naked body so close to his. He pulled the satin sheet up to cover her so that she wouldn't feel the chill of the morning air. He looked at her beautiful face, now washed with the pink-lavender of the sunrise, and his crystal blue eyes filled with regret that he was not able to make her respond to him. He rose from their bed and was puzzled by his emotions. It must be the guilt that he felt knowing that the day was hastening when Elise would learn the truth; knowing he wouldn't be able to repair the broken heart for which he would be solely responsible. He gazed at her once more before dressing for his long day.

Twelve

ELISE wanted to cry, but couldn't. Christopher must have been sickened by the sight of her. He had covered her up with the sheet! Elise dismissed any other explanation. To a man like Christopher, who had known so many women, she must be sorely lacking in the necessary physical attributes. If only I weren't too tall or if my breasts were larger . . . maybe then he would be proud of me. But I can't cut off my legs or do anything about my freckles or the size of my bosom.

But I can learn to dress exquisitely. Maybe that will please him. She almost laughed aloud. And just last night, she thought, I was protesting the plight of women and their subservience to men. But this is different. I want to do this to please the one I love; surely that's not merely being submissive. If I'm only fooling myself in thinking that, then I guess I shall be love's number-one fool. I must make him proud of me.

Exhausted from her sleepless night, she floated into a dream world where Christopher loved her with all his being.

Christopher silently left the room in an effort not to disturb his sleeping wife. He walked down the stairs, bracing for the day's events, and strode into the breakfast room. For some reason, he loved this large, square room. Hannah kept it filled with lush green plants. There was a round dark table in the center of the room, surrounded by six Windsor armchairs. He sat at the table reading the morning paper. Presently, bearing a large white ironstone coffeepot, Hannah entered the room. She placed a white cup and saucer in front of him and filled it with steaming liquid. He sipped it easily.

"Good morning, Hannah. I trust you have not been too upset with the turn of events in the household?" he asked.

"Oh, no, sir. You know I've wanted you to settle down for years. Although I don't know the missus yet, she has been very friendly—and quite lovely, even if she is so tall," Hannah said.

"You think she is? I guess I don't think much about it, really," thinking of her fabulous legs. "I imagine that I rather like the way she is."

"I should hope so! You married her," Hannah chuckled.

"Please take a breakfast tray up to Mrs. Mann. She doesn't know her way around the house yet, and I have an early appointment today. Otherwise I would do it myself. Oh! And Hannah. As soon as the shops open I want you to have some workmen come here and clear out all the pink garbage in the old study."

"Mr. Chris! None of us knew Miss Worthington would take such liberties. We were all so busy with all that was going on we just didn't pay any attention."

"Don't worry, Hannah, I know it wasn't your fault. It's over and done with now. But I do want that room made over into a sitting room. And this time the color will be lavender. I want all the furnishings to be the finest in French antiques. I also want some space near the windows left for an easel. I think you could call my friend Mr. Salem at the La Galerie and have him suggest proper paints, canvases, and any other equipment that artists use. I want that room renovated by the end of the week even if it takes every workman in the city of New York."

"The new missus, she paints, is that it?" Hannah asked.

"Yes, she does. But I don't want anyone to say anything to her about what is going on. Do you understand?" Christopher asked her as he sipped his coffee.

"Yes, sir. Now would you like some breakfast or not?" Hannah asked as she poured a second cup of coffee.

"Yes, I'm famished. I'll have sausages, eggs, some potatoes, and some strawberries, if you have them."

"Oh, yes sir. And they're very nice ones."

"Good! Put some on Mrs. Mann's tray too. And lots of cream for her too. And, she loves croissants. Send to the bakery for them," Christopher said, smiling at his house-keeper.

"I'll make them myself, sir," she said as she left the room.

Christopher put the paper down and stared at the Welsh cupboard that was filled with white ironstone. This room was so homey, and was perpetually filled with the good smells of Hannah's cooking and baking. He wished his childhood home had been like this. It was warm here, and was the only room in the mansion where he could be himself. Here, he wasn't the eligible bachelor of New York's society. He didn't have to prove himself to anyone. He didn't have to contend with pressures of his political and business commitments. He pretended he was a little boy as the aroma of the sausages and hot breads wafted into the room. He gazed out the large wall of windows that faced the small, perfectly groomed gardens.

"Hannah, come here!" he yelled.

"Yes, sir?"

"Hannah, when you see the gardener, have him re-place the pink roses with white ones, and some yellows," he said, and smiled at the thought of Elise's face sur-rounded by white roses.

"Sir? Mr. Chris! You can't be serious! These roses are in beautiful bloom, and it will be a year before new plants will be able to bud!" she exclaimed.

"Well, do it anyway. Then call the florist and have cut white roses sent to the house every few days for Elise to arrange in bouquets. I don't think that will be too difficult a task for you to handle, now do you, Hannah?"

"No, sir," said Hannah. She left the room thinking how much Mr. Chris was in love with his new wife. She hadn't believed it would ever happen. Whatever it was, she was glad Miss Elise was here now; Mr. Chris certainly needed someone to love him.

Christopher noted the hour and bolted down his food. Shouting the last few instructions to Hannah, he grabbed his valise and rushed out the door.

Elise finished her toilette and sat before the mirror try-ing to do something elegant with her tresses. Exasperated, she gave up and simply slicked her hair back from her face and pinned the long curls into a bun toward the back of her head.

Lord! She wished Crystal were here. She could certainly do more than this. She wondered if anyone in New York wore their hair like this—she certainly never had. She couldn't even get a straight part down the center of her head, much less do anything else with her hair. She hoped no one would laugh at her. She looked at her reflection. She seemed older and more sophisticated this way. Her eyes looked larger, and her cheekbones were more prominent.

Good heavens! She looked underfed! What a joke. As a child she had always been so fat, and had been taunted by the boys who lived a few streets away from her. Hardly for the first time, she recalled the day, when she was eleven, that she had been walking home from school and three boys she knew came out on the front porch of a white frame house and threw stones at her and called her insulting names. In an effort to run away she did not hear all they said, but she had heard them call her "fatty" and "tub of lard." Those words had remained in her mind every day of her life. She could not escape them when she looked at her body in the mirror. All she saw was the grotesqueness they had seen. As she grew older, it was even worse. She was round in the wrong spots, and straight up and down in the spots that should be round. Her physical shortcomings had always bothered her, but never so much as now, when she wanted to please Christopher. Elise was lost in her thoughts when she heard the knock at the door.

"Yes, who is it?"

"It's Hannah, Mrs. Mann. I brought your breakfast tray," she said.

"Come in, I'm sorry. I just didn't know who it could be. You didn't have to do that, I could have come downstairs."

"Oh, no, Mr. Chris said to bring this to you. I hope I have some of your favorite things here."

Elise looked at the tray and was surprised to see the strawberries, croissants, and strong hot coffee before her.

"How did you know?" she asked Hannah.

"Mr. Chris said you like the French rolls and your coffee was to be strong. I don't know how to prepare New Orleans coffee. If you can tell me, I'll try to get all the right ingredients," Hannah said.

Elise poured a generous amount of thick cream into the white cup and sipped.

"This is just fine, Hannah. Lots of sugar, cream, and strong coffee will do. It's supposed to have chicory in it, but that was hard to find even in Mobile. This is lovely. The croissants are perfect. I'm more than pleased, Hannah."

As the housekeeper left, Elise pondered Christopher's keen observations. How had he known so well what she liked? It was curious. Why in the world would he have noticed such things? She finished her favorite repast and thought of the shopping spree she would begin today. She dressed quickly in the only suit she owned, clutched her reticule, and rushed from the room. She reached the reception area and realized she had no idea where she would start. She had heard that Saks Fifth Avenue was a nice store. She might as well start there. She certainly didn't want to have to ask Deanna's advice. She would rather make her own mistakes than to acquire bad advice from her rival.

The chauffeur drove her to Fifth Avenue, and she marveled at the curious structure the chauffeur referred to as the Flatiron Building. It was located on Twenty-third Street where Broadway crossed Fifth Avenue. It was built in the shape of a triangle and she laughed at the fact that it really did look like a flatiron. Mobile didn't have anything like this! She asked the driver about the building, and he explained that it had twenty-one stories. She felt as if she were seeing one of the eight wonders of the world. Just the sight of Fifth Avenue was almost more than she could comprehend, for there were so very many beautiful shops, hotels, churches, clubs, and museums. Now the car stopped at Saks Fifth Avenue, and Elise told the chauffeur she would call for him when she had finished her shopping.

When she entered the store she was assaulted with a myriad of merchandise and she had virtually no idea where to begin. She approached a man who was giving directions and advice to some customers.

"I'd like to see the latest designs in evening apparel, if I may. Where would I find the items I'll require?"

The man, noting her déclassé appearance, asked: "I

must have your name before I can send you upstairs to the haute couture department. You are . . . ?"

"Mrs. Christopher Mann," Elise replied.

The man's jaw dropped three inches, Elise thought.

"Why, Mr. Mann is a very good customer of ours. I'll have someone down immediately to escort you and tend to your purchases," he said.

He couldn't believe his eyes or ears. For years, Christopher Mann had been buying gifts for some of the loveliest female creatures in New York. Here, suddenly, was a shabbily dressed Southern girl who had not an ounce of sophistication and was really much too tall. They would have their hands full trying to outfit this one.

Presently a stout, gray-haired woman appeared and introduced herself as Mrs. Anderson. She was beaming a friendly smile, and Elise trusted her immediately. They rode up several stories. Elise didn't know how far up they had gone, she was so fascinated with this contraption the lady called an "elevator."

"New York is a very interesting city," she said to the lady.

"Here we are, dear. Now let's get to work and see just what your needs are," she said.

"I need five or six evening gowns that will be suitable for dinner parties and theatre. I'll also need shoes, purses, and any other accessories you feel are appropriate. For daytime wear I'll need skirts, blouses, suits, and more shoes, of course. Hats too, I believe. I'll need some winter things as my husband and I are embarking for a year's trip to Europe in a matter of a few days. So, you see, I will need these things almost immediately. I realize some things will require alterations," Elise said.

"I think we can satisfy almost all your needs at this moment. Aside from alterations, we should have no problem completing your wardrobe. We'll start with your day wear if that's suitable to you."

"Thank you, Mrs. Anderson. I'm anxious to begin."

"Of course, Mrs. Mann."

Elise sat down in a Louis XV chair and selected various articles to try on later. Mrs. Anderson seemed to know just the colors that would enhance Elise's best features. Elise followed her to a large and well-lit mirrored room. She stood on a small round platform as Mrs. An-

101

derson aided her in discarding her old navy summer suit.

"Mrs. Anderson, would you please take that out and dispose of it."

"Yes, Mrs. Mann," she replied, picking up the suit and handing it to one of the black maids.

"I'll just wear something home that I purchase today," Elise said.

Elise chose a beige linen skirt that fit quite snugly over her hips. To wear with it she selected a beige silk shirt with a bow at the throat. To alternate with this skirt she purchased a blue and beige striped shirt of cotton, and a yellow and cream striped shirt of silk. She chose three summer skirts of white, sky blue, and soft yellow linen. There was a gray flannel suit with silver fox cuffs and collar, and a matching muff that Elise adored. She selected a gray velvet suit with a snowy silk blouse and matching ascot. Mrs. Anderson persuaded her also to purchase a black velvet theatre suit. Elise liked a sky-blue wool suit and Mrs. Anderson coordinated the blouses and scarves she would need for all her choices.

Elise ordered a winter cape of black velvet lined in silver fox. She also ordered a shorter cape in heavy chocolate brown wool lined in champagne beige mink for daytime. There was a day dress in white linen, one in brown linen with a sky-blue vest and skirt, and a beige silk blouse to go with the brown suit and vest. She ordered the appropriate hats, shoes, and gloves for all her outfits. For winter wear she selected a heather-green flannel skirt with two front pleats, a matching vest, and jacket with gold buttons.

Elise felt exhausted already, and she hadn't even begun to try on any evening gowns—and she would need one for tonight! Mrs. Anderson had the maid bring them a light lunch and some white wine.

"I never knew it could be so much work to build a suitable wardrobe! Is it always like this?"

"No, it's usually worse. Right now you are procuring your basics. After this you will sometimes have a specific item in mind and you will find it most distressing to shop and shop, knowing just what you need, and no one will have it in stock or be able to make you what you need when you need it," Mrs. Anderson stated knowingly.

"Ugh! I don't know if I can cope with all this! But I do

know it's imperative that I have the perfect gown for our dinner engagement this evening. We will be dining with my husband's business associates. However, I want something to make me look anything but the country mouse that I am."

"Mrs. Mann! I'm shocked! You have an excellent sense of color, and with some training you'll increase your knowledge of fashion. You're very fortunate to be the height you are. The clothes fall so gracefully on you. I know I could certainly never wear the things you can."

Elise smiled at her reflection in the mirror.

"Thank you, Mrs. Anderson. Now, let's get back to work," Elise said.

Mrs. Anderson returned her smile and then dispatched two clerks to bring her the finest gowns in the store. Within minutes there were nine gowns hanging in the room. Elise chose the beige one first. For some reason, beige and white looked best on her. Mrs. Anderson agreed with Elise. These colors heightened the blue of her eyes and accented the red highlights of her hair. The beige gown was made of the silkiest crepe de chine Elise had ever touched. It was cut high at the neck with a simple collar and had long sleeves with lace cuffs. A large sash tied simply at her waist, and the fabric clung to her body, enhancing all her curves. Elise had to admit the back view was grand. It was starkly elegant.

The next gown was white organza with a white taffeta underdress. Tiny tucks ornamented the front of the bodice, and the skirt was slightly fuller than most. The sleeves were tightly fitted organza with wide cuffs. Elise thought the dress was beautiful, but perhaps more suited to a bride than a matron. She chose instead a black taffeta gown that was cut low in front and bared quite a bit of her shoulders and back. It had an extremely tight fitting bodice and waist, and the skirt fell gently over her hips with a flare at the bottom. The skirt had panels of lace that added some detail to the simple lines.

Her final choice was a soft lemon-yellow silk, which had a sheen to it that reflected the light and made the beams dance about her. She usually didn't care for yellow, but this color was so delicate that it made her hair shine with golden lights. This was the dress she would wear that evening, she decided. Its round neckline was deeply cut, as was the back. It, like the others, fit closely to her breasts and revealed their delicate contours. Luckily, she wasn't so thin that her ribs showed through the fabric. The full skirt cascaded over her hips, outlining her derriere, and then, just below the thighs, billowed into a soft, bell shape.

Tonight she would wear her hair in Grecian curls, as she'd worn it the night she met Christopher. Mrs. Anderson brought out some soft yellow kid slippers to match.

"Would you please fetch me a light wrap of some type? Perhaps a small cape just to cover the shoulders."

Mrs. Anderson returned with a white lace capelet that was utterly perfect for summer nights.

At this point, even if she needed more things, she couldn't go on; she had to get some rest before the dinner that evening. She bid Mrs. Anderson to call for her chauffeur and made arrangements for the delivery of her other purchases. She took the yellow silk, slippers, and lace capelet with her. Mrs. Anderson made an appointment for Elise to return in five days time to select from the new items that were to arrive by then.

On the way home, Elise felt much reassured. Mrs. Anderson had been just the person she needed to talk to. But she needed to find someone to dress her hair. She chided herself for not having insisted that Hannah find her a personal maid quickly. If worse came to worse, she could always shock New York society and wear her hair down in its natural state. She laughed mischievously and decided right then and there that was exactly what she would do.

Christopher was late in arriving home and barely had time to change into his tuxedo. Elise was bathing when he entered the room, and he didn't wish to disturb her. He changed quickly, and as he tied his tie, he yelled through the bathroom door.

"Elise, I'm home! I'll wait for you downstairs, I have some calls to make before we leave tonight."

"Yes, Christopher, I shouldn't be too much longer," Elise said.

She smoothed the perfumed body lotion over her arms, legs, and breasts. She started to put the wrapper on, then went back to the jar of silky cream and rubbed it into her stomach and hips, enjoying the wicked feeling of total self-indulgence.

She entered the room stark naked, picked up her chemise from the bed and put it on. She sat in the chair and bending from her waist, brushed her long hair until it gleamed red-gold. She stood up and let if fall naturally about her shoulders. She pulled one side back from her face and fastened it with a simple tortoiseshell comb painted with soft yellow roses. Taking the yellow gown from the bed, she stepped into its shimmering fabric and pulled it up. The drape of the material over her long body was splendid. She fastened the buttons, slipped on her yellow shoes, and placed the capelet over her arm. She spun before the mirror to give herself one last inspection. She was pleased with the results, but was quite unsure of Christopher's reaction. Before she thought about it too long and made herself nervous, she headed for the stairs.

He was standing in the reception area, tapping his foot on the white marble floor as he waited for her. Crushing his cigar into the large brass ashtray on the center table, he quickly glanced up to see if Elise was coming yet.

He was overwhelmed at the sight of her. She was breathtaking; he had never seen a more beautiful woman in his life. The crystal chandelier rained down beams of light that caught in Elise's hair and eyes and in the silk of her gown. Her eyes were the bluest he had ever seen. Her gown was not vulgar in the least—it was very simple in detail—but her body was most provocative. He wanted to pick up this radiant form and carry her upstairs and make endless love to her. Speechless, he could merely walk to her side like a dumb puppy and hold out his arm to her. As she placed her arm in his, he patted her hand, leaned over, and kissed her soft cheek.

"You look very nice tonight, my dear," he said. Dammit! Why couldn't he say something more appropriate than that? He was acting like a schoolboy with his first crush. He could hardly get out even those insipid words. He found nothing to criticize about her appearance; in fact she was perfection itself. And yet, he couldn't tell her so. Why not? The least he could do was compliment her on her hair. He knew she had worn it that way just for him. It was so long and lustrous, and he wanted to play with the soft curls that fell about her shoulders. More, he wanted to bury his face in its lavender scent and drift with her to a land where there was no one but the two of them.

She must have taken great pains to find this gown in such a short time. He wondered if she had purchased anything else. If this was a preview, he thought he would be very much interested in what else she had chosen. He held her capelet for her, and as she turned her back to him for him to place the white lacy fabric on her shoulders, he noticed the back of the gown. My God! he said to himself. Every line of her back was revealed to his gaze. Now he was filled with even more desire than before. This was not the time for such thoughts, he told himself; but his body found it more difficult to respond to common sense.

Halfway through a rather boring evening, Elise pondered her fate: Would all their parties and dinners be like this for the next two weeks? How can any of them stand the life they lead? Don't they ever want something more for themselves? she thought.

Elise wanted to be free—free from all the mundane chatter, business associates, and meetings. She longed to ride her horse; perhaps, that was all that was wrong. Whenever she had felt penned in at home, she took Sandy for a long ride on the beach. But there was no beach here in the middle of Manhattan. She couldn't go for long walks, nor could she even leave their bedroom at night to walk in the garden. There must be something she could do. Then she remembered that she didn't have any paints with her, and she wanted to sketch these city scenes. Tomorrow she would purchase some charcoals and some paper. She didn't have to see Mrs. Anderson for a few days, and she desperately needed an escape from her role as the perfect wife.

While she waited for Christopher, he was making their apologies for an early departure to their host. Elise was relieved that they wouldn't have to remain any longer, for she was exhausted from her busy day. She thought she could sleep for the next three days. They thanked their host and hostess and quietly left. The ride home was peaceful until Christopher spoke.

"I'll be late to bed tonight. I'm expecting a visitor and will have some business to conduct in the library, so you might as well just get some sleep. You look as if you could use it," he said, looking at her half-lowered eyelids. He put his arm around her and drew her next to him, then gently laid her head on his shoulder.

"Try to rest for a while, we have a long ride yet."

Elise felt his warmth through his clothing, and from her angle she could see the night lights of Manhattan. It was spectacular. She had felt that day that no sight could equal that of the hustle of Fifth Avenue at midday, but she had been greatly mistaken. New York at night was utterly fantastic. She wished she and Christopher could view these marvelous scenes together every night. The lights began to spin by her vision, and she felt her lids lower. She fell asleep. Christopher stroked Elise's arm and back as she slept peacefully. He kissed the top of her head and ran his fingers lovingly through her hair. Too soon, they reached home. Elise awoke as the car came to an abrupt stop.

They were just giving their outer wraps to Bailey when they heard the sound of the brass knocker against the front door.

"This must be my appointment," Christopher said. "You might as well go up, Elise, I have no idea how long this will take. Don't try to wait up for me."

Elise was halfway up the staircase when Bailey opened the door and Elise heard him announce: "Miss Worthington to see you, Mr. Mann."

Elise's ears burned as they were assaulted with the words the butler spoke, and she flew up the stairs before she would have to subject herself to any of Deanna's ridicule.

"Chris, darling! I couldn't wait any longer!" she purred as she swished into the room before Bailey could shut the door to her. She almost threw herself at Christopher, and pressed her mouth against his.

Christopher watched Elise out of the corner of his eye as she finished her quick ascent of the stairs. Christopher grabbed Deanna's arm roughly and ushered her to the door as he said: "Now get this straight, once and for all. You are not welcome in this house day or night. I have a wife now and don't need your services. Deanna, if for some strange reason I find I do need you, which I seriously doubt, I'll call you. I still haven't forgiven you for the liberties you've taken with my home," Christopher stormed.

"Chris, I only wanted to please you. I had no idea you'd walk in with a wife! I thought you loved me!" Deanna cried, becoming unsettled. "I thought you wanted to marry me!"

"I never led you to believe I would do any such thing. And in any event, Deanna, I am married now. But more important, I will not let you or anyone try to rule my life or my home for me. Now, please, go. I have a meeting here tonight and I don't want anyone to see you," he said, opening the door for her.

"All right, all right, I'll go. But Chris, if you don't send for me soon, I may not be there when you do need me," Deanna said.

"I'll take my chances," Christopher said with a smirk as he shut the door. He knew he should go up to Elise and explain that this wasn't the appointment he had scheduled for that evening. He bounded up the stairs and flung open the door. She stood in the middle of the room with her hands balled into fists; she was fuming with rage.

"Elise . . . I—" he began.

"Don't say another word! I don't want to hear it. I'm very well aware of Miss Worthington's position in your life! So, why don't you just go back to her!" she wailed in furious tones.

"I *was* going to say something else! But now seeing the mood you are in . . . I doubt my words would do any good. Until you calm down, I'll leave you to your ill temper!" He stormed out of the room and banged the door behind him.

She burst into tears, took off her shoe and threw it at the door.

"Damn you, Christopher! I don't care what you do!" she huffed. Then she took a breath, and as the anger abated, she whispered to the walls: "But I *do* care . . ."

Downstairs Christopher poured himself a drink and tried to forget about Elise . . . and Deanna. The knocker sounded, and Bailey opened the door to Wilhelm

Schmidt. Christopher crossed to him and greeted him warmly, then sent for a light supper for his friend.

"Before I get into the reason for my trip here tonight, I want to give you this letter. It's for Mrs. Mann from her friend, Jesse, in Mobile. I promised I would deliver it. It was faster than the mails," Wilhelm said.

"Something has happened that has caused you great concern, hasn't it?" Christopher inquired.

"I'm not sure. I think there is a leak somewhere. Or perhaps one of our employees has become greedy. Our last few runs have been anything but smooth," Wilhelm replied.

"Sit down, please. Start from the beginning and tell me just what is going on," Christopher said, handing Wilhelm a glass filled with three fingers of whiskey and branch water.

"The night you left Mobile, we ran four loads of machine guns. I felt everything was going well on the trip from Birmingham to the waterfront at Mobile. It was at that point that things started to go awry. Our regular dock foreman was not present, and his replacement informed us he had taken ill. It was my own fault—I should have recognized the danger at that moment, but I didn't. It was an extremely dark night, perfect for our operations. We were able to load the boats easily, and did so in record time. This was a larger shipment than usual, and I was pleased with our speed. It was only slightly after midnight when we were ready to embark for Dauphin Island. We found nothing strange or out of the ordinary in our transfer operations at the island. Even though our small cruisers were weighted down with the load, they still were able to gain a fair amount of speed quite quickly. As we moved away from the island and began our voyage down the Florida coastline according to our charted route, I noted some unusual traffic in the St. Andrew Bay area near Panama City, but it didn't seem there was anything to be alarmed about, so we stayed far enough away from shore to avoid detection." Wilhelm paused and took a long drink.

"What happened then?" Christopher asked as he lit a cigarette.

"Just past Tampa Bay a pair of fast cruisers entered the gulf. At approximately the Sarasota area these other boats picked up speed. They weren't regulation Federal Patrols, but they had that unmistakable air about them. I could just feel that something was wrong. We gave chase, and frankly I didn't know how we did it. Our boats were much heavier than theirs, but luckily you have seen to it that ours have far better equipment. Thanks to our superior boats and skilled helmsmen, we were able to stay ahead of them till we reached the Florida Keys. Our four-day schedule was reduced to three days. But because of the black night, the still waters, and our hidden refueling bases in the keys, we were able to make it. I think that the fact that our boats carried that second refueling on board was what saved us. We threw the empty barrels overboard, and that lightened the load somewhat. We had gained enough distance when we reached the keys that we backtracked a bit and lost them completely before we reached our base. The trip to Cuba was as usual, and we encountered no problems."

Wilhelm finished his whiskey, poured another for himself, and continued.

"I don't mind telling you, Christopher, that I was gravely concerned, although the next shipment three days later met with good results. So far, our luck has held. I decided not to schedule any further shipments until I spoke with you. My sources inform me that the substitute foreman has been dealt with. I still haven't been able to find the leak, and was hoping you could authorize someone to accompany me to Mobile to investigate. I realize it is most imperative, that these shipments be delivered on schedule, and to the proper customers. At this point we need to increase our shipments, and we can't afford any misfortune. Do you agree?" Wilhelm asked.

"Yes. I'll handle everything. We can't afford to have federal or state interference now. It'll only be a matter of weeks until I establish our foreign offices. How long until you hand down your position in Mobile to Sellers?" Christopher inquired. "And do you feel he is capable of doing the job?"

"Oh, yes. I trained him myself and trust him completely."

Christopher glanced quickly about him. "And when do you leave for Bosnia?"

110

"In the morning, if I don't need to return to Mobile."

"No, you don't. It isn't necessary."

"I'm taking my mistress to Lisbon. From there she will go to Zurich, where she owns a chalet. It's perfect for my operations. I can handle just about all my territory from there. I'll be at our rendezvous point on the evening before the accident, unless you change any of the plans."

"There is always that chance, but for now we'll keep to this plan," Christopher stated with an assenting nod.

"So, unless you have more information for me . . . Oh! and I do realize that there won't be any further communication between us for the time being," Wilhelm said.

Without saying a word, Christopher rose and very quietly walked to the library doors. He flung them open. Bailey straightened and stood erect.

"Is there anything you need, sir?" he asked sheepishly.

"Yes, please bring another bottle of cognac. Then you may retire, Bailey. I don't think that we'll need you anymore this evening," Christopher said sternly.

"Yes, sir," Bailey said, retreating into the kitchen.

Christopher and Wilhelm conversed until after three o'clock in the morning. By that time, Christopher was so exhausted when he closed the front doors after Wilhelm that he stripped off his vest, shirt, and shoes, and fell asleep on the leather sofa.

Thirteen

ELISE awoke from a fitful sleep with a thundering headache. She gently pressed her fingertips against her temples and felt the quick tempo of her pulse. The pain throbbed more with each beat. Why did she feel so awful? She rolled on her side and looked at the place in her bed where Christopher slept; she realized he hadn't come to bed all night! She sat up quickly and blinked at the bright sun that shone into the room. She tried to forget her pain in an effort to recall last night's events. Then she remembered. Deanna! She had come to Christopher, and had even said she couldn't wait any longer! When had he arranged their rendezvous? Oh, God in heaven! He wouldn't make love to that woman here in this house, would he? Could he possibly be that cruel?

At this moment she believed he could. She trembled with rage as her tears streamed down her cheeks, and she jumped from the bed and ran across the floor to the door that led to Deanna's rose-and-eyelet room. She turned the brass knob, but found the door had been bolted. She pushed and jiggled the knob, but it was no use. She didn't pound on the wood, as she wanted so desperately to do. She realized that they must be in there at this moment, although it was late for Christopher to be in bed. Perhaps he was so spent from his night of ecstasy that he couldn't awake. Was Deanna still with him? Elise's back slid down the door, and she fell into a heap on the the floor and sobbed.

"God help me, please! I can't bear this and I don't know what to do anymore. I know he finds her more

112

pleasing, but why must he torture me so? What have I done to him that makes him treat me like this?" she wailed. Her melancholy grew until she felt herself sinking into a deep depression. With an enormous effort, she gained control of herself.

No, I won't fall into that pit, she promised herself. No one and nothing will ever again make me lose control like that. I've got to make myself immune to his cruelty toward me. This is my chance to control my fate. I can at least learn to master my own emotions. If he wanted Deanna last night, then I'll have to deal with it somehow. But I've got to be much stronger.

"Christopher, my dear," she said as she rose from the floor. "You are certainly the best teacher I've ever had. One way or another I will survive. Damn you, Christopher!" she swore as she stormed into the bathroom to begin her toilette.

Christopher awoke to Hannah's scolding words. "Mr. Chris! What are you doing down here? What time did you get to sleep, anyway?"

Christopher rubbed his bloodshot eyes and looked up at her.

"My God! I never even made it upstairs! I feel rotten. What time is it?" he asked.

"It's half past nine and the antique dealer is here with the furniture for the study. We were fortunate in that he had everything we needed. He wants you to approve these items. The painters left last night before you came home. We don't have the upholstery or the draperies in, but there's nothing left that's pink. The easel was installed about an hour ago. I hope the rest arrives either today or tomorrow. Mrs. Mann will be surprised, won't she?" Hannah was pleased with the progress she had made.

"Hannah, you are a wonder! Let me see these things so they can take them upstairs right away."

Christopher followed her to the reception area, where a small, elderly man waited. "How do you do? I'm Christopher Mann."

"How do you do, Mr. Mann? I'm Anthony Blake. I don't have everything you requested, I'm afraid. I was able to procure the wood pieces, a Louis XV fauteuil in a lavender and white toile print that I hope you will find suitable. I took the liberty of choosing a Louis XV sofa in white raw silk that blends nicely with the chair," Mr. Blake said.

"It all sounds good to me. Hannah can order the draperies. Let's see what you have," Christopher said as they went out the front door to the large truck parked in front of the house.

"Since there was such a rush, I brought several items. You may choose what you like," Mr. Blake said.

Christopher purchased the upholstered pieces that his visitor had described, a hand-carved French armoire, a small secretaire, and a cherry Louis XVI chair in blue and white striped taffeta. These items were immediately taken upstairs under Hannah's supervision. Christopher thanked Blake and went to the breakfast room for a cup of coffee before awakening Elise. He was reading the morning paper when she silently entered the room. He glanced up at her and noted the firm set of her jaw.

"Christopher, I would like to know if I may have some money for some purchases I wish to make today," she said sternly.

"And what purchases do you intend to make? I thought you did your shopping yesterday," he said, turning the newspaper nonchalantly.

"I need some paints, charcoals, and art paper. And I think I'll need some money," she said, angry that she had to ask him for it.

"I have a friend who will be most happy to help you out, Elise. Here, take this card and have the chauffeur take you to this address. John is a good friend, and the owner. I'm sure he can find you what you need. He'll just send me the bill," Christopher said, smiling to himself.

Elise took the card from his hand, glared at Christopher, and spun on her heel to leave.

"Elise! Don't you want some breakfast before you go?" he asked.

"No thank you! I don't have the stomach for the company I'd have to share it with!" And she slammed out the front door.

Christopher knocked over his chair in an effort to run after her and catch her. As she drove away he said, "What in the hell is the matter with her, now? I've never seen anyone whose mood changes so quickly! Women! Who needs them?"

Elise was still furious when the driver stopped in front of La Galerie des Beaux Arts. When she went inside, she was delighted. She thought she could spend hours gazing at the beautiful artwork all around her. As she slowly passed by several paintings set on gilt easels, she felt horridly inadequate. Who was she to think she could even attempt to paint anything when she saw the perfection of Degas, Monet, Manet, and Renoir! The Impressionists were her favorite painters, and she hoped that she and Christopher would go to France so she could tour the Louvre. She would love to see all the places that these great men had known: the Seine, Notre Dame, the Champs-Elysées. Oh, to walk the streets they had walked!

Presently a tall, handsome man with soft brown eyes approached her.

"May I help you in some way?" he asked her.

"Why, yes. I'm Mrs. Christopher Mann, and my husband has informed me that a friend of his here would help me," Elise said quietly.

"Of course! How is Christopher? I'm John Salem, and I'd be happy to help you," he said, smiling at her.

"I would like some art supplies. I'm afraid I don't know my way around New York yet, and I had no idea where to purchase anything. I realize this is a gallery. So if you could just direct me—"

"I most certainly will not!" he broke in. "There is a shop not far from here, and I'll take you there myself." He paused to give brief instructions to an employee; then, taking her arm, he guided her back to her motorcar.

They arrived at a small art shop and John entered the vestibule and rang the bell. Elise had never seen a shop like this before. The vestibule had three glass window walls heavily draped in dark blue velvet. Presently, the carved oak door was opened for them by a valet, who ushered them inside a beautiful room. One entire wall was of glass, and even the ceiling had glass panels in it. Elise was fascinated by the effect that had been created. It was as though she were standing outside while still being inside. How could they capture the sky like this? She viewed the trees and clouds and felt her spirits soar.

"This is marvelous! It's so open and beautiful here!"

"You don't mean to tell me you have never seen an art studio before?" John asked, amazed at her naiveté.

"Is that what you call this? No, I haven't! But I wish I would never have to leave this room. I feel as if I could catch the clouds in my hands!" she exclaimed. Looking back at John Salem, she blushed.

"I'm sorry. Forgive me for carrying on so. I have never seen anything like this before. In fact I've never seen anything but Mobile in all my life. I'm finding that New York is a strange and wonderfully exciting city. Everyday I experience something new."

Salem was delighted with the unaffected honesty of this girl and found that his heart went out to her. No wonder Christopher married her!

"Mrs. Mann, let me select some paints for you. These are the finest quality, I assure you. Let's start with some charcoals. I have three sets of watercolors here. Some colors are repetitive, but you'll use them all, I'm sure. But I didn't ask you, which medium do you prefer?"

"I've only worked in watercolor to this point. I've always felt oils were too heavy, and I much prefer the delicate touch of the waterpaints," she replied.

"I want to give you a few oils for you to experiment with and see what you think. There are some new blends that we like, and you may discover something quite intriguing when you get used to them. I sense that your tastes are more inclined toward the pastels. So I'll give you a dozen tubes of white and you can mix the white with this set of primaries that I'll assemble for you. You'll need a dozen brushes, canvas, sketch pads, stretchers, art paper, hammer, tacks. What else . . . ?" he murmured, looking at the stocked shelves in front of him.

"Mr. Salem! I'm sure you can think of all the materials I need more adequately than I. For the moment, I would like to take some paper and charcoals with me. The other supplies I'd like to have sent to our house. I thought I'd try to sketch some of these fabulous city sights."

"That will pose no problem for us. May I suggest you have your driver take you to Central Park? It's beautiful there this time of morning. Unless you wanted to sketch the buildings and street scenes of Manhattan. If that's the case, I'd be most delighted to let you do so from the gallery. There's a spectacular view from the courtyard area under the awning. We could set out a table and chairs for you. Please, let me do this for you, Mrs. Mann," he said pleadingly. "I'm most anxious to be of any help to Christopher and to his wife."

"Please, John, call me Elise. And I'd like very much to do my sketching from the gallery. Then, if I have time I could go to Central Park this afternoon." Elise beamed at him. She had found a new friend in John Salem. She saw kindness and honesty in his eyes, and she had known instantly that she could trust him. Now she had two friends in New York—John and Mrs. Anderson. New York was not as cold-hearted as she had feared.

She wondered, though, how Christopher could have such diverse friendships. All his business associates seemed secretive and false toward her, but then there was this man, John, who was as sensitive as she. Elise found it difficult to imagine Christopher and John ever being close. Was she misjudging John? Or was there something about Christopher she didn't know? She almost laughed at her own stupidity. She didn't know anything about Christopher at all.

Lost in concentration on her work, Elise was surprised to look up and see John standing beside her at the little round wrought iron table with a bottle of wine and two glasses in one hand and plate of fruit and cheese in the other.

"Don't you think it's about time you took a break? Put your things away, now. You can always come back tomorrow." His smile was warm.

"I had no idea it was lunchtime already! I'm famished," she said while he uncorked the bottle.

"Lunchtime? It's after three o'clock! You really have been lost in your own little world, haven't you?" he asked.

"It can't possibly be that late! After we finish this lovely treat, would you please call the chauffeur for me?"

"Certainly. Now," he said filling her glass with cold white wine, "to an enchanting new artiste. May this be the beginning of a great career for you." He touched her glass with his own.

This had been one of the most memorable days of Elise's life. It was certainly the nicest day she'd spent in New York. John's kindness had touched her deeply. She quietly hummed to herself as she entered the mansion with her sketchbook. Hannah was just leaving through the vestibule area when Elise spied her.

"Hannah, what's that you have there?" she asked.

"Oh, Mrs. Mann. There you are. I was afraid we had lost you for good," she chuckled. "These flowers just arrived for you. Would you like to arrange them?"

"Flowers? What kind of flowers?" Elise asked as she opened the huge box. "Why, there must be five dozen roses here. And they're all white and yellow. Oh, Hannah, look at this apricot color. Aren't they beautiful? Are there any silver bowls?"

"Yes, ma'am, there are."

"Good. I love yellow roses in silver bowls. And the white ones in crystal bowls. I'll put the apricot roses upstairs so I'll be able to see them when I'm dressing this evening. Oh! I just love roses! And these are unusually fragrant."

"Hannah, who ordered these?" she asked with a frown.

"What a silly question. Mr. Mann, of course. He ordered them for you, child," Hannah said as she left the room to fetch the containers Elise wanted.

Appeasement! He was pacifying her again. Did he think that a bunch of roses would make up for his night's frolic with Deanna? A black mood hung over her. She scowled fiercely as she jammed each delicate bud into the silver container. She felt nauseated, and her head was pounding. She finished her task and gave Hannah instructions where to place the flowers.

Elise stormed upstairs to bathe and change for dinner. God! She felt awful. All day long she had been able to escape the hurt and anger she felt, but now it was all back again. Elise took off her brown linen suit and sat on the blue and white Oriental rug clad only in her pastel blue satin chemise. She took out her sketches and picked up a piece of charcoal. Her hand flew across the surface of the paper in an effort to improve her rendition of a city scene. She flipped through the stack, found another sketch, and embellished its tones also. While she worked, she reflected on her wonderful afternoon with John Salem.

Hannah found a pensive Elise sprawled in the middle of the floor. "Mrs. Mann! I thought you'd be dressed by now!"

"Why? What time is it?"

"It's after eight o'clock, and Mr. Chris should have been home by now. He called half an hour ago and said he'd be home presently, just as soon as he delivered some legal documents to the Worthingtons. He should be here any minute," Hannah said as she hung Elise's freshly pressed white organza and taffeta gown.

Elise winced at the mention of Deanna's name. Just how often did he see her? When Hannah left the room, Elise quickly filled the tub and raced through her toilette. She didn't want to keep Christopher waiting. She couldn't win him from Deanna if she became a screaming banshee, she knew. She would have to curb her anger. She wished she could understand why he was so cruel to her. But, in spite of that, she was inexplicably drawn to him. His touch, his voice, his presence were magic. The night grew darker, and clouds streamed across the face of the full moon. She finished dressing and began to pace the room nervously as the hour ticked away. Where was he?

"What a stupid question, Elise! He's with Deanna and even tonight's dinner engagement couldn't pull him away. You are a fool, Elise. A fool! When will you ever learn? God!" Elise cried as she slumped into one of the wing chairs to wait for her husband to come home.

The grandfather clock chimed the late hour as Christopher dragged himself up the stairs. He opened the door and saw his wife sleeping in a chair. The silver moonlight played over her slender form. She was fully dressed in a white gown he hadn't seen before.

"Oh, Christ! She didn't get my message! Or did I forget to send one? Damn!" he cursed himself. "How could I have been so inconsiderate?"

He padded quietly over to her and kissed her cheek. Even though he was stirred by her vulnerability to him, he didn't wish to wake her. He gently lifted her into his arms and tenderly placed her on the bed. Covering her with a light blanket, he gazed at her face for a moment before he left the room and went downstairs to the library to sleep.

Elise was awakened by thunder. The rain was beating against the windows with great force. The ebony night was broken by jagged lines of lightning. She had always been terrified of storms, and the power of nature's potential destruction panicked her. She cried out and reached toward Christopher. When she did so, she realized he was not with her. The storm shook the walls, and its reverberations played with the delicate prisms of the chandelier until, quite suddenly, the thunder rolled away into the distance. The racing tempo of her heartbeat slowed, and tears of relief cascaded down her cheeks. Gradually she drifted back to sleep.

The early dawn light greeted her.

Elise sat up and swung her legs off the bed when she realized she was still fully dressed. When did she get into bed? And where was Christopher? Then, as she remembered the horror of the storm, she gathered her courage and decided she couldn't keep her frustrations bottled inside any longer. She had to tell Christopher how she felt. Before she left his bedroom, she tried the door to Deanna's room and found it still locked. Her fury rose again. She would find him immediately and tell him how abominably he had treated her. But she wouldn't look in Deanna's room first. She could not endure *that* rejection. She stormed down the stairs into the breakfast room.

He sat at the round table with his head in his hands. He had obviously slept in his clothes. He looked up as he heard her come into the room. Her face was filled with pain and anger.

"Good morning, Mr. Mann! Did you finally decide to come home? I do believe we will be a trifle late for our dinner engagement. Or did you escort Miss Worthington in my stead?" Her smile frightened Christopher. "Or perhaps she's still in her room upstairs? How can you be so callous as to bed your mistress in the room next to me?" she cried hysterically.

"I've just about had enough of your temper tantrums, *Mrs. Mann!*" He grabbed her forearm and pulled her up the stairs. He unlocked the door to the study and pushed Elise inside. She stumbled and almost fell to the floor before she caught her balance and glared at him. Sensing something strange, she turned slowly and observed the room around her.

"It's gone! All the rose is gone!" she exclaimed as she saw the newly painted lavender walls. The crown molding and chair railing had been lacquered in white, and on the dark oak floor lay an Aubusson rug in pale blues and yellows. She walked over to the fauteuil chair and ran her hand over the lavender print fabric. Exquisite French antiques filled the corner opposite the wall of the windows. Turning toward the sunlight that streamed into the room, she exclaimed: "The windows! There aren't any draperies! It's like the art studio! I can see the trees, the gardens, the sky!"

Elise was like a small child on Christmas morning as she flitted around the room investigating all the changes. When she saw the easel near the windows, her eyes filled with grateful tears.

"You, you did all this for me, Christopher? It's just like home! Only better!" Her voice fell to a whisper as she gazed up at his face.

For the first time since the night she met him in Mobile, she once again saw his eyes as crystal blue. Gone was the steel door blocking her entrance to his soul. She glided toward him and stood in his gaze. She felt herself fall into the depths of his eyes as she slid her arms around his waist and pulled herself close to his warm body.

"Thank you for all of this, Christopher. I'm so very glad I was wrong and had misjudged you . . ." she breathed softly as his lips covered hers. Her heart was so full of love for him, and she wished to tell him so. He held her close to him, gingerly at first, but then his kisses became more demanding and her body responded to his.

"Christopher, my darling, I—" she had begun, when they were interrupted by Hannah, who appeared at the door.

"Mr. Chris, excuse me, but there's a gentleman downstairs who is carrying on something awful about seeing you. He says it's urgent. I'm sorry for bursting in like this," she said.

Christopher held Elise close for a minute and said, "It's all right, Hannah, I'm coming." He started after Hannah and then, remembering something, took a small envelope out of his vest pocket and handed it to Elsie.

"A messenger brought this for you, and I almost forgot

121

it. And, Elise, hold the thought. I'll be back," he said, smiling at her, and then he left.

Elise watched his magnificent form disappear down the stairs. Glancing down at the note, she saw that it was Jesse's stationery.

"Jesse! Now it *is* really like being at home!" She peered around the lavender room in which she stood. "What kind of man am I married to? He's been so distant and cruel until now. But it's a beginning. I wonder if he'll trust me enough to let me into his heart?"

She sat serenely on the fauteuil chair and ripped open the heavy, cream parchment envelope. She almost wept as she saw Jesse's familiar, delicate script.

My Dearest Elise,

I have so much to relate to you that I am confused as to how I should begin. I do suppose that the beginning would be a proper place. At your papa's birthday party, I met a most extraordinary man. He is most pleasing to my eye, Elise, and you know all too well how discriminating that eye is. His name is Wilhelm Schmidt and I have found myself deeply in love with him. We are sailing shortly for Zurich, Switzerland. My parents know nothing of our plans as they do not approve of Wil because of his German heritage. Please, my friend, find it in your heart to be happy for me and pray for me. You are so often in my thoughts. I wish we were all children again playing silly games in Mobile. That is not to be. I trust in Wil and I pray you have found a love as wonderful as mine. You know my address in Zurich should you need to contact me. Perhaps on your honeymoon? What a delightful thought! I will wait to hear from you, my dearest friend.

Lovingly,
Your Jesse

Elise's hand fell heavily to her lap, and she began to tremble with the sobs that racked her body. Everything in her life had changed so quickly. She was amazed to realize that only two weeks ago she and Jesse were playing lawn tennis and talking until midnight on Jesse's can-

122

opied bed. Only two weeks ago they had confided in each other just as they had done since they were tiny girls. They had been children just fourteen days ago, and now they had both cast their fates into the hands of men they hardly knew. But Jesse had the love of a man she was leaving with. The thought was painful to Elise.

She scanned the letter again quickly. Nowhere had she seen any mention of an elopement, wedding, or marriage. My God! Jesse was his mistress! What was she thinking of? No wonder she didn't want her parents to know. Jesse must have lost her mind!

"No, she didn't lose her mind," Elise said aloud as she calmed herself. "What she lost was her heart, just like I did. I may have Christopher's name, but that's all I have. Jesse has Wilhelm's love, but not his name. What have we done? What made us both such fools?" Elise lamented.

She sat in the chair, gazing at the celadon canopy of leaves that swayed in the warm June breeze outside her open window, and mourned the death of her childhood.

Fourteen

THE past week's events flashed through Elise's memory. She had managed to visit Mrs. Anderson at Saks Fifth Avenue twice and had assembled an extensive wardrobe. Christopher hadn't mentioned the bill when it came, but he did comment on the numerous deliveries to the house. She and Hannah carefully packed the winter clothing in large steamer trunks. The gowns she would need aboard ship were packed in lighter suitcases. Elise was quite pleased with her new things, and wished Christopher had been more interested in how much she had accomplished in just one week. When she wasn't arranging her wardrobe, she worked at her easel in the study. She had transformed one of her charcoal sketches to soft pastel watercolors. She laughed to herself when she thought of how unrealistic the colors were. Her paintings were certainly not true to life, but they were a product of herself.

On two sunny afternoons she had gone to John's gallery to sit under the awning and paint. She made a valiant attempt to learn the proper usage of these oils. He said she had progressed under his tutelage, but she was unsure. She was such a novice, and had to work quite diligently to accomplish the simplest tasks he gave her. But she wanted to please him and prove to them both that she did have some small talent. John was teaching her much about the art world.

He said that the finest talents flocked to Paris to learn new techniques and that he himself had been there just after New York's 1913 Armory show. He said he had been shocked by this new art, but then, as his awareness and appreciation of the painters grew, he had become enthralled by the work of the Spaniard Picasso, the Russian Chagall, and the French Marcel Duchamp. Duchamp's painting *Nude Descending a Staircase No. 2* was John's personal favorite.

Elise made a true effort to understand this modern art mode, but she decided she was just not sophisticated or intellectual enough to fully appreciate these painters. She still loved the Impressionists. Perhaps if she ever went to Paris and spoke with these new artists, as John had, or investigated their work more thoroughly, then she would understand what they were hoping to accomplish.

John had been such a thoughtful friend to her. It seemed that when she was most frustrated and ready to give in to defeat, she would look up and he would be standing next to her. His smile was warm and genuine. It still puzzled her that this wonderful man was Christopher's friend, yet they never saw each other. Every evening when they went to dinner with friends and associates, she hoped that John would be there. She looked for his face everywhere, but in two weeks, he hadn't appeared. John spoke endearingly of Christopher, and just this morning her husband had inquired about John. Christopher had told her that John was his most trusted friend and that he thought of him as a brother. She couldn't understand the situation at all.

Elise finished packing her art supplies in her satchel and placed it on top of the last suitcase that Bailey would take to the motorcar. It was late, and she hadn't dressed yet.

She was soaking in lavender-scented water when Christopher walked into the bathroom unexpectedly.

He hadn't seen her in the bath before, and it was broad daylight. He folded his muscular arms, leaned against the doorjamb and grinned at her wickedly. He was so handsome with his white cotton shirt open at the throat. His tan trousers seemed molded to his thighs, and he wore polished white shoes with tan leather on the toe and in a square patch around the lacings. He'd been outside a good deal lately, she thought, for his face was a golden brown. His eyes flashed blue mischief at her, and she lost her heart to him once again.

"I was about to come up here to scold you for being so

slow. Everything seems to be in order except for you, Mrs. Mann. However, I don't believe I can take my anger out on such a bewitching vision. I think I'll just watch awhile."

"Christopher! Do get out of here, I . . . I don't have anything to cover myself with! Please, go away. I don't want you to see me like this," she pleaded.

"You're my wife and I can look at you anytime I damn well please. Just don't forget that, Elise. Now, hurry up and get dressed. Ships don't wait for vain little girls," he said, scowling as he turned and went into the bedroom.

"Little girl? Vain? You callous brute!" she hissed.

"Damn! Damn!" he muttered to himself. He could feel his hands on her breasts right now. What was it about her that made him act like a schoolboy? He could never say the right thing to her. They didn't have long until it would be time to depart, and now he wished they had time to make love.

He cursed this last week of business arrangements, meetings, and dinners that had kept him out till very late every night and away from her bed. She had been so pleased with the studio, and he had wanted to share it with her. It was his own fault he had constantly been away. He was looking forward to their seclusion on board ship for the next week. He would make it up to her. He would . . .

Christopher! For God's sake remember your priorities, he reprimanded himself. *You're getting too involved again and too close to her. You'll both end up getting hurt. It's up to you to control this relationship.*

He left the room abruptly and went to the library for a drink. Sitting on the window seat, he sipped his bourbon and stared out the window at the animated summer scenes.

A girl in a white middy dress played hopscotch just outside his gate. Her brown-haired friend, dressed similarly in navy blue, was jumping up and down in glee over her friend's success at the game. A boy in knickers sat across the street playing with a Yorkshire terrier. He was shouting at the girls, who pretended not to hear him. They whispered and clasped their small hands over their mouths, giggling uncontrollably. One little girl spun on her heel, grabbed the other child's arm, and pulled her

126

out of sight. The little boy looked sad as they disappeared, but as the girl with the red-brown hair popped back into sight and smiled at him, he stood up and waved. She was gone again in an instant. The boy put his hands in his pockets and stared after her for quite some time. Then, whistling to himself, he picked up his dog and went into his house.

Christopher gulped down his drink and gazed at the trees that grew close to the windows. How he wanted some response from Elise! He knew it wasn't good for him to torture himself this way. He was responsible for her just as he was responsible for the shipment of guns to Germany and the other Central Power countries. He must keep reminding himself that Elise was simply a part of a plan. He had needed her to speed up his business affairs, and she had done just that. Actually, she had already served her purpose. It was true that their traveling as honeymooners would place him above suspicion by the authorities; but he *could* leave her here, where she would be safe.

Perhaps he was being overly concerned about his feeling toward her. If he were truly involved with her, wouldn't he insist that she remain in New York? Where they were going it could be physically dangerous for her. Christopher hadn't really thought of this before. He had concerned himself merely with the emotional pain he would inflict on her. He knew she was infatuated with him, but he knew she didn't love him. And his own feelings were merely protective, he told himself. It was his responsibility to care for her needs. Many times in her presence he felt an oppressive guilt, but she had never responded to him, or reached out to him. It was possible he was worrying needlessly.

Now he was angry with himself for being such an idiot. It eased his conscience somewhat to know that he was not getting as involved with her as he had earlier believed.

He heard her delicate heel tap the marble floor of the reception area and then heard the muffled voices of Hannah and Bailey. Hannah was saying she knew it would be lonely without Elise around the house.

He placed his glass on the silver tray, gathered up his valise, and started to leave. Abruptly he stopped, turned, and went back to the desk. He took out a small brass key

127

and opened the top desk drawer. He reached into a concealed compartment and withdrew a revolver. He opened the valise and inserted both the gun and a box of cartridges. He relocked the drawer and joined his wife.

Elise stood before him in a white linen dress with long sleeves that ended in thick cuffs; black buttons ran the length of the skirt. She wore a small brimmed white cloche hat that hid her hair. She appeared quite striking, and the hat emphasized her cheekbones and eyes, but he much preferred to see her hair streaming down her back. She was impatiently slapping her white cotton gloves against her hip, waiting. Upon seeing him, she stopped and smiled.

"I trust we are ready to go?" he asked her.

She walked over to him, still smiling sweetly, raised her foot, kicked him in the shin, and said: "I am *not* vain!" And with that she stalked off to the waiting motorcar.

"Hurry up, Christopher, or we'll be late," she called to him.

Christopher rubbed the spot where a welt had begun to rise. He wanted to turn her over his knee and spank her. What a little spitfire! No! What he wanted to do was make love to her over and over until he couldn't breathe anymore. He shook his head, laughed, and earnestly tried to remember his earlier resolve. He must take care to find some outlet for his frustrations while on board ship; he was finding it increasingly difficult to harness his emotions. Every time he took a noncommittal approach to the situation, something happened that made his body overrule his good judgment.

Elise was fascinated with the New York harbor and its great variety of ships. She had seen cargo ships and barges in Mobile, but nothing to compare with these ocean liners. Riding to the pier, she grew homesick and wished she were sailing for home instead of Europe. She wanted to see Mama and her sisters. Then the thought of Papa's hideous betrayal banished her happy memories. She clutched her gloves and twisted the fingers in her trembling hands. She felt closed in, overwhelmed by a sense of panic. Just as she felt herself about to scream, the chauffeur stopped the auto.

"This is our pier. Elise, is something wrong? Are you

128

ill?" Christopher said, shaking her shoulder gently with his steady hands.

"I'm all right. Just nervous about the voyage, I guess," she lied.

There was an inordinate commotion. Passengers, porters, chauffeurs, and the ship's crew milled about them. Christopher was occupied with a steward. Elise was pushed and shoved by those about her. Several times she nearly lost her balance, and she had a difficult time remaining composed. When Christopher walked over to her and offered his arm, she quickly grabbed it. She felt as if she were drowning and he was her life preserver. Her fingers pressed into the fabric of his jacket and found the security of his muscular arm. Christopher looked at her and patted her hand as he led her up the gangplank.

The gray ship was enormous. The hull was topped by three stories of cabins, which extended the long expanse of the ship. There were two huge black smokestacks, the tall foremast, and the aftmast. But all Elise could see from her vantage point was steel, and it seemed to surround and engulf her. Everywhere were large steel walls and doors. Steel doors! Just like the steel door she had seen in Christopher's eyes that first night she met him. She felt panic-stricken.

They stood on a large deck and leaned over the railing to view the people below. Everyone was waving and shouting and yelling. She saw both sorrowful eyes and happy smiles on the faces of those on land. Streamers, confetti, and flowers flew through the jubilant air. The excitement of all those about her only seemed to intensify her gloom and sense of dread. She needed desperately to lie down. Christopher appeared to be enjoying himself, and she didn't want to disturb him. Ordinarily, she could stand for hours and just watch him. But today, something was wrong. She was afraid and uncertain of everything. She was more unsure of him than she had been. She knew him no better now than on that first night in Mobile.

Christopher mumbled something to Elise as he steered her toward the interior of the ship and away from the railing. She was glad to get away from all the people; she had the eerie sensation that all their shouting was not what it seemed. Her mind perceived the noise as cries of human pain and suffering. It was as if they were all dying about her. Why would such a morbid thought enter her mind?

They were walking down a flight of steel stairs and were now in a narrow passageway. They stopped at a gray door, and Christopher opened it while the ship's cabin boy brought in their luggage.

The stateroom was larger than Elise had expected. She giggled to herself when she realized she had anticipated small bunks and hammocks hung in tiny windowless rooms deep belowdecks. But they were on one of the uppermost decks and had a beautiful view of the ocean. There were two beds and a sitting area near the windows. The door to the left led to the bath area. She opened the louvered doors to the closet and started to unpack when Christopher spoke.

"Let the cabin boy do that. I want you to rest awhile. I'll be back shortly. We're having dinner at the captain's table tonight, and I want you to look especially nice!" He tipped the cabin boy and left.

Elise sat in a blue chair and drummed her fingers against the dark wood of the round table before her. She gazed about the suite. The walls were pale gold velvet, the carpet a gold blue and pink floral design. On the dresser across the room sat an enormous basket of fruits and a bottle of champagne. It was tied prettily with a large white satin bow. She took the small square note off the basket and read his script.

To my dear friends, Christopher and Elise. May you have a safe and happy voyage. My thoughts are with you both.

Affectionately,
John

Elise felt the tears sting her eyes. She was leaving another good friend. Would life always be like this? It seemed she was forever leaving life's treasures behind and heading toward more unknowns. She began to blame Christopher for the pain she felt, even though she knew it wasn't his fault. If she wanted to blame anyone, it was Papa. He had sold her into this bondage. But there was

130

nothing she could do about it and the adult thing to do was to accept her life. At least she was with Christopher; and whether or not he wanted her, she wanted him.

The cabin boy finished and left promptly. Elise wrote a quick note of thanks to John and dispatched it before they left port. While she was bathing, she felt the movement of the ship as they sailed out toward the open seas. She had always sought solace in these steaming baths. They were her remedy for her tensions and frustration, her private oasis.

She dried off with a large white towel and slipped on her turquoise peignoir. As the ship continued to roll, Elise felt bile rise in her throat. Her stomach began to churn, and she felt light-headed. Her knees and legs tingled and buckled, then suddenly she slumped onto the bed. She lay down, threw her arm across her damp forehead and swore at herself.

Damn, Elise, she thought, you are a true marvel! Your first ocean voyage and you get seasick only two hours out of port. Christopher is going to be livid.

She didn't have much time to ponder the matter any longer; she ran to the bathroom. It was at this point that Christopher entered the room.

"Elise, are you all right?" he asked, and then he realized her predicament. "Are you seasick? I'll go to the ship's doctor and get some medication for you. You'll be just fine. Don't you worry," he said, pressing a cold cloth to her forehead. Elise watched him leave, and the wry thought came to her that seasickness had some benefits: This was the most concern she'd seen from him since the day they'd met. As her stomach rolled over again, she wondered if the price was worth paying.

Realizing that his wife would not be able to attend dinner, Christopher sent for a tray with toast and tea while he dressed.

"If we weren't having dinner with the captain, I would stay here with you. But I feel I should go. I hope you don't mind too much. Do you?"

"No, no. You go ahead and enjoy yourself. I'm sure I'll be fine once the medication takes effect. When you return you can tell me all about it," she replied in listless tones.

The first-class dining room was located in the center of the ship. Christopher left the cool evening breezes of the promenade deck and entered a large wrought iron railed landing area. A curving staircase wound down to the opulent dining room. The room was lit by large antique brass chandeliers. The heavy red velvet draperies and the red, black, and gold floral carpeting complemented the red flocked wallpaper. There were approximately one hundred round tables covered in snowy linens. The steward led Christopher to the captain's table and seated him next to the captain.

"How do you do, Mr. Mann. I'm Captain Sanders. I'd like to introduce you to Mr. and Mrs. Charles Smythe, Mr. Alan Chesie, and Miss Liza Garrett," the captain said.

Pleasantries were exchanged while the appetizer and wine were served. While the wine was poured, Christopher had a chance to observe the young woman next to him. His eyes widened in pleasant surprise as he realized how beautiful the red-haired girl was. She looked up at him and smiled. Incredible! She had flawless skin and a magnificent figure; her low-cut satin evening gown was the same color green as her eyes.

Tonight wouldn't be a total loss after all, he thought. Their conversation was lively and stimulating. He had no desire to let the evening end.

"Miss Garrett, would you accompany me upstairs to the ballroom for some dancing? The captain assures me that the orchestra is excellent, and I don't feel sleepy just yet."

She answered both his question and his smile. "Why, I'd be most happy to, Mr. Mann. I've never been on an ocean voyage before, and I intend to explore all the delights this ship has to offer."

Christopher helped her with her chair, gave their thanks to the captain, and ascended the circular staircase. The orchestra was engaging, and Liza Garrett was an accomplished dancer. While dancing, they met three couples who joined them later in the gambling room. Liza was enthralled with the game of roulette, and Christopher delighted in advising her which numbers to play. He had to admit she did not need much help; in fact she seemed to do better without his aid. He watched her accumulate a tidy sum before she decided to quit.

"Do you suppose we could play some poker?" she asked him.

Christopher had to close his opened mouth quickly so she wouldn't see his shock at her words.

"Well, I suppose so. Perhaps we can get together a table. Let me talk to the steward and see what I can do," he said, amused by her independence.

In twenty minutes, Liza was dealing a second hand to six men. Christopher had folded and sat watching in amazement. He wondered what she would do next. It wasn't long before she pulled an imported cigarette from her gold mesh evening bag and asked him for a match. Christopher laughed, lit her cigarette, and kissed her on the ear.

"Gentlemen, guard your wallets," Christopher said. "I think the little lady may charm their contents away from you." Then he sat back for the next three hours and watched her do just that.

Christopher kissed Liza on the cheek at her cabin door and headed back for his own cabin. He gently opened the door so as not to disturb Elise. After undressing, he got into bed next to his wife. He fell asleep thinking of the red-haired Liza, who had made his first night on board such a memorable one.

Christopher awoke with a start when he felt Elise shaking his arm.

"I'm famished! Could we go to breakfast soon, Christopher?"

He peered at her through his fogged brain and pulled the sheet over his face. "It can't be morning already!" he groaned.

"But it is and we've missed the first call to breakfast," she replied as she pulled on the sheet. "I thought I'd go on deck afterward and sketch, if you don't mind."

"Fine. Just give me a moment to dress," he said as he carefully rose from the bed. His head throbbed, and he thought he could feel the crash of every wave inside his brain. He was sure he hadn't had that much to drink. But then, he mused, it had been a late night.

Elise finished packing her satchel with her oils, papers, and charcoals. She thought she would blend the colors that John had selected for her.

Christopher emerged from the bathroom dressed in white trousers and a white open-necked silk shirt whose sleeves he had rolled up to bare his tan arms. God! Did he always have to look so handsome?

"Shall we go now, my dear? I could use a little repast myself!" he said cheerily.

As they left the room, Elise wondered how many more nights would pass before he would come to her. It seemed like it had been an eternity already, and she would just as soon return to their stateroom now. He took her arm, and she trembled at his touch. In that moment, she lost her appetite for food.

My God, Elise, she said to herself. Don't be such a wanton! It's the middle of the morning! But what should I do when I want him so?

The afternoon passed uneventfully. While Elise dabbled in her paints, Christopher sought Liza's company. As the sun set in the west, Elise realized how late it was, and she decided to dress for dinner. After putting away her art things she rose from the deck chair and was seized by a wave of nausea. She couldn't be going through this again! At this rate she would never have dinner with Christopher. He would be furious. She had been fine all day long. Why did it always hit at dinnertime? Did she have a secret aversion to being with Christopher? Was her body reacting to the stress she felt? It was so strange . . . she felt weak and so faint. . . . That was her last conscious thought as she fell to the deck.

Four passengers hovered over Elise's body. She was ashen in color, and her eyelids were closed. She was very still, and her breath was quite shallow. The ship's doctor felt for her pulse. Finding it, he pulled some smelling salts from his leather bag. Her eyelids fluttered slightly, and she uttered a low moan. The doctor raised her head in his arm and held the salts beneath her nostrils once more.

"What happened? Where am I? Who are you?" she asked him. Then she felt the throbbing lump on the back of her head and winced.

"Miss, are you able to stand up? You fainted, but I believe you are perfectly fine now. I'm Doctor Mills. I'd like you to come to sick bay for a more thorough examination. Fainting spells can be very serious. I wouldn't want to know that any passenger was seriously ill," he said.

Elise merely blinked at him. She had heard only bits and pieces of what he was saying to her—something about her fainting and that she was sick. With his aid, she stood up and was ushered to a medical examination room of some sort. Lying on the examining table, she tried to answer Dr. Mills's questions.

Christopher had been shooting skeet all afternoon with Liza Garrett, and she had bested him three out of four times. He liked her nonchalant attitude toward all her undertakings. He had been walking with her on the promenade deck when one of the stewards came up and informed him of his wife's illness. He excused himself and went directly to the sick bay. He arrived just as a pale Elise was leaving. The doctor had his arm around her shoulder and was handing her another vial of the same medication that Christopher had procured for her the previous night.

"Oh, Christopher! Now that you are here Doctor Mills needn't walk to my cabin. Thank you, sir. I'll do just as you say," she said to the doctor as she took Christopher's arm.

"Take care, Mrs. Mann. I'll be here if you need anything. Please don't hesitate to call on me," Dr. Mills said.

"You caused quite a stir on deck," Christopher said. "Are you all right? Perhaps it's just exhaustion. We have had a busy few weeks. You may need more rest."

"Yes, that's just what Doctor Mills said. Too much excitement on top of seasickness. I don't think I'll join you for dinner tonight either, Christopher," she said weakly.

"I can well understand that. Let's get you settled in first and make sure you are comfortable. We can have a tray sent up if you feel you can eat something. How does that sound?" Christopher asked concernedly.

He opened the door to their cabin and sat Elise on the edge of the bed. He unbuttoned her jacket and hung it in the closet. He took off her shoes as she stared down at the top of his dark hair. The medication Dr. Mills had given her was taking effect; she didn't feel nauseated any

longer. She unbuttoned the back of her skirt, then stood
and let it fall to the floor. As she sat back down, Christopher picked up the skirt and put it away. He unbuttoned
the gray pearl buttons of her silk blouse, and as he did so,
he glanced up into her eyes. She lifted her arms to pull
the pins from the tight knot that held her hair. It fell
about her and the setting sun turned it to gold. After he
pulled the blouse off her shoulders, she sat clad in a short
white satin-and-lace chemise. Her eyes were filled with
desire. His hands tenderly grasped her hair and he
brought her head toward him. His lips brushed hers
softly, and he felt the tingle of their light touch. His mouth
covered hers, and he knew he couldn't stop. His hands
moved to her shoulders and pushed the strap of the chemise down her arms. The chemise fell and bared her
breasts. His mouth moved down her soft white throat then
to her nipples. He feasted on her beauty; on the loving
gift that was Elise. He clasped her waist tightly as her
breasts heaved against him. He removed her chemise before divesting himself of his own clothes, and then, while
gazing with passion at her long-legged body, he lay beside her and caressed her flat stomach, moving his fingers
ever lower. Her legs parted and he filled her with himself.
She moaned softly as her hips rotated with the rhythm of
his penetrations. Her moans became louder, and her
breathing quickened. She put her hands on his strong
back and caressed him. She pulled him closer, and as
she cried out his name her legs moved around his and
covered his flanks. She tilted her hips up to him, and at
the moment of his explosion she whispered his name repeatedly.

His body relaxed, but she held him tighter and closer
than she had before. He made a start to leave her, but
she clutched at his back, and he held her as close as he
could. He wished he could hold her forever; he wished
she could hold his soul as she now held his body. Tears
rolled down her cheeks, and Christopher rolled to his side
and put her head on his broad chest. She had not eased
her hold on him, and now she flung one of her long legs
over his thigh in order to be even closer to him. He lay
with her for hours and after she slept, he felt tears in his
hot eyes. No one had ever held him so close; nor had

anyone needed him so much as this frightened girl who was his wife.

Elise spent the rest of the week battling the nausea that seemed to come and go. She certainly hadn't been good company for Christopher. She had managed only one dinner with him. She didn't know what he did while she rested, but he was uncomplaining and was forever checking on her. He was so kind and considerate. She wondered what had come over him. He had even sat in a deck chair to read one afternoon while she painted. He teased her mercilessly about her simple designs. He walked her around the promenade deck and held her hand. And every afternoon after lunch they had come back to their stateroom to make love. It was actually beginning to seem like a honeymoon. Except for her spells of illness, it couldn't be more perfect.

Elise had not been able to go to dinner that night because of the nausea, and now she found that Dr. Mills's medication was gone. Elise was glad they were only a day away from port. But there was tonight to get through; she must go to Dr. Mills and get some more medicine. She dressed quickly and decided to walk out on the deck. Perhaps the night air would help clear her head and calm her stomach. Maybe that was all she needed—just some fresh air. She had been cooped up too long.

The full moon was a beacon in the starlit sky. The silver gleam on the surface of the rippling sea was breathtaking. Elise did feel better just being outside again. She started down the companionway stairs to the next deck. At the landing she stopped dead in her tracks.

She backed into the shadows lest the intent couple sense her intrusion. A red-haired girl gazed into Christopher's handsome face. She was dressed in midnight blue silk that blew in the breeze. He held both her hands quite tightly, and the beautiful girl was crying. He moved a hand upward to remove a tear. Then he kissed her forehead. She pulled away, nodded her head twice, and sobbed under her breath. Then the strangest thing happened. He pulled a large envelope from his inside jacket pocket and handed it to the girl. She took it, kissed him lightly on the lips, and walked away.

Payment! It was some kind of payment! Elise thought in shock. *Why does he need to buy a prostitute?*

She felt herself start to tremble. She really was not enough for him. She had failed him again. What could she do to please him? He obviously needed something she could never give. All her hopes and dreams of the last few days were shattered. Even the fact that she carried his child would not be enough to win his love.

Fifteen

ELISE had always wanted to visit Rome. The Coliseum was the first thing she wanted to see. Christopher rushed them through the city so fast she had not seen anything. They were due at some airstrip in one hour —and they were not going to be late, he'd said. Their luggage would arrive in Sarajevo by rail in a few days. They each carried only a small valise. Elise feared she would be sick again once they were airborne. She was beginning to think her legs would never touch land again.

They were rushed to the biplane by a short Italian man who was most concerned about their schedule. She couldn't understand the need for such expediency, but Christopher also appeared quite concerned. They experienced an easy takeoff, and Elise didn't feel ill in the least. Gazing at the lush countryside below her, she was able to view the city and the Italian farmland and villages from a vantage point that was denied most tourists. She decided she may as well enjoy herself, especially since there was little enough cause for elation these days. Although Christopher treated her with consideration, she knew he felt her a fool. She was horridly depressed.

She had wanted to tell him about the baby, but couldn't do it now, knowing about the red-haired girl. First it was Deanna; now this one. How many were there? Would she ever know? Why was it that some men had to have so many women? What was it Christopher needed? It certainly wasn't her. She couldn't blame him, though. Deanna and that other girl were both quite beautiful, and she had been foolish to think that she could do battle

139

with them. Now she knew better—but "now" was too late. She was in love with him and was to bear his child.

She still couldn't believe it. Nobody gets pregnant on her wedding night! It even sounded indecent. She'd heard Mama say lower-class girls did that, and one should exercise more self-restraint than a rabbit. God! This was such a mess. She had no one to blame but herself. She should have fought her emotions; she shouldn't have been so quick to give in to him. But all he had to do was look at her, speak her name, and she couldn't resist. What makes a person react like that to another? No one else had ever affected her the way Christopher had. Why did she lose all reason when she was around him? Half the time she could barely speak; she was still tongue-tied when he asked her the simplest questions. She should be livid at the knowledge of this new mistress, but she only felt inadequate. Maybe she didn't have the energy to get angry because she had been ill. Maybe if she could eat a good meal, she would feel like she could beat him with her fists. She laughed out loud at the thought, and since only the wind was witness, she laughed harder and let bitter tears streak her face.

Christopher landed the plane in a barren field. Two old men came running up to assist them. They ushered Christopher and Elise to another airplane. Christopher talked to the men, who nodded their heads. Then Christopher piloted the plane into the sky once again.

"Just how long is all this going to go on?" Elise asked the wind.

They flew for hours and landed again at another countryside airstrip. There was a small house off in some trees, and Elise and Christopher were escorted to the sparse abode. Inside, a stone fireplace covered the expanse of the far wall. The floor consisted of some loosely nailed planks and upon this sat a crude table. A large bowl of fruit and cheese rested in the center with a bottle of red wine and two tin mugs. A rich aroma filled the room; near the hearth Elise saw three loaves of freshly baked bread. A four-poster sat in a corner beneath a small window.

Elise didn't know if she was more tired than hungry, or vice versa. Christopher lit a small fire to take the chill

140

out of the air, then poured them each a mug of wine. He took a deep gulp and broke off a piece of the bread. He silently stared into the fire as he ate. His mood appeared to darken and Elise noticed that his grip on the tin cup had tightened. He drank the wine quickly and filled his mug again. Elise put her cup down and very quietly went over to the bed, where she collapsed on the down-filled mattress.

As he stared at the dying embers, Christopher contemplated the gruesome task that lay before him. He thought of Elise and how he could shelter her. He saw no answers in the flames.

The motor was running as Elise took Christopher's hand and ran to the waiting plane. This was their last day of travel. She had certainly been glad to hear those words. She was stiff from the night's sleep. Tonight they would be able to stay at a nice hotel—one with a hot bath, she thought, as she rotated her stiff neck and sore shoulders.

It was a beautiful day. Already it was quite warm, and the farther south they flew, the warmer it became. But what a honeymoon! Whoever heard of flying all over the peasant countryside in a biplane and staying in a shack overnight? At least Christopher never bored her, she thought ruefully. Unfortunately for her, most of his surprises caused her pain. She was trying to avoid her feelings, to become indifferent to him. If she could order her heart to be numb, he could do as he pleased and she would not feel so desolate. But it was no good. She was just as lovesick as a schoolgirl.

They must be crossing the Adriatic Sea. The soft blues, teals, and turquoises of the waves tempted Elise's artistic eye. How wonderful to be able to capture those colors! If only they could set the plane down on the white sands of the beach just long enough for her to mix some oils. Her fingers longed to hold her palette and brushes. She made a valiant effort to lock those pigments precisely in her mind. The sunshine skipped across the small white-capped waves. Flying this low, she swore she could see some starfish just beneath the surface of the sea. The sun warmed her face as she turned her gaze heavenward. The wind blew tendrils of her dark hair about her face.

She opened her eyes and observed a group of clouds that looked like horse-drawn chariots careening across the sky.

Elise's attention was focused on nature's sideshow when she moved her gaze to the sights below her and was surprised to find that they were over land. Christopher executed a perfect landing, as usual. Elise was growing used to his expertise.

A sleek black motorcar was parked at the end of the airstrip. As they walked toward the car, she said, "Are you going to leave the plane in the middle of the field?"

"Don't worry. A crew will take care of the plane and see that it's in order." He helped her into the car. "It's not a long ride into the city. I think you'll be intrigued with Sarajevo, Elise. The Moslem influence is quite interesting. I want you to be sure to see the Begova Mosque. I think you may find some unusual subject matter for your sketches."

The automobile rattled down the dusty road toward the city.

The streets of the Old Town were quite narrow, and many of the buildings had their windows shuttered against the heat. As they drove past the Begova Mosque, Elise noted the massive dome and the minaret. Behind the mosque were the souks—the name, Christopher told her, for these greatly tangled narrow streets. It was in the souks that the tradesmen kept their shops. The peasant men were dressed in vests and jackets and wore fezzes on their heads. The women were veiled in black. The peddlers in Mobile had not appeared as poor as these people did. A small group of tradesmen occupied themselves with unloading their oxcarts and arranging their wares on rickety tables and benches, while small barefooted children slept inside the carts. Elise wondered if any of them had a real home. She viewed lush, juicy-red strawberries, eggs, and fresh radishes, onions, and other vegetables.

Slowly they rode past the coffeehouses, where old men sat at minuscule round tables in the sunshine. The indoors must have been stiffling in the heat, Elise imagined, for the narrow doors could offer but little ventilation. Groups of dirty children ran through the bazaar bearing cups of sweet coffee to the waiting parents. Elise could smell garlic, and Christopher explained the odor came from the cook stands to their right, where women were grilling lamb patties or *patlyan*. Elise hoped their hotel wasn't located near the mosque. It was picturesque, but the foreign odors caused her nausea to return.

"Don't worry, we have a lovely hotel suite reserved for us," he said, reading her thoughts. "After all the traveling we've done, we'll need some rest and a good meal. Did you think we would spend all our days like we did last night?" he laughed. "You did think that, didn't you? Well, perhaps such surroundings are enchanting and romantic for one evening, but I, for one, prefer the finer amenities life has to offer. A good hotel suite is one of them."

Elise was surprised at his words. Something about last night must have truly bothered him. He had been lost in thought when she fell asleep, and she now noticed that his black scowl was still present. What sort of business did he have in this country? Until a few days ago, she had never even heard of Bosnia, much less Sarajevo. She would have preferred the romance of Paris to these very foreign sights, sounds, and smells. Everything from the exotic mosque to the haggard faces of the peasants made Elise uncomfortable. The air was permeated with a tension that unnerved her.

She couldn't identify exactly what was wrong, but it was more than just finding herself in an unfamiliar land. Had she developed a sixth sense that warned of danger? She was suddenly seized with fear. It was much the same as the chill she experienced during thunderstorms, but far more intense.

She closed her eyes to the city scenes and concentrated on the feeling within her. She saw black and red—the colors of death. Her eyelids flew open at the realiziation. She shouldn't feel such dread when she was in Christopher's presence. But the ancient biblical words "the angel of death" would not leave her mind. She shook her head to clear the dark mood. Why did she experience things like this? The frequency of these forebodings had markedly increased recently. Not only had her body awakened to nature, but her soul had been introduced into an eerie realm of supernatural forces. She knew she was being warned of some impending catastrophe. And she knew it was connected with Christopher, but she didn't know how.

She shivered in the torrid heat of the June afternoon. She found her jacket, wrapped it around her shoulders, and hugged herself. Her teeth chattered so hard that her jaw ached. Never had she felt such extreme cold. Her breath came in short gasps, and she couldn't breathe normally. She hugged herself tightly, and the pressure in her back increased as her eyes became saucerlike. She tried desperately to blink, but all she could do was stare straight ahead. In her mind's eye she saw nothing but death around her as they drove. The buildings were crumbled and disheveled, as if they had been bombed. She saw flashes of red fire, then black smoke. Her ears heard screams of agony and pain, and the booming and thundering mingled with the sounds of human anguish. She wanted to cover her ears, but her arms were glued around her and she knew that even if she freed them to block her ears, she would still hear the wailing and crashing. She smelled blood, rotting flesh, gunsmoke, and sulfur.

The icy fingers of the spell that possessed her slowly loosened their grip, and the tension in her back eased and the air grew warmer. Her lungs finally filled themselves with air. She blinked and felt her heart beat normally once again. She screamed.

"Stop the car, Christopher! I'm going to be sick!" She cried as she tried to open the door and vomit. Instead, all the blood rushed away from her brain and her head fell with a thump on the halfway opened car door and she tumbled into the red brick street.

"Elise, my God! What's wrong?" Christopher yelled as the car came to an abrupt halt. He jumped out of the car and ran around toward her still form. He panicked when he touched her cold skin. Her bluish lips were opened, and it looked as if she would scream even in her unconscious state. Her complexion was deathly pale. He laid her on the backseat and gently slapped her cheeks and rubbed her hands to warm them. He had never seen anyone faint like this before. After a few moments the color returned to her cheeks; her eyelids fluttered. She stared blankly at him with her beautiful, but frightened deepblue eyes. Simple breathing was an effort for her. She

144

was still quite cold, and he raised her to himself, hoping to warm her. Her heart beat rapidly against his chest. He was utterly confused. He had been pointing out the sights of the city, and then all of a sudden she was ill; but to his mind it was as if she were trying to escape from the moving car. The look on her face was so strange. Finally she warmed in his arms, and mumbled something into his neck.

"What is it? Are you sick again? It's all my fault, Elise. I've pushed you too hard with all this traveling."

"Please, how much longer until we get to the hotel?" she asked.

"It's just up the street. I'll hurry. You lie here and rest until I have everything ready for you."

They had driven a bit farther when he told the driver to stop the car in front of a small hotel. Presently he returned with two porters. He carried Elise to the elevator. One of the porters closed the two mesh-and-wrought-iron doors and held her on their swift ride up two stories to the red-carpeted hallway. The second porter had the door to their room open, and fresh air washed away the stuffy hotel room smell. Christopher placed his wife upon the large brass bed. Her last conscious thought was of Christopher as he left her side, and she wondered if he had business to attend to once more.

A soft, motorized whirling sound like a low drone of a housefly fell on her ears. It created a hypnotic trance that she almost fell prey to, but the dull ache in her abdomen would not let her pass into that blissful, carefree state. The long wooden blade of the ceiling fan pushed the hot air down to touch her skin. Her body lay immobile. She was clad in a white satin and lace chemise that was thoroughly sweat soaked. Perspiration ran in rivulets down her forehead, neck, and breast. Her nipples, stomach, and navel were plainly visible through the now transparent wet satin. Her mouth opened to emit a low groan of pain. Between her legs a small pool of thick red blood formed. Sounds of pain rumbled low in her throat. There were no cries of anguish, just soft whispers of hurt.

The old man wearing thick glasses over his bulging brown eyes smoothed back his white hair as he gazed at her and ordered Christopher out of the room. The old man placed his black leather medical bag on the bed and took out his stethoscope. He placed the cold metal against her damp skin. Her eyelids fluttered open. She saw the instrument of his trade and focused upon the gleaming metal as she fully awakened. She felt his hands press against her abdomen and winced in pain. He placed her hand in his.

"Are you pregnant?" he asked in a quiet whisper.

"Yes, only a month, if that. Please, don't tell my husband. He doesn't know," she replied faintly, her eyes pleading.

"It's his right to know, especially now that you are ill."

"Not yet, please. I need more time. How bad is it?"

"With rest and care, you'll be fine, and the baby also. I'll give you something to make you sleep. And be assured I will not tell your husband." He smiled compassionately at her.

She swallowed the sleeping draught he gave her, and once again her body was immobile. She was aware of Christopher, but she couldn't open her eyes, He was questioning the old man, who reassured him she merely needed rest. The old man replaced his instruments in his black leather bag and shuffled out of the room. Christopher followed him out and locked the door.

When Elise awoke again it was to the rays of the early morning sun. Her body had not moved an inch throughout the long pain-filled night. The white linens were still neatly folded at the foot of the bed. The down-filled pillow beneath her head was quite damp, and the linen pillowcase was stained with sweat. Her hair was matted around her face and neck. Her arms felt like dead weights, and with a great effort she finally raised her arm to brush the hair away. Her other hand moved to rest on her abdomen. It felt the same. She caressed the soft skin with a slow, gentle, circular motion. The chemise was thoroughly soaked.

Her thoughts came in fuzzy rushes and flashes. She had difficulty in reconstructing the events of the past day. She was uncomfortable in the damp chemise, and she thought of how ugly she must look. She needed a bath to cleanse her body. She endeavored to focus her eyes on her surroundings. The bed she was lying upon was massive. It

146

was elevated on a platform and that entire area was heavily curtained in white chiffon. At the hem was a wide border of Greek key design embroidery in gold thread. The curtains shimmered in the pink dawn as the circulating air from the ceiling fan ruffled their deep pleats. The ceiling was edged in a deeply carved crown molding, and to either side of the bed were long narrow windows shuttered in white louvers. Because she couldn't see beyond the chiffon draperies, she experienced a feeling of suspension in both time and space. She felt like a tiny child.

The events of the last day came back to her as she remembered the doctor's visit. Placing her elbows at her side, she pushed herself into a sitting position. The pool of blood had dried completely, and no new bloodstains were in evidence. She breathed a heavy sigh of relief and lay back down. To her left sat a dark wood tea cart. A large silver tray with covered silver dishes rested upon its surface. In a crystal bud vase stood a single yellow rose, and the napkin was of a lavender colored linen. Tears streamed down her cheeks as she realized she didn't have the energy to walk to the tea cart, nor to pull it to her bedside.

Although Christopher appeared self-possessed as he drank his morning cup of coffee at the small café, he felt the sweat of heat and nerves dampen the back of his shirt. He waited for Wilhelm Schmidt and could think of nothing save his task. Elise was well cared for, and it was just as well she stay in bed for a few days. He didn't need any encumbrances at this point.

Christopher saw the blond German approaching with a jaunty step and friendly smile. He extended his hand in a warm gesture, and sat down next to Christopher. They ordered hot coffee and sweet breads. Two young Bosnian girls passed by and made quite an effort to catch the eye of the handsome men who seemed to be engaged in casual conversation.

"I trust you and Mrs. Mann are comfortably settled in by now," Wilhelm said.

"Mrs. Mann is exhausted after a trying voyage and those godawful flights. I hope she'll feel fit enough to attend the dinner and ball on Friday and Saturday night.

I would like her to have the chance to meet the archduke and his wife. It's sure to be a gala affair," he said dryly. "Now that the pleasantries are out of the way, Wil, what do you have to report?" Christopher said as he watched the two girls pass again.

"Some disturbing facts have come to light, but fortunately, between Serbian and Austrian ineptitude and the precipitous payment of our monies to the key people, disaster has been averted. Pasic discovered that Princip, Grabez, and Calerinoric were members of the plot against the archduke. He issued orders that they be intercepted at the border. Luckily, we were able to see to it that the esteemed Serbian prime minister's orders were not carried out. Pasic knew all along that the plot was on, but he failed to notify Vienna, and he did nothing to bring the mob in," Wilhelm said.

"How much did it cost us to buy his dalliance?" Christopher asked.

"Only twenty thousand dollars. He probably had gambling debts. He did try to warn Vienna merely through his ambassador, but Jovan Jovanovic wasn't at all pleased with his mission to Vienna. So he paid a call on Finance Minister Bilinski. Over drinks he suggested that the archduke should not attend the Feast of St. Vitus and the annual manuevers here. Bilinski thought it was not a matter for him to concern himself with and dismissed the entire affair. I tell you, Christopher, I really worried over that one when I heard the details. But I think our money was well spent."

"I know it's extremely important to the archduke that he and Sophie attend the inspection of the two corps of Austrian Army next to the border—especially because it's their fourteenth wedding anniversary. He's devoted to her and their three children. She's been snubbed by the court all these years. Seems petty to me, but then I don't pretend to understand this European caste system. This is the archduke's one chance to give her a place of special honor on her anniversary. He'll get his wish, won't he? She'll be immortalized in history." Christopher's words were cold and flat, and he shivered as he spoke them.

"To get on with my report, as my time is precious today, if you don't mind? In our propaganda sheets we have taken full advantage of the suspicions of the Serbs against the archduke. Because of our influence, we have led the Serbs to think that if he were to rule, there would never be a great Serbian nation to rise to the forefront. We've convinced the Serbians that he's the most evil villain in history. Vienna feels that if they send him here this weekend, they can smooth some of these ruffled feathers. I, for one, am proud that our undertaking in those newspapers had such far-reaching effects. Power of the press, eh, Christopher?" Wilhelm asked as he winked at the brunette who was strolling by their table for the third time.

"Do you suppose she is enamored of me, old boy?" Wilhlem chuckled.

"I doubt it, but it's a pleasant diversion in any case. Now, tell me about the men we've employed."

"First of all, there are seven Serbians, and all are very much nationalists. One is a carpenter, one a printer, one a teacher, and there are four students. Five of these men are under twenty-five, the eldest is twenty-seven. None of them has a police record, save one who had the misfortune to strike his teacher. This will be the first time they have worked together, and they will disband when this is over. I'm afraid they aren't as skilled in weaponry as we had hoped; still, their talents should be adequate. In any case, there's nothing we can do about it now. Also, we won't need to worry about any of them celebrating an early victory the night before the fact. Most of them have never touched alcohol, and none are gamblers. All have kept their debts paid.

"Incidentally, we have infected them all with tuberculosis. It helps to keep the brain clouded, and the fever distorts their judgment and creates true zealots. They all claim it is their duty to die heroically for the cause of Serbian nationalism. Since the Feast of St. Vitus is the symbol of Serbian resurrection and victory over the Turks, emotions will be high," Wilhelm stated.

"I have sent our payment to Colonel Dimitrievic—you will recall he is the chief of intelligence of the Serbian Army," Christopher said. "His knowledge had been invaluable. It will be on his orders that weapons will be supplied to the conspirators. The bombs, Belgian pistols, and cyanide for any necessary suicides will be brought across the border. At midmorning on Sunday each man will be armed, and each has been assigned to a separate position along Appel Quay. At that point there's nothing else we can do. No one will be able to prove anything. It's in the hands of purchased fate."

Sixteen

THE setting sun left Elise's hotel room in darkness. No lamp had been lit to ward off the gloom that surrounded her still form. She groaned and curled into a fetal position. Hugging her knees to her chest, she realized she no longer felt any pain. As her eyelids opened, she focused on the silver tray beside her. She pulled herself up to sit on the edge of the bed.

Weakly, she pulled the tea cart toward her. She poured cold dark tea into a cup and drank thirstily. Slowly, with unsteady fingers, she selected a piece of coarse dark bread from the silver tray and devoured it. Next to the lavender napkin was a bowl of strawberries that were limp and soggy in their own juice. She ate all the berries and another piece of bread. Embarrassed by her own greediness, she finished the last of the tea and slowly lowered herself back to the pillows. Her eyes roamed the unfamiliar room. She felt her energy return, and with it a desire to explore her surroundings. She rolled to her right and discovered a small French table with a lamp resting upon it. She raised her arm and pulled the cord, and as she did so the room was bathed in a soft beige glow of electric light. The drapes fluttered softly as the cooler night breezes entered the room, and with the aid of the fan the temperature of the room dropped to a more tolerable degree.

Elise rose from the bed and walked slowly, cautiously across the tiled floor to an elegant sitting area. The walls were whitewashed panels of carved wood embellished with thick moldings. The damask wallpapers were gray on white. A huge brass chandelier with lily-shaped glass shades presided grandly overhead. A silver brocade settee sat before the black and gray marble fireplace. There were green palms in every corner of the room, and a silver bowl of yellow roses sat atop a cherry tea table near the settee. Two gold-leaf occasional chairs were upholstered in gray moiré. Elise walked to the glass-paned double brass doors at the end of the room and pushed them open. In the center of the tiled room was a sunken gray marble bathtub. She couldn't wait to bathe. She stripped off her blood-stained chemise and then thought to hide it in a corner of a drawer. She didn't want Christopher to have any idea that she was carrying his child. She wasn't even certain why she didn't want him to know, she knew only that the secret must be hers alone until she understood more about him. She eased herself into the lukewarm water and rested her head against the back of the tub. She was vaguely aware of numerous visits by the chambermaid, who must certainly have been acting upon Christopher's instructions. He obviously cared enough about her not to leave her completely alone during her illness, and for that, she was grateful and touched.

She had finished washing her hair when she sensed a presence behind her. She turned cautiously to see Christopher gazing down at her. He wore navy trousers and a white shirt, and his hair was damp with sweat. He appeared to be out of breath.

He looked at her pale body and wanted her desperately. He needed a refuge from the hideous world he was creating. Yet he couldn't imagine her having any compassion for him.

"You must be feeling better to be up and about. I saw that you finally had something to eat. I didn't come back last night, I had business," he lied to her. He had been back and had watched her sleep for an hour before falling upon the settee in exhaustion. He wanted her to be strong now, both for her sake and his own.

"Since you needed rest, I took the liberty of doing some shopping for you. If you feel up to it, tomorrow night is a dinner party for some heads of state that I thought you'd enjoy. Saturday night we are obliged to attend the Royal Ball at the embassy. It's the eve of the Feast of St. Vitus, and you'll meet Archduke Francis Ferdinand and his wife, Sophie. Do you think you'd like that, Elise?" he asked as he watched her in the water. He kept expecting her to order him from the room.

"It's fine, Christopher," she said wanly. She felt she would faint from the effort it took to speak. How could she possibly go to a ball?

"Christopher, I'm very hungry. Could you send for some supper? I don't feel like going downstairs, but I must have something to eat."

"Certainly. I haven't eaten yet either, even though it's past nine o'clock. Is there anything else?"

"Just a towel, please," she said.

He handed her a towel that was as large as a blanket, and left the bathroom. She felt worn out, and it frustrated her to know that although she was ill, Christopher's business would not allow her a proper convalescence. Perhaps when she had something to eat and another night's rest, she would be fine. She felt somewhat restored by her bath.

Christopher reentered, holding up a new wrapper for her. It was floor length and consisted of yards of heavily reembroidered white lace. Pink ribbons ran through the cuff, neck, and hem. Over the shoulders was a capelet of more lace and ribbons. She had never seen anything so luxurious in all her life. It must have cost a fortune. And where did he find it?

She entered the sitting area and saw a round table covered in a white linen cloth. Christopher stood tall and handsome, clad in a wine-colored smoking jacket with black satin lapels. He was opening a magnum of French champagne. On top of the pale yellow flowered china plate was a long-stemmed yellow rose. She picked it up and sniffed its delicate scent. He aided her with her chair, and a waiter appeared at the door pulling a dinner cart behind him. He served them each a large filet mignon.

"Unheard of in this country," Christopher said.

There was asparagus with hollandaise sauce, flaky rolls, a strawberry mousse, cognac, and hot coffee. Elise ate everything on her plate and Christopher's dessert.

Throughout dinner she kept glancing at the yellow rose and its perfect duplicates in the silver bowl on the tea table. Of all the gestures he had made while she was ill, this was the one that touched her the most. She still wondered how he knew that she loved them so. Even in

New York he had sent white and yellow roses. She felt her heart swell with love for this man whose child she bore within her. He could be so thoughtful and giving at one moment, and then in a split second storm at her about the way she looked or some silly thing she had done through her ignorance and naivete.

Why couldn't he trust her enough to tell her what was wrong? He looked so completely lost at times, and he seemed to have no one with whom he could share his burden. Elise knew it was deep relationships with others that gave her own life meaning. She plucked at the pink ribbon on her sleeve and wondered how Christopher could be drawn to the beauty of such a garment, but unable to see the loveliness of the companionship she wanted to offer him.

She wished they had never come to this strange country. Christopher's mood had been blacker than usual. No, that wasn't correct. He appeared numb, as numb in soul as Elise had been in body. She had lain, feeling lifeless, for two days. Was his soul lying prostrate and lifeless even now? His eyes seemed opaque, and he had slumped in his chair. She had no idea what to say to him. She finished another glass of champagne and felt quite lightheaded. She picked up the rose and ran the soft petals against his cheek.

"I think perhaps I should get some rest, but I find I can't make it to the bed under my own power," she said, smiling at his morose face.

Without a word he walked over and picked her up—carefully, as if she were his most cherished treasure—and carried her to the bed. He knelt beside her and looked into her eyes. He pulled the soft sheet up to cover her and kissed her moist lips.

"Elise, please get some rest. You'll need your strength for tomorrow. I have to go out for an hour, but I'll be back," he said.

He walked to the door, closed it softly behind him, and leaned his back against its carved wood. He turned his eyes upward. *God help me! I don't know what to do!*

He couldn't stay with her. She was fine and good; the more he learned about her, the more he realized it was so. He could not ask her to share his torment.

He stood in that position for what seemed like hours;

154

his hands clenched into fists against the rage that coursed through his body. He turned the shiny brass knob on the door and cautiously reentered the room. He silently crossed the room to the draperied platform and looked inside.

She was asleep. There were dried tears on her cheeks, and the pillowcase beneath her head was still damp. He lay down next to her and gathered her up into his arms and breathed in her sweet fragrance. As the fan hummed overhead, he fell asleep with his lips against her hair and forehead.

The dry heat ripped across the room in waves. The day was new, and Christopher had gone to meet it headlong. On his departure he sent a maid to Elise to aid with her toilette and breakfast.

As she finished her last cup of morning coffee, she walked to the window. Quaint coffeehouses across the street were filled with people. A trio of young men were erecting flags and banners along the sides of the street. She guessed this was all in preparation for Sunday's Feast Day events. Brilliant red geraniums and white petunias bloomed in large tubs and in pots of crockery placed before most stores and shops.

Already the town assumed a festive air, and just witnessing the preparations filled Elise with hope. She felt stronger now, and the mirror showed that her color had returned. Her spirits renewed themselves at the thought that her child was safe; perhaps God was truly watching over her and her life. She would not give in to despair. If she bricked her pain and fear behind a sturdy wall, she believed they could not escape to create further havoc.

Tonight she would do all she could to please Christopher. He'd told her that he had purchased new gowns for her while they were in New York, and if it took her all day, she would be beautiful for him. She had never said anything to him, what with all the wedding plans, the crossing and her illness, but today was her birthday. She was twenty years old and as she thought of her baby, she believed she was now beginning to learn what it was to be a woman.

She placed the china cup on the tea table and crossed to the closet to investigate the new treasures awaiting her.

Once again, Christopher proved that his taste in all things was impeccable.

The first gown was made of a heavy pearl-gray crepe. The inner bodice, cut low and straight across the breasts, was heavily reembroidered with silver sequins and crystals. Even inside the dark closet, the dress glittered. It was belted at the waist with a rose-colored silk sash, and the narrow skirt formed a tulip effect at the hem. Elise twirled the dress around and stared aghast at the low back. The spangled piece would barely cover her waist! Perhaps on a shorter woman the dress would be more appropriate, but Elise was positive that a great deal of breast, back, and lower leg would be revealed. She couldn't wear a camisole or chemise with it, and she decided that apart from her gray silk stockings and garters, she would wear no underclothes at all. Obviously, Christopher was not satisfied with her present style of dress.

On the small gold stool were a pair of silver-gray long gloves and sparkling silver shoes. For her hair he had chosen a cluster of white feathers attached to a silver comb. She would wear her hair in curls tonight. She rang for the chambermaid and arranged for a hairdresser. She laid out her clothes, and as she picked up her shoes, she noticed another pair, these worked in gold sparkles. She slipped the second gown off the rod and realized this was the gown for the ball on Saturday night.

It was cut very much like the first dress, but this time the bodice was executed in gold sequins and the fabric underneath the thousands of beads was sheer organza. This dress had no sleeves at all, and a band of spangles would encircle her breasts and rib cage. The tiny straps of the garment were made of twisted gold silk. The dainty capelet was made of golden chiffon shot with stripes of gold thread. From the tightly fitted waist fell a wrap skirt of the same gold striped chiffon, which was lined in gold taffeta. Even so, she thought the outline of her legs would be clearly visible. She smiled to herself at the thought. What a delight to wear such beautiful clothes! She was doubly delighted, for she pretended they were her birthday presents, but as she thought about the care and amount of thought Christopher had put into these garments, she wondered if perhaps, somehow, he did know what a special day this was. And she was more baffled by him than ever.

She tensed slightly as she thought of the ball. She had never been presented to royalty, and she wondered what one said to an archduke. She would have to inquire about protocol. She was learning so many things so quickly these days. Where had she been all her life? Christopher had opened so many doors for her. He accepted all these things so matter-of-factly. She was easily awed by the beauty of a rose or a beautiful day, and even though he made these things more precious to her, he traveled in a sphere that to her mind made all she had ever done seem quite mundane. He was so worldy and cultivated—she doubted it was in her power to reach such sophistication. She only knew in her heart how she felt, and she prayed she had enough wisdom to follow those feelings. She might not know much of the world and its workings, but she was honest enough to sense her own needs and be compassionate toward those around her.

While she was lost in thought, the midday sun transformed the elegant hotel room into a blast furnace. She felt perspiration travel the length of her spine to her hips. It was difficult to breathe in the weighted air. These sensations revived her experiences of the last days. She went into the bathroom and, dropping the heavy lace robe, stepped into the tub, then filled it with ice-cold water. She let her head rest upon the rim of the marble and felt her misgivings dissipate.

Christopher leaned against the filthy oxcart and kicked at the dried manure and dirt that clung to the wooden wheel. The smells of the bazaar were intensified by the torrid afternoon heat. He couldn't decide which was worse, the stench of unwashed humans or that of uncared-for beasts of burden. After half an hour his contact had still not arrived. Christopher didn't relish handing this money personally to a peasant emissary. He believed he should not have been involved in this part of the transaction at all. The less he was seen, the better. Unfortunately, circumstances required him to contact this member of the Black Hand. There were too many discrepancies in their arrangements lately, and his anxieties had multiplied. He had wanted to forestall any informa-

157

tion leakage. He didn't need interference from government forces; experience in Florida had made him wary.

Luckily, they had been able to overcome that particular problem. The reports he had received that morning had laid his fears to rest. His pilots and crews were now running a three-day schedule.

A sickly child peered at him and begged for money. Guiltily, Christopher dropped a coin into his hand, wanting the urchin to be gone. For reasons he could not understand, the child made him think of Elise. His feelings for her were beginning to complicate his plans. He knew he was spending far too much time worrying about her. What if this spell of illness was some sort of exotic virus that no one would be able to treat effectively?

Stop it, he told himself, she's just tired and you're being melodramatic. She'll be fine.

He hoped she would feel well enough to attend the dinner that night. Not only did he need her there to complete the picture of the happy honeymoon couple, but he found he desired her company. He was startled at his own observation. Just what were all these emotions he was feeling?

"I'm just not good enough for her, even though I do love her," he mumbled as he stared down at his muddy boot.

My God! What am I saying? I am in love with her, and I didn't even know it! What a fool I am!

He guessed that because he had never truly loved anyone in his entire life, it had been almost impossible for him to know what he felt. His discovery baffled him, and now he was anxious to complete his task here in the bazaar and return to Elise.

A young boy clad in dirty slacks and a baggy dark khaki shirt approached him. The youth walked just past Christopher, stopped, glanced about him, and cautiously returned to the oxcart where Christopher stood.

"Your shoes are dirty, perhaps you should have them polished," the youth said in a melodious voice.

Christopher handed over a thick yellow envelope that the boy promptly tucked inside his shirt. All at once Christopher connected the soft voice and the peculiar fit of the shirt and realized this was a girl! He smiled at her

158

then turned his gaze toward the sunset. When he looked back, the girl had disappeared.

Nonchalantly, he whistled an old love song he had once heard, and strolled out of the bazaar. He purchased a small handful of deep-purple violets, wondering whether they might cheer Elise. He vowed she would never learn of her father's involvement in the assassination. He would find a way to keep his own participation a secret, too. Wasn't he Christopher Mann? He could do anything! He jauntily made his way to the hotel where she was waiting for him.

Elise stepped naked into the silver gown and fastened the buttons at the waist. She padded over to the French gilt mirror. The silver-spangled fabric was snug against her breasts. She ran her hands over them and was pleasantly surprised that her pregnancy had begun to show in such a delightful manner. She wondered if Christopher would notice. Quickly she placed her hands on her abdomen. She breathed a sigh of relief as she realized it was still just as flat as before. As she turned, she noticed that a flash of long leg was quite evident, but it was the fall of the crepe fabric over her derriere that proved to be the gown's most provocative aspect. She smiled at the thought of Christopher's face when he saw the explicit outline of her hips and legs in this dress. The satiny skin of her back in the low-cut gown glistened in the soft lamplight. Never had she felt so womanly or so beautiful.

She bent down to retrieve a silk stocking when Christopher entered the room. He stopped dead as she sat down and pulled on her stockings. He felt his passion rise as he crossed slowly to her with the violets in his outstretched hand. He felt like a child, unable to say a word although many sophisticated phrases came to mind. She placed a shoe on her left foot and looked up at him with her startling blue eyes.

"I brought you some flowers, Elise. I hope you like violets. They were all I could find. And I thought the color would go well with your gown." His breath caught as he felt the bulge in his trousers.

"I'm going to clean up. I've sent for some wine to cool us. Let me know when it arrives, all right?" He leaned down and kissed her lightly on the lips; then he went into the bathroom and shut the door quickly behind him. He looked down at his hands and realized they were trembling. He was filled with more than just desire. The emotions that possessed him now were so powerful that it seemed he was losing control of his very being. He could feel his heart race as if he had been running for a long time. He couldn't understand how Elise could become more beautiful to him every time he saw her. And now he had the strangest thought: He would like to take her, just as she was, and place her in some suspended, frozen state. Then he could possess her and nothing would ever change. He could have her all to himself.

But that wasn't enough, because what he truly desired from her was her warmth and her love. He sighed as he felt a great pain in his chest. He had treated her with such cold disdain and had avoided her so much! He had killed every chance he might have had to win her love. Everytime she looked at him he could see the fear in her eyes. He placed his head in his hands and roughly ran his fingers through his hair. What had he done to her? And to himself? Now he was in love with her, and how foolish he had been not to see it coming!

He was certain she couldn't love him. He saw too much pain in her eyes now. If she had felt love for him, it hadn't lasted long; he had seen to that. He felt as if all the joy had gone from his life.

Then, as he saw his own mournful reflection, he determined to push aside this unwanted despair: He had to hope that he could find a way to alter their present course. It was up to him. And there was tonight.

"God! I'll make this the best night of my life and hers. All is not lost," he said, reassuring himself.

Christopher had just finished buttoning the jacket on his black tuxedo when he heard her light tap on the door.

"The wine has arrived, Christopher," she said timidly.

He opened the door and was mesmerized by the sight of his beautiful wife.

She turned to bring him a glass of wine and he saw every muscle in her thighs and hips as she glided to the silver ice bucket.

"Oh, my God! I'll never make it through dinner seeing her in that dress!" he muttered to himself as he felt his pulse quicken again and his blood heat.

"Elise, I have a gift for you. Stay right here while I get it." He went to the bureau and brought forth a narrow green box. "Here, open it. Happy birthday, Elise. Your mother told me. . . ." He clutched for explanations. "I thought it would look nice on you. Uh, with your, uh, gown, I mean. The color was suitable, is what I meant," he stammered. Hell! When would he get control of himself, he thought, and handed her the gift.

Carefully, Elise opened the box. She gasped as she picked up the bracelet of blue diamonds from the black velvet. "Christopher, these are exactly like the stones that Papa gave me on my wedding day," she replied sadly and placed the bracelet on her left wrist. "It's the loveliest birthday present I've ever had, Christopher. Thank you. You didn't need to buy me anything so expensive," she said as she desperately wished he would offer her his love and not these "suitable" blue stones.

With an effort, she cast aside her gloom. This was to be a night of gaiety and it was up to her to dispel the tension in the room.

As he passed the large-bowled wine glass to her and filled it with the cool white wine, he realized that he had been correct in his earlier assuption that she did not love him. If she had, she would have been pleased with his gift; obviously, she was not pleased. She hadn't made any gestures to indicate to him that she cared. He had spent two days talking to every jeweler in Sarajevo in his attempt to find these blue diamonds.

Now, Christopher believed it had all been a waste of time. Nothing he did at this point could make amends to Elise for his abominable treatment of her. He'd been unable to show her that he was concerned about her when she was ill. When he had found time to visit her, she had always been asleep; she had never known that he was in the room. He gulped down his wine and checked the ornately carved walnut grandfather clock that stood at the far end of the room.

"It's time for us to go, Elise. Do you have all your things?"

"My gloves! Oh, yes, here they are," she said. And they left the room.

* * *

The dinner was held in the dining room of the hotel. Because Elise had been ill upon her arrival, she hadn't seen any of the hotel except for her suite. She was overwhelmed by the richness of the furnishings. All the doors were polished brass with glass panes. The ceiling must have been over twenty-five feet high, she thought. They entered the room through the tall doors and stood on a raised landing that encircled the dining room. The landing was separated from the main floor by a railing forged of solid brass. To the left of the room were twenty-foot windows, each topped with a semi-circular window, and all were draped in white chiffon fabric. The chandeliers were of heavy brass with tulip-shaped glass shades. Circular tables were skirted in floor-length white Damask. The dark green floral carpeting was a dramatic backdrop for the golden gleam of the flocked wall paper and abundant brass fittings of the room. The china was white with gold rims and the royal crest of Austria had been hand-painted in the center of each dish. Christopher took Elise aside and pointed out various members of the aristocracy and European dignitaries that occupied the best tables in the room. She was most anxious to see the archduke in person, but for that she would have to wait.

Elise and Christopher were escorted to their table by the headwaiter. Christopher ordered a glass of wine for her and a whiskey for himself. He immediately excused himself as the other guests began milling about the room. In the absence of her husband, Elise introduced herself to the others at her table. She scanned the room, looking for Christopher, as she sipped the cool wine. At a table in the far left corner sat a pretty red-haired woman who, from the tilt of her head, looked familiar to Elise. She raised her glass to her lips again and realized with a shock that this was the woman from the ship! She couldn't see Christopher anywhere in the room.

What did this mean? Elise immediately thought that an idiotic question to ask herself. She knew very well what was happening. Her hand traveled to her abdomen in an unconscious gesture to shield her unborn child from the agony she felt.

The elderly woman at the table did not miss the movement. She leaned over to Elise and said, "How far along are you, dear?"

Startled out of her reverie, Elise said, "I don't know what you mean."

"The baby, of course. How many months pregnant are you?" she asked.

"I'm afraid you are mistaken. I'm not going to have a baby. I've been ill with stomach problems ever since our crossing. I guess I'm having a difficult time adjusting to this country and the great deal of travel I've had to endure. I'm feeling much better today, however." She tried to smile convincingly at the woman. The lady returned her smile and nodded knowingly at Elise.

Christopher returned to the table just as the first course was served. As soon as he sat down, he began a lively conversation with the others at the table. Throughout the evening he enchanted the ladies with his charm and impressed the men with his knowledge of politics and business. Elise found it difficult to do more than pick at her food and smile wanly. She wasn't becoming ill again, she was sure. She just felt so empty and alone. She couldn't wait for this all to be over. For the first time since she'd met him, she wished she were anywhere than by Christopher's side. But she was determined to see the evening through.

After dinner there was to be dancing in the main ballroom. Elise didn't think she would be up to the waltzing, but she refused to let Christopher attend by himself. The red-haired woman was escorted by a very handsome blond man. He too appeared familiar to Elise, but she dismissed the thought as her attention returned to the woman. She was quite poised, and very sure of herself.

The music permeated the air, and immediately she felt her spirits rise as Christopher took her in his arms and swirled her about the dance floor. At this moment she felt that everything was right with the world. Lately it seemed her emotions were either at very high peaks of joy or very low valleys of melancholy. She prayed that her conflicting thoughts and sensations were due merely to the pregnancy and not to her growing suspicions of Christopher's involvement with this other woman.

As the music rose, she clung to his muscular arms and peered deep into his eyes. Holding his gaze, she once again felt herself being pulled into the depths of his eyes. She was lost inside him and didn't care if he desired an-

163

other. For now, he was with her, truly with her. She could sense his body responding to her touch, and as the music slowed, he pulled her closer to him; she yielded willingly. His arms held her tight to him, and she could feel her breath coming quickly. It took her a moment to snap back to reality and realize they were in the middle of a ballroom dance floor and not alone in their suite.

"Elise, let's go upstairs. I've tired of these festivities. Wouldn't you like that?" She felt her skin tingle and goose bumps rise all over her body.

With his arm encircling her small waist, he led her to the elevator. As they rode upstairs, he took her in his arms and brought his lips down upon hers in a gentle but fervent kiss. The elevator stopped, and he pulled back the wrought iron doors for her. When she walked past him, he could smell the lavender scent of her hair. He unlocked the door to their room, and she gazed at his black hair shining in the light from the brass wall sconce above his head. She walked inside and turned toward him as he kicked the door shut. He came to her and placed his hands upon the small of her back and pressed her body to his own. He brought his hands up and began to remove the pins from her hair. The curls tumbled down her back as his eyes bore into hers. He unbuttoned the back of her dress and carefully slid it down her shoulders. He gasped when he saw that she was stark naked.

"Why, Elise! You wicked creature! No wonder that dress looked so provocative. You were the talk of the men this evening," he said, grinning wickedly.

She was embarrassed at his stare, but still, peering into his face, she felt her nipples harden even before he touched her. She kicked off her shoes and peeled off her stockings as he stripped himself of his tuxedo. They stood naked together in the middle of the room, each mesmerized by the eyes of the other. He pressed his lips to hers, and as he kissed her, he picked her up and carried her to the bed where she had known only pain and tears.

He lay beside her and caressed her stomach lovingly as his mouth devoured her swollen breasts. He moved his hand slowly downward and heard her moan with increasing intensity. He covered her long, slender body with his own and entered her soft depths. His muffled sounds of passion filled her ears. He felt heat blaze within him as

she rose to the tempo of his rhythmic thrusts. He clutched her hips and sent himself into her very soul. They spun in each other's arms, in tune with all the sensual pleasures of God's universe.

He lay spent at her side, and she watched his eyelids flutter and his breathing deepen. She pressed close to him and placed feathery-light kisses upon his hair and ears. She ran her fingertips almost imperceptibly over his chest and flat belly. He uttered soft sounds of pleasure as he felt himself consumed with an electric fire. He gathered her up into his arms and feasted hungrily upon her mouth. He swept the length of her velvety skin with his smouldering lips until she was aglow with the volcanic fires of the pleasure only he could create within her. He could not deny his need any longer, and as he filled her, she wrapped her legs about his hips and held him there. Once again he brought her to ecstasy. He held her close to him and refused to let her escape his embrace; he wanted her this near to him for the rest of his life.

She lay sleeping in his arms as he stared open-eyed at the ceiling above them and contemplated what he must do. Even tonight he must leave her side to play his part in making the final arrangements for the assassination. For the first time in his life, he felt torn between his duty and his need he felt to remain at the side of the only person in the world he loved. He had always believed that if he ever fell deeply in love with a woman, the experience would be the happiest and the most wondrous of his life. It was true that he felt blessed with some great, precious gift, but now he knew the pain that accompanied the sweetness of love. Had any other man known such soul-piercing agony? He sought to capture that euphoric state of bliss that should be his at this moment, but all he found was torment as the hour of his departure drew near.

He commanded his body to move away from her, but not a muscle obeyed his mind. Ultimately, he knew there was no choice. He was bound by the chains of allegiance to this destructive path he must pursue. With an all-pervading sense of loneliness and anger, he rose from the bed and passed through the gold-embroidered draperies away from her world and into one whose very existence he despised. He dressed in solemn silence and left the room.

The sound of the heavy door clicking shut brought Elise to consciousness. Her mind refused to recognize the sound, and her body eased its way closer to the space where her lover had lain. Her arms reached out to embrace him once more, but they encircled a void. She jerked into a sitting position. She felt the trembling of the bed beneath her and feared that the earth had quaked. Once again he had left her side, and she was certain he was now with the gorgeous red-haired woman. Why didn't he just send Elise back to her family and friends in Mobile? She would not have to try so very hard to please anyone at home. But her heart told her she could never return; she would always be impelled to stay with Christopher. She prayed for strength. Perhaps she could put him from her mind and her heart. She wished this trip were over and they could go back to New York. There she could speak with John, and she knew he would console her and assuage some of her pain and heartache. As she lay listening to John's imaginary words, the ceiling fan droned louder and the night grew in age and the world outside her room fell into the abyss of sleep.

Alone physically and mentally, she dared the dawn to come to her and rescue her from doubt and fear. As her lungs filled with the cooler night air, she waited for them to cease functioning. She commanded her heart muscles to end their pumping. She lay perfectly still and began to build yet another brick wall around her pain.

Seventeen

ELISE sat sketching the early-morning activity of Sarajevo from the balcony of her hotel suite. She was fascinated with the coffeehouses and the faces of the old men who frequented them. The heat had begun to creep its way across the city. She pulled at the lapels of her aqua wrapper in an effort to bare more of her skin to the last cool morning breezes. Christopher hadn't returned all night, and although it couldn't be eight o'clock yet, he had failed to send word regarding his day's schedule.

She was ravenous with hunger and guessed she would be forced to fend for herself. She decided she would dress and go to the dining room alone, rather than have something sent to the room. She didn't want to see Christopher when he arrived. Perhaps after she ate, she would explore some of this quaint Bosnian city; she might never have the chance to see it again. But mainly she was disgusted at her own self-pity and felt a desperate need to take charge of her own life. Since he didn't care about her, it was up to her to boost her own morale.

Elise bathed and dressed with great speed, snatched up her art satchel, and went to the breakfast room. She was seated at a small table near the tall windows, where she had a breathtaking view of the formal gardens. She finished her breakfast and asked the waiter if she could take her coffee outside and sketch under the large cypress trees. He assured her that she would find it perfectly delightful in the gardens and asked to view her sketches when she finished.

As she sat on the stone bench near a fountain, she re-

flected upon how much like Mobile it all seemed. Of course this was far more grand, but a sense of peace descended upon her and she reveled in the calm. At this point in the day, the weather was much like hot summer days at home.

She must have sketched for quite a while, for she saw a number of people enter the hotel dining room, eat, and then depart. As the heat intensified, Elise decided to take a nap before exploring.

She entered the lobby from the veranda and spied Christopher in the elevator with the blond man she thought she had recognized the night before. She certainly didn't want to go upstairs now if Christopher was going to be there! She needed time to herself if she were to endure the embassy ball that night. Once she was sure he was out of sight, she crossed the lobby and went out into the hot afternoon streets of Sarajevo.

Christopher was frantic with worry. He had come back to the room before seven-thirty to find Elise gone. He questioned the maid, who stated that Elise had failed to call her that morning; no breakfast had been ordered. Christopher was sure Elise was not physically strong enough to do much by herself. He couldn't understand where she would possibly go. All manner of ominous thoughts invaded his brain. He feared that she was kidnapped by some crazy Serbian or that she had become ill again. He summoned Wilhelm's aid early in the day, and together they visited the doctor but Elise hadn't contacted him. Their only course now was to hope she was shopping and would return shortly.

Christopher ordered a bottle of whiskey and lunch sent to the room for them, and Wilhelm did all he could to calm his friend.

"Christopher! For God's sakes, quit pacing! You'll drive us both mad. She's fine. If something underhanded had occurred we would have received word by now. If there was to be a ransom we should have had *that* news by now," Wilhelm said, trying to convince himself as much as his friend.

Christopher poured two large drinks and gulped his down as he ran his hand through his black hair. It seemed to Christopher that the hours took forever to pass. With

only a little help from Wilhelm, he had finished the entire bottle of whiskey, but he remained stone sober. He had never been so terrified. He was wild with frustration when the brass knob on the door turned; both men stopped breathing and tensed.

She pushed the door open and was startled to see the two men staring at her with anticipation, joy, and rage.

"Elise, where the hell have you been?" Christopher demanded.

Defiant at his anger toward her, she said sweetly, "I was out sketching the city. I was tired of being cooped up in this stuffy hotel room with you—or do I mean *without* you? Why? Is something wrong?"

"Goddammit! No wife of mine is going to be gallivanting around a strange city unescorted! From now on, if you want to go somewhere, you let me know and I'll take you. Do you hear me, young lady?"

"Yes, I hear you. But how can you show me the city when you are never here with me in the first place?" She spit the words at him, turned on her heel and went into the bathroom, slamming the door so hard the prisms on the wall sconce tinkled.

"Jesus! Isn't she great?" Christopher said, and smiled at Wilhelm.

"You're both insane, if you ask me. I'm getting out of here and get ready for tonight. I've wasted too much time already. Tomorrow is the day. I'll inform you tonight at the ball of all I transact," Wilhelm said, and he put his drink down and left.

Elise tore the linen suit from her body, ripping seams and popping buttons in her anger. She picked up the brush and tore at her hair. She looked at the brush and, as she threw it against the wooden door, hissed: "You are worse than my own papa, Christopher Flynn Mann!"

She filled the tub with very hot water and dumped every bottle of bath salts she could find into the water. Then she flung the empty bottles across the room and watched them shatter in a pile beneath the potted palm in the corner. The water reeked of jasmine, lavender, and lily of the valley.

"Maybe now, I can at least smell like the whores Christopher seems to prefer," she cried angrily as the rushing water drowned out her words.

169

She ignored Christopher's pounding on the door.

"Elise, please," he begged when she ignored him. "Are you all right?"

"Yes, I'm just dandy. What do you want?" she demanded.

"I heard all that crashing, and then silence. I just wondered. Well, never mind. Hurry up. I need to bathe myself, you know," he said.

"You'll just have to wait your turn," she said. She spent an hour washing and drying her hair.

She opened the door, and he merely gazed at her strangely. She was wrapped in a large towel, and she looked positively delectable to him with her damp hair hanging down her back and that defiant look on her face.

"Your bath awaits you, sire," she said curtly.

He went to the tub and filled it with cold water, then poured the water over his head in an effort to clear away the now significant effects of the whiskey from his brain. God! He loved her even when she was furious with him. He was even amused by the pile of broken glass in the corner.

Elise had finished dressing in the golden dress that Christopher had purchased for her. Because the evening was still quite warm, she didn't wear her chemise, and the silky fabric made her skin quiver as it caressed her body. She tied her hair up with gold ribbons and waited for her husband to finish dressing.

The Embassy was resplendent with light from the dazzling crystal chandeliers. Elise had never witnessed such extravagance and wealth. The mammoth ballroom was filled with exquisitely dressed women whose husbands were high-ranking members of the Empire. She immediately recognized some of the faces from their dinner at the hotel. But when she finally saw the archduke and Sophie in person, she was thrilled beyond her own expectations. They were resplendently dressed and carried themselves with an innate though casual grace, a deportment which set them above all others. She wondered how and why she and Christopher were included in such auspicious company. Tonight she would not question a thing; she would simply enjoy herself. The champagne flowed

freely, and the thirty-piece orchestra played constantly. Elise was awed by the royal court. She'd never dreamed she would stand in the same room with an archduke and his wife. Elise felt positively giddy as she whirled about the room in the arms of many admirers. She and Christopher had not completed their first dance together when a sandy-haired young man cut in and waltzed her around in breathless circles. She had danced for hours, with a new partner each time the music changed, before Christopher came to take her in to dinner. He stopped a waiter who was carrying a large golden tray of glasses filled with champagne.

Elise was quite warm, and she was thankful she hadn't bothered with any underclothing. She almost gulped the cool wine.

Christopher escorted her into the long, darkly paneled dining room. This room was more softly lit, creating a more intimate atmosphere for dining. Christopher suggested they take their plates to the terrace, where the night air might cool them. The array of food was astounding, and Elise wished she were hungrier. She was having such a wonderful time that nothing but the music filled her thoughts. What a soothing balm to her earlier pain! They sat under a large cypress tree at a small table in whose center had been placed a small crystal bowl of tiny yellow sweetheart roses. She cautiously tasted the strange-looking foods before her and found, much to her surprise, that they were quite good. Christopher raised his wine-glass to his lips, sipped the champagne, and adored her with his eyes.

How he wanted to reach out to her and tell her everything that was in his heart. That was what he should have done that afternoon, but instead he had rebuked her. No wonder she refused to speak to him tonight. He truly was the master of stupidity! Whenever he attempted to show her or tell her how he felt about her, he inevitably said and did the opposite. He still could not comprehend this inability of his to command the situation when he found himself in her presence. Elise possessed an uncanny ability to be provocative and vulnerable at the same time. She sipped her wine, and as she did so, she let her velvet-blue eyes travel up to his; she held him there and gazed

at him knowingly. He reached out and touched her hand and held it tightly within his own. Just as he was about to tell her that he loved her, he felt a tap on his shoulder.

"Excuse me, Mrs. Mann, I'm very sorry to interrupt your dinner—but I must speak to you, Christopher. It's urgent. There's a library downstairs on the main floor. I'll meet you there. This shouldn't take long. Again, I apologize for intruding upon your evening, Mrs. Mann," the tall blond man said.

"Elise, believe me, I didn't want this to happen. The last thing I wanted was to discuss business, tonight of all nights. I'll make it up to you, I promise."

"It's all right, Christopher. I understand. In fact I'm getting used to it," she said bitterly.

She watched him pass through the French doors and wondered again why this blond man looked so familiar to her. Something in the back of her mind kept gnawing away at her suspicions. She took another sip of wine and decided she would follow them. She walked past the rows of tables, feeling foolish but determined to carry out her whim. She floated down the wide circular staircase, but all she saw below were the huge oak library doors, which were slightly ajar. She stood off to the side and could see the two men. Straining, she could make out their conversation.

"Well, I don't know. Do you think this will alter any of our plans at this points?" Christopher asked.

"Nothing can be changed now, Christopher, it's too late. Every detail has been arranged, and all we can do at this time is become the observers we are pretending to be," Wilhelm said.

"Just what the hell does Justin Kendall think this is, anyway? A family outing? He can't dictate to us at the eleventh hour. The assassination is set for tomorrow afternoon," Christopher said as he lit a cigar and sat in a leather chair.

At the mention of her father's name in connection with the word *assassination*, Elise went pale. She leaned closer to the door.

"It's my feeling that Justin had second thoughts for some reason. Fortunately, he has not ceased the munitions operations. In fact, his production has increased by over

fifty percent. Our reports on his efforts are excellent. We've had two very large shipments arrive in Germany. If anything, we seem to be ahead of schedule, and all subsequent shipments will be on time. Justin has received his payment, and believe me, he has already doubled his initial investment; I don't understand what's troubling him. It certainly can't be his conscience," Wilhelm said.

"I doubt he has one. I've always wondered what compelled men to sell their souls for money. Something must have happened to him long ago to twist his mind like that. I knew he was devious when he handed his daughter over to me, a perfect stranger. At the time, I almost laughed in his face."

Elise clutched the door to steady herself. She had to flee from this place; this world. Her mind wanted to scurry away into a secret cave deep within the labyrinth of her soul. Groaning inwardly with an animal pain, she employed every ounce of her strength to move across the reception area. In numb shock she propelled her leaden body to the door and then ran in the direction of the hotel, leaving a startled doorman to call out after her. Her instincts guided her; she had lost all sense of how far away her refuge was or how long it would take her to get there.

Back at last in her room, she sorted out the gruesome knowledge she had gleaned. She sat upon the settee and stared at her cold, shaking hands.

Her papa had sold her to Christopher. Yes; she knew that. Papa had paid for a hired killer. This killer would accomplish his task tomorrow. Now what was happening tomorrow? Oh, yes, now she remembered. It was the Feast of St. Vitus.

"The motorcade! The archduke!" she exclaimed as she stood up straight.

"It's all beginning to make sense now . . . No! It's not *possible* for something this insane to make sense! And Christopher is just as guilty as Papa!"

She just couldn't believe this was all happening. She must still be in delirium, or perhaps this was some sort of horrid nightmare! She prayed she would awake soon. Her mind could not endure much more. Would they all die? She remembered her baby. What would happen to him? She was not so sure she wished her child to be born into this appalling world.

And who was this man who was always with Christopher? She knew she had seen him before. But where? It was before they came to Europe, she was sure. She reviewed every detail of the past month, and then she remembered.

He was with Jesse at Papa's birthday party and then again at my wedding. Oh, God! Jesse! You have been betrayed, too!

This must be the man she had run away with. But then, where was Jesse now? She said she was going to Zurich; but *he* was *here*.

Could she be in Sarajevo?

More questions filled her mind and confused her the more.

How could something like this happen? She fought to stay in control of herself.

She wondered if she could stop the course that history was taking right now. She knew she didn't have enough details to go to the authorities. And she couldn't speak the language, and doubted anyone would believe such a story. She knew no one in Sarajevo. The only person with whom she had come into contact here was the doctor.

He'd never believe me! She concluded. He'd think I was still sick with fever or delirious! But I've got to try!

She raced for the door, and as soon as she opened it, she closed it.

"No, Elise," she said aloud. "He won't believe you. No one will. It's all moving too fast, and you can't stop something like this . . . I feel so powerless." She let her head fall into her hands.

She felt as if she were sinking in a quagmire. No one could rescue her. Everything she had believed in all her life had been shattered. She stared into the black abyss and felt the same icy wind sweep over her that she had experienced when she and Christopher had first arrived in Sarajevo. Her blood froze in her veins, and once again she saw the vision of the crumbling, bombed buildings. Terror filled her as she realized all too well that what she had foreseen would come to pass; it was inevitable. She couldn't stop the course of destiny any more than she could stop the earth from spinning on its axis. She was helpless. They all were.

She was positive that she must escape from Christopher and the destructive forces he represented. "Now how do you propose to run away from him?" she asked herself angrily. She had no money, no place to run to, and no means of getting there. There had to be a way. She couldn't stay anywhere near him, not now. Not after knowing what he was and how little she meant to him.

"Damn, Elise! Here he is the devil himself, and you still wish that he loved you. What a fool you are," she cried as tears of desperation flowed down her panic-stricken face.

Her eyes darted nervously about the room, searching for something to give her an avenue to freedom. She stared at her hands and she spied the diamond bracelet. Her jewels! That was it! And Christopher must have some money in the room. He would have had no reason to take much money with him tonight.

She ran to the bureau, yanked the drawer open, and ransacked it, tossing clothing about her as she did so. She had searched three drawers before she found a brown leather pouch in the back of the fourth drawer. She sat on the floor and opened it. There were hundreds of dollars here. She couldn't take all of it, she reasoned, because he would miss it and would wonder where it had gone. But then she could make the room look as if it had been burglarized. No, then the police would investigate, and that might impede her flight. She would take as much as she could without it causing any concern. She straightened the clothing in the drawers and carefully replaced the pouch. She put the money and all her jewelry in her purse.

Now she had the means to pay for her escape. Where would she run? Madame Renaud! Of course! Those notes in her art satchel. She raced to the closet and opened the satchel. She dug deeply into its interior and found the note. Here it was! Paris! She would go to Paris. Lord! How far was Paris from Sarajevo? She had no idea. Maybe it would be too far. She could go to Jesse! She knew where Zurich was. But, no. Wilhelm knew where Jesse was, and Christopher could easily discover her whereabouts through him. No, it had to be Paris; it was all she had. She could never return to Mobile. She didn't know if anyone could stop her from killing her own father. He would never be "Papa" to her again.

Poor Mama! Elise knew that Dorothea was unaware of any of this. How could he do this to us? How could she ever love or trust anyone again? Everything had been a lie.

It must have been comical for Christopher to watch her fall in love with him. She had fallen prey to his every word—and oh, yes, to his touch! Even now, with all she knew, just the thought of him lying with her sent quivers of pleasure and anticipation across her skin. It was going to be impossible for her to ever forget him. But she had to leave him now; that much she knew. She couldn't respect him. She feared him, in fact. He had said with his own lips that he wanted to laugh when he had asked her father for her hand. Now, even she laughed. She became hysterical. She laughed through hot, salty tears as she beat her fists against the wall. "I've got to calm myself," she told herself, rubbing her tears away.

She must ready herself for her journey. It was impossible to pack, for Christopher would be suspicious. She'd have to leave all her clothes behind. When would she do it? During the procession, of course! Everyone would be preoccupied with the execution. In all the confusion she could easily lose herself in the crowd and then . . . And then *what?*

She needed transportation. She couldn't buy a car or hire a carriage or even take a train. Christopher would be certain to trace her. A horse! She would need a horse. She remembered seeing a livery stable near the bazaar. She was sure she could buy a horse there. She had enough money for that. Then she would ride through the countryside to the north and board a train at the next railway stop. She would pack only necessities in her art satchel and tell Christopher that she wanted to sketch the motorcade. He would indulge her, she knew that much. He had delighted in her painting; he'd even made a studio for her. Thinking of that and all the problems that she faced made her heartsick. She huddled on the bed and fell into an exhausted sleep.

Christopher burst into the room and almost wept with relief when he saw Elise on the bed. He had felt panic-stricken when he returned to their dinner table and been told she had left some time ago. An elderly woman told him that she had risen quickly from the table and looked a trifle ill. What was wrong with her lately? She was constantly escaping his grasp. For the second time in one day he had feared for her safety. She had known he would be in the library; why hadn't she simply come for him? If she were ill, he would have seen her home. Seeing her here like this, he knew she must have been very sick. How long had she been lying here? Had she fainted?

He bent down and swept the damp locks tenderly from her forehead. As he did so, he was shocked to discover that her skin was ice-cold, yet her gown was thoroughly soaked with perspiration. It made no sense. Her breathing was very shallow, and he felt for a pulse. He couldn't find one in her wrist, and in dread he felt her throat.

"God, don't let her die. Don't let any harm come to her," he prayed. *There it is! It's faint, but I can feel the pulse!*

He kissed her and sat on the bed rocking her in his arms. As he held her, he felt the warmth return to her skin, and her cheeks and lips became pink again. He gently laid her upon the white linen sheets and rolled her onto her stomach in order to unbutton her gown. He peeled the material from her arms and shoulders and once again was startled to see that she wore no lingerie.

"God, Elise, you're a minx even in your sleep," he whispered.

He leaned against the brass headboard and gathered her into his arms. He placed her head upon his chest and held her close to him as he stroked the soft skin of her back. Her breathing became normal again, and he sighed with relief that she was safe. He kissed her brown hair. He fondled her breast and felt the nipple harden at his touch. She must be gaining some weight, he thought absentmindedly, for her breasts felt larger. He caressed her smooth hips and long legs, thankful that he did not have to leave her alone this time. Even if she was asleep, he didn't mind. This way she could not refuse his love, and he reveled in the subtle responses her body made to his loving touches. He held her as close as he could without waking her.

He thought of the years they would have together. As soon as he could, he would take her back to New York,

177

where she would be safe from this war that was soon to begin. He would buy her anything she wanted. They would visit every art gallery on the eastern seaboard if that was what would make her happy. He would take her to the finest restaurants, the ballet, the theatre. There was so much he wanted to do for her. He wondered if one lifetime would be enough for them; he doubted it seriously. But he could fill their life with love and happiness. He was certain no man had ever loved a woman as much as he loved her.

Right now all he needed was the chance to show her how much he cared for her and wanted her. They needed time. His job wouldn't demand that much from him now that the assassination was imminent. At the most, he surmised he had but a week here in Sarajevo. There was a trip to Paris, and then he could arrange to go back to the States. He didn't have to supervise international matters. He would contact his superiors and resign. He thought of the magnitude of his duty and wondered if he were deceiving himself. So much and so many depended upon him and his ability to carry out orders. Wilhelm was a good man and his performance was excellent, but Christopher knew he could never handle everything alone. It was so easy for a contact to be lost or for some pertinent information to fall into the hands of the enemy. Lately every negotiation had become critical, every minute detail demanded constant attention. The pressure had mounted until, at times, he feared he would break. This was certainly no time to lose his control. He had been able to command the situation until now, and he must pursue it to the end. But then, when this all began, Elise had not been part of his life. And it hadn't been her presence that complicated matters; it was his falling in love with her. But he would not—could not—relinquish his feelings for her or throw away his opportunity to create a full life for them. Nothing on earth could make him do that. He pleaded with God to grant him the time to give Elise what she deserved from him, which was a heart full of love.

He still couldn't believe this had all happened to him. It both dumbfounded and delighted him. He wished that he could think of a word that could encompass all that he

178

felt for her. To his mind, the word *love* wasn't powerful enough. It had been used and misused so much by so many that it had a hollow ring to it. As he racked his brain, he could still find no word that served his purpose. He pulled her closer to him. Someday she would know how much she meant to him.

Eighteen

ELISE awoke to find herself in the circle of Christopher's embrace. He was staring at her with those crystal blue eyes, and she smiled sleepily at him. She raised her arm to lift her hair away from her damp neck. He lowered his face toward hers and pressed his hungry lips to her. She felt his hand tighten around her waist, and for the first time it dawned on her that she had no clothes on, nor was she covered with a sheet. How had she forgotten to don a negligee? Her thoughts were confused as she tried to piece together the events of last night, but his demanding kisses pushed all logic from her mind. As his hand cupped her breast and her skin tingled at his touch, her memory was jogged and the painful knowledge flashed across her consciousness. She relived the shock and devastation of her father's participation in this great conspiracy of Christopher's. She was lying with the deliverer of her destruction. His hands were passing over the length of her, and she trembled in morbid fear. Thinking it a response of pleasure, Christopher pressed himself against her. She experienced both terror and need. She must break away from him! She couldn't allow herself to be used by him or any other man for his demonical aims or perverted pleasures. She could not arouse his suspicions, but she had to do something now.

"Christopher, how did I get here? I don't remember how I got home!" she cried.

"Elise, you must have been quite ill. I was so worried about you. A woman who sat next to us at dinner told me you didn't appear to be in good health. Are you all right now?"

"Yes, a little weak and quite tired."

"Something must have happened on that cruise. You haven't been well for quite some time. Is there something you are not telling me? Have you always been in such poor health?"

"There's nothing wrong, not seriously anyway. I'm just having difficulty adjusting to the heat. And the traveling was a little hard on my constitution, I guess. Right now I think I need a cool bath. If you wouldn't mind, could we have breakfast sent up to the room? I'd like lots of fruits, if that's possible. Could you please do that for me, Christopher?" she asked in her sweetest tones, smiling timidly.

"Anything you want, Elise. But wouldn't you rather stay here in bed with me for a while, hmm?" he asked, desire filling his eyes.

It took all her power of self-denial to refuse him. She rose from the bed and walked quietly to the bathroom, locking the door behind her. She wondered if she could ever quench this raging inferno he always managed to create in her body. Just what kind of a fool was she to respond to a man like Christopher? After all, she knew the truth now. When would logic and reason return to rule her body? She filled the tub, and as she sat in the water she realized that this would be the last day of her life that he would touch her body or, she hoped, spirit. In only a few hours she would be gone from him; she would no longer have to be reminded of his treachery. The burden of her father's betrayal would be with her always. She could never forgive either of them for what they had done. She lathered with the sponge and sweet-smelling soap, and rinsed. She shampooed her hair three times. She had no idea how long it would be before she would have a chance to indulge herself like this again.

She would be embarking on a journey not only to a new land, but to a new way of life. She had always lived under the protection of a man. She had gone from her father's house to Christopher's home. Now she would be alone; responsible only for herself. She had always desired to command her own destiny, and now she would. She thought of Sadie and how proud Sadie would be of her. But she was petrified at the thought of riding out across the countryside by herself. All kinds of dangers could await her there, but surely they could be no worse than what lay in store for her here with Christopher. She could not tolerate such a life, living with such a man. She was not sure he was even human—could a human being have such little regard for life? He couldn't possibly believe in God or life or love.

When she returned to the sitting area, she saw that their breakfast had arrived. Luckily, there was a vast array of food. She felt she should eat heartily, since she had no idea when she would eat again. She didn't even know the name of the next town, and she wondered just how she could find out. She pulled the sash of her blue wrapper about her and sat down opposite Christopher, who was pouring their coffee.

"I'll just have coffee right now, until after I shave, Elise. You have something to eat while it's still hot," he said as he sat down.

Elise piled her plate with sausages, eggs, and three pieces of dark bread, and she filled her bowl with berries and hunks of melon. She spread a large quantity of marmalade on her bread and ate with apparent relish. Christopher held his cup to his lips and watched her devour the food. He had never seen Elise do more than pick at her plate. What was the matter with her? She never ceased to astonish him. Everytime he thought he had learned her habits, her likes and dislikes, she did something completely unexpected. His eyes grew larger as he watched her reach for more sausages from the server. Where was she putting it all? Perhaps after her illness, her body truly craved the food and the energy she would gain from it.

"I can order more for you, if you wish. You seem to be inordinately hungry today, my wife," he said with a chuckle.

Elise winced, afraid that he might discover her true intentions. She put her fork down and smiled up at him.

"I guess I was making a pig of myself. I can't understand why I was so famished. I'll get dressed now," she said, and began to push her chair back.

"Don't be silly. I was only teasing. You eat. I'll go bathe and dress," he said as he rose and left the room.

Elise breathed a sigh of relief and waited till the door

the bomb had struck her face. She was not the only one to be injured. He could see several spectators screaming and scurrying about. He looked behind him to the third motorcar in the procession and noted that Count Boos-Waldeck, Colonel Erik von Merizzi, and even Sophie's attendant, Countess Lanju, had also been wounded. Fearful that Sophie would be even more distressed were he to say anything, he kept his thoughts to himself.

Wilhelm watched Nedjelko Cabrinovic as he took a small cyanide capsule out of his pocket, swallowed it, and then dove into the Miljacka River. Wilhelm smiled to himself. He knew the cyanide would only make him vomit, for its formula was not strong enough to kill him. He had prepared those capsules himself, as the plan did not call for the death of these assassins. Not just yet, anyway. If all the conspirators were to die of cyanide poisoning, then the authorities would not be able to capture them. The New York group had been quite explicit about the fact that these young men were to remain alive, and were to be imprisoned. After all, in order for the world to sympathize with Serbia, there must be proof, and enough prisoners for Vienna to make a case against the little country. No, there must be conspirators left very much alive, and they must talk at the proper moment. Wilhelm looked at Cabrinovic as he raised himself up from the water and retched into the river that was too shallow to allow him to drown.

Christopher watched as the first two cars of the motorcade came speeding up the street to the city hall. In so doing they passed too quickly by three of the conspirators, Vasco Cabribovic, Cvijetko Popovic, and Danilo Ilic; it was impossible for them to do anything. Christopher noted that although something had happened to those in the third car, the archduke was very much alive. The cars stopped at the city hall, and the burgomaster alighted his car and stood before an angry Archduke Francis Ferdinand, who stormed at him.

"One comes here for a visit and is received with bombs. Mr. Mayor, what do you say? It's outrageous. All right, now you may speak!"

It was obvious that Fehim Effendi Curcie had no idea what the archduke meant, and he slowly began to read his prepared speech:

"Our hearts are filled with happiness . . ."

Christopher couldn't hear all the words, but he could tell that the burgomaster had no intention of apologizing for the bombing or even stating that he was happy that there were no serious injuries.

The archduke took command of the situation and gave his speech, which he closed with the words: "I assure you of my unchanged regard and favor."

The archduke did not want to continue the motorcade. However, the military governor, General Oskar Potiorek, believed that no one would dare attack again. He endeavored to persuade the archduke that all would go according to earlier plans. But the archduke had opinions of his own; he felt it his duty to venture to the local hospital, where the dozen or so injured spectators had been taken. He wanted to inquire about their injuries. He was most concerned with the Countess Lanjus and the others in his motorcade. But he believed the trip was too dangerous for Sophie, and he pleaded with her to remain behind, in safety. But she insisted on going with him.

He knew there was no dissuading her. The mayor entered his own car, the archduke and Sophie rode in theirs, and they began the drive up to the Imperial Bridge.

Christopher watched as the two cars approached him. They drove past Trifko Grabez, who stood stock-still and did nothing at all. That was the sixth assassin, Christopher thought. It was beginning to look as if the whole plan would be a bust. Damn! The archduke's car followed that of the burgomaster's auto. The next intersection was Appel Quay, but the cars turned to the right onto Francis Joseph Street.

"What's this?" Potiorek said. "We've taken the wrong way!"

At his words, the chauffeur slammed on the brakes and tried to turn the car around.

Even from this distance, Christopher could see that the motorcars were only five feet from Gavrilo Princip, the last of the assassins. Christopher wondered if seven would be a lucky number. Gavrilo pulled out his pistol and fired two very quick shots. Christopher saw that the archduke has been hit in the neck, even though he still sat bolt upright. He couldn't see where Sophie was shot, but he guessed somewhere in her upper torso. He saw Potiorek turn around and glance at his two royal charges. The military governor must have believed they were safe, because he was giving some kind of directions to the chauffeur and they were turning around to go back the way they had come. Both Sophie and Francis Ferdinand continued to stare straight ahead of them. Suddenly, as the car started on its way, the archduke's mouth opened and a stream of blood spewed out.

Christopher watched as Sophie slumped down into the car. Potiorek made an effort to raise her. His hands trembled in shock as he heard the frightened voice of Francis Ferdinand.

"Sophie dear, Sophie dear, don't die! Stay alive for our children!"

Then he too slumped, and Potiorek asked if he were in pain or if he suffered.

"It is nothing. It is nothing. It is nothing."

The Archduke Francis Ferdinand had uttered his last words.

Sophie died before anyone could get to the car, and the archduke lingered only a few more moments.

Elise kept her eyes glued on Christopher's tautly pensive form as he and the other spectators watched the confusion ahead of them. They had barely heard the shots, but the scurrying policemen and the young assassin, who was quickly captured, held everyone's attention. Elise dropped her paper and charcoals, picked up her art satchel, and crawled behind the cypress tree. Still watching Christopher, she backed down the little knoll to the sidewalk. When she was sure no one would see her, she walked as quickly as possible toward the bazaar and the freedom she knew she must find.

Nineteen

Lacking enough energy to walk very far without resting, Elise had feared she would not be able to escape undetected. But already she had reached the almost vacant souks. It was not far to the stable, she remembered. But she felt a sense of panic, because all the souks looked alike. No! She should turn left. Or was it to the right? She took the right turn, and there, about four blocks ahead, was the livery. She quickened her pace and stopped just outside the large wooden door. Suddenly she realized she could not communicate with these people! She didn't know their language. Well, she would have to find other ways to make her needs known—and fast! The toothless, white-haired man, who sat on a wooden stool, had friendly eyes. She used her hands and gestures to indicate her needs. He kept smiling, but shaking his head, until she waved some bills under his nose. She found money expedited communication.

The horse was beautiful, a chestnut brown with white markings and white hooves. He had to be fifteen hands high, Elise thought. She purchased a hand-tooled leather saddle and bridle, and a bedroll and saddlebag. The old man helped her mount her steed, and she galloped toward the dirt road that led to the north of the city and into the woods and rivers of Bosnia.

It was a beautiful day. The blue skies were cloudless and now that the wind blew in her hair and about her body, she didn't mind the heat quite so much. The countryside was scattered with colorful meadow flowers and grasses. Farther outside the city, a carpet of tiny pink flowers grew in thick fluffy rows; for miles the terrain resembled an eiderdown quilt.

As the afternoon passed, Elise grew weary. She passed small farms along the way and took great comfort in viewing the freshly tilled and planted earth. Perhaps this would be a friendly land after all. She felt free now that she had put the past behind her; with each beat of the horse's hooves, the old pains and lies were drummed out of her mind and beaten into the earth beneath her. She prayed they would never rise to haunt or torment her again.

Christopher watched with great interest as the assassin turned his executioner's weapon upon himself. A quick-acting bystander knocked the pistol from Gavrilo Princip's hand. The crowd and a few policemen crowded around the young Serbian. He was shoved, pushed, and beaten before the police halted the rough treatment. Christopher saw Gavrilo take the cyanide capsule from his jacket pocket and swallow it before he was searched by the authorities. After a few moments, the assassin retched and clutched his belly. Christopher smiled and crossed his arms over his chest; Wilhelm had done fine work in preparing those pills. The conspirators would live.

He moved his eyes to the motorcar where Sophie and Francis Ferdinand lay, and his eyes changed to steel as he shut his mind to the pain and terror he had helped to create here today. He scowled deeply, and his shoulders slumped. He took a few steps backward and wished he could walk back into time, not just space. He sought the courage to cast away his wretchedness.

"Elise, did you see that?" he said, not taking his eyes from the murdered royal couple. "There has been an assassination attempt on the archduke and Sophie. I think they have been badly hit. I don't know yet if they are dead. Elise? I said . . ."

He turned to look down at her and found her gone.

Confused, he stooped over to pick up her charcoals and art paper. He rose again and scanned the crowds to see if he could catch a glimpse of her; she must have walked down closer to the street to get a better view of the confusion.

He pushed his way through the rows of people lining

the street and looked up and down the boulevard. She was nowhere to be seen. He looked up past the bridge. She was not on the knoll. Could she have become ill? He had been so intent upon the assassination that even if she had called out to him, he doubted he would have heard her. She must have returned to the hotel. He searched the faces of the crowd once more; positive she was not among the spectators, he walked briskly toward the hotel. Why would she have left her charcoals and paper? Fearing she was in some danger, he increased his speed. The crowds made it impossible for him to hurry.

It seemed like hours before he reached the hotel lobby. He pressed the bell for the elevator and tapped his foot impatiently as he waited. Finally he heard the whirring of the elevator cable, and it stopped before him. He threw back the steel and wrought iron doors, entered, and pressed the lift button. He ran to his hotel room door and searched frantically for his key. He found it in his coat pocket, dropped it on the floor, retrieved it, and fumbled further in his effort to unlock the door. Elise just had to be inside! He flung the door open and called her name.

"Elise, Elise. Are you here? Are you ill?" he called as he ran into the bathroom searching for her. He raced to the draperied area about the bed. He tore at the chiffon drapes and stared blankly at the empty bed. Where was she? Had she fainted along the way? Perhaps she was downstairs having a cool drink! But as he arrived at the dining room, he noted that there was not a single patron there. He ran out onto the terrace; no one here either. Then he went to the front desk, leaving word that when she returned, she should wait for him in their room.

He retraced his steps to the Imperial Bridge. The crowds had begun to disperse, and still he couldn't see her anywhere. He arrived at the knoll and racked his brain to make some sense of what had happened. If she were in trouble or ill, where would she go? She had no friends here in Sarajevo. That too was his fault.

As before, he was impelled to visit the doctor. Yester day he had sensed that the doctor had some knowledge that he refused to share with him. What could he know? Was Elise gravely ill? There was definitely some mystery here, and he intended to discover just what it was.

He walked down the street and turned left onto Appel

Quay, which would lead him to the hospital. There was sure to be mass confusion there now, what with all the injured people from the bombing. It was dangerous for him to be seen there, but he couldn't lose Elise now that he had just found her. He began to run, and was breathless by the time he reached the square granite building. He entered, and went up to the nun dressed in a white cotton habit of her order.

"I would like to inquire if a Mrs. Christopher Mann was admitted here today," he said, out of breath.

The young, pretty, green-eyed nun looked at him quizzically.

Christopher, his tension now extreme, could do nothing to make her understand him. Finally, after repeating his name several times, she nodded and went to the desk. She flipped through a list of admittances and shook her head.

"Not here? God! Where can she be?"

He turned and was heading for the front door when he recognized the doctor.

"Doctor! Please one moment. May I speak with you?" Christopher asked.

"Mr. Mann, we are extremely short-handed today, and with the bombing surely you realize . . . Isn't this something that can wait?"

"It's my wife. She has vanished again, but this time I'm truly afraid for her safety. I was wondering if she came to see you?" Christopher asked.

"No, she did not. And I haven't seen her at the hospital. I'm sure she's safe at your hotel by now. She does need rest and care, Mr. Mann. She shouldn't have been out in this heat," the doctor said, throwing Christopher an accusing look.

"That's another thing! You keep telling she needs rest and that she is ill, but no one has bothered to tell me what the hell is going on. Both you and she have been quite secretive about her health, and I want to know what all the mystery is about."

"I can't go into it here, right now, Mr. Mann. If you'll wait for me in that reception area while I see to my more urgent patients, I'll be back as soon as possible," he said as he turned to leave.

"I'll be here," Christopher said curtly, angry at being put off. But at least he would soon discover the reasons behind Elise's strange behavior. He sat on the hard wooden chair and looked straight ahead at the long, wide crack in the plaster of the dull-gray wall. Christopher's shirt became soaked with sweat. This must be hell, he thought. Could anything be worse than helplessly sitting here?

He was in the stuffy room for what seemed like an eternity before the doctor arrived and sat down next to him.

"I promised your wife I wouldn't tell you, and this is the first time in forty years I have betrayed the confidence of a patient. I hope you understand that I'm doing this against my better judgment," he said in a low tone.

"Yes, I understand. But please tell me before I go insane!" Christopher exclaimed as his tension mounted.

"When I came to see your wife, she was bleeding. It wasn't merely exhaustion. She is pregnant with your child, and her body is trying to abort the baby. I don't think even she realizes the seriousness of her case. She isn't very far along, and this can be a most difficult time for both mother and child. She must stay off her feet as much as possible, and she will require good nourishment. Your wife is in a weakened condition. However, don't let me paint the picture too bleak. The bleeding did stop quickly, but it wouldn't take much strain or stress to have a recurrence. Mrs. Mann was most insistent that you not be told of the baby or of any of her medical problems. If she is having difficulty now, please search me out again. I will do all that I can for her."

"Thank you, doctor. I appreciate all that you have done for us both already. My main problem now is that I can't locate her. If she does come to you, please tell me. I'll keep in touch," Christopher said as he rose and extended his hand to the doctor.

He walked into the street and moved down the sidewalk in a daze. He couldn't believe it. She was carrying his child! They had been married only a little over a month. Had it happened on their wedding night? He smiled at the thought. In all his life he had never even thought of children or what it would be like to have them. But now the idea appealed to him. Yes; it appealed very much to him. Then his mind flashed back to reality: He had to find Elise. She was gone, and he couldn't fathom why she would vanish as she did. She must have been terribly upset at the assassination; she bore a new life within her, and all around her was death. He walked the streets of Sarajevo until the sun began to set. He had combed every side street, the banks of the river, the coffeehouses, even the Mosque and the churches. He went back to the hotel and learned that no one had seen her since morning.

Christopher ordered a bottle of whiskey sent to his room, then went upstairs and unlocked the door. He tossed the brass key onto the tea table, sat on the settee, and hung his head. He ran his hands through his hair and rubbed his temples.

It was obvious now that night had settled over Sarajevo that his wife had left him. But why? Did she hate him that much? Was it because she carried his child? She knew the risks she was taking if she tried to travel now in her condition. Her loathing of him must be quite intense if she wished so desperately to rid her body of his seed.

He jumped at the knock on the door, and then remembered the whiskey he had ordered. He opened the door to the bellboy, who placed the tray on the bureau, accepted the tip Christopher offered, and left the room. Christopher filled his glass almost to the rim and gulped the fiery amber liquid. He must take action tonight if he had any hope of finding Elise. If she had planned to run away, she must have packed suitcases. She would have needed money, train tickets. He could track her down, but he needed to start now. He crossed to her closet, opened the door, and was surprised to find that there seemed to be nothing missing. Where was she going that she would not need clothing? Perhaps she hadn't left Sarajevo at all; maybe she planned to come back to the hotel later and pack her clothes then. Or—his hopes lifted—she didn't plan to be gone long at all.

He crossed to the bureau and searched for his wallet. It was possible she could have found it. He checked: Half the money was gone. This meant she planned to travel quite a distance and thought to be gone for quite some time. Perhaps she was trying to sail back to America! He knew she had been terribly distressed at leaving her family. But no; she had not taken enough to get her to America. Her jewels! He had almost forgotten them. He searched her drawers until he found the velvet boxes, one square and one long. Both were empty! If she had procured an agent to buy her jewels, she would have more than enough money to buy passage to the United States. He would need to send some telegrams—one to John Salem, surely. If she did arrive in New York, Christopher knew John would be the first person she would contact. He hesitated to wire Justin Kendall. There could be repercussions there if the Kendalls thought that Elise was unhappy or that the marriage was not sound. No! He would wait for now. If he found it imperative to cable Justin, he would do so when the situation seemed bleak enough to warrant it. He prayed it would not come to that.

He needed to contact Wilhelm; he was going to need some help this time. He would have to check the railway station first. She would take the train, he was sure of it. She didn't have a car or know anyone who would drive her to her destination—whatever that was.

"Where could she go?" Wilhelm asked.

"I can't figure it out. I was so sure we could trace her by the tickets she must have purchased," Christopher said.

"Well, I mean to tell you, I'm baffled. You don't suppose her disappearance yesterday was a trial run for today, do you?" Wilhelm asked as he stared wide-eyed at Christopher.

"That must be it! But what would she have been out looking for? How else could she leave but by train? She can't walk to America!" Christopher said.

"No, if that's where she was going. I'm not so sure it is. We still have no idea why she has left, you know. We need to determine that first. When she left you at the embassy ball, where did she go?" Wilhelm asked.

"Just to the hotel. I told her she should have come to the library and I would have escorted her home. But no! She just left on her own!" Christopher said as he lit a cigarette.

"Are you sure? Perhaps she *did* come to the library. . . . You don't suppose she heard any of our conversation, do you?"

"Oh, my God! My God! She couldn't. No, please dear God in heaven! Don't let it be true! . . . But it *is* true, Wilhelm. *I told* her to come to the library—and she did! My poor Elise. . . . No wonder I found her unconscious.

194

I'm surprised the shock didn't cause her to lose the baby right there," Christopher said as he sank to the grass of the knoll under the street lamp. "What have I done to the only person I love, Wilhelm? I've destroyed her faith in her family and any chance I ever hoped to have to possess her love. She must despise me and my child. How she must be disgusted at the thought of me! And I don't blame her. There are no words harsh enough to describe how reprehensible I find myself."

Wilhelm pulled his friend to his feet, and together they walked slowly back to the hotel. Both were exhausted. Once inside the hotel room, they drank large amounts of whiskey and contemplated the dreadfulness of the day they had created. Christopher was terrified at the thought of Elise out in the night somewhere, unprotected.

Flashes of her crossed his mind, and he remembered the first time he had been entranced by her. She had been sketching on the beach, and the sun had played so lovingly on her hair. And the way she rode away into the sunset, her regal bearing and her tresses flowing in that coppery haze . . .

"That's it! Wilhelm! Why didn't I think of it before? A horse! She loves horses. She must have gotten a horse somewhere," Christopher said, elated with the possibility that all was not lost.

"But where would she buy a horse? It's too late now to go out and start asking questions of sleepy stable owners. But we can start at the break of dawn," Wilhelm said.

"I doubt I'll sleep tonight, but I do have hope now," Christopher said. "We will find her. We will!"

Twenty

THE Emperor Francis Joseph had just finished his demi-tasse when General Count Paar, his chief aide, entered the room with a grave expression on his face. The emperor thought this was not the time for bad news, no matter what it was. He had thoroughly enjoyed his vacation here in Ischl, and he didn't wish to be disturbed. He had full intentions of turning General Count Paar away, but something in the man's eyes cautioned the emperor, and he decided against it.

The general leaned over and carefully chose his words. The assassination would come as a shock, and Paar did all he could to lessen the blow. The emperor appeared as if he had suffered a stroke at the news, for his eyelids fluttered against his cheeks and he spoke nothing for quite a few moments.

General Count Paar was about to check for a pulse in the still old man when the emperor opened his eyes and said, "Terrible! The Almighty cannot be provoked!"

Paar thought this quite an ambiguous statement for him to make, and stared at the old man with a puzzled look upon his face.

Suddenly, the emperor said, "A Higher Power has restored that order which unfortunately I was unable to maintain." The Emperor Francis Joseph commanded his aide to see to the funeral arrangements: They were still a family, and they would care for their own.

The General Count Paar walked away incredulous at his emperor's attitude. There had been not a single recrimination or anger at the Serbian killers. He had taken the entire situation quite matter-of-factly and appeared to be most concerned with the ability of the House of Hapsburg to profit by the incident. If anything, it was as if the emperor felt Francis Ferdinand got just what he deserved for being so careless.

Christopher and Wilhelm were rudely awakened by the mounting sounds of violence in the streets of Sarajevo. They immediately raced to the window and raised it. Small bands of people entered the main street and soon became a mob bent upon destruction.

"Who are those people? Can you tell?" Christopher asked.

"Moslems mostly, and some Croats, I'm sure. As far as I can tell, they're attacking only Serbian establishments," Wilhelm said.

Bricks, stones, homemade bombs, and boards flew through the air. People covered their heads and ran for shelter wherever they could find it. It was difficult to tell the number of wounded. Christopher and Wilhelm had a good vantage point from their window, but they could not see all of the city. The smashing and looting lasted for another two hours before the mob dispersed; Christopher had no idea how long this had been going on, but he judged it was approximately four hours. They couldn't venture outside until the rioting died down. He hoped that in the aftermath of all this destruction he would still be able to trace Elise.

Christopher searched one end of town and Wilhelm took the other. Christopher walked through the souks and inquired of the peasants through a mixture of hand gestures and a crippled usage of Serbian and French dialect, if they had seen his tall brunette wife. At last, an old woman nodded and directed him down one of the curving streets. He gave her some coins in thanks. She smiled toothlessly as he hurried away. He came upon the livery stable at just about the same moment that a sweating Wilhelm arrived stating he had come up with nothing. An old man sat on a three-legged wooden stool rubbing saddle soap into the deep brown leather saddle that rested upon his scrawny legs. He glanced at them and grinned.

Wilhelm described Elise to the old man and asked if he had seen her. The man smiled and nodded. He described the horse and saddle he sold to her. Christopher asked the man which way she had gone. The man was not sure; he had not paid any attention. They thanked him and walked away.

"Where the hell can she go on horseback, Wilhelm? She knows nothing of the countryside or the dangers. My God! Riding horseback in her condition! The baby! Is she trying to commit suicide?"

"Calm yourself," Wilhelm said. "We'll get a motorcar and search every inch of Bosnia if we must. We'll find her."

Elise, riding like the wind, noted that night was beginning to fall. She had passed into a forest of tall evergreens, and felt the blackness envelop her. She must find some place to stay; surely there would be an inn somewhere. She could always take out her bedroll and sleep under the stars, but she feared wild animals. As she rode further with no sign of a town or even a farmhouse, she doubted the wisdom of her decision to escape. How foolhardy had she been? She gently urged her horse onward with the firm muscles of her thighs. Suddenly the horse reared and bucked. She clung to his mane and neck and strained her eyes to see what had frightened him so.

Ahead she saw what it was, and was filled with a dread she had never known. Cold perspiration broke out over her forehead as she stared at three pairs of red eyes—animal eyes. The hungry eyes of a wolf pack stared back at her. Bracing, she dug her knees into her horse and turned him to the west and sped away. She had no idea if the wolf pack had followed, but she rode for quite a distance before even venturing to look back. Then she saw the the lights of a little cottage ahead. She pushed her panting and exhausted horse on to the lights and safety. She stopped in front of the house and shouted to raise the attention of the inhabitants.

A tall, muscular man stepped onto the porch with a long rifle pointed directly at her, and he pulled back the hammer and aimed the shotgun at her face. Elise screamed. The door behind him opened slowly, and a pretty young woman ran to his side. She gently placed her tiny hand on his huge arm and urged him to lower the weapon. He didn't move an inch, but the young woman walked cautiously up to Elise's horse and patted his nose. Taking hold of the reins, she led the horse up to the porch. The man put his gun down, and Elise sighed with relief and slid off the saddle. The handsome couple helped her walk to the cottage. Elise fell into a heap on the wooden rocker that sat before the cold fireplace.

"Thank you. Thank you. I was being chased by a pack of wolves. I've never been so scared in all my life," she said as she laughed nervously at her own terror.

The couple looked at her blankly, not understanding a word she said. How would she communicate with them? They were extremely wary of her; all they did was stare. Elise smiled at them and nodded. She rose and walked to the woman, took her hand in her own, and held it. The woman's lips parted slowly into a smile, and she nodded at Elise. Elise took the man's hand and put it over those of her own and the woman's, and they all smiled at each other and began to laugh softly. Elise knew now that once again, God had sent her a friend when she needed one.

The young woman conveyed to Elise that her name was Stephania and her husband's name was Martin. Stephania drew out a loaf of very dark bread, some berries, and some dark, sweet tea, and they all sat at the narrow table and shared the meal. Elise was ravenous with hunger, but she ate lightly as she gratefully realized that this was the best meal they could offer her. When she yawned for the third time, Martin left to go outside to tend to Elise's horse and bed him down for the night. Stephania led Elise to a small cot in the corner and handed her a quilt. She thanked Stephania and was asleep before Martin had returned from the barn.

A cool morning breeze entered the tiny cottage through the open windows, and Elise rubbed her eyes and looked at her surroundings, making a valiant effort to remember just where she was. It didn't take long, and she smiled to herself at the thought of her new friends. They were obviously very poor, and Elise didn't want to impose on them any longer than necessary. But then she remembered the money she had in her purse. She could pay them. Yes! As she sat on her cot, Stephania entered the room with a bucket of fresh water. Elise jumped up to help her carry it to the table, but immediately she felt the room begin to spin; the colors faded to black and the earth rose to meet her skull.

A woman screamed something inaudible, and then Elise's body seemed to float about the room of its own accord. Soon it lowered itself onto a colorful cloud, and there she floated once again.

Elise awoke to find herself lying upon an eiderdown patchwork quilt that rested upon a down-filled mattress. No wonder she thought she had been floating! She had fainted, and she surmised that Martin had brought her in here. Her hands went immediately to her abdomen and covered it. She raised her wide blue eyes in alarm and looked questioningly into Stephania's face. Her new friend smiled, nodded, and patted Elise's stomach. Her child was safe! She rested for most of the morning, and it was not until after the midday meal that she had the energy to venture into the other room. Stephania was shocked to see her up and urged her back to bed, but Elise insisted she was fine. As they sat at the table cleaning some green beans and making every effort to communicate, Elise discovered that sometimes words could be a hindrance. She relaxed, and smiled as she helped Stephania prepare the meal.

Elise remained with Martin and Stephania for over a week. She had been able to teach them some English words; they were apt pupils. She wished she could say the same for herself. She had always had difficulty in her French classes at the academy. She guessed she was not good at languages, and she so desperately wanted to learn, if only to please these two good people.

Elise had learned that they were very near the village of Vlasenica, only ninety miles from Belgrade. Once she reached Belgrade, she could take the train to Zagreb, pass the border into Austria, and continue from there to Switzerland. At the thought of that country, she remembered that Jesse would now be in Zurich, and the temptation to see her was overpowering. But she didn't want to have to break Jesse's heart by telling her of Wilhelm's involvement in the assassination. These thoughts caused Elise great pain, and she put them from her mind. She had difficulty in dealing with the problems of the present, and her mind could not dwell on the loss of her family or Christopher. Martin gave her a list of names of family and friends of his and Stephania's who lived in Belgrade; and there was a distant cousin of Stephania's in Zagreb, should she encounter any difficulties and need assistance. Martin had gotten maps and rail schedules for her; after the previous evening's meal they had all sat around the table discussing the most direct route to France. She had no passport, having left it in Sarajevo. That oversight might prove her undoing: If Christopher knew she didn't have the document, he could easily track her down. Elise dismissed the idea; she still doubted he cared enough to pursue her for long. And she had hidden her passport in the back of the bureau drawer in case of robbery in the hotel; there was the chance he might not find it.

A visa could be obtained in Belgrade with the aid of Martin's brother, who was clerk in the city offices there. Once she had that visa in her hands, she would rest a little easier. The train system here was quite good, from what she could gather of the information that Martin gave her, but she had no idea what the condition of the train itself would be. She was glad it was not winter, for she had no warm clothing to protect her. She had no clothing at all, she lamented thinking of the beautiful things she had left behind. She had washed and ironed her suit and underthings. Stephania had given her an old dress to wear, and it had kept her cool on these hot summer days.

She was sitting on the little front porch cleaning vegetables for their supper when she realized it was the Fourth of July. Tears welled in her eyes as she reminisced about past summer holidays in Mobile. There would be picnics and parties with all her friends, and Mama would have the cook and maids scurrying every which way. There were always lots of guests for the Fourth at the Kendall household. She imagined that Sadie and Andrew were probably playing croquet this very moment. And Jack Beauvais was undoubtedly stealing kisses from Violet under one of the oak trees in the gardens. She wondered whether Mama had decorated the terrace and gardens in the traditional red, white, and blue and whether there were clusters of tiny flags and red roses on the terrace tables. The bachelor buttons would be blooming now, she mused. And Mama had always served homemade strawberry ice cream; Elise could taste its icy sweetness even now. How she wished she were anywhere but here! But

201

what was even more distressing was that more than just miles separated her from that world of childhood. For now, she knew of her father's treachery and lack of integrity. What had compelled him to do such a thing? She only had one answer, and that was money. But why did he need so much money? Was it his love for Mama? Did he love her so much that he felt insecure and felt he must give her even more, Did he love her so much he would sell his soul and his principles? It was impossible to fathom; but then she remembered how deeply she loved Christopher. Love could make a fool of anyone.

For the first time, she felt the ice in her heart begin to melt. Yes! Her papa did love that deeply and that completely. What he had done must torture him more than she could know. Somehow, someone must have placed Papa in an untenable situation, and this must have been his only escape. She felt great compassion now for her father, because she knew what her love for Christopher had forced her to do. Yet, knowing the truth, she could never live with her husband. She was taking all these risks to free herself from him, and yet she could never run away from her own heart. Christopher would always be with her. She carried him with her even now. She placed her hand over the slight swelling of her abdomen.

She finished preparing the food and waited for Stephania and Martin to arrive. Tomorrow she would go to Belgrade. Martin had wanted to ride with her, but she declined his offer. Now she wasn't so sure. Perhaps she shouldn't take any more risks than necessary. Her journey to Paris would be a lengthy one. She had been foolish too many times, she thought as she remembered the wolf pack. She decided they had better go together. Stephania had begged Martin for a trip to Belgrade for months, or so Elise thought from the parts of their conversation she could understand. Perhaps it would be fun. She could give them a holiday. They had refused the money she offered them, so perhaps she could repay them with a little gaiety in the city.

After their meal, Elise, with her very limited vocubulary and many hand gestures, accepted Martin's offer to accompany her to Belgrade only if they would both accept her hospitality once they arrived. Stephania threw her arms around Elise and hugged her tightly. They went to pack the things they would need as Martin smoked his evening pipe and stared contentedly at the blazing July sunset.

It was still dark when they began to load the wagon they would take on their journey to Belgrade. Martin had tied Elise's horse to the back of the wagon, but she insisted he put the horse in the barn. He would be her gift to them since she now had no need for a horse. Martin refused, but when he looked at Stephania's eyes, he shrugged his shoulders in surrender. They all sang songs as they started on their journey in the first rays of morning light.

Twenty-one

CHRISTOPHER had spent four days searching for Elise. He had been on horseback, riding as swiftly as he could, trying desperately to discover any clue to her whereabouts. Wilhelm had taken an automobile and was covering the north and eastern areas around Sarajevo. Christopher had gone south to the Adriatic Sea, hoping she would have booked passage on a ship. When that proved fruitless, he circled back to Sarajevo. He hadn't slept and had eaten very little. He arrived at the hotel exhausted and filthy, and very much alone; never had he felt such desolation. His only hope was that Wilhelm would return with good news. For now, he needed a bath, a stiff drink, and some sleep. He decided that as soon as he and Wilhelm finished their current assignments, they would conduct a more thorough search.

He bathed and ordered whiskey sent to the room. As he drank the soothing liquid mixed with water, he found some consolation in the apparent fact that she had not sailed from the port, although that was clearly the most logical escape route. He ran his hand through his hair and thought out loud, "There's not an ounce of rationality in her!"

But he knew he had forced her into flight. If she had heard even the smallest bit of the conversation at the embassy, it would have destroyed her whole world. He had been the instrument that had shattered her dreams. If he had given her even a kind word in the weeks he had known her, he couldn't remember it. Even though he had tried to show her that he loved her, he had always done the opposite. Remembering their wedding day and the week preceding it, he winced at his callousness. He remembered the way she had looked on their wedding night when she had been silhouetted against the French doors, bathed in a lavender cloud. Even now he could taste the sweetness of her skin against his lips.

"Oh, God," he groaned in agony. "What have I done to her?"

He downed the rest of his drink and flung his head back against the chair, overwhelmed by sorrow and regret. Grief clutched at his heart and blacked out any other thoughts.

His dark reverie was interrupted by an insistent pounding on the door. Christopher roused himself from his melancholy and unlocked the door. He clutched at Wilhelm's shoulders and pulled him into the room. "Well," he demanded, "where is she? Did you find her? Is she safe?"

Wilhelm was stunned by Christopher's appearance. He was pale, and his eyes were lusterless. "Sit down," he said quietly, urging him toward a chair. "Please calm down. I'm sorry, Christopher, but I found no trace of her. There's only one clue, and it's a very small one. A farmer said he saw a lone rider heading north into the woods the day Elise left. The horse matches the description the old man gave us, but the farmer was certain it was a man. He rode astride and was quite tall in the saddle. It is all I have. I'm so sorry," Wilhelm said as he poured himself a drink.

"But don't you see? That could very well have been her. She never rides sidesaddle. And she is tall! Which way did you say she was going?" Christopher asked as his hopes rose once again.

"*If* it's her! Remember that. To the north near the woods," Wilhelm said.

"What the hell would she be going that way? Let's see, north. Belgrade is north of here. Why would she go there? She doesn't know anyone in Belgrade. But let's go check it out. Come on!" Christopher said, rising from his chair.

"No!" said Wilhelm as he grabbed Christopher's arm and pulled him back. "We can't. We have work to do here. Or did you forget about our commitments?"

"To hell with commitments! I'm no one's slave. I can't lose Elise a second time. Isn't there some way you can take care of things for a few days? You only need to pay that idiot judge. Vienna has given him full reign in the inquiry. All you have to do is make sure there's no proof of our involvement. There shouldn't be any trouble at all. I'll come back in a week. If I haven't found her by then, we'll both leave for our new posts. Then I'll hire detectives, if necessary. I know you want to get to Zurich, but I can't let this chance go. We'll fly out of here in seven days. The planes will be ready by then. Agreed?" Christopher held his breath as he waited for his friend's reply.

"Agreed. I know how I'd feel if I lost Jesse. And I have a feeling if you don't leave, you'll go berserk. You go ahead. And, my friend, take care. You haven't slept in days and you look as if you could use some rest," said Wilhelm.

"I won't sleep until I find her. Thank you, Wilhelm. Remember, seven days!" Christopher said as he threw things into a suitcase, then darted out of the room.

Christopher started the engine of the car that Wilhelm had used. There was plenty of petrol. Good! He could drive to Belgrade. His renewed hope revitalized him, and he began contemplating all the places Elise could be going. Passing farms and tiny villages in his quest, he drove on and entered the forest.

Twenty-two

ELISE, Stephania, and Martin could feel the cooling breezes off the Sava River as they approached the city. Elise didn't know what she expected Belgrade to look like, but she had not envisioned this metropolis. The main streets were wide, and autos, pedestrians, and horse-drawn carts clogged the intersections during the busy noon hour. The spires of the city's churches reached toward the hot sun and glistened in its light. The smaller cafés and restaurants were crammed with shop girls, businessmen, and elegantly dressed ladies. Much of what Elise witnessed reminded her sadly and fondly of New York. Martin had decided that after taking the wagon to the livery, he would visit his brother and arrange for Elise's visa while she and Stephania had luncheon at one of the cafés.

Presently, Elise spied a small restaurant that she believed Stephania would enjoy. They sipped wine under the red and white striped canvas canopy. Giant cobalt-blue urns filled with colorful summer flowers were placed about the red brick terrace area. The patrons enjoyed their light fare while engaging in bright conversation. Elise noticed a young man and woman in a far corner who held hands and gazed longingly into each other's eyes. She felt a stab of pain in her heart as she wished that she and Christopher could have found such a care-free love. It took all the effort she possessed to strike from her mind the thoughts of him and what could have been. She kept telling herself it was over and that she would never see him again. It seemed that Christopher had destroyed everything she believed in. The idea that she

207

might become as cynical as he made her tremble. If she lost her compassion and vulnerability, she would lose her own self and nothing would move her again. It was better to be naive and foolish than to be empty and cruel as he was. She would never reject her basic convictions. Perhaps others would brand her foolish, but so be it. As she looked at Stephania's excited face, she felt her heart warm. If she had become a cynic she would never have experienced the friendship of these wonderful people. There was no point in bemoaning the fact that her vulnerability had made her easy prey to Christopher's silver lies.

Martin strolled up the sidewalk whistling to himself. He waved enthusiastically when he recognized the lovely face of his wife. The waiter brought another glass of wine, and he shared their lunch. Elise watched him for about ten minutes and could stand the anticipation no longer. She tapped his arm and, through gestures and the phrases she had learned, asked if he had been able to procure a visa for her. He looked at her strangely; then, realizing what she asked, he smiled, sipped his wine very slowly, and nodded his head. Elise threw her arms around him and exclaimed, "Thank you! Thank you, my friends!"

Martin asked the waiter where they could find suitable lodgings. He wrote down the names of three hotels on a scrap of paper. Upon finishing their dessert, they set out on foot to explore Belgrade.

After signing the hotel register, Christopher went to his room and ordered that a bath be drawn. Half an hour later, wrapped in a white towel, he gazed out his hotel window at the busy streets; the café down the street was filled to capacity with its noontide crowd. Groggy with fatigue, he sat down on the bed, still watching the crowd at the café. His weary eyes could no longer focus, and as he leaned back onto the pillows, he imagined he saw Elise and another young woman rise from a table at the café. A handsome young man had an arm around both women. He slumped into the pillows and was asleep at once.

Elise entered the lobby of the elegant hotel and knew that she could not possibly afford two rooms. She still had not sold her jewels, and until she did, she would have to

208

be more than frugal. It *was* beautiful. The flooring was the most exquisite white and pink veined marble she had ever seen. She had heard that some of the finest marble in Europe came from quarries near Belgrade. It possessed an incandescence from within, almost as if it were electrically lit, she mused. The wood of the walls had been highly polished, and the antique furnishings gleamed with beeswax polish.

Out of curiosity she inquired of the hotel clerk what the daily rates were for two rooms and bath facilities. It was difficult for her to converse with him and she therefore thrust her hand, containing all she possessed of local currency, at him. He sighed and shook his head at her. Elise had known she couldn't afford the rooms, but still she had hoped. She thanked him and left. It was imperative that they find a buyer for her jewels.

They all walked on, stopping at little shops along the way. They arrived at the second hotel on their list. It was clean and pleasant, though not as grand as the first, but Martin and Stephania appeared to be quite pleased with it. Elise started to register, but as she began to sign her own name, she hesitated. Sensing her difficulty, Martin took the pen from her hand and signed the name of a relative of his, then entered his own name and Stephania's. He placed the pen on the counter and turned to Elise, put his huge hands on her shoulders, smiled at her, winked, and said: "Sonya." They took their keys, and as the two women went up the wooden staircase, Martin went to the livery to fetch their luggage.

Elise and Stephania took turns going down the hall to the bathroom. Stephania gave Elise the coins she would need to put in the little gas water heater that hung on the wall in front of the copper bathtub. Elise had not seen one of those heaters since before Papa had the house renovated, years ago. She was beginning to realize just how fortunate she had been in so many ways. She had never thought much about money or the cost of things. But now, if she could not sell her jewels, she had no idea how she would go on. She needed money for her rail passage to France, and she would need enough money to live on once she arrived. The magnitude of her plight began to depress her as she laid her head back in the hot water.

"I will find a way! I have to think of the baby and not just myself. I can find employment as a governess or seamstress. I could even try to sell my paintings," she said as she prayed that her decision to leave Christopher had been wise.

Her eyes misted with tears. Was it possible for a woman alone to care for herself and her child in this world? Would her foolhardiness affect her baby? She cast her morbid questions aside and scrubbed herself vigorously. Back in her room, she took out her clean linen suit and decided that tonight they would all have a delightful meal. Tomorrow she had a lot of work to do if she wanted to leave Belgrade on Thursday morning. She needed visa, tickets, clothes, and, most importantly, money.

She opened her purse and regarded the bracelet; she hoped that it would bring a high price. She laughed nervously as the lump rose to her throat and she tried to choke it down. She had paid a high price for the bracelet already. She took the earrings and necklace. "The gifts of my betrayers," she said aloud. Her heart was cold.

Elise started at the knock on the door. She opened it to her friends, who were eager for their holiday to continue. Their happy mood dispelled Elise's gloom, and the three almost skipped down the stairs and out into the July evening. They had not gone far when Elise spied a large, gaily lit restaurant. They went inside and Martin ordered dinner, and Elise ordered a bottle of champagne to celebrate. Stephania giggled at the bubbles that tickled her nose, and Elise delighted in the fact that she had presented them with a new discovery. During dinner Elise endeavored to explain to Martin that she needed to find a purchaser for her blue diamonds. After much discourse, he realized what she needed, and he nodded assent. Their dessert arrived, and Elise discovered a raspberry and chocolate torte she had never experienced before, and she exchanged her last glass of champagne with Stephania for her dessert portion. They giggled in pleasure, and Martin looked protectively at both his charges.

Christopher awoke with a start and sat bolt upright. He looked out the window and realized that it was quite late. It could even be past midnight, for all he knew. He remembered his dream. His eyes darted to the brightly lit café down the street. He stood up and pulled back the lace curtains with a jerk. It was the same café! He squinted his eyes and strained to get a better look. It had not been a dream. But who were those people, and how could Elise possibly know anyone in Belgrade? It must have been a dream; he must be on the verge of insanity. He considered that he himself was in Belgrade only because of some flimsy clue from a farmer about a man on horseback, and he had been foolish enough to believe the "man" was Elise. He jumped up from the bed, whipped the towel off his body, and went to the closet. Dammit! She was here and he would find her. Dressed in a shirt and trousers, his jacket over his shoulder, he strode out of the hotel room into the night.

The next morning, Elise stood nervously before a jeweler who was taking extreme care in passing judgment on the quality of her jewelry. He was an extremely good-looking middle-aged man with jet-black hair, tanned skin, and deep, dark eyes. His black mustache gave him a roguish air that unnerved her. She must take care lest he try to cheat her. He spent a great deal of time examining the bracelet. She thought he was pleased with the cut and brilliance of the stones. Luckily, he spoke some English, and they had been able to establish communication. He looked up at her and flashed her a smile.

"Mademoiselle, these are lovely. I am sure we will be able to find a price that will be, uh, how you say, good to us both," he said.

"I do certainly hope so. Do you wish to purchase all three pieces or just the bracelet?" she asked cautiously.

"Ten thousand?" Elise said, making an effort to check her exultation.

"Yes. You had thought it would be more? I'm sorry that is the best I can do," he said.

"In that case, I'll keep the earrings and the necklace for now. Could I have the money in the form of a bank draft?" Elise asked.

"Of course, mademoiselle. However I would like to purchase these other stones. I'll give you six thousand for both the necklace and the earrings," he said.

Elise thought it was a great deal of money, but her instincts told her not to sell.

"No, I think I'll keep these, but I will sell the bracelet. I hope that is satisfactory."

The jeweler gave her a case for her necklace and earrings and had his assistant take Elise to the bank, where all further negotiations would be handled.

When Elise arrived at the hotel, Martin had her passport and all the papers she would need while travelling throughout the Empire. He took some bills from Elise and left for the railway station to purchase her tickets. While he was gone, Elise told Stephania that she wanted to buy her a gift to thank them both for caring for her. Elise played upon Stephania's need to please Martin in order to entice her into accepting. With a measure of reluctance and excitement, Stephania followed Elise to the dressmaker's shop.

Elise purchased a traveling suit of blue heavy linen with a bolero jacket trimmed in thick black braid. There was a matching hip-length capelet that would keep her warm as she crossed the Alps. She purchased two blouses and new undergarments. She had no idea how long her journey would be and where the train would take her. She knew the main stops along the route, but she possessed only a sketchy knowledge of European geography. She knew nothing of the climates of the countries she would pass through. This would surely be a valuable education, she thought. Elise turned to inspect the suit and was astonished at how tightly the jacket fit.

"My goodness! When does it all stop?" she wondered when she envisioned herself in another seven months.

Out of the corner of her eye she saw Stephania approach her. She was attired in a light blue linen suit; the hip-length jacket was piped in thin gold braid. Her blouse was white heavy lace, and a thin blue ribbon encircled the ruffle at the throat. She was enchanted at the prospect of owning something so fine, Elise knew.

Elise paid the dressmaker, and the two women returned to the hotel juggling their boxes. After Stephania modeled her suit for Martin, they all went downstairs to the dining room as the evening sun began to drown itself in the western horizon.

Christopher had checked every hotel register in town and had found no Elise Mann or Mrs. Christopher Mann registered in the city. He thought she might have used another name, but he didn't see her handwriting in any of the hotel records. He had been to the train station to see if she had purchased a ticket, but again, no woman fitting her description had been seen. The shops had been closed for over an hour now, but tomorrow he would go to every jeweler in the city. She had those jewels, and she would have to sell them. He wondered if she planned to remain in Belgrade. But why would she want to do that? Perhaps she did have friends here that he knew nothing about. He felt weary at the futility of his search, but he couldn't give up. He sensed that she was quite near him. He didn't know why, but at times he thought he could feel her presence. He laughed at himself as he realized he was trying to believe in something that could only be described as supernatural. Ridiculous! He put aside his foolish thoughts and went downstairs to dinner. He sat at a small table in the corner of the gold-appointed dining room. The crystal chandeliers had been turned down, and the room was bathed in the romantic glow of candlelight. A gentle rain fell outside, and Christopher stared out at the blackness through the etched glass of the large window. The raindrops hit the windowpane and trickled down the glass. Christopher placed his finger against the window and followed the course of a single drop until it met with another bead of water and together they ran swiftly together down the terrain of the glass.

Oh, Elise, I want you with me in the rain, holding you as we listen to it fall. We would live in a world of our own with no problems to haunt us. Just the two of us. I would make love to you through the night and never let you go.

Elise sat next to the door in the small hotel dining room and gazed at the soft summer shower. As the raindrops fell against the glass of the French doors, Elise touched the glass delicately with her fingertips and then moved her hand to her cheek. She placed her tear on the window and sighed.

Christopher, where are you? Do you ever think of me? Could you ever need me as desperately as I need you?

And the rain beat with greater force against the glass and washed away the tiny droplets.

Twenty-three

ELISE hugged her new friends as the steam escaped from the engine and swirled about the trio. Once again she was departing into the unknown, and she was very unsure of herself and her abilities to cope. It would be easy for her to stay here with Stephania and Martin, but she could no longer burden them with her problems. And something, an inner voice perhaps, impelled her to go to France. She knew not why, but she had to follow her intuition. She boarded the train clutching her purse, art satchel, and a small valise she had purchased the day before.

The train pulled away from the station, and Elise waved until she could no longer see her friends. Her eyes were dry, but her heart writhed with the pain of loneliness. Elise walked dejectedly down the passageway to her private compartment. She rolled the door back and entered the small room, locking the door behind her. She pulled the shade down over the glass of the door and slumped onto the seat. She flung her head back, stared at the ceiling, and let the tears flow.

When the light tap at the door came, Elise had no idea how much time had passed. The conductor checked her passport and her tickets. He directed her toward the first-class passengers' dining car. It was slightly over two hundred and fifty miles to Zagreb, the next main stop, and they were scheduled for arrival shortly after the lunch hour. Elise peered out her window and stared at the countryside, but saw only a hazy vision of Christopher's face in the glass.

Christopher stopped in front of the little jeweler's shop and prayed he would discover something tangible as to Elise's whereabouts. This was the last jeweler in the city. Christopher's greeting was returned warmly by a swarthy middle-aged man.

"Good day to you sir, may I help you with something?"

"Yes, I would like to see something rather special for a most intriguing woman. You wouldn't happen to have any blue diamonds, would you?" Christopher asked.

The man flashed him a surprised look and unlocked his large jewel case. "I have a most exquisite piece here. Perhaps this would please you and the lady both," he said.

Christopher gasped in amazement as he looked down at his bracelet! His heart rose and sank all at once. Now he knew she had money—but how much?

"It is nice. Do you have anything else? Some earrings, perhaps?" he asked.

"I'm sorry. This is all that I have. Perhaps some other diamonds with sapphires would be more suitable?" the man asked hesitatingly.

"No, I'm afraid not. If this is all you have, I'll have to take this. How much is it?"

"Fifteen thousand," the man said greedily, as his broken English became more distinct.

"Ten thousand," Christopher countered without moving his eyes from the man's face.

"Twelve thousand," the man said.

Christopher walked into the street clutching the jeweler's box. Now he had to check every route out of the city as quickly as possible. He drove to Sava River and inquired among the passenger boatmen about his wife. He was instructed to journey to the piers on the Danube, where many boats paddled and steamed upriver with summer vacationers. Perhaps she had taken one of those boats. He spent the rest of the day combing the banks and wharves for any information he could garner, and was exhausted by the effort. He spoke a little bit of many languages, but it was often hard to make himself understood. And the answer was always the same: No one could give him the smallest hint as to Elise's whereabouts. As he headed back to the hotel, he passed the University of Belgrade. He parked his automobile in front of the administration building. It was a shot in the dark, but since Elise loved art and books, perhaps she had enrolled here. It was, he knew, a farfetched idea, but he was desperate.

The registrar informed him that no classes were in session until September and no one had enrolled in the last week. Christopher left an address where he could be reached should his wife approach them.

He stared out the window of his parked automobile. He could see the old fortress that kept watch over Belgade. The city was spread beneath it along low hills, and now, as the evening settled over it, the lights were going on in each home and building. It resembled a twinkling Christmas tree with long, low branches spreading warmth and happiness over the land; but Christopher felt no mirth or gladness in his heart this evening.

After a restless night, Christopher once again rode to the railway station. This was the main rail center for all trains passing from Western and Central Europe all the way to Istanbul and on to Thessaloniki. It only made sense that he would go back to Sarajevo and aid Wilhelm. Christopher arrived at the station and talked to two different ticket agents, who could tell him nothing. A bribe enabled him to check the list of travelers, but Elise's name didn't appear anywhere. He was convinced she was using another name, but he had no way of discovering what it was. He left the station with a strange sensation. He had not seen her name, but he knew somehow she had been on that train. He came away not with a sense of futility, as he had believed earlier he would feel, but with a renewed sense of hope.

He drove back to the hotel, packed his few belongings, paid his hotel bill, and began his journey back to Sarajevo.

The train had stopped at Zagreb for less than an hour, and Elise did not leave the compartment, preferring to stay and sketch the cone-roofed towers and church spires that shaped the city's skyline. She had learned from the conductor that the walls of the city had been built in the fifteenth century, and although she found the fact quite intriguing, she couldn't make herself venture outside. Her hand moved rapidly across the paper as she tried to capture as much as she could in the time she had.

They were now only half an hour from Ljubljana, and as the locomotive raced along the track, she embellished her sketch. As she listened to the rails clicking beneath her, she remembered the grandfather clock at home in Mobile and thought once again of Jesse. She would be passing right through Zurich, and knowing that her friend was so near was too much temptation for Elise. She grabbed her art satchel and rooted in its depths for Jesse's note. She desperately tried to remember the address of her little chalet on the edge of the city. The view from the balcony was splendid, Jesse had told her. As soon as they stopped in Ljubljana, she would telegraph Jesse that she would arrive tomorrow. Elise needed a friend to confide in. It would be like going home. Elise had to remember to guard against saying anything about Wilhelm, however, for she didn't want to upset Jesse. It would be a good visit, she was sure.

When the train stopped at Ljubljana, Elise elicited the help of two English-speaking Serbian students whom she'd met on board. They were able to translate her wishes to the conductor and she was able to send her cable to Jesse. They also informed her that they would be crossing the Austrian border soon, passing through the Carnic Alps; the scenes would be breathtaking especially as the sun set in the mountains. The train would stop in Innsbruck overnight, and the conductor recommended a fine restaurant with a view of the Alps he was sure she would enjoy. Elise thanked him, and as he left she took out more paper and continued her sketching.

Christopher and Wilhelm finished talking with their informants and sent their respective reports back to New York. Christopher contacted the man who maintained his airplane. The man assured him it had been properly checked and fueled, and in the morning he would be ready to assist Christopher and Wilhelm with their flight plans. The charts and rendezvous points had been established. Wilhelm was not so sure they could leave the next day but the man assured them that the following day would also be satisfactory. Christopher was adamant about waiting no more than two days.

"Believe me, Christopher, I'm more anxious to flee this

hell-hole than you are, but I'd rather make certain we've absolutely finished here. I refuse to come back in a month because we rushed away too soon," Wilhelm said.

"I agree. There's nothing I can do about Elise right now. And I know how you want to get home to Jesse. I don't blame you. She certainly caught my eye when I first saw her!" Christopher said.

Wilhelm spun around on his heel, his eyes blazing with surprise, if not a trace of jealousy. But then remembering the Kendalls and their flare for entertaining, it was no doubt true that Christopher would not allow a beauty like Jesse to escape his eye. Wilhelm could tell that Christopher's teasing had elicited the response he'd expected, for Christopher was chuckling to himself.

"Too bad, old boy. And believe me, I don't want to escape! Can you think of anyone more desirable than Jesse?" Wilhelm said, grinning wickedly.

Christopher's eyes clouded over. "Yes, I can . . . Elise." He picked up his files and stacked them in his valise, locked it, and went to the bureau and poured two deep whiskey-and-waters. He handed one to Wilhelm, walked to the window, and looked out over Sarajevo.

"I'm sorry, old friend. I just wasn't thinking. We'll find her. If we have to comb the entire landscape of Europe, we *will* find her," Wilhelm said. "She has to have some destination in mind. She just wouldn't get on a train and travel all over Europe for the hell of it. Not in her condition. Now where could she go?"

"I don't know. I've racked my brain and come up empty every time. The whole thing is so illogical. Just like a woman!" Christopher lamented.

"Oh, my God! We are so goddamn blind! I can't believe what asses we've been!" Wilhelm exclaimed.

"What? What are you talking about?"

"She's gone to Jesse! She's gone to Zurich. I swear that has to be it. It makes so much sense. In New York I brought that note from Jesse for Elise, remember? They were always so close. Jesse told me they were like sisters. Well, Jesse must have told Elise where to find her. Doesn't it all make sense now?" Wilhelm asked.

Christopher had brightened immediately. "Of course. Jesus! Why didn't we think of this before? Where are the maps? How long till she arrives in Zurich? By plane we can be there at almost the same time!"

Wilhelm and Christopher clinked their glasses together and toasted the night. They went downstairs whistling as they strode into the dining room and ordered the finest French champane the hotel could offer. It was a grand night, for it was filled with hope.

Twenty-four

THE mountain air of Innsbruck was quite chilly, and Elise was glad she had a jacket. A group of taxis awaited the passengers to take them to the resort area for food and lodging. As she rode with some of the other passengers, everyone marveled at the breathtaking sunset that evening. Never had Elise witnessed such beauty. The tops of the mountains were still snowcapped and studded with darkest green pine trees. Some of the peaks were purplish in tone, and the juxtaposition against the blue and flame of the sunset was an artist's dream. Elise wished she possessed the talent to capture such splendor. The emerald hills rose and fell about the base of the mountains, and little wood and stucco chalets with brightly colored shuttered windows dotted the area around the lake that mirrored the scene. The taxi driver explained that when the lake froze over, people from the town came to skate till late at night.

As the sun disappeared behind the mountains, huge outdoor lamps were lit that bathed the restaurant and the surrounding trees and evergreens in filtering light. A festive mood permeated the air. Elise sat at a table with a well-traveled elderly couple who were obviously very much in love with each other. They were English and lived in London. Agatha stated that they spent every summer on the Continent, moving about wherever they felt like going. Although she and Stanley were wealthy, they both believed that under the skin they were ardent vagabonds. Many times even now, weather permitting, they would sleep under the stars. They traveled only with one another, for none of their society friends could share their gypsy predilections. Elise, fascinated by their commentary on Europe, asked numerous questions about France and Switzerland. Stanley expounded on Paris, one of his favorite cities. If not for the Moulin Rouge and Maxim's, he said, life would be worthless. He wrote down the names of restaurants, toasted their good fortune, and with that they ordered dinner.

After a marvelous repast, they ventured to their hotel. The building, erected in the fifteenth century when the Hapsburgs frequented Innsbruck for royal vacations, was small and elegant. Even though she was briefly drowsy from the heavy evening meal, she was much too excited at the prospect of seeing Jesse to sleep. She tossed and turned for hours and only managed to keep herself awake. The empty space in the bed beside her made her think of Christopher. She had not been gone from him for two weeks, and already her body craved his touch. Elise called out for him as her arms reached out to grasp the chilly air. The only warmth she felt this night was the burning need that pulsated within her loins and breasts.

The blinding dawn sunlight rescued Elise from the night and its punishments. She gazed at herself in the mirror and thought how ugly she looked—ugly, tired, and so lonely. Even though this was the day she would see Jesse, her heart was weighted with depression. She crossed to the door to leave, then looked back at the bed once more and wondered if she would feel this way every night. She opened the door and prayed she could leave Christopher's ghost in this room when she closed the door.

Elise and her new companions ate a light breakfast of fruit, raisin bread, and hot chocolate on a sunny terrace that afforded them a spectacular view of the blooming meadows and foothills. Elise hoped someday to return during winter. She had never seen snow, and she hoped she would one day bring her child to this beautiful place to ride in a sleigh and skate on the frozen water of the lake. What fun they would have! She gazed at the lake and imagined herself teaching her child to skate; Elise would need as much instruction as he. She could see herself constantly falling upon the ice. She would try to stand, and Christopher would be there and place his hands about her waist and lift her effortlessly from the frozen surface. . . .

The train whistle blew three times, breaking her reverie. She went to the lobby to procure her valise and followed the anxious travelers on to the boarding platform. Once inside her compartment, she took out her art paper and sketched the rustic scenery about her as she looked forward to her visit with Jesse.

The train passed through the small country of Liechtenstein and made a short stop in Vaduz. Knowing it was only fifty miles to Zurich now, Elise was very excited. The conductor had told her it would be less than an hour. The train seemed to move at a snail's pace. Couldn't they go any faster? This part of the journey was so long! After what seemed an eternity to Elise, the conductor knocked on her door and told her Zurich was ten minutes ahead. Elise nearly flew off the seat and crammed her art papers into her satchel. She smoothed her hair and skirt and held her hands in her lap, trying desperately to control herself. Only ten minutes! She gathered her belongings and left the compartment to stand in the companionway. She wanted to be the first off the train. She didn't want to get lost in a crowd of rushing people and be left on the train as it pulled out for Paris.

Suddenly she was jerked forward and then back as the train began to brake.

"We're here! It's Zurich!" she yelled out loud, and then sheepishly glanced around to see if anyone had heard her. Aided by the conductor, she walked down the little iron steps. Off to her right stood Jesse, her long blond hair flying as she waved and jumped up and down with the same excitement Elise was experiencing. They ran to each other's arms and hugged one another tightly. They squealed with delight and simultaneously began chattering. Jesse hired a carriage to take them to her chalet, and they held hands and talked incessantly the entire way. Elise saw nothing of the city they drove through; she saw only Jesse's beautiful face and sparkling eyes and basked in the glow of their friendship; it was as if they had never been apart. Elise felt as if she had known a hundred years of sadness in the past weeks, but now, with Jesse, her spirits soared. The carriage stopped at the base of the hill, and Elise looked up to see a large chalet of wood and stucco.

Three large second-story balconies jutted out over the hill. Many of the windows were leaded glass, and there were two sets of French doors opening onto the largest balcony.

"You call this a little chalet?" Elise asked in surprise. "Why, it's much larger than I had imagined it would be."

"You know I don't like anything small, Elise. Well, don't just stand there, come on! Wait till you see how I furnished it. I've been so busy while Wilhelm has been away on business. He'll be so surprised! I hope he likes it. I have no idea what his tastes are, besides a love for the very best. He chose me, didn't he?" Jesse laughed with glee. "I guess we chose each other. There was never any question. The first moment I saw him, something passed between us. It was like a magnetic force. I've always dreamed of a great love, Elise—the kind you read about in stories and poetry. Well, it's much more wonderful to live it."

Jesse led Elise up the stairs to the large open living room, where heavy wooden beams stretched across the width of the high ceiling. The massive stone fireplace to the left soared to the top of the pitched ceiling. The French doors opened onto the balcony, and Jesse had filled every piece of crockery available with brightly colored summer flowers. The flooring, composed of large square parquet blocks, was covered with three Aubusson carpets. Directly in front of the fireplace lay a white sheepskin. Elise, bewildered, looked at the sheepskin and then at her friend. Jesse, noting Elise's reaction, laughed loudly.

"Wait till you lie on it naked, Elise. It's marvelous, really!"

Elise blushed, grinned, and said: "Not alone, I hope!"

"Oh, God, no! Never alone!" said Jesse, and they laughed the more and hugged each other.

Jesse went to the kitchen to open a bottle of wine to celebrate, and Elise gazed about the room. She sat on one of the two enormous tan leather Chippendale sofas flanking the fireplace. In the far corner was a game table with four French ladderback chairs with cane seats and thick down-filled cushions covered in palest blue moiré. In the other corner were two bergère chairs in pale blue velvet; reading lamps stood next to each chair. Scattered about

223

the chairs were pots of yellow daisies. Jesse had obviously designated the area near the kitchen as a dining room. A large dark Louis XV parquet-topped table was surrounded by chairs upholstered in a blue and white striped fabric. An armoire stood against the wall, and the doors were open to display an exquisite collection of blue-and-white porcelains and china.

Jesse glided into the room with a copper tray filled with summer fruits, cheeses, Swiss chocolates, and two very large wineglasses.

"The days of tea and cakes are over, Elise! Isn't this grand? I just wish Wil were here so you could get to know him. On second thought, then I would have to share you with him. Perhaps it's better this way. Here's to us. The best of friends, ever," Jesse said as they clinked their glasses together. "I haven't completed this room yet, but what do you think so far?"

"Well, if Wilhelm is everything you say he is, that sheepskin is all the furnishing you really need!" Elise giggled.

Jesse laughed and agreed. "He won't care about anything but me, I hope!"

"I do love the room, truly I do. But then you were always so much better at those things than I. I should think it would be difficult to make one large room function as three or four all at once," Elise said, looking at the sheepskin.

Jesse caught the look. "Elise! I do have bedrooms!"

Elise laughed until her sides ached. "I don't know when I've laughed so hard," she said.

"Speaking of which, when are you going to tell me just why you are alone and not with that gorgeous man you married?" Jesse asked.

Elise's mirth vanished.

"Jesse, I don't want to burden you with all my problems. Not now. Not today. Perhaps tomorrow."

"Elise, that's why I'm your friend. You can tell me anything. You know that. But I don't want to press you. I'll be here if you need me. All right?"

"Yes. It's painful for me, and I need to laugh some more. I've had too many days of tears," Elise said.

"Oh, Elise! It can't be that bad! Can it?" Jesse asked.

"Yes, it can. But let's not talk about it. Tell me what

you have planned for us to do. Jesse, I can't stay for very long, but if it's possible, I'd like to go shopping. I need clothes desperately."

"I was going to ask you where your luggage was. Did you have it sent on?" Jesse said, biting into a pear.

"This is all I have," Elise replied.

Jesse nearly choked. "What? You can't be serious! What in the world is going on? You cable not even twenty-four hours ago and say you are arriving. You haven't told me where you are going. You say you can't stay long, and you are without your husband or any clothing. I assumed you were coming here to stay in Zurich. Elise, please tell me what has happened," Jesse demanded.

"I've left Christopher. It's as simple as that. I discovered something about him that is unforgivable. I had to leave my clothes behind." Elise paused, fighting tears. "I can't stay long because I'm afraid he might follow me here. I won't tell you where I'm going. For the first time in my life, I have to keep this from you. I know you would never tell anyone, but I can't take the chance. Christopher can talk anybody into saying or doing anything," Elise said.

"You still love him, don't you, Elise?" Jesse asked, knowing what her friend's reply would be.

"Yes, with all my heart. And that's not all. I'm carrying his baby."

"Lord! You must have gotten pregnant on your wedding night!" Jesse laughed, looked at Elise, and said, "My God! You did, didn't you? But nobody does that!"

"I did!" Elise said, and they both burst into laughter again.

They finished their luncheon and talked until the sun went behind the mountains. Most of what they said was idle chatter, but it mattered little what the topic of conversation was; they were together and sharing.

Twenty-five

A tiny silver bell tinkled as Jesse pushed open the door of her favorite apparel shop. She passed by the sitting area to speak to a petite blond woman of middle age who appeared to be quite thrilled at their arrival. The woman greeted Jesse effusively while Elise investigated the shop. The thick carpeting was baby blue and blended nicely with the walls' white paneling. Ceiling-high glassed-in cases ran the length of the room on either side. The cases were filled with the finest handwork in Switzerland. There was little in daywear, as the shop specialized in party dresses, evening gowns, furs, and, most important, lingerie. Elise had finished most of her shopping and was pleased with the two suits she purchased. She at least now had a change of clothes for Paris. Jesse was here to select a special negligee and peignoir for Wilhelm's imminent return. Her statement of this fact alerted Elise to the necessity for her departure. She didn't want to see Wilhelm or run the risk of Christopher discovering her location or, worse, her destination.

Jesse introduced Elise to Maria, the proprietress. The two girls followed Maria to an elegant fitting room. Jesse began to disrobe while Maria brought a group of night things from which she could make a selection. Elise was shocked when she realized how revealing these gowns

226

were. Jesse flipped through them and immediately settled on the white gown of sheer silk.

"Jesse, you aren't serious about wearing that scandalous thing, are you?" Elise asked.

"Of course! It reminds me of a harem costume. Where's your sense of adventure and romance?" asked Jesse as she stepped nude into the diaphanous gown. The silk was so sheer that Elise had to blink to see if it truly existed. There were no sleeves, and the garment buttoned with one tiny button at the throat. Two large medallions of lace covered Jesse's breasts, but her entire midriff could be seen. Just below her navel began a band of the lace that extended in back to cover her derriere, and one sheer layer of the silk fell to the floor.

"Jesse, it's risqué, but you look so beautiful."

Jesse herself was thoroughly pleased with the effect of the gown. She wanted to look most desirable and yet elegant, and this negligee was perfect. She stepped out of the gown, dressed, and thanked Maria once again.

As they walked out of the shop and headed for lunch, Elise told Jesse she would leave in the morning. Jesse protested vehemently, but Elise could not be swayed. They shared a quiet meal in a pretty café, though neither felt much like eating. When they left the restaurant, they were already experiencing the pain of separation.

"Jesse, please don't be so sad. We only have a few more hours together, and I want us to have a wonderful time. I've cried so much these last few days. . . ."

"I'm sorry, Elise. I wish I knew more about what has happened to you so I could really comfort you. But you're right. We should be glad we've had this reunion. We still have a chance to do lots of things here." She smiled brightly into Elise's solemn face. "Come on," she said, "there's still the bakery, the perfumery, the florist—a hundred places to explore."

Arm in arm, they set off to enjoy the summer afternoon. They rode a carriage to the chalet and required the aid of the driver to unload their parcels. By the time they went tripping up the stairs, their earlier happy mood had returned. They made a pact not to think of Elise's departure until after the train had left.

Christopher, alone, paced up and down on the carpet with his hands jammed inside his trouser pockets. He was expecting a call from the flight engineer, as Wilhelm referred to the man who scheduled all the flight rendezvous he would require in order to arrive in Zurich by dawn tomorrow. Christopher was becoming unnerved, and his patience had left him thirty minutes earlier. According to his calculations, if Elise had been on that train, she was in Zurich. He and Wilhelm had experienced one delay after another; nothing had gone smoothly for the last two days. He still was not positive Elise was in Zurich. Now he wished he had called Jesse and left word that should Elise turn up, Jesse must make every effort to detain her until their arrival. He had not done so, for fear that Elise would flee again.

"Ring, dammit!" he yelled at the silent telephone. He should have been in the air hours ago. He lit a cigarette, then stamped it out. He jumped as the telephone bell pierced the air of the stifling hotel room. He picked up the receiver and braced for the bad news.

"Mann here," he said tensely.

"Christopher, grab your bags. We're ready to roll!" said an exuberant Wilhelm on the other end of the line.

"Right!" Christopher said as he slammed the receiver down. He glanced around the room, pulled on his navy jacket, snatched his briefcase and valise from the settee, and rushed out the door.

He paid the hotel bill and left a large tip for the efficient staff. He jumped over the closed door of the open-topped automobile and sped to the improvised airstrip just outside Sarajevo.

Wilhelm leaned against the biplane; he was dressed in his flight trousers and an open-necked white shirt. A white silk scarf fluttered about his neck, and he smiled broadly as his friend drove up. He ran to the car and took Christopher's luggage, placing it in the small cargo hold under the pilot's seat.

"You can't be any more anxious than I to leave. I'm glad we waited, though. There were some major difficulties with the propeller, and I would have hated like hell to have it fall off over Austria somewhere," Wilhelm said with a laugh.

"Everything is repaired now, I hope!"

"We wouldn't be taking off if it weren't."

They climbed into the plane as the little man started the propeller for them. Christopher taxied to the end of the strip, revved the engine, and built up his speed as they raced down the strip. He pulled back on the stick in front of him, and they left the ground and Sarajevo behind them. The sky was a brilliant blue that day—much the color of Elise's eyes, Christopher thought with a pang. He didn't know what he would say to her once he saw her; he prayed the right words would come to him.

Why had it always been impossible for him to say what was in his heart? Was it pride? Or the fear of rejection? Christopher suddenly realized it was both. He had never loved before, and the intensity of the emotion overpowered him. He thought of Wilhelm, who sat behind him, and wished his relationship with Elise could be as simple as the love Wilhelm and Jesse had for each other. What magic truth had they discovered that he found so difficult to grasp?

Christopher nosed the plane downward toward the landing strip that was located just north of the little Italian village of Udine. The ground was flat, and only a few shrubs were scattered about the area. After refueling they would pass over the Venetian Alps to the northwest, over Liechtenstein and then on to Zurich. There would be three more stops along the way; but if this stop proved typical, they would merely run from one plane to another and would waste no time on land.

If they didn't make every minute count, they would have to stop for the night, as it would be much too dangerous to fly over the Alps. Christopher judged that if they could make Vaduz, they could spend the night there; but since Zurich was only another forty minutes to an hour from Vaduz, they both agreed to try to push on. They hopped into the plane and once again were airborne. There was enough time to make the entire journey before nightfall, barring any unforeseen circumstances.

Both Christopher and Wilhelm spent the next hours in a state of numb suspension. Their eyes were glued to the horizon when not checking their charts or anxiously marking their seemingly slow progress. Actually, Christopher determined, they were making better than eighty miles per hour. He pushed for more, but the little plane was delivering its utmost. The board had financed the ultimate in equipment and planes for all their undertakings, and for this, Christopher was grateful. But his stomach churned as he thought of what he had been forced to do, and immediately he was deeply depressed. Through circumstances beyond his control he had been placed in an untenable position; he'd had no decision in the matter.

He would never be able to erase the memory of the blood gushing from the mouth of the archduke. Christopher cursed himself and the world. His mind clouded with remorse, he peered into the skies ahead and through sheer force of will, it seemed, pressed the plane onward.

Elise and Jesse clung to each other, wanting never to let go. This was the most difficult farewell Elise had ever experienced. The burning lump in her throat and eyes was nothing to compare with the void in her heart.

She stumbled into her compartment and ran to the window; she could see Jesse still standing in the same spot with her arms outstretched. Through the fogged glass Elise cried Jesse's name over and over, until she could no longer see her friend.

Only with Jesse could she be so natural, so human. Jesse accepted her with all her faults. With Jesse, she could be totally free. She could say or do anything, no matter how ridiculous or silly it might seem to others, and she knew that Jesse would always stand by her. Even in her present circumstances, Jesse had not lectured her or expounded on Elise's duty to her husband. She had simply offered her the love and warmth Elise so desperately needed right now.

She experienced the gamut of emotions as she remembered their few short days together. She laughed once again at Jesse's sheepskin and cried all the more at their recent leave-taking. Elise laughed louder, and her laughter became high-pitched as she choked back her unrelenting tears. Her breathing quickened as her lungs burned within her and her hands began to shake. Her knees buckled, and she dropped with a thud to the floor.

Elise's eyelids flew open as she heard herself scream in

panic. It took several minutes before she fully realized where she was and what had happened. She placed her hand on her forehead and was surprised to discover it was drenched in cold perspiration. A dull ache moved through her abdomen. She wrapped her arms around her belly and moaned with the pain.

"No. God, don't let it happen. Please, I beg you. Don't take this child from me! It's all I have. Let me keep my baby!" she cried over and over, in time with clicking of the rails.

Trying to relax, she took deep, steady breaths, and she lay as still as she could. She pulled her cape about her and raised her knees. After slipping her valise and art satchel under her legs to elevate them, she rubbed her abdomen in slow, circular motions. She stared at the overhead light. She concentrated on that light and counted her breaths. The pain began to subside, but still she did not move. She fought all the negative emotions that tried to control her; she clutched for the calm and peace that always seemed just beyond her reach. Finally the pain fled her body, and once again she was master and her child was safe. There was no blood. God had given her a reprieve. She would not give in to melancholy: Even though her plight was depressing, she vowed to put from her mind all thoughts but those of her own and her child's safety. She made no attempt to rise from the floor.

When the conductor knocked on the door during his routine passenger check, he found Elise in this position. She merely looked at him and said: "I need a doctor."

The conductor raced from the room without a word, and returned in less than five minutes with a very young man. He looked too young to be a medical doctor, but he assured Elise he was fully qualified. He was Parisian, but because his command of English was quite good, she was able to understand most of what he said. He gave her a sleeping tablet, telling her that it was extremely mild and would only make her drowsy. After they reached Paris, he would give her his address in order that she could call upon him if she needed his services. He told her to stay in bed for at least a week and do nothing that might be upsetting. He asked if she had someone to help her once she arrived in the city. She assured him that she did, although she was not so sure.

She felt as helpless as a small child. The doctor told her that when the train arrived in Paris, he would personally see her to her residence. The conductor returned, breathless, bearing the extra pillows and blankets the doctor had ordered for her. Now he told the conductor to bring her a light lunch; it was imperative she eat correctly. The doctor remained in the compartment with Elise while she ate the toast, tea, and fruit, and he reminisced about his childhood in Paris. His soothing voice and the warm tea lulled her to sleep.

When she awoke, she realized that all the other passengers had departed. She had slept almost the entire trip. The doctor knocked on her door and rolled it back. The conductor, directly behind him, carried a blanket. It was quite warm in Paris, and Elise had already kicked off the covers she had needed earlier. Her chills had come from within, and now that the crisis had passed, she saw no need for a blanket.

The conductor picked up her luggage and headed toward the boarding area. As he stepped from the compartment, he said, "The doctor has ordered a taxi for you, Mrs. Mann."

The doctor leaned over and lifted Elise in his arms as if she were weightless. She was surprised at his strength. She put her arms around his neck; and when she felt her head begin to spin slightly, she placed her head on his capable shoulder and closed her eyes lest she pass into unconsciousness once again.

The brilliant July sun almost blinded Elise. The doctor placed her upon the seat of the taxi and asked her for the address. Elise looked at him blankly and then remembered the note in her art satchel. She took out the note and handed it to the doctor. He sat next to her and held her hand as he gave the instructions to the taxi driver. He gave the note back to Elise, and she looked at the name of Madame Renaud's cousin—Madeleine Gérard. She had intended to wire ahead and tell Madame Gérard of her arrival, but it was too late to worry. She wondered if the woman would take her in. What if she was not home? What if she had taken a holiday? Now Elise began to worry once again. Then she looked at the doctor.

"All this time you have been caring for me, and I just realized that I don't even know your name."

"Henri Brusard," he answered with a friendly smile.

She returned his smile and was comforted again by his warmth.

Presently the taxi stopped before an elegant stone and marble building. The neighborhood was fashionable, and very quiet for this time of day. Dr. Brusard helped Elise from the taxi, and together they walked up and rang the bell on the heavy wood door at number 83 rue du Faubourg-St. Honoré. The wide, tall windows were embellished with marble carvings at their apex. Above the door, heavily carved moldings and cupids executed in dark fruitwood adorned the area about a circular window. Elise noted the elegance of the strollers and shoppers on the sidewalks. They were very near the heart of the city. Once again during her journey she realized that she had formed false expectations. She had been prepared for a small house on the outskirts of the city that although poor, would be clean and tidy. Although Madame Renaud had not told her anything about her cousin, Elise had assumed that the woman was perhaps a seamstress, or occupied in some similar capacity. She pictured a woman much like Madame, complete with her same station in life. Perhaps she was merely a housekeeper of this grand residence, or a member of the household staff. The door opened slowly, and they were greeted by an elderly butler dressed quite formally in black. He glared at them suspiciously. Dr. Brusard spoke to the butler, who ushered them into the vestibule and left through glass doors to the left.

Elise regarded the exquisitely hand-painted tiles that composed the ceiling. Plump cherubs in the four corners each held a garland of pink and blue flowers. At the midpoint of each section were tall golden urns overflowing with gold, pink, and blue blossoms. The center area was painted sky blue, and a chandelier of solid brass with tulip-shaped shades of milk glass hovered over their heads. The walls were paneled in dark cherry.

Presently the doors opened and Elise and Dr. Brusard were greeted by an impeccably dressed woman in her late thirties. She was of medium height and quite slender, and her black hair was elegantly coiffed. It was delicately touched with the lightest hint of gray, which seemed to accent the friendliness of her face. Her blue-green eyes sparkled with anticipation and delight at seeing Elise.

She glided forward with her arms outstretched, and she took Elise's hands in her own and said, "Mes amis! You have brought word from my cousin! She wrote to tell me that I may be so fortunate as to expect a visit from you. You are Elise and Christopher, no?" she said, beaming at them.

"No, this is Dr. Brusard. My . . . my husband did not accompany me here today." Elise stumbled over her words.

"No? Where is he?" Madeleine said.

"He had some pressing business matters. I'll explain them all later, if I may. I was taken ill on the train, and the doctor was so kind as to offer his aid in bringing me here. I'm afraid I must impose upon my friendship with your cousin and ask if I might possibly stay with you tonight until I can find suitable lodgings for myself tomorrow in Paris. I do so hate to ask such a tremendous favor. I'm afraid I'm not as strong as I had thought."

"Certainement! You shall remain with me as long as necessary. Do not think this is an imposition. It is not. We shall do all we can for you, my dear. I shall have Gilbert bring your luggage to your room. Dr. Brusard, merci. I am sure we are both grateful for your concern," Madeleine said to the young physician.

Elise turned to him, placed her hand against his cheek, and said, "Thank you. Someday I hope that I may have the opportunity to come to your aid. Truly, I do not know what would have happened to me had you not been there for me."

Dr. Brusard kissed her hand and spoke slowly in English. "I shall be back often to see to your progress. You rest. If you need me, please come to the address I gave you. Madame Gerard, if for some reason you feel you cannot care for Madame Mann, please let me know. However, I sense that she is in the most capable of hands." As he departed, he turned once and waved to them, and then was briskly on his way.

Madeleine turned to Elise and smiled. "You are most

fortunate. Now, come, off to bed with you, and you may tell me tomorrow all the news of my cousin in America. And also, how it is that you come to be in Paris without your husband. It is a good story, no?"

"It is a good story, yes," lamented Elise as she followed Madeleine up the wide gold-carpeted staircase.

Twenty-six

As Christopher took their suitcases from the seat opposite him and closed the door, Wilhelm paid the carriage driver and stood at the base of the hill watching Jesse as she sat on the balcony. The French doors to the interior were flung open, and the summer breezes flapped the draperies in and out of the doors. She was sipping from a teacup and gazing pensively at the piece of stationery in her hand. The wind lifted a long tendril of her honey-gold hair and she passed her hand under her eye as if to wipe away a tear. As he approached her unnoticed, he saw that she had been crying.

He raised his arm and waved. "Jesse! I'm home! I've come back to you, my Jesse!"

Her head turned quickly, and as she saw him, a joyful smile filled her face and the color rose in her cheeks. She rose quickly from the table and leaned over the railing on the balcony.

"Wil, my darling, run faster!"

He flung his jacket over his shoulder and ran up the hill into the chalet.

Jesse ran into his arms and laid her head on his shoulder and pressed her body close into his. He took her face gently in his hands and kissed her, softly at first and then deeper as he probed her sweet mouth with his tongue. As he pressed himself to her, he suddenly remembered Christopher.

Christopher had stood riveted to the spot at the base of the hill as he watched the intimacy between Jesse and Wilhelm. He lowered his head when he couldn't torture

236

himself any longer by intruding upon their privacy. He ran up the hill hoping that Elise was here. He bounded up the stairs, and as he came into the large room he scanned the expansive area, frantically searching for her.

She was nowhere in sight! Perhaps in one of the other rooms, he thought. He raced down the hall and looked in the two bedrooms. Empty. He walked back into the large room, and the moment he saw Jesse's face, he knew.

"I'm sorry, Christopher. She isn't there. I was just reading a note she had left for me." Jesse said, feeling his pain.

"Then she was here?" he said.

"Yes, but only for two days. We had a wonderful visit. I miss her already."

"When did she leave? Where did she go?" he asked.

"I can answer almost any question you would ask me except that one. I don't know her final destination. She wouldn't tell me for fear you would somehow discover it. She left just this morning on the train for France. I know it goes all the way to Marseilles. She never came right out and said it, but I don't think she'll sail for the States. She kept saying something about never being able to go back home again. I couldn't understand what she meant, and I'm afraid I failed to comfort her. She was terribly upset, Christopher. She didn't tell me what happened between you, either. But certainly you *can* straighten things out between you! Can't you, Christopher?" Jesse looked at his face and saw utter dejection.

"It *couldn't* have been that insurmountable! What happened? Is it that awful?" Her gaze went to Wilhelm's face, and as she realized the magnitude of the situation for the first time, her face went ashen at the thought of her friend alone in France.

"I'll follow her there," Christopher said. "I can stop at every town on the train route and inquire about her. I have to be in Paris at the end of the week to take over the management of our new offices there. So I have until then. When does the next train leave?"

"Not until midday tomorrow. It's too late in the day now to do anything about it. Why don't we all go into Zurich for dinner and try not to worry about what we can't help?" Jesse asked.

"Jesse, it's kind of you to offer, but I just can't sit here and ruin Wilhelm's homecoming for you. If I hurry, I could catch that plane before nightfall and then backtrack if I have to," Christopher said as he crossed to Jesse and kissed her cheek.

"Thanks, both of you," he said as he shook Wilhelm's hand. "I may need your help again. I'll keep in touch and let you know what I find. Next time we meet, let's hope there will be four of us together," Christopher said.

Jesse and Wilhelm waved to Christopher from the balcony, where they stood with their arms around each other. Wilhelm pulled Jesse to him and said in low, gruff tones: "I thought he would never leave!" He brought his mouth down and covered her moist, parted lips as he pulled her blouse out of her skirt and moved his hand up to fondle her breast. She gently removed his hand and led him back inside the chalet.

"I would rather not all of Zurich witness our reunion. Besides, I have a very special evening arranged for us, if it meets your approval. I've made reservations at a very posh, but intimate restaurant in town. It's a favorite of mine and I've never taken anyone there. I've only gone by myself. I hope you don't mind our having dinner first?" she asked.

"Jesse, I could feast on the sight of you alone. Since you have gone to so much trouble, I guess we could go early—very early, Jesse, so that we can come back here all the sooner," he said as he buried his face in her hair.

"Wil, what happened to Elise and Christopher? Can you tell me? He didn't *tell* her, did he?"

"No, he didn't, and for the life of me, I can't understand it at all. It would have cleared up everything for them, I'm sure. I suppose he is concerned for her safety —although at this point I don't see much sense in it, since she's all by herself someplace. But in any event, he's in a more dangerous position than I and has more responsibility. I don't know what I would do in his place. You didn't tell her about us, did you? I know how tempted you are to tell her everything," he said.

"No, I did not! For all she knows, we are having a glorious affair. She has no idea that we are actually married," Jesse said as they lay on the sofa together and Wilhelm stroked her back and played with her long tresses.

"Christopher knows, of course, but I think even he forgets sometimes, especially when he sees my lecherous look when your name is even mentioned. I feel badly that all your family and friends believe you to be a fallen woman. I swear, Jesse, I'll make it up to you. I never want to hurt you." Wilhelm said as he kissed her again.

"I would rather be with you than back in Mobile waiting for this all to be over and carefully guarding my reputation. But I'm glad we are married. I'm still old-fashioned enough to think I wouldn't make a very good mistress. Oh, Wil, I'm so glad you are back with me," she said as she hugged him tightly.

"My only wish now would be that Christopher could find his wife as I have found mine," Wilhelm said.

"Even if he finds her, Wil, in her present state of mind she won't even talk to him. You still haven't told me why she left him." Jesse said.

"I can't give you all the details, but she believes Christopher is responsible for the assassination, and to top it all off, she discovered her father's involvement."

"Oh! My poor Elise! How devastated she must be! No wonder she didn't want to tell me anything. Since she doesn't know that you and Christopher are government agents, she must believe he's the most despicable person in the world. To be so stunned must have been her undoing. She told me how ill she had been. Now I fully understand what she's been going through. Why doesn't Christopher tell her the truth? You told *me!*"

"Because the world believes you are my mistress and of not much importance to me. They are married and everyone knows it. The enemy could kidnap Elise and break Christopher. Especially now with the baby coming. He is beside himself. I don't suppose she told you she left Sarajevo on horseback? Can you believe that?"

"No she didn't! Wil, how could she be so foolhardy?"

"It's possible she was so anxious to get away from him that she felt the risks were justified. Or perhaps she truly had no idea just how dangerous it was. Or both."

"I just wish Christopher had told her the truth. Then all of this could have been avoided," Jesse said as a frown crossed her face.

"Let's not talk about it anymore. Let's go find that restaurant you love so much. I hope the food is good. Suddenly that's all I can think of," Wilhelm said.

"All? Just food?" said Jesse as she moved her body closer to him.

"Well, perhaps not all," he said, and once again moved his hand under her blouse. As she moaned softly in pleasure, he jumped up, grabbed her arm, pulled her up from the sofa, and said, "Come on, Mrs. Schmidt, let's go take a bath together! Since we have to pretend we are having an illicit affair, we may as well play the part. What do you say?"

The restaurant had only a dozen tables. At a glance, Wilhelm recognized the clientele as Zurich's elite. In the dim light, he saw two barons. a count, and a marquis. He wondered if Jesse had any idea that the men here were accompanied by their mistresses and not their wives. Knowing Jesse, she probably did; it was all part of this little game she played. The waiter brought a bottle of vintage wine. Wilhelm ordered creamed herring for their appetizer with their wine. Jesse was not as hungry as he and chose broiled fish, while he ordered beef en croûte, mushrooms, and fried sliced potatoes, and had an enormous serving of apple strudel. Wilhelm gazed longingly at Jesse, who sensed his mood. She took his hand in hers and squeezed it tightly.

"Wait till you see the surprise I have for you," she smiled.

"What is it?" he asked.

"Oh, just a little bit of nothing."

He looked at her quizzically, shrugged his shoulders, and beckoned to the waiter, who brought the bill. They left the restaurant and stepped into the cool night air. Wilhelm hailed a taxi, and they rode nestled in each other's arms as the air grew quite cool for July.

Wilhelm went to the kitchen and took out a bottle of wine. He sat down on the sofa, opened the bottle, and filled the two crystal glasses with the deep-red liquid. He began to sip the wine while waiting for Jesse, who was bringing out his surprise. He leaned forward slightly and rested his forearms on his thighs as he held the glass. Then he spied it. He looked at the white fluffiness. He reached out, touched it, and felt its sensuous tickle against his skin. He took a sip of wine; and as he raised his eyes from the sheepskin, he beheld an apparition in snowy gossamer.

At first glance, he thought she was nude and somehow was encircled by fog or a cloud. The cool summer breeze from the balcony door fluttered the silk about her voluptuous body. The honey-gold of her long hair shimmered in the silver of the abundant moonlight that was the room's only illumination. Her thick tresses were scented with jasmine. He was so intent on the delightful show that he found he couldn't move.

"God, Jesse! You are so magnificent!" he said as he felt desire's fever race through every nerve and vein in his body. "I've dreamed of this night for so long. I want my arms always to be filled with you. I love you."

Twenty-seven

CHRISTOPHER answered his eighth telephone call of the day and lit his fourteenth cigarette. He had spent the last weeks establishing his contacts, setting up his offices, and continuing his search for Elise. He still could not fully believe that he had been unable to track her down. She had left the train here in Paris, and then, for some reason, all his leads had ended in blind alleys. What was happening to his expertise? He had been unable to contact the driver of the taxi that took her and some man to their destination. The taxi driver had been substituting for a relative, who had been ill that day. The stand-in driver was the family reprobate and an alcoholic to boot, and had vanished into thin air. The most upsetting knowledge had been that Elise had been in the company of some man. He discovered from the conductor that the man was a doctor who had given her medical aid while on board the train. He didn't know the doctor's name, only that he had remained with Elise for the entire journey. The conductor thought they had known each other, judging from their demeanor. Christopher had searched all the hospitals for word of Elise. If she had been so ill, she would need much care. But she was not registered at any hospital in the city.

He was baffled. She knew absolutely no one here, he was positive. She was not registered at any of the hotels. Although he was convinced she was using an assumed name by now, he didn't have any way of discovering what it could be. He was running out of ideas, and now that his "business" obligations were demanding more of his time, he feared he would not be able to conduct his search single-handedly; he would need to hire some professional aid. That would not pose any problems for him, as he had informants all about the city and the countryside. But he was now faced with the prospect that she could have left Paris. Perhaps she was now somewhere else in France and all his efforts here were in vain. He *had* to believe she was still here. He had yet to investigate the colonies of artists on the Left Bank. Whenever he could, he went to the art galleries and museums. If she were in Paris, sooner or later she would visit them, he knew.

She had dreamed of the great artists all her life, and it would not be like Elise to abandon her talent. It was as much a part of her as the child she carried. At the thought of his seed in her womb, he closed his eyelids to force back tears. His stomach churned with loneliness and the hollowness of his life without her. He wondered if she hated his child as much as she despised him. So far, it appeared to him, she had purposefully taken as many chances and risks as she could to bring on a miscarriage. He still couldn't believe she had left Sarajevo on horseback. Did she want to end her own life? Oh, God! he thought. She could not have taken her own life!

The thought had not crossed his mind until now. He rose from his chair and stared out the window at the splendor of Paris, the city of romance.

"What a joke! Romance! God in heaven, I've never asked for anything but please do not let such a thing come to pass. Keep her safe. Even if she should never be mine again, let no injury befall her," he prayed as he slumped against the wall.

She was alone somewhere, with no one to refute her evil thoughts of him.

Madeleine rustled into Elise's room, where she sat gazing out at the rain and the lights of rue du Faubourg-St. Honoré. Elise glanced up at Madeleine and gasped at her beauty. She was magnificent in a crimson silk evening gown. It had a plunging neckline, and the fabric was

243

caught up at each shoulder with a cluster of red feathers with gold clasps. The skirt fitted close to her narrow waist and fell gently over her hips. She wore a cache of feathers at the back of her black hair, and on her feet were red satin slippers. She was pulling on the second of her long red gloves as she smiled affectionately at Elise.

"Tomorrow night, we will have no excuses," Madeleine said. "It will be a special night. We shall all go to Maxim's; this is a promise. You have had much rest and too much sorrow. You need some gaiety. The baron says it will be his treat. Only the loveliest of women are even allowed into Maxim's. And the baron says that with two beautiful women, one on each arm, he will certainly be assured of an excellent table. Just so that you cannot refuse our invitation, I have ordered a dress for you. No excuses! Now, I must go. Rest well. Tomorrow will be a big day."

"Oh, Madeleine, you look so beautiful! Are you so sure you truly want me to impose upon your evening tomorrow? Wouldn't you rather be alone with the baron?" Elise asked.

"Ordinarily, yes. But I want you to see some of Paris. This stuffy little room is not Paris. We must make your heart light and happy once again. I do not like to see you so sad. It's not good to be gloomy in Paris!" she said as she crossed to Elise, hugged her tightly, kissed her cheek, and was out the door in a flurry of red silk.

Elise looked after her and, watching the door close, smiled to think of the comfort Madeleine had given her. She chuckled to herself when she thought of the impressions her own mind had created prior to arriving in Paris. Madeleine was certainly nothing like what she had imagined she would find; this house alone was nothing like what she had imagined. Every piece of furniture, every carpet and drape, every glass and piece of china was exquisite. Madeleine had told her the history of the house.

In 1840, it had been the pied-à-terre of William Thackeray. To think that the great writer had lived here and walked in these rooms gave Elise a thrill of excitement. This house, as many others along this street, had been inhabited over the years by the mistresses of the royal courts of many countries. Elise found it hard to believe that Madeleine was the mistress of a German baron. She had been raised to believe that such women were wicked and heartless and destined to burn in hell. However, she had never met anyone so full of love and warmth as Madeleine. Elise had come to her a total stranger, and Madeleine never questioned for one moment Elise's presence or her motives for being in Paris. She had taken her in and had spent those first days and nights at her side, holding her hand throughout those long nights of pain and fear. She had asked nothing of Elise, but gave all that she had and saw to her needs.

Madeleine was desperately in love with the baron, and he with her. He had been the victim of an arranged marriage, the benefactors of which were hardly the pair involved. Even his wife had her own lover in Germany. Madeleine could never be openly recognized by society. But then, Elise knew Madeleine loved the baron deeply, and although it must hurt her at times not to bear his name, she did appear to be blissfully happy. All she asked was to be first in his thoughts and love and to be with him as often as possible. Elise briefly wondered if such an arrangement would be enough for her. But she knew it would not. They were two different people living in two different worlds. Madeleine seemed to exemplify all the romance, gaiety, and warmth that was Paris.

Elise rose from the chair and crossed to the dainty antique writing table. She sat down on the cane chair and took a deep breath.

Throughout her weeks of convalescence, Elise felt she must compose a letter to her parents. She knew Mama would fret endlessly if she did not send some sort of word to her, but she couldn't possibly relate all that had happened to her. Not only was it too painful; she knew her mother would want her to return to Mobile, and that was something she could never do. She would have to devise some sort of explanation that would not let Mama know how miserable she was. Elise vowed she would do everything in her power to shelter her mother from ever learning about her father's involvement in the assassination. It was imperative that her family believe that she and Christopher were enjoying the splendors of romantic Europe.

Over an hour had passed and Elise crumpled the fourth

sheet of cream-colored writing paper in her hand. Then she picked up her pen and started once again.

Dear Mama, Papa, Violet and Sadie,

Just writing your names makes me feel so much closer to you all. Even though Christopher and I are enjoying the beauties of the Continent. I want you to know that I miss you and think of you often.

I have been fortunate, though, because Christopher has kept me so busy that I sometimes feel I haven't enough time to breathe!

Our trip here to Paris was delightful and our rail accommodations were quite nice. Unfortunately, we were not able to stop in Zurich as I had hoped, for Christopher was pressed for time since he felt it imperative we come here to Paris as soon as possible.

I loved traveling through the Alps. What marvelous magic God worked when he created those mountains! I was spellbound at their beauty. I laugh about it now, for it seems that Christopher has opened so many worlds for me. Ones that I never dreamed existed. I wish you all could have been there to experience it all with me.

We dined at the quaintest little chalets while en route. I must say that though I have tried a great many new dishes here, I still miss my café au lait as I used to enjoy it in the cool mornings on the terrace with you and Violet and Sadie. That was such fun, wasn't it? I cherish those memories.

But, now, Christopher says that we are making new memories. And they are just as dear to me. Isn't that the way it should be when we are so very happy?

And how could I ever begin to describe Paris to you? It is breathtaking. We have been to the opera, ballet, and theatre. My greatest thrill was touring the Louvre. It was my dream come true. I was more than awed by the works I saw. It delights me to see such talent from mere mortals. And yet, I realize how lacking my own works are. It does provide me with the impetus to strive for perfection, even though

I know I could never accomplish what they have. At least I am willing to try. Sometimes I think that may be half the battle, don't you?

Well, Christopher just came into the room and now I really must end this letter, but I promise I will write to you all again quite soon.

> *Your devoted daughter*
> *and loving sister,*
> *Elise*

Elise let the pen fall from her hand. It was all she could do to write just that short note. Perhaps later she would be able to write in greater detail.

"Detail?" she laughed bitterly. "God! Such lies! It's all lies! When is it going to get better for me? Will I ever be happy?"

She wondered how long it would be before she could finally tell them the truth. How many months? And what about the baby? She would have to tell them that they were going to be grandparents.

She closed her eyes and wished that things could be different. How she wanted all this pain to leave her! If only it were possible for her to go home . . . with Christopher. It could have been such a joyous occasion.

Her shoulders quivered and jerked with her cynical laughter. She rubbed her forehead and temples with her fingertips as she thought of how ironical her situation was. For so many years she had believed she was nothing like her mother. And yet, both women were in love with men who had betrayed them. Thank God her mother was ignorant of her circumstances. Dorothea was a woman blessed. The knowledge, Elise knew, would destroy her mother. It sometimes took every ounce of Elise's strength to continue on with life knowing the truth.

Elise pondered the tragedy of their similar situations. Elise was young and had not invested decades of love and devotion to the man she loved, as Dorothea had. Were her mother to discover the appalling facts concerning Justin's secret life, the devastation would be unbearable; she would have no one to turn to, no place to go. Elise had grown enough to realize that she was more independent than her mother had ever been. She doubted that her mother, because of her background, training, and emotional dependency on Justin, could break free and do all that Elise had done on her own. Dorothea's agony would be more intense, since she had the entire family to consider. No matter what it would take on Elise's part, she would protect her mother. Mothers were precious creatures that too often were left vulnerable to malicious onslaughts and barbs from even their own children. And in Mama's case, her pain would spring from the person she trusted and loved most in the world.

"God! Must reality always be so unmerciful? Why have I been denied the happiness of my own dreams?"

Her honeymoon should have been a glorious whirlwind of romance and gaiety, but life had hit her headlong with waves of disillusionment and even cruelty. She was supposed to be happy. Things weren't supposed to happen like this! It wasn't fair, her heart screamed.

In some ways she knew she was responsible for her own predicament. She had left Christopher. She had been the one to make the decision. But it had been his murderous role in history that had forced her into that decision—and it was irrevocable. What a dubious future she pursued! Was she strong enough to survive?

Elise allowed her thoughts to flutter over the remains of her girlhood dreams. She shook her head and pondered the reasons for her current dilemma. She yearned for the smiling faces of her sisters and parents. So often, she knew, families were a shelter from the storms of loneliness and pains that were inevitable in life. And yet, to grow and know oneself, those ties sometime had to be strained.

"But, Lord in heaven! Why does it have to hurt so much?" she sobbed.

She let her forehead rest on her hands and sat immobile, forcing her mind blank.

Suddenly she heard a light tap on the door.

"Yes? Who is it?" she asked as she crossed to the door and opened it.

"Mademoiselle Elise, your dress is here," said the maid as she handed her a large box. It cheered Elise to realize that after only a few weeks in Paris, she was truly beginning to understand French. She was still hesitant about speaking, but she understood much of what she heard.

"Merci," Elise said. She placed the box on the bed and pulled off the ribbon and lid. She dug through the tissue and lifted out a midnight blue gown. She held it up to herself in front of the mirror and marveled at the enlivening effect the hue had upon her own blue eyes. Madeleine was right! She had been sad and despondent much too long. It was not her nature to dwell on her problems, and even she was disgusted with herself lately. Perhaps it was time to come out of her hiding place and begin to live again. Elise felt the crepe de chine of the gown and the softly gathered full skirt. It had dolman sleeves, and the square neckline was cut low. She immediately thought of her expanding waistline and feared the dress would be much too tight. She untied the wrapper and stepped into the gown; she had no difficulty fastening it.

"How could Madeleine know my size so perfectly?" she said to her puzzled reflection.

She was pleased that so much of her bosom was revealed in the dress. Perhaps no one would notice her thickening midriff. Yes! This dress and the evening out would do her nothing but good.

The following evening Maxim's was glowing with the soft light. Elise was dazzled by the ornate decor. Heavy hand-carved beams and moldings embellished the ceilings. Numerous arabesques executed in stained glass of greens and honey-toned hues contributed to the ambience. On the burled mahogany paneled walls hung enormous beveled glass mirrors, many of which were joined by "garlands" of mirrors, plating and brass scroll. Elise thought the effect was much like the waves at sea.

The headwaiter escorted the trio to a long red velvet banquette. Elise gazed about her in wonder: This was pure elegance, and she felt her heart lighten. She could detect the air of impertinence that pervaded the restuarant. Waiters and patrons alike possessed an unmistakable snobbishness that one would only expect in such a legendary establishment.

Elise gazed at the handsome baron, who was discussing

the menu and wines with the waiter and the wine steward. He was so attentive to Madeleine, and obviously cared deeply for her. Elise was happy that her friend had found love and was able to share her joy with someone special. She only wished she could find such happiness.

Karl leaned over to Madeleine and kissed her on the cheek. As he took her hand he said, "Perhaps you should tell Elise about Maxim's. It has quite a history."

"Mais oui! Many things about Maxim's have been almost unsavory, but that is what makes it all so very romantic!

"Originally," she told Elise, "Maxime Gaillard purchased the building from an ice cream vendor named Imoda. Maxime had little money at that time and was forced to borrow from friends to purchase the building at 3, rue Royale. To attract the affluent English clientele, Gaillard dropped the *e* from *Maxime*. Gaillard almost went bankrupt his first year until Irma de Montigny, a star at the Palais de Glace, a vaudeville theatre, had been refused a table at Weber's. At the time, Weber's had been one of the most elegant restaurants on the rue Royale. Since she liked Maxim's so well, the next time she returned she was accompanied by Baron Arnold de Contades. Their patronage made Maxim's fashionable and assured its success. It was in 1900 that Maxim's was decorated like this. The frescoes above us are originals by Martens and Sonnier, Elise. Aren't they lovely?"

Elise agreed wholeheartedly.

"Now, my story. Monsieur Gaillard died in 1895 and left Maxim's and her unpaid bills to Eugène Cornuche, the headwaiter. Recently, in 1907, I believe, he sold it to a British company. It was a mistake! No longer does Maxim's have the romance it had only a few years ago. It is now too proper, too restrained. Everyone wants respectability these days. Elise! You would have loved Maxim's then. It was wine, women, and sin. The most beautiful women in Paris dined here with kings and princes. Of course, all the women were of dubious reputation, as I am, so society politely referred to them as 'les grandes cocottes.' The most exciting and wealthy men from all over the world—sultans, spies, and maharajas—came to Maxim's. And the reason they came was to view les dames de chez Maxim's," Madeleine said as the waiter poured champagne into the crystal wineglasses.

"Where did these grandes cocottes come from?" Elise asked, enthralled by Madeleine's tale.

"Ma cherie! They were the ballerinas, actresses, and music hall stars. Oh, you should have been there! Each one was dressed more elaborately and fashionably than the next. They all possessed a mad penchant for jewels. In all your life you shall not see such jewels! Every night just past midnight, when the theatres had closed, they would appear in the door, escorted by rich men, handsome men, famous men, titled men. There were kings and princes here, but everyone came to view only the ladies. Maxim's was so exciting! Some of the women would provoke the gentlemen into duels that were fought at the Bois de Boulogne. After dueling they would return to Maxim's for a reconciliation breakfast."

"My goodness!" Elise exclaimed. "It's terribly romantic. Imagine living only for pleasure."

"My dear, tell Elise of Caroline Otero. That is a marvelous story and happened not so long ago," the baron said.

"Oui, Karl. It seems Caroline had many admirers, including Kaiser Wilhelm II, the Prince of Wales, and the Grand Duke Peter of Russia. But, it was the Baron Ollstreder who gave her so many fine jewels he went bankrupt. Then Caroline left him. And why not? There would be no more jewels!" Madeleine laughed and sipped her champagne.

"Liane de Pougy was her archenemy. She was so jealous of Caroline because of her jewels that one night she walked into this very restaurant wearing not a single solitary gem—just a plain dress. Then, her maid, who had followed her in, took off her coat and displayed Liane's vast array of jewels. The patrons were stunned. Caroline and Liane had a terrible fight right over there," she said, pointing toward the center of the room.

"You do know that *The Merry Widow* had an entire act set in Maxim's? It serves to whet the appetite for the forbidden fruit," Karl said.

Elise was fascinated. She thought of all the museums, palaces, houses, and other gathering places in Paris and pondered what exciting history might have been born in them, as in Maxim's. She was thinking of the great artists when the waiter brought their filet de sole amandine. Elise ate with relish; everything at Maxim's was positively the ultimate. Karl watched the young girl with a fatherly concern and then moved his eyes to Madeleine. He reached under the table and stroked her thigh as he beckoned for more champagne.

Twenty-eight

Elise sat in the yellow and white breakfast room sipping her café au lait as she watched the early-morning antics of birds just outside the bay window. She loved this room more than any other in Madeleine's house. Everything about it appealed to her and stimulated her cheery disposition.

Her benefactress was a master at forcing bulbs. There were a dozen white china jardinieres resplendent with yellow tulips and daffodils. A new pot was always in bloom, and Elise smiled at the presence of spring flowers in the last warm days of summer. As she gazed at the blue heavens filled with voluminous white clouds, she found it difficult to believe that the winds of war were passing over all of Europe at this very moment. Events had moved so quickly. Although she only knew what the headlines told her, she realized that the Continent was about to be plunged into an awesome and catastrophic war.

Every time she saw a newspaper, she trembled. Resolutely, she pushed from her mind all thoughts of Christopher and her father. She had enough problems of her own without feeling guilt and despair at the realization that the two men in the world who were closest to her had manipulated the events of the summer so that war would ravage Europe; she would not permit herself to dwell on things that she could not change. She would think only of herself and her baby.

She knew that it was time for her to make her own way in life. She felt guilty at having imposed upon Madeleine's good nature so long. The first weeks she had been too ill to do much about procuring her own quarters. It was now well into September, and with autumn approaching she needed to make a home for herself and her child. She vowed that it would be as much a real home as she could create, even though the baby would not have a father. She buttered a croissant and had begun formulating her plans when Madeleine came into the room attired in a soft yellow linen skirt and white silk blouse. She made herself a cup of café au lait, pouring simultaneously from the two silver coffeepots.

"Bonjour, Elise! Isn't it a pretty day?" Madeleine said with a delicate lilt to her voice.

"Yes, it truly is," Elise replied. "Madeleine, I have been thinking about my circumstances. You are my dear friend, but I don't feel I can remain here much longer. There is no way I'll ever be able to repay your kindness."

"Ma cherie, please do not say such things! I have come to love you dearly and would miss you so terribly. Why do you want to go away?" Madeleine asked, as tears welled in her eyes.

"I'm not leaving Paris! Please don't think that I would go away from this city. I must make a home for my child and myself, and I need to paint again. I'm sure I could sell a few things to supplement the monies I have. Later, I'll have to find employment—although with the war now, that might be difficult. But I can't intrude any longer on the baron's good graces. I realize that he has said nothing, but this is his home and yours, not mine."

"Elise, Karl adores you and is awaiting the birth of your baby almost as if he were the father! He will be most disappointed at this news. He would never dream of turning you out. There just is no need for you to leave. There's more than enough room for you and your baby," Madeleine pleaded.

"You have done so much for me, but I feel uneasy at not paying my own way. And I must paint again. I thought perhaps I could find an apartment that could also serve as a studio for me. Do you think Karl would know someone who might find such an apartment?"

"If this is what you truly desire, I won't stop you. Karl and I will help you in your house hunting. We will make it an adventure."

Elise was touched by Madeleine's attempt to hide her sadness. As she reached to embrace her friend, Madeleine said, "Elise, if you ever need me, you have a home here. Never forget that." She kissed Elise's cheek and squeezed her hand. "I'll speak to Karl tonight. So what are your plans for today?"

"I thought I might do some watercolors. I want to capture this beautiful day," Elise said. "I'm eager to work, but it's also been my dream to see the homes and favorite gathering places of the famous painters. I guess that since I am actually here in this marvelous city, I should take advantage of it. Would you like to go with me to see some of those spots?"

"But, of course," Madeleine responded. "And perhaps today too we shall find you the perfect house, yes?

"Oh, yes," said Elise, glad that Madeleine would be joining her in her quest.

The Baron Karl von Gotlieb came bounding up the steps to 83 du rue Faubourg-St. Honoré, clutching a long white envelope. He was out of breath, but all smiles as Madeleine embraced him. He looked down into her face and dancing eyes and pulled her as close to him as his strong arms would allow. He pressed his lips to hers.

"Mon cheri," Madeleine said. "Your kisses steal my breath away even after all these years!"

"I want to make love to you now, Madeleine. However, I have another purpose to my visit this afternoon. I have here the address of a delightful studio for Elise. I have a taxi waiting for us this moment. I will escort my two pretty ladies," he said as he moved his mouth to her ear.

"Don't torture me so, if I must wait until this evening." She smiled at him over her shoulder as she mounted the stairs on her way to Elise's room.

"Elise! Karl is here. There is a studio for you to view," Madeleine said, beaming at her friend.

"How wonderful! Are we to leave this minute?" Elise closed the book she was reading.

"Yes. Hurry now."

The baron escorted the two ladies into the waiting taxi. Elise loved to ride up the rue de Rivoli. It was such a beautiful boulevard. The air was much drier these days, and she could feel a hint of autumn in the air. The trees along the Seine had just begun to acquire the slightest tinge of color. The row of trees closer to street level leaned gracefully over the water, and their colors were reflected in the blue ripples of the river. Elise loved the way the ivy cascaded over the retaining wall between the two rows of trees. There was so much to see in Paris.

In the past weeks, Elise had discovered much about the city. Like any other visitor, she fell in love with the area between pont du Carousel and pont Sully. She loved to visit the Louvre. She loved the structure itself as well as the works of art contained within its walls.

As they rode, Elise noted all the strollers in the pont des Arts enjoying the enchanting view of the Seine. Elise had spent many an afternoon browsing in the flower and bird markets and the bookstalls.

The taxi had entered the Champs-Elysées, and Elise sat up straighter to view the chestnut trees that lined the wide boulevard. The gardens to either side of them were filled with small children and their white-frocked nannies. A large group of happy little faces were enjoying a puppet show. Not far from them a rotund man was handing a large red balloon to a dark-haired young girl dressed in a white-trimmed navy blue dress. The ribbons on her straw hat streamed down her back and fluttered in the breeze. Three little boys laughed merrily as they rode in a goat-drawn cart down the narrow path. It was a lovely scene, and Elise thought of the days when she would bring her child to play in these gardens. She watched the young lovers walk slowly among the huge trees and autumn blooms. As she mused about the days to come with her child, her thoughts wandered to Christopher, and the pain in her heart deepened. She wondered where he was and if he were safe. She squeezed her eyes shut and fought the lump in her throat. She still loved him, although she found it difficult to forgive him. She opened her eyes once again, and this time noted that most of the young men escorting their ladies in the gardens were in uniform. She prayed to God that it would be a short war and that none of these young men would be killed.

She looked to Madeleine and Karl, who were engaged in lively conversation, and she wondered if they would survive the war with their love intact. Karl had already encountered much difficulty because he was German. He had been questioned frequently by the authorities, and the only reason he was here with them today was that he had influential friends in the French Ministry. All who knew Karl, knew that Madeleine was the only reason for his remaining in Paris. Elise had overheard Karl say that he was certain they were being followed, but that he could understand the precaution.

Just as they passed the Rond Point, Elise noted the very old town houses, luxury shops, and cafés. The taxi pulled off to a side street and stopped.

"Here we are, my dears. This is the best apartment I could find. I think it will measure up to your standards, Elise," the baron said as he aided her out of the taxi.

"It's lovely, and its location is heaven! I can walk anywhere I want to go. And the parks are so close! I can paint under the trees!" Elise exclaimed with excitement.

A large middle-aged woman answered the bell and immediately recognized the baron. She beckoned them toward the wide green-carpeted staircase. They followed her upstairs as she chatted brightly about the weather. Just off the second floor landing, the woman unlocked the oak door, and they saw another small set of stairs.

"Elise, you go up first. If this is to be your home, you should be the first to view it," Karl said as he stood back for her to mount the steps.

The wood of the stairs and the flooring had been bleached, Elise thought. The woman told her it was known as pickled oak. As she slowly came to a stop at the landing, Elise gazed about her with great surprise. It was an art studio! The sunlight poured into the room and filled it with warmth. The walls were the same carved oak paneling as the flooring, which gave the room an illusion of spaciousness. Opposite a wall of windows was a day sofa upholstered in a turquoise and white striped taffeta. Two lamps rested upon tulipwood tables. A larger tulipwood table with oval-backed chairs sat in the corner near the minuscule kitchen area. The woman informed her there was a bedroom off to the far left, and the bathroom facilities were connected to the bedroom. Elise and Madeleine went to look at the bedroom as Karl discussed rental details with the woman.

Upon entering the bedroom, Elise was surprised to see a small cradle in the alcove near the brass bed. The cradle was suspended on two tall posts and was heavily draped in white organza. She quietly walked over to the cradle, and as her breath caught in her throat, she pulled the feather-light fabric that fell from the canopy away from the wood of the cradle and saw a hand-embroidered pillow and comforter of white satin and lace. She felt tears fill her eyes as she looked to Madeleine.

"It's a gift from Karl and me. I worked on the pillow and comforter while you painted or slept. He spent weeks searching the antique shops for the cradle. We wanted to buy the baby's first bed for you. I hope you don't mind our presuming so much," Madeleine said.

"Oh! Madeleine! How can you say such a thing? It is so beautiful, and I love you both dearly for doing this for me and my child. It's just like you to be so thoughtful. What a wonderful surprise! Karl was right, this is the best apartment one could hope to find." Elise went to Madeleine and embraced her lovingly.

"Thank you, Madeleine. I have so much to thank you both for."

Elise went back to the studio area and smiled at Karl, who saw the happiness in her eyes and beamed back at her.

"Karl, words can never express my gratitude. The cradle is beautiful. And this room is exactly what I had hoped for. I had seen an art studio in New York that had these windows, and I was fascinated by them. It brings the outside into the room. I can set an easel here by the windows. Just look at the view of the parks and gardens!"

"So you think we shall move your things here?" Karl asked.

"Oh, yes! But first, Karl, we must discuss the financial arrangements. I don't know how much this apartment will cost." Elise looked up to see that the woman who had shown them the apartment had discreetly retreated to the hallway.

"Don't be silly, Elise. I am familiar with your finances and I would not have brought you to an apartment that would be beyond your means. You have invested your money well, and I am sure that you will be able to sell your paintings to augment your income.

"I have spoken with Madame Chevonnier while you and Madeleine were in the bedroom and agreed on the rent. I promise you it is well within your means. We can talk of all that later." He signaled to Madame Chevonnier that she could return to the room.

"Oh, Karl, thank you again. I'm so glad that I have you to help me with my financial decisions. Your advice has meant a great deal to me."

"I am always here to help you, dear Elise," Karl said with a bow. "Now to celebrate, I would like to escort my favorite ladies to dinner this evening. Although I hope it is not our last, it still will not be the same as it once was," he added sadly.

No, Elise thought, nothing is ever the same. The war was closing in around them, and they were helpless. Once such forces were put into motion, there was very little one could do to halt their course. History had proven that much to Elise. All they could do was to watch and wait.

Twenty-nine

CHRISTOPHER turned off the ignition and sat in his auto in front of the large town house that had been leased for him on the rue Cambon. He looked at the rather stark exterior of the stone residence that had been erected in the mid-eighteenth century and contemplated the ivy-covered courtyard spotted with exquisite statuary dating from the same period. The gardeners had left the day before, and he almost laughed at the absurdity of his having been so concerned with the upkeep of his grounds when this house and all of Paris was in danger of being overrun by the German armies at any moment. The event of the past week should have alerted the citizens to the seriousness of the city's plight. However, it was not until the first day of September that the inhabitants had begun to react with panic to the horrors that would imminently befall Paris. Before now, only a mild sense of dread had struck the minds of the higher Allied officials, much less the citizenry; today, it appeared that the government was about to leave the city. Alexandre Millerand replaced War Minister Adolphe Messimy, and Millerand placed Paris under the command of General Joffre.

Christopher had read all the reports of the Germans' invasion of Belgium, and even he was startled at their swift advance into France. German forces were just out side the city of Paris. French troops were rolling into the city in taxis. The garrison and the capital were being fortified, bracing for the onslaught. Christopher thought that finally, after the past month of Allied losses and defeats, they now appeared to be building a collected front against the progress of the German armies. Even now, the Germans seemed to be spread thinly over most of Belgium, Luxembourg, and the northern portions of France to the Oise River just north of Paris.

Christopher left his automobile and entered the house. He went straight to the main salon on the first floor. He sat at his desk and rustled through the stack of memos and communiqués he had received that day. He poured himself a large cognac and pondered what reply the government would give to the crowds that had clamored for a declaration that Paris be an open city. As he placed his head on his folded arms and slipped into an exhausted sleep, he wondered if they would all wake to a German occupied Paris.

Christopher awoke with a start. As he jerked to an upright position, he spilled his cognac onto the ruby Oriental rug. He rubbed his stiff neck as he peered at the late-morning sun streaming into the splendor of his home. The jangling of the telephone bell pierced the still atmosphere. He grabbed the receiver before it had a chance to ring again.

"Mann here," he said gruffly. At the other end of the line was one of his American agents.

"Good morning, sir, I trust you slept well," the man said.

"Not any better than anyone in Paris could, considering the current situation. What have you to report?" Christopher asked, staring at the cognac as it seeped into the carpet.

"Sir, although the rumors in the streets are that the Germans are surrounding the city, my information is that they have bypassed Paris and headed east. For some reason General Kluck defied his orders as flank guard. It appears he is headed for Château-Thierry, which, as you know, is a considerable distance from this city. He hasn't rested his troops. The German General prefers to gain a little glory for himself," the agent said.

"And the French Ministry?"

"Joffre has forced the government to flee. They are packing up now. Obviously, he feels he will lose the city.

Gallieni had had his people tacking up his orders on the billboards all over the city, and there was no mention of surrender. That's all I have on the current situation," stated the agent.

"Then in your opinion there will not be any conflict here in Paris?" asked Christopher.

"No, sir, I don't believe so. Not at this time, anyway," the agent said.

"Very well. Keep me informed of new developments." Christopher said, and laid the receiver in its cradle. He lit a cigarette and leaned back in his chair. Now that the conflict in Paris would be averted, he must get back to matters at hand. He had a dispatch ready to go back to New York, but more importantly he had the report to send to Washington, D.C. As he stared at the thin folder before him, he recalled his first meeting with the small group of senators in whose employ he now found himself.

It had begun two years ago at a festive New Year's Eve dinner at the home of a friend in New York. It was one of those white-tie affairs that Deanna always loved to attend. They had been in high spirits all day after ice skating in Central Park. It had taken him quite by surprise when, after the elaborate meal, the senator had approached him and had asked Christopher to join him and two others in the small library. Christopher had no business or social dealings with these men, and he had found it odd they seemed so serious on such a gala evening. After introductions and pleasantries, the senator had spoken for the trio.

"Mr. Mann, I am a blunt sort and there is no way around this except to state our purpose. Unbeknown to you, you have been observed for quite some time. Please don't take offense. Let me finish," he said to the astonished Christopher, "then you may judge us and our intentions. We have investigated your background quite thoroughly. We have been pleased with our findings," the senator said.

From that point on, the conversation had been entirely one sided. Christopher remembered his incredulity upon discovering that his every action for six months had been documented and scrutinized by government agents.

Apparently they had been impressed with his qualifications and connections in many areas. They had known of the arms conspiracy for two years and had searched for the "proper candidate to infiltrate the group," the senator had told him.

Christopher had been flattered that they should choose him, but he also had been angry at their invasion of his privacy. He remembered feeling victimized when he learned of their actions, but he soon realized that all their investigations were merely part of normal procedure and they had no other choice. The senator had insisted that Christopher would need to enter the group at a high level so he could immediately be aware of the extent of the machinations of its members.

It was to this same party that two conspirators had been invited. Justin Kendall and Albert Winston were introduced to Christopher that night. He had utilized his wit and intelligence to earn their trust. It hadn't been easy, but they had never doubted his motives. Looking back, he realized that Justin was easily impressed by money and social position; he had been the key to influencing Winston, who was the unacknowledged leader of the group. Once Christopher had won those two men to his side, the rest had not been difficult at all.

It was on that night that he had cast his lot, and now he felt he would never again command his own life. So much had happened to him as a result of his acceptance to that appeal from Washington. The past two years had been his entrance into a sphere of devious minds and deeds he found intolerable. The effort of displaying himself as friend to such men sickened him. His burden of guilt over the assassination and the loss of Elise devastated him. He doubted he was strong enough to withstand the pressure of the emotions that flogged his mind.

He believed he could not possibly give any more of himself to anyone or anything. Truly, he felt spent, for there was nothing left of himself to give. From what mysterious source would he derive the strength to continue? He conjured up a vision of Elise before him. There was no other woman that could fill his heart and mind as she had done. His chest constricted with the loneliness that consumed his life. His eyes still closed, he placed his arm over his forehead and made a great effort to erase Elise's visage from his mind; but the effort was in vain. She would always be with him—and yet she was not with him at all.

Even if the whole world were blown apart in the coming days, he would find her. Paris wasn't that large, and if it took every bit of his energy and every dime he possessed, he would find her again.

Thirty

FOR the past seven days, the skies around Paris had been filled with the red, gold, and orange explosions of small-arms fire. The stench of sulfur and smoke pervaded the September air. Elise's hands flew to her ears and covered them in an effort to block out the sounds of war. She closed her eyelids and prayed that it would all be over soon. The reports she'd read in the newspapers stated that the fighting extended from Verdun in the east, and all along the length of the Marne River. Every day costly battles were being fought over seemingly unimportant ground.

When she had ventured into the street, she was astounded to see taxis full of troops. Over luncheon yesterday at Madeleine's home, the baron had informed her that Gallieni had amassed over a thousand taxicabs. The citizens were already calling the onrush of reinforcements in these cabs "the miracle of the Marne." Elise knew that Gallieni would become famous for this one endeavor if for nothing else. Today, the ninth of September 1914, the news came to the city that the Germans had begun their retreat back to the Aisne River. Their armies were tired and beaten. Because the Germans had repeatedly attacked without full support from their artillery, they had suffered great losses.

As she stared out the window at the large chestnut trees, she wondered how long this war would continue. She felt instinctively that it would be lengthy and bitterly fought.

She wondered where Christopher was now. Was he

behind German lines? Was he with his friends of the Central Powers, even now? The vision of him in the arms of the red-haired woman came to her, and she fought the sorrow it caused in her heart. Wherever he was at this moment, she knew, he would not be alone; he would find someone to fill his hours and his bed. She doubted that he would have time to let a thought of her enter his mind. The tears spilled over her lashes as she thought of the fascinating women he had known intimately. How could she ever have been fool enough to think, even for a day, that she would win his love and keep him satisfied? And when would she learn from her mistakes and not dwell on something that was never meant to be? She wrapped her arms around her abdomen and cried to her unborn child. She rocked slowly back and forth, lulling herself to sleep.

Elise awoke as the sun warmed her face. She was still hugging her abdomen, her arms locked about herself. Her neck was quite stiff, and only with a great effort was she able to pry her arms away from herself, so tightly had the mucles constricted. She knew she would need a very hot bath this morning to soak away these aches. If only a leisurely bath could cure the pain in her spirit! She rose from the settee and crossed to the expanse of glass to watch the city come to life. An inordinate amount of traffic clogged the Champs-Elysées and the side streets. She wondered how many more troops were being rushed into the city. The foot soldiers appeared in Paris quite suddenly, and just as quickly they were whisked away. Generals were seen everywhere in Paris—especially frequenting the finest restaurants and theatres, which enraged her. Although she was not naive enough to believe that the generals were solely responsible for this war, they were the ones who would order young men to their deaths. It was a devastating thought that so much death, pain, and sheer waste would result from the depraved schemes of greedy, vicious men who, even now, sat amid luxury and contemplated the rewards they would reap.

Elise shuddered. There was absolutely nothing she could do to turn the tide of history. What she must concern herself with was her own survival. There must be some manner in which she might utilize this frivolous attitude of the high command to her advantage. She may very well be forced to make compromises, but she hoped they would not be totally against her principles. Recalling her studies of history, she remembered that there were a few commodities that always sold well during wartime: women and luxuries. She would never compromise enough to sell herself; she was not that desperate for income, and prayed she never would be. If they were to appeal to the ladies who would be entertaining the military in the months to come, perhaps some of these men would purchase her art as gifts for their lovers.

She brightened at the idea. Now she must obtain a dealer. She would want to sell only through a prestigious gallery whose customers would be most able to afford such luxuries.

Karl had once mentioned the name of one of his friends who owned a gallery not far from her residence. As she began her morning toilette, she made the decision to visit Madeleine and broach the subject. She finished dressing while contemplating the changes in her life and the new course she was about to embark upon.

It was shortly after ten o'clock when she rang Madeleine's bell. Elise was surprised when Karl answered the door.

"Why, Elise! What a delightful surprise. Come in. Madeleine and I were just talking about you over our morning coffee. Please come and join us," he said as he put his arm around her shoulders and ushered her into the breakfast room.

Madeleine's gaze was focused upon the gardens outside the window. She appeared lost in thought, and Elise felt like an intruder. At the sound of their footsteps, Madeleine turned her head. A smile of pleasure spread over her face and she almost jumped from her chair to embrace Elise.

"Ma cherie! How wonderful to see you! You cannot know how much I have missed talking to you in the mornings. Come and join us."

"Thank you. I must apologize for not telephoning before I came, but I didn't know that Karl would be here. I don't wish to interfere with your times together," Elise said.

"Don't be silly, dear," Karl said. "I was just about to depart. You and Madeleine will have all day to discuss whatever it is you ladies talk about for hours on end."

"Please don't leave just now, Karl. Actually, I came here to ask a favor of you. You don't mind, do you?" she asked. "I find I'll require some additional income. Although the situation is not grave, I thought if I might sell some of my paintings I could save the money and I'd be assured of meeting my bills once the baby arrives. I have the time to paint now, but later I may not. I was wondering if you would be good enough to speak to your friend who owns the art gallery you mentioned. Do you think he would be at all interested in an unknown artist?" she asked.

"Elise, all artists are unknown at one point. I admire your work tremendously. I'm most certain others will value its qualities as I do. I'll do all I can to help you. I will speak with Jacques this very afternoon. Don't fret, Elise. Just paint lovely scenes for us to enjoy. I shall tend to the business affairs for you. Now, I must be off. I'll let you know what Jacques says as soon as possible," he said as he rose and kissed Madeleine.

Madeleine poured the café au lait while she and Elise discussed the news of the battle that raged about Paris. Madeleine told Elise that Karl had given her some sound advice about how their lives would be altered now that the war had come so close to the city. Even though they had been spared for now, they must not pretend that the future was secure. They passed the morning sharing their thoughts and fears as friends do.

Thirty-one

CHRISTOPHER flipped his desk calendar to November twenty-seventh. The past two months had been the longest and loneliest of his life. His work load had multiplied with the war. The shipping arrangements of the smuggled guns to the Germans behind the trenches had become increasingly difficult in the last weeks. His communiqués from Wilhelm were almost nonexistent. His suspicions had been aroused of late. Something was amiss, but he couldn't identify it. He had been awakened by a telephone call from Liza Garrett, who had just arrived from Washington carrying his next instructions. Maybe she could provide him with information that would help him discover what was wrong.

After all these months, he still found himself awestruck at her abilities as an undercover agent. She was extremely intelligent, not to mention beautiful. Perhaps the fact that she was a woman was what always caught him off-guard; that was very likely the key to her success. Most men did not accept women as thinking individuals, and Liza was able to play upon that prejudice and use it to her advantage. Recently, she had become his most valued agent. She managed to procure necessary information that the others failed to discover. Not one of her reports had contained an inaccuracy. He was pleased with her work, and lately believed that without her information he might have been discovered. He had an uneasy feeling that something had gone awry. Perhaps it was simply that in this line of work a single overlooked detail, a character misjudgment on an agent's part, or a lost communiqué could be vital not only to the completion of a mission, but to an agent's life. It was as though the days of his life formed a rosary of crucial seconds and precarious moments.

As he rose from his chair, he lit a cigarette and walked to the window that faced the gardens. The trees were devoid of foliage, and the brown bare limbs created a stark picture against the gray November sky. The snows of last week had blanketed the city, but now an icy sleet covered the sidewalks, and he could tell that traffic either on foot or by auto would be treacherous. Feeling a cold chill, he turned to glance at the dying coals in the fireplace. He added more coal and stoked the fire. It was not long before the room warmed once again. He thought how fortunate he was not to be stuck in a trench along the Aisne. There were now four hundred miles of trenches across the face of France.

In late September the Germans had fortified their troops under General Falkenhayn. Concrete pillboxes had been built on the slopes of the hills. The trenches encompassed vast areas, and horses and men resided in the dugouts. For most of October, bombardment between the French and German troops continued day and night, but gained nothing for either side. It was during October that Antwerp fell to the Germans. But it was the Battle of Ypres, which began October twentieth, that ended the German drive to reach the Channel. An important center of communications, Ypres was greatly needed by the Germans, for all roads in the area met in and radiated from this city. The roads extended out of the city to the ports on the English Channel, and if the German armies could hold Ypres, they would be able to cut Allied use of this network. However, after almost six weeks of battle the November blizzards halted the violence. The armies were spent, but the Germans redoubled their bombardment of Ypres. The artillery fire was aimed at the gates of the canal, and finally the flood waters crashed through and inundated most of the low-lying areas.

Reports from the front line indicated that the situation had stalemated. The troops lived like rodents in their underground homes as they braced for the coming winter, and the inevitable fighting. Christopher stared at the maps that spread over his desk, and he marked the line of trenches on the paper. He would have to route his shipments through the port of Ostend, Belgium, now that it too lay behind the German lines. He threw down his pencil and fervently wished this entire business were over. He still hoped that this was one of the last duties Washington would require of him. There was the possibility that Liza's orders were for him to terminate operations here in Paris. The last communiqués he had received implied that the government was about to close in on the gun-smuggling operations. Perhaps those arrests had been executed by now. He hoped this was true, for he found it more difficult to cope with his dual role as each day passed and the casualties mounted.

The pounding of the heavy brass knocker on the front door broke in on Christopher's thoughts. A taxi driver handed Christopher the sealed envelope. He ripped it open and read Liza's directions. He grabbed his wool coat and umbrella from the hall tree and followed the driver to the waiting cab. As they rode toward the hotel where Liza had taken a room, Christopher noted that it was thunder he heard rolling in the distance, and not war guns. The skies had filled with black clouds laden with icy rain and snow. The wind, increasing its velocity, had shifted and now blew out of the arctic northeast. Against the almost black sky, jagged spears of electricity shot across the horizon, and the thunder boomed as the storm moved closer to the city.

The taxi pulled up abruptly in front of the hotel. Christopher opened the door and was about to leave the cab when Liza appeared and got into the taxi.

"The weather was getting rough, and I thought I'd wait for you in the lobby. Anyway, I didn't want anyone in the hotel to see you call for me."

"Very astute, young woman," he said as he smiled for the first time in days. "So, tell me. What instructions have you received from Washington?"

"Much of what I have to relay is what you have been waiting for. It seems your assignment has been terminated. However, you have one last duty to perform. You are to complete the necessary transactions for this last shipment of Justin Kendall's machine guns, then report to your American contact, who, by the way, is me. I will relieve you of the reports they give you. I'll go back to Washington, where I intend to spend the duration of this

271

horrid war behind a desk. I've had enough of this cloak-and-dagger life for quite some time. I can hardly wait to to have a day when I say to myself that I am bored. Just imagine!"

"I thought this day would never come. After more than two years, it will all be laid to rest. Thank God! I don't believe I could tolerate much more, you know?" he said as he turned his anguished eyes toward her.

She looked deep into his eyes and felt the pain that had been his. She pulled him close to her. He rested his head on her shoulder, and she cursed the destiny that had caused this man so much grief.

Elise carefully placed each booted foot in front of the other in an effort to keep her balance on the ice-covered sidewalks. She hugged her paintings close to her body. She was determined to deliver them that afternoon. Jacques, the owner of the gallery, had promised her a large payment upon his acceptance of them. And she needed the money now. She still hoped she would not have to sell the last of her jewels, and this sale was the only way to prevent that.

The frigid wind whipped her muffler into the air about her head as the sleet beat against her body. Tiny pellets of ice stung the delicate skin of her face and left small red marks. She heard thunder in the distance and squinted her eyes in an effort to see the gray of the horizon. The lightning streaked against the sleet-filled ebony clouds. All the terror of her childhood dreams rushed over her soul, and she felt the presence of death. This feeling was different from the atmosphere that the war created in Paris these last weeks. The power of the forces that filled her body and spirit chilled her more than the winter winds that blasted her. The tears that formed in her eyes froze, and her very being was devoid of warmth. At that moment she raised her face to the wind in an effort to defy the unearthly power that engulfed her. A taxicab moved slowly against the storm. Just as it was about to turn the corner, Elise saw his face in the window. Christopher! She opened her blue lips and screamed against the howling wind.

"Christopher! Christopher! Christopher!" she shrieked as loudly as her tortured lungs would allow, and struggled to command the muscles in her thighs to move her legs. She ran toward him, slipping on the ice patches. The taxi stopped and slowly pulled to the side of the street. When it did so, someone alighted from the auto. It was the red-haired woman!

Elise came to a dead halt and stared in shock through the sleet. She spun on her heel and tore down the sidewalk. The wind at her back pushed her over the ice as she heard thunderbolts crash in her brain. Her mind screamed silently as it reeled in a black whirlpool of pain and horror.

Christopher had heard his wife call his name from out of nowhere. At first he thought it was his agony beckoning to him. He directed the driver to pull over to the curb. It was then that he saw her. The look on her face was ghastly, but it was Elise. He jumped out of the cab and ran toward her. His heart leapt for joy; and then she turned and was running away. She had called to him. She had wanted him! Why was she fleeing him once again? He watched as her sleet-soaked clothes impaired her flight and she began to slow as he drew near to her. Then her leg twisted underneath her and she sank to the pavement. She lay sprawled on the ice as the sleet pelted her face and body. He hovered over her unconscious form in an effort to shield her from the elements. As he gently slipped his arm under her head, he noticed the blood that trickled down her neck.

He screamed. "No! Don't let this happen! I've just found her! I won't let you die, Elise. I can't. All the words I haven't spoken, all the love I haven't given . . . No! Don't die."

The taxi pulled up next to him, and Liza picked up the paintings that were scattered about Elise. Christopher lifted her effortlessly and placed her on the seat of the cab. He and Liza got in, and as the driver sped to the hospital, Christopher stripped the wet coat from Elise's body. Liza gasped, "You never told me she was pregnant! Christopher, I'm afraid for her. This can hardly be good for the baby. Here, put my coat on her, too. Her skirts are icy and wet. And her feet! They look frostbitten! We'll put my dry shoes on her. Oh, Elise! It's all my fault. She wouldn't have fled if I'd stayed in the cab."

"Don't blame yourself. She's been trying to escape me

273

for a long time. It's no one's fault but my own. Right now my only concern is getting her to the hospital in time. Driver! Allez-vous-en!" Christopher cried in panic.

The taxi sped down the streets and presently stopped at the entrance to the hospital. Liza ran into the building ahead of Christopher to call for help. Two young men in white came dashing out into the rain with a stretcher. They gently placed Elise upon it and whisked her inside to the awaiting doctor. Leaving Christopher behind, the doctor and the two attendants disappeared down a long corridor.

When the doctor had not returned for over an hour, Christopher began to despair. Liza sat twisting her hands in her lap as Christopher paced the floor praying that Elise was safe. God! Why did all this have to happen? He couldn't tolerate the thought that the innocent Elise was bearing this pain because of him.

Liza saw the doctor approaching from the end of the corridor. He was pleasant looking, though he seemed haggard from fatigue and stress.

"Mr. Mann? You are the patient's husband? Is that correct?" he said.

"Yes, that's right, Doctor . . . ?" Christopher asked.

"I'm sorry. Let me introduce myself. I'm Doctor Bienville."

"Doctor, how is Elise? Is it serious?" Christopher asked, his anxiety taking firm hold of him.

"Please. Don't worry. She has a slight concussion. The blood you saw was from a deep cut on the back of her head. This has been sutured. She regained consciousness not long ago. However, we have given her a sedative. I would like her to rest for the night."

"The baby. Is the baby all right?" Christopher asked.

"We don't anticipate any problems. She hasn't started labor, and there's no bleeding. However, because of the impact of her fall, there is still danger. The next twenty-four hours will tell us a lot. She is being moved to a private room for now. If you wish, you may see her for a while. I must apologize, but I have many patients to see, soldiers are being brought in every minute. Please excuse me, Mr. Mann," the doctor said.

Christopher shook his hand and thanked him for all he had done for his wife. The nurse directed Christopher

274

and Liza toward Elise's room. Liza told him she had appointments to keep and would meet him after his scheduled rendezvous with the German courier.

He turned around to face the wooden door and pushed it open with the palm of his hand. The yellowed roll shade had been pulled down over the window, and the dim November light that fought its way into the hospital room cast an amber hue. She slept immobile upon the raised iron bed. Slowly he walked toward her, afraid to even breathe lest he awaken her. Her dark hair, a red-gold aureole, spilled over the white pillowcase. Her skin was more than just pallid, he thought; it was transparent. He could make out the network of deep-blue veins in her face, arms, and chest. Her breathing was very shallow, and he had to strain his eyes to detect the slight movement of her chest.

Hestitatingly, he reached out his hand and gingerly pulled the blanket down to her knees, and then he lifted her hospital gown. He tenderly placed his warm hand against the cold flesh of her distended abdomen. At his touch the life within her moved ever so slightly. He leaned over and placed his lips against her abdomen. Then he slowly eased himself onto the bed at her side. Since she had conceived in June, possibly even on their wedding night, he surmised that, this being the end of November, Elise must be six months pregnant. She still appeared quite thin to his eyes, except for the small mound in the center of her abdomen.

He didn't like it; there was something wrong. He could sense it. It wasn't natural for her to be this small.

He sat staring at her bluish pallor. He placed both his hands upon her and massaged her skin in slow, circular motions until it became warm once again. He thought he felt the baby move against his gentle caresses. He could not stop the tears that came to his eyes. He pulled the thin hospital blanket up over her breasts. He took her fragile arm in his hands and rubbed the skin until it regained its former glow. The purplish tint that had settled over her eyelids and lips faded before his eyes. Slowly her head moved slightly, and he held his breath as her eyelids fluttered. He leaned close to her face and touched her eyelids with his warm lips. She muttered his name in a voice so low that he would not have heard it if he had not been this close. Her face twisted into a frown of anguish as her body convulsed in her nightmare. She shuddered and screamed.

"No, Christopher, no!"

Alarmed, he raced to the door and called for the nurse. Elise's body was shaking uncontrollably. The nurse ran to the cabinet and pulled out three blankets. She tossed one to Christopher.

"Quick, cover her with these. She must be kept warm. I'll get the doctor," she said as she vanished from the room.

Christopher put the blankets over her as she groaned in her unconsciousness. The convulsions increased in intensity, and he gently held her shoulders as she pitched and jerked in the iron bed.

"Oh, Elise, what is wrong? Does my touch cause you such pain?" he whispered sadly.

As the doctor came into the room followed by the concerned nurse, Christopher rose and stood at the foot of the bed, grasping the cold metal of the footboard. He braced for the bad news. The doctor felt for her pulse and listened to her heart. He lifted the blankets and noted a small pool of blood seeping from between her legs. He covered her again and ordered some medication that the nurse brought immediately. The convulsions appeared to release her body from their control. Each spasm became less acute, until finally she rested. Christopher noted that her skin was devoid of color and had again acquired that transparent quality that frightened him immeasurably.

"Mr. Mann, I think she will rest more comfortably now," Doctor Bienville said as he folded his stethoscope and placed it in his pocket.

"What is it?" Christopher asked despairingly. His eyes did not leave her sleeping form.

"It's an involuntary muscular reaction. I am concerned about the bleeding. But she is not hemorrhaging, which is a good sign. All we can do is watch and wait," he said as he turned to leave.

Christopher's senses told him that there was something the doctor had not told him. He started to ask if the baby was still alive, but the doctor had gone. He went around to the side of the bed and slid his hand under the blankets until it rested upon Elise's abdomen. He felt no movement. He knew very little about pregnancy or childbirth and had no idea whether the baby was safe. Surely the doctor would have indicated something if the baby were in danger. However, this thought did not ease his conscience.

He looked around the room and spied a wooden chair. He pulled it close to the bed and began the long night's vigil. He held her icy hand in his own, and although he rubbed it, it remained cold to his touch. The sun died in the western horizon as Christopher sat and waited, powerless in his inability to divert her pain to himself. He laid his head on the edge of the bed and passed into a turbulent realm of nightmares.

The nurse, dressed in a sparkling-white cotton uniform, entered the still room and lifted the roll shade. As she did so, the brilliant rays of dawn dazzled Christopher's sleep-laden eyes. He blinked at the pain the light caused him. The nurse came over to him and handed him a small cream-colored envelope.

"This was delivered by messenger for you just a few moments ago. Also, the doctor will arrive soon and will want to give Mrs. Mann a thorough examination. I'm afraid you'll have to leave at that time. But you may remain with your wife until the doctor is here," she said. "Could I get anything? Some coffee, perhaps?"

"No. Nothing," he said absentmindedly as he opened the envelope. It was a message from Liza reminding him of his appointment this morning at the café. He had almost forgotten about it in his concern for Elise. He checked his pocket watch and realized that he must leave in thirty minutes.

God! This couldn't be happening to him again! Once before he had left her to tend to business, and he had almost lost her. Would he be so lucky as to return and find her still here? He knew her condition was not critical at this point, but she was not out of danger.

Once again he was aware that he was compelled to fulfill his commitment to his duty. That this was his very last transaction did lessen his consternation, but only minutely.

He looked at the message once more and thought that he might be able to return within an hour or so. A simple financial transaction was all he need be concerned with today. After relaying his report to Liza, he would be free of this untenable responsibility for all time. His life would be his own once more; he would no longer answer to the unrelenting force that held him captive.

He crossed to the bed and gazed at the still form of his wife. Her color had not improved during the long night; in fact he thought he detected a slight enlargement of the blue veins that lay beneath her pale skin. All his reason commanded him to remain here. He bent over and placed his lips upon hers, and a chill traveled down his spine at the lack of response. If he hurried away, he would return that much sooner. He turned on his heel and walked quickly out the door, closing it softly behind him.

Elise moaned in her sleep as her spirit fought against the black fog that crept into her mind and filled her with fear. From the far side of her being, she felt the warmth even before she saw the light. She thought her legs were paralyzed as she made a desperate effort to run toward the light before it faded away and left her in the dark clutch of fear. She could not reach the light, she knew. With a great force of will, she beckoned the light to come to her. The warmth spread about her, and the small, flickering beam grew as suddenly she raised her eyelids and the sunshine flooded into her vision. She awoke to find herself lying in an unfamiliar bed. Her head pounded. She knew she was not in her apartment or at Madeleine's home. Then where was she?

The room was stark, and the walls and ceiling were painted in a chalky off-white. The iron rails of the headboard and footboard of her bed were also white. The mattress was somehow elevated, and she could tell she was far above the floor. She knew if she sat up on the edge of the bed, her long legs would not touch the floor. It did not matter, Elise thought, because her head ached so terribly that she could not raise it from her pillow. It was then she realized that she was in a hospital. How had she come to be here? The sheer effort of recall caused her much pain.

Suddenly the door to her room swung open as Madeleine entered with a grave expression upon her face.

"Elise, ma petite! How are you?" she said, taking Elise's

hand in her own and leaning down to brush a light kiss on her pale cheek.

"Madeleine! I am so glad to see you. I don't know how I am or how I got here. I'm afraid, I truly am! I can't remember a thing! How did you find me?" she inquired.

"Dr. Brusard saw your name on this morning's admittance roster of new patients, and he telephoned me. I rushed over as fast as I could. How do you feel? Has Dr. Brusard seen you yet?"

"I have no idea. I have this horrid headache, and I can feel such pain at the back of my head!" she said as she reached to touch the spot. She felt a bandage instead, and the sting of the sutured wound. "Oh, Madeleine! What is this on my head?"

"You have some sort of injury. Are you sure you can't recall what happened?" Madeleine was worried by Elise's apparent amnesia.

"Well, I was on my way to the gallery. I do remember that. And the sleet storm. I'm so terrified of storms, you know. It was so cold . . . and . . . the taxi!" exclaimed Elise as that devastating moment screamed across her memory.

"Oh, my God, Madeleine! He was with her again! After all this time, he was still with her! He never felt anything for me and he never will. I wish my life were over. Why didn't I die? Why did I try so hard to recover when I could have just slipped away?" Bitter tears burned their path down the sides of her face.

"Who was in the taxi? And with what woman?" Madeleine asked.

"Christopher. He was with that beautiful girl from the ship. I saw her in Sarajevo, too. He keeps her near to him always. Why does he hurt me so? What does he want from me? If only he would just leave me alone. Oh, Madeleine. I can't bear to be without him, though. What am I going to do?" she sobbed.

Elise felt the strange tremors course through her prone body. Her legs quivered slightly, and as the muscles along her spine constricted, her arms began to jerk off the bed. Though she fought to stop the seizure, she realized with great alarm that she couldn't control her own body. Panic gripped her mind and increased the force of the convulsions.

Madeleine raced out of the room to search for the nurse, who was already on her way to Elise's bedside with new medication. Dr. Bienville entered the room a few moments later. Noting the intensity of the seizure, he doubled her medication.

"Doctor, what is happening to me? I can't stop this shaking!" Elise said as her teeth chattered; and in the next moment she discovered she could not even speak. Her eyes widened with a look of horror and pleading as her eyes darted to Madeleine and then to the doctor. Never had she been so helpless.

"This is a small seizure, Elise. I won't keep the truth from you. You have started labor, and since you are only six months along, from what I can judge from the size of your uterus, there is a possibility that the baby might not live," he said in a low voice.

"But he's not dead!" she said, finding her voice again. "I can feel him! He's alive!"

"We'll do all we can to still the tremors and halt the labor. I want you to rest as comfortably as possible and try not to worry. Your emotions will play a great part in your ability to control these convulsions. I want you to stay warm, and please, nurse, keep those blankets on her. I'll return after a while and look in on you," he said as he patted her hand and then left.

"Madeleine, please find Dr. Brusard for me, if he is here. Would you do that for me?" Elise asked in a whisper.

"Of course I will, cherie," Madeleine said as she kissed Elise's cheek and left the room.

Elise felt the last of the tremors leave her body. Finally she was in command of her own muscles. She lifted her hand to her face and wiped away the tears. Afraid for the life of her child, she could only stare at the stark white of the ceiling above her. She noticed the glass of the round electric light above her, and she focused her eyes upon it as she felt the dull ache spread over the expanse of her abdomen and on to the small of her back.

With the stealth of a predatory panther, her oncoming ordeal moved toward her and loomed over her body with bared sharp teeth. She felt the sharp claws rake her abdomen and jab at her sides. At the stench of the beast's lethal breath, she felt nauseated and vomited bitter green

280

bile onto the sanitary hospital bed. With all its animal cunning, the panther padded silently away and poised for the next strike. It focused its flaming red eyes upon her defenseless form and mesmerized her, then pounced upon her again and ripped at her insides, shooting lances throughout her midsection. After this attack, it did not allow her to rest, but continued the assault until she gasped with painful lungs for the small amount of air that seeped into her throat. She could not spare the energy to scream, for she knew she would require what fortitude she possessed for the battle ahead.

She and the animal pain grappled ceaselessly in the silent room. Through swollen eyelids, she saw blurry white forms approach the arena she lay in. They were powerless in their effort to annihilate the predator. As it clawed mercilessly at her stomach, she felt herself being moved to some other room. The hazy patterns of the ceiling had changed, and this room was filled with harsh artificial light. The structure they laid her upon was extremely cold and caused the muscles in her back to contract and send more tremors of agony through her body. Her legs were raised and placed into icy metal stirrups.

At the next assault, the bile rose in her throat, but she choked it down. She never uttered a sound except to laugh at the inability of the torturer to overpower her. She refused to succumb to its will. She felt someone place her hands around cold metal grips that extended outward from the sides of the labor table. With all her strength, she grasped them tightly when the beast lunged at her again.

For hours the duel ensued, as neither contender conceded the struggle. Blood had spilled upon the floor with the amniotic waters. Elise's eyelids were swollen shut; she could not see the wounds in her palms where she had ripped the skin open on the metal hand grips whose purpose had been to relieve pain, not to cause it. The muscles in her left thigh cramped and shot burning rays down her leg. She opened her parched, swollen lips to mumble something to the figure she felt standing next to her.

"My leg . . . a cramp . . . left side," were the only sounds emitted from her throat.

Gentle fingers massaged away the cramp, and she breathed deeply as the panther came to her again. She

281

would never surrender. Never would she let him take her child to his deathly lair. She could still feel the baby moving within her, and she knew her child was still alive only through her determination. Then her mind closed itself to all thought save this contest. No one could wage this war but she. The hours of the day passed slowly, and although she could not see, through her pain she heard the strange voices of the changing medical staff as morning faded into afternoon. It was evening when she heard the reassuring voice of Dr. Brusard through the haze of pain that surrounded her spent body.

"Elise, I'm sorry I didn't come to you sooner, but I'm here now. Dr. Bienville tells me you are fighting against what nature demands of you. Elise, you cannot keep the baby. I know that it is difficult for you to accept this, my dear. You have been living for this child. It was not meant to be. You will only endanger your own life if you continue this struggle. Let your body go with the contractions. When you feel the need to bear down, don't try to stop it. You have lost much blood, and this should have been over for you hours ago," he said, concerned for her safety.

"Dr. Brusard, I can't give up," she mumbled almost inaudibly.

"Elise, let me help you. I don't wish to frighten you, but you will not be able to fight much longer. You have shown great strength, but the battle is over. Please, little one, let us help you," he said, issuing instructions to the staff. Elise only shook her head.

The attacker came to her another time, and he had gained momentum and great strength during his short retreat. She felt his teeth. She held her breath for an abnormally long time, and her hips lifted into the air with the excruciating pain. The skin covering her body turned blue as her veins bulged close to the surface. She felt her hips fall back at the animal's final lunge, and life within her escaped in a pool of warm, sticky blood.

There was much scurrying all around the weakened form of the young mother whose baby had been born dead. Elise uttered a low, mournful sound as her abdomen constricted and the afterbirth was delivered from her. The nurse lifted the stillborn child into her arms. Unbeknown to Elise, the Catholic girl baptized the boy and carried him out of the room. Cold and almost bloodless,

282

Elise slipped away to a merciful dimension where no pain would follow.

She awoke, and it was only with an effort that she managed to open her swollen eyelids to form narrow slits. The first thing she saw was a large bouquet of miniature yellow tea roses resting upon the bedside stand. She tried to roll over and retrieve the card that lay next to the flowers, but she found her arms were locked into a bent position. Her muscles ached with the soreness of her long ordeal. Her bleeding palms had been treated with some sort of salve. The skin was blistered, and her fingers felt as if they had been burned. She could hear the door open, and turned her stiff neck toward the sound of Madeleine's delicate footsteps.

"Madeleine? Is that you?" she asked in a low whisper.

Madeleine gazed in horror at Elise's appearance. It was as if she had been ravaged by some beast of prey, she thought. Her face was swollen, and so blue that she appeared bruised around her eyes. The flesh of her hands was mangled, and the veins under her transparent skin gave her a deathlike countenance. Madeleine could think of nothing to utter but inanities. Shocked at Elise's condition, she realized how very close this girl had come to death. It was miraculous that she was still alive.

"Mon petit chou! I am so happy to see you." She choked out the words through her tears. She rubbed the icy skin of Elise's forearm.

"Oh, I see that the florist has delivered my flowers to you. You see? I remembered. Yellow roses. You love yellow roses, don't you?"

"Yes, Madeleine," Elise said as she tried in vain to smile back at her friend, who seemed upset about something.

Elise passed her trembling hand over her flat abdomen and realized what had occurred.

"I wasn't dreaming, was I, Madeleine?" she asked as her tears careened over her cheeks. "Oh, God! Why? Why did You do this to me? Madeleine, why did He take my baby?" she screamed as she grabbed at her friend's arm, her fingers biting into her flesh.

"It must be very difficult for you to realize, but the baby was not strong enough, Elise. There was a reason, cherie. There's always a reason for everything," Madeleine said, knowing no words could give comfort this time.

"What good reason could there ever be for something like this? My baby is all I have! Am I to have nothing? Why should God take everything from me? Am I so repellent to Him that I should endure this? I have no family, no husband, no home, and now I do not have my child?" She became hysterical as the impact of her loss turned her heart. She trembled as her tears pushed their way out of the slits of her puffy eyelids. As her sobs became more vehement and the bed began to shake with her tremors, Madeliene ran to find the doctor.

After administering a sedative, the doctor left instructions for the nurse to remain with the tortured girl. As Elise fell into a disturbed slumber, Madeleine found she could no longer bear witness to Elise's agony; she turned and fled the room, shaken at the scene in the stark hospital room.

Thirty-two

Aʟᴛʜᴏᴜɢʜ the November sun was bright, it did nothing to warm the air that swirled the colorful autumn leaves into tiny whirlpools on the red brick terrace of the little café. Two young men in uniform stood chatting easily with a pretty blond nurse. The wind lifted her navy-blue cape about her slender body as she laughed at the joke her friend was telling. The trio turned and, arm in arm, strolled jauntily down the sidewalk. Taxis filled with businessmen, soldiers, and shoppers whizzed past the café on their way to their various destinations. The icy patches on the streets and sidewalks slowly began to melt as the sun climbed in the sky.

Christopher waited impatiently for his foreign contact, who was quite late. A sense of foreboding passed through his mind as he glanced at his pocket watch. Something was not quite right. Of all times for him to be late, he thought as he sipped his hot café au lait. All I want to do is get back to Elise.

He hated himself for leaving her side. He had no idea how she was recovering now. He prayed that she was safe and no harm would befall her or the child. He felt his heart swell with hope and pride at the thought of his child within Elise's womb.

Out of the corner of his eye he saw the man approaching. He was dressed conservatively in gray flannel, and he exuded a self-assurance that might lead on the onlooker to believe he was a wealthy banker. He greeted Christoper curtly and seated himself across the round table. He beckoned to the white-aproned waiter and ordered beignets and café au lait.

"Do you always partake of your breakfast in the open air?" he asked Christopher nonchalantly.

"It's rather chilly this morning; however, I prefer the security of open spaces. Experience had taught me not to trust anyone or anything but myself. I prefer not to take any unnecessary chances. Surely you can understand that," Christopher said as the waiter arrived.

"You have nothing to fear from me, Mr. Mann," he said.

"I hope not. However, one never knows for certain, does one?" Christopher said. "Now, I understand you have an order for a shipment of goods. Is that true?"

"Yes," the man said as he drew a long envelope from an inside coat pocket. "I have the order, instructions for delivery, and your payment."

Christopher took the envelope and pocketed it.

"There have been some minor alterations in our pre-arranged shipping destinations," Christopher said. "Because of the conditions along the western front and the battle at Ypres, we will have to dock at Ostend. We have no other options. If this doesn't meet with the approval of your board, please inform them that we will have no recourse except to cancel the order. We can't give you any more direct route than that. It'll be difficult enough maneuvering through the English Channel with the British warships sending troops to France."

"I don't anticipate any problems. I trust your decisions on these matters. All our dealings have been handled with the utmost efficiency and discretion. You are to be commended, Mr. Mann, on your thoroughness. It's been a pleasure to watch you operate in these affairs. You have a brilliant future ahead of you, young man. I do hope you take full advantage of all opportunities that come your way. There are those here in Europe who have taken a great interest in you and would be most anxious to assist you in reaching any personal and financial goals that you might have. All it would take is the word from you and I will speak to these benefactors, if you desire such an opportunity," he said as he spread his hands on the table.

"I'm quite flattered by all of this, but you will understand if I don't respond at this moment. I'd like to have some time to think this through. There are certain things right now that require my attention. If you need no further information, I believe I will take my leave," Christopher said as he rose and left the distinguished-looking man to his breakfast.

As he strode away, Christopher thought it odd that his contact should be so concerned as to his future. The hairs on the back of his neck prickled as his suspicions grew. He went over the entire conversation in his mind and could detect nothing. His sixth sense told him to guard his activities, but perhaps he was just imagining things. He was very worried about Elise and the baby and was so anxious to return to her that he was tense about everything.

He chided himself for being too cautious. That same attitude had caused his lack of communication with Elise and eventually led to her flight. He did glance behind him several times, unable to shake the feeling that he was being followed. In the past two years he had learned to watch for such things. Today there was no one lurking in the shadows. Try as he would to dispel it, the feeling remained with him.

He crossed the Champs-Elysées and hailed a taxi. He directed the driver to take him Notre Dame. As he rode toward his meeting with Liza Garrett, he thought how good it would be once all this responsibility was lifted from his shoulders. This was his last assignment. God! He had feared this day would never arrive. For over two years not a single moment had been his own. At last this damn nightmare was over. He took out the envelope and stared at this final transaction, sickened at the thought of all he had been involved in.

The taxi pulled up in front of the great cathedral. She stood waiting for him under the center archway. The stained glass of the circular window high above her reflected the morning sunlight. He strolled up to her nonchalantly, and as he took her hands in his and kissed her cheek, passersby noted the happy reunion of two lovers. He stood close to her as he passed the envelope into her purse.

"How is Elise, Christopher? Is she going to be all right?" Liza inquired.

"For now, there does not seem to be much we can do but wait. I have the feeling the doctor knows something he is not telling me. I don't like it. I can't believe that she and the baby are out of danger. As soon as I leave here I'm headed to the house to send off the last wire to Washington. Then I'll go straight back to the hospital to stay with her as long as she needs me," he said.

"Did she regain consciousness while you were there?" she asked.

"No. She did call out my name, and then she had some sort of convulsions. I don't understand it at all."

"I'll feel much better about it myself when you return to be with her. She needs you now. And although she may tell you to leave, don't do it. Stay with her until you can explain everything. She has so many misconceptions, and you have to win her trust again. You'll have to tell her about me. I'm certain she thinks I am your mistress," she said, watching for his reaction.

"Liza! You can't be serious? Elise doesn't even know you. This isn't your fault. How could you come up with such an absurd idea?"

"Christopher, I don't know when she saw me for the first time. Sarajevo. The ship, perhaps. But, I'm telling you that when she saw me get out of that taxi yesterday, she recognized my face. I know that look. You were too surprised at finding her to realize that she tore off running before she even saw you. You were still in the cab when she started to. So it *was* my fault. She was afraid of me for some reason. I think it's because she thinks you and I are having an affair," she said.

"I find this preposterous, Liza."

"You think about it! Sometimes you men can be so damn thickheaded. It's a wonder any woman puts up with you. Everytime you see me, even today, we put on the appearance of lovers to avert suspicion. What if just once, only one time, she saw us like this? Then too, she hasn't seen you for months, she is going to have your baby, and she's in a strange city. And yesterday, out of the blue, there you are in a taxi, with me of all people! If I were in her situation, I would be thinking a lot worse things than what I've just told you now. I think you should prepare yourself for some accusations. She has probably convinced herself it is the truth," Liza said.

"I guess I just never thought about it. If you're right, she has this haunting her besides all her other suspicions about me. God! but I have been a royal ass about all this. I seem to manage business so easily, and I haven't handled matters with my own wife at all!"

"Well, old friend, you certainly have your work cut out for you. I don't envy you your task in the least. And, standing here talking about all of it is not going to win her back. It goes without saying that I wish only the best for the two of you. You've earned your retirement from this work. We all are aware of what you have accomplished and the sacrifices you have made for your country. I guess I'm having a difficult time finding the right words to express what I feel. You know what I'm trying to say, don't you?" she said, looking up into the blue eyes of her handsome and dejected friend.

"I know. I do. But you've worked just as hard. I'll miss you, Liza. I must say I'll rest easier when I know you are safe back in the States. Things here are going to get pretty rough, and I'd like to know that all my friends are safe from harm. Take care, Liza, and if I can, I'll send you word on our situation here," Christopher said as he leaned down and kissed her forehead. He turned toward the sun and walked quickly away from her.

Christopher hailed a taxi to take him to his house on rue Cambon. As the driver pulled up in front of the stone residence, Christopher once again experienced uneasiness. But he was anxious to complete his business so that he could return to the hospital, and did not see the sleek black automobile parked behind the evergreen to his left. He placed his brass key in the lock, turned the latch, and entered the house. He went immediately to his desk in the main salon and gathered the files he had sorted the night before. He threw the papers into the metal container at his foot, struck a match and tossed it onto the stack.

"I wouldn't do that if I were you, Mr. Mann," the handsome middle-aged German said as he stood in the doorway with a revolver in his hand. He waved the gun at Christopher and ordered the two men with him to douse the flames.

"We'll need that information, if you don't mind, Mr. Mann. Erik, bind Mr. Mann's hands behind his back. We won't gag you just yet," the German said.

A man came around to a stunned Christopher and roughly grabbed his arms and pulled them behind him, tying them together with a leather strap.

"Just what the hell is going on here? Who are you and how did you get in?" Christopher demanded.

"Patience, please Mr. Mann. Let me introduce myself. I am Baron Karl von Gotlieb. You will get to know me and my associates quite well in the weeks to come. We have been observing your operations here in Paris for quite some time. Your acumen in the business world is commendable. Unfortunately, foreign intrigue is not your forte. You lack a certain finesse that is required to accomplish your tasks without detection. And, by the way, you should lock your doors more securely," the baron said.

"And what exactly do you want from me?" Christopher asked.

"It has come to our attention that you are not what you appear to be, Mr. Mann. We have learned of your communiqués to Washington. My superiors in Munich are not pleased with this information. They are not happy at all with your double dealing and divided loyalties. Such acts of treachery must be dealt with harshly, don't you agree?" the baron said condescendingly.

"I doubt you have proof to support these accusations," said Christopher, hoping to buy time.

"Hardly. We have intercepted all your missives to Washington for the past two weeks. We have replaced them with similar, but misleading, information. And, Mr. Mann, I think it will interest you greatly to know that your wife was a guest of mine in my home for many weeks," the baron taunted Christopher.

At these words, Christopher bristled and glared at Gotlieb.

"Save your lies!" he shouted. But the thought of Elise living with the baron had visibly disturbed him.

"It is no lie. Elise is a beautiful woman and a delight to have around every morning. I admire her courage at facing the world alone. In fact, I purchased a cradle for her child. You must ask her about it. She was thrilled with it and was, er, most grateful," he said, noting with pleasure the torment his words were causing Christopher.

"You're a liar!"

But Christopher was stunned. Could Elise have been

so desperate that she would seek the protection of a man like this? It was incomprehensible.

"Unfortunately, you will not be able to communicate with her anytime soon, because we have certain plans for you that do not include a reunion with your lovely wife."

"Damn your soul to hell if you ever lay a hand on her! I'll rip your depraved heart out of your body if you do," Christopher vowed as he struggled to free himself.

"I don't think I would say anything more, Mr. Mann. Oh, yes, I almost forgot! Hans is a devout and religious man, and as he left Notre Dame Cathedral after his daily visit, he just happened to run into your Miss Garrett. I thought you should know that she is in our protective hands. We'll take care of all the ladies in your life," the baron said as he nodded his head to the man who held Christopher in his viselike grasp.

"Erik . . ." the baron signaled, and the enormous German hit Christopher over the head with the butt of his revolver.

Christopher's last thoughts as he sank into a heap on the red Oriental carpet were of the evil Baron holding both Elise and Liza captive.

The two men pulled Christopher's unresisting body into the waiting auto. The baron issued orders to his driver and the two other men. He closed the door to the auto and reentered the house to retrieve the files and records. He was quite proud of his exploits today, and he knew that he would be greatly rewarded for his success. He walked down the street, hailed a cab, and ordered the driver to take him to the nearest florist. Elise would like some fresh spring blossoms on a cold November day like this. Something cheerful, he thought. He and Madeleine could convince her to move back with them so that they could care for her more properly. He thought perhaps he should purchase another gift for her, chocolates or a book, perhaps. No, not just yet. He would wait.

Christopher moaned as he opened his eyes. His head throbbed. He moved his hand to the back of his head and winced with the shooting pain caused by merely touching the tender area. He was having difficulty focusing on anything clearly, but he could smell the stench of manure, and he heard the neighing of a horse. A barn! He must be in a barn! But no. He was moving. He heard the clicking of the rails beneath the train wheels. He was aboard a freight train. But where was he headed, and how long had he been unconscious?

As though through a fog, all the day's events came back to him as he focused his eyes upon the straw beneath him. His hands were untied, but he found to his dismay that his legs were shackled to the wall of a car. A large ring was riveted to the wall, and from it a heavy iron chain was suspended; two large iron cuffs encircled his ankles, and they were soldered to the chain. He was trapped. But even more than his own predicament, the fate of his wife and child weighed heavily on his mind. He refused to believe the baron's words that Elise was his mistress. She would never compromise her principles so much as to ingratiate herself with someone like him, much less prostitute herself.

"Oh, Elise, what horrors have I brought upon us both?"

He rolled onto his side, and the hay and manure clung to the back of his jacket. The monotonous clicking of the rails marked the passage of time and distance. As the sun set, the freight car became increasingly cold. He wrapped his arms around himself in a vain effort to warm his chilled body.

He lay motionless upon the hay-strewn floor of the rail car. At last, in total despair, he succumbed to the cold and his own overwhelming fatigue.

Thirty-three

E LISE gazed at the wilted Valentine roses that Madeleine had miraculously produced a week ago. She tapped a dry blossom and stared as the withered petals rained down upon the freshly polished mahogany of her desk. The flowers reflected her unholidaylike mood! No fragrance remained, only an acrid stench from the water in the cut crystal vase. No sunlight filtered through the windowpanes. And no warmth rose from the blazing fire. She tugged at the lapels of her heavy woolen sweater but still fell victim to the chill within herself. She struggled to cry —to let all her loneliness escape—but nothing happened.

If only she could receive some word from home! She knew then she would feel better. But with the war engulfing every facet of daily life, it was understandable that letters from home would easily be lost or held up. Surely Mama had sent numerous letters, perhaps even a lacy Valentine card—just something to surprise her. Mama always managed to do just that with the smallest things.

"Yes, she did," Elise said sadly, as she choked down the large lump in her throat.

Since she hadn't received any sort of communiqués from Mobile, she wondered exactly what they thought of her life in Paris. They surely knew her whereabouts and address by now since she had written at Christmastime. Elise hoped that she would hear from them the next day. Even at her darkest moments, she always believed that her prayers would be answered. She hoped for many things. . . .

Though she forced herself not to think of him, her

thoughts naturally wandered to Christopher. Undoubtedly he was in regular communication with her father. Papa would request detailed accounts of Christopher's business. Surely her husband had not informed her parents about their separation. To do so would be ludicrous! Christopher was probably forced, as she was, to relay only bits and pieces of news. Justin would never tolerate anyone's mistreating his daughter, regardless of all else he was responsible for. Elise did wonder how much Christopher had lied. Where had he told Justin that they were living?

Obviously, Christopher had provided little or no information at all, because if he had and their stories hadn't matched, Elise would have heard from her mother immediately.

She smoothed the writing paper with the palm of her hand and wondered just what her parents were thinking about her at this time. Undoubtedly, they would expect her nights to be filled with dinner parties. Of course, only the most distinguished and interesting people would attend. The meals would be delectable, war or no war. And the conversation would be clever and stimulating. She was sure Mama had been as spellbound by Christopher and his social prowess as she had been. Perhaps they thought she would have a quiet evening now and then, but mostly they would expect the honeymooning couple to surround themselves with merriment. She also thought that in her letter she should include details about the latest fashions. No. She couldn't do that. Mama always was too well informed about such matters and due to the cold realities of her situation, Elise didn't know what was au courant this season. She would work around that and just not include authentic details. Her plan now formulated in her mind, she began her letter.

Dearest Mama,

I want to apologize for not writing to you since I sent my Christmas card. I find it hard to believe that the holidays have come and gone, and it seems I have accomplished nothing of consequence. I have been quite remiss in all my correspondence.

Naturally, December was extremely active for me. There were so many parties and dinners that we were expected to attend. For days, it seemed that all

I did was to sleep, eat, and prepare for yet another ball. I did manage to order some beautiful but much too expensive gowns. Christopher was sweet about it, though. He never reprimanded me for the money I spent as long as my purchases met with his approval. (Which they always did.)

Even with the war all around us, Paris during the holidays was gayer than I have ever seen her. The officers were so very handsome in their dress uniforms. I sometimes think they thrive on these festivities. I suppose it takes their minds away from the current conflict.

It has been quite cold and dreary this winter, but with my social obligations, painting, and occasional needlework, I have been able to occupy myself and not think so much of home. It was difficult to celebrate Christmas Day so far away from the family. I think I missed our Christmas dinner together the most. Ours was lovely and I really should not complain, but it wasn't the same. I missed watching Sadie and Violet argue over their gifts. I had always thought that they were being selfish, but now realize that they did so in jest. Perhaps it was their way of keeping the childhood days of make-believe alive for all of us.

Mostly, I do long to see you, Mama. I try to be strong now that I am a woman and wife to a man. But, it's not easy to be on the other side of the world, especially at Christmastime, which now more than ever before means family time to me. I'm sorry. I should not let you think that there is anything wrong. I suppose I just fell prey to a bit of homesickness.

Our holiday decorations have all been packed away and now it is time for us all to concentrate on the new year. I pray every day that this war will end, as I'm sure you do, too. Christopher is extremely busy with his business affairs, but we managed to attend the theatre every so often.

I promise to try especially hard to write to you more often than I have in the past. Even when I have not sent word, remember that not a day passes that I don't think of you and home. You are all so

*close to me in my heart. Nothing can ever change
that.*

> *Your devoted daughter,*
> *Elise*

Elise folded the letter, addressed the envelope and
sealed it, then left the house to mail her fabrications to her
mother.

Thirty-four

TRUDGING through the March rains, Elise clutched her parcels in one hand and shielded her body with the umbrella she held in the other. Thunderstorms no longer frightened her. She thought that for the rest of life nothing would move her to either fear or love. She was a shell, devoid of spirit. She knew no joy, no laughter, no happiness. After her baby died, all her reasons for living had been taken from her. She had been forsaken by her husband and by God. She wondered why she still existed; there was no purpose to her life.

At Madeleine's insistence she had given up her apartment and moved back to the rue du Faubourg-St. Honoré. In truth she had been glad to leave the apartment, for it was too painful for her to confront the corner where the cradle had been. But she knew that her presence cast a pall over Madeleine's home and ordinarily jubilant life. Even the baron had ceased trying to please her with little gifts and surprises. Her depression was now pulling her friends down with her, but she was powerless to stop it. Had it been within her power to control her emotions and her life, she simply could not make the effort. She did wish that she need not depend upon Madeleine and Karl for her livelihood.

She had, from some unknown inner region, found enough strength to paint and sketch. But the products of her current attitudes were political essays on the war. No longer could she find it within herself to depict the smiling faces of—oh God! children—or sunny landscapes. When she gazed upon the world about her, she saw only death.

Ambulances loaded with maimed and mangled bodies of French soldiers rolled into Paris each day. Only the strongest survived. They were patched up, and many were sent back to the lines before they could fully recover. Her loss was insignificant when she thought of the mutilated bodies of the moaning men in the corridors of the under-staffed hospitals. She wondered how long the atrocities would last. It was hard to believe that over a million and a half Allied soldiers had already perished; the war was only six months old. She knew it was foolish to hope for an early end to the struggle. She thought of the photographs she had seen of the homeless Belgian families whose eyes were shadowed with pain, hunger, and desperation. These were the faces that she transferred to her canvases.

Once, long ago, she believed in man's inherent goodness; now she knew that humans could be as debased as they allowed themselves to be. She could not decide if it was the war or her hollow, loveless life that altered her opinions. Perhaps she was growing up and this was part of the process; this steeling of oneself against the sometimes hideous realities of life. She knew she could never be happy again, not now that everything she had ever cared about had been wrenched from her grasp. As she turned the corner and stepped toward the door of Madeleine's home, she thought of the two remaining friends she had here. Soon she must leave them.

She entered the house and took the bread, coffee, and spices to the kitchen. These were becoming luxuries in Paris, and she wondered just how long it would be until even these necessities would vanish from the shops. Only through the sale of her war scenes had she been able to purchase these few staples for Madeleine. Luckily there was a great call across the ocean for just such contemporary art as hers. All the world was clamoring for news of the war.

She put away her rain-drenched coat and went to the main salon to warm her legs by the dying coal fire. She stirred the coals with the poker and replenished them. Her mind wandered to faraway places, and for the first time in months she allowed herself to think of Jesse. The pain was so deep that tears came to her eyes and she laid her head upon the back of the bergère chair.

298

"Jesse, I can't bear this alone. No one can help me but you, and now more than just miles separate us. Will I ever see you again? The war, time and the loss of my self keeps me from you. Jesse! Has this war dealt you such cruel blows? Are you still the same? Jesse! Can you help me? Oh God!" she cried despairingly.

The sudden ringing of the door bell startled Elise out of her lamentation. She sprang from her chair and wiped the tears from her cheeks. In the foyer she stopped to regard herself in the oval mirror. She was aghast at her appearance. What had happened to her? Hadn't she even looked at her own reflection all these weeks? Her eyes were gray and lusterless. There were lines and deep circles under her eyes. Her cheeks had lost their youthful fullness and glow, and her cheekbones appeared quite prominent. There were furrows in her brow. She thought she had aged ten years. No wonder Madeleine always seemed to be hovering about her, telling her to eat and rest properly. She thought her face was an accurate reflection of the condition of her bleak and devastated soul. She crossed to the door and opened it to Dr. Henri Brusard.

"Elise, hello! You look so pretty; you must be feeling better today," he said as he entered the foyer. Elise looked at him incredulously and beckoned him to follow her into the salon. She was happy to see him; she needed to talk to someone about anything except her troubles. She told him she needed to find something to keep her occupied, because her art was not enough for her. She wondered if she could aid the war effort by joining one of the ladies' hospital groups.

"No, Elise," he said. "That is not enough for you and you know it. But this is the reason for my visit. I would be very grateful if you would accompany me as my nurse's aide to one of the field hospitals."

"But I know nothing that could really help you."

"Elise, we need any volunteers we can get. We'll be going to the hospital at Neuve-Chappelle, and the wounded men are in dire need. The medical staff is extremely small and overworked."

Elise listened as he explained that word had come to him that well over a thousand men were suffering. He was being dispatched with supplies and hospital volunteers to man the hospital.

Henri explained that the Germans had thinned their own forces at the front to such an extent near Neuve-Chappelle that they had almost invited the Allied attack that ensued. The Germans had reduced their manpower to six companies, and General Haig of the Allies had reinforced his troops so that the number of soldiers was well over forty-eight battalions. The Germans had left only a dozen or so machine guns to cover the entire area, whereas Haig had well over forty medium howitzers, sixty batteries of light gun, and eighty-two pieces of heavy artillery.

The bombardment that started the fighting lasted only thirty-five minutes, but it was overpowering. For three days the battle raged and the Allied troops were able to break through the enemy lines; but the attack failed, for it lacked the key ingredient of surprise. The generals had been much too cautious.

"What a waste for so many to be sacrificed for a stalemate. It seems we never hear of victory, nor do we experience any real defeats," Elise said. "I have nothing to keep me here in Paris any longer. If you truly think I can help you, I'll do what I can. I don't have any nursing experience, Henri, but—" She stopped as she noticed him smiling and shaking his head.

"Willing hands are what I need most, dear Elise. If you can take over some of the more menial chores to free the trained nurses for other jobs, it would be a great blessing. We'll leave in the morning," he said as he rose to leave.

As Elise closed the door after him, she felt the first stirrings of renewed purpose. Perhaps if she couldn't help herself, then she could give a small measure of comfort to those who desperately needed her. She had started up the stairs when Madeleine rushed in the door shaking the rain off her umbrella. As she placed it in the brass stand, she noticed Elise.

"Ma cherie! Don't rush away. Come and have some hot tea with me. It is so cold and rainy today. Let's sit by the fire," Madeleine said as she swished out to the kitchen to prepare the tea. She returned with a silver tray and the delicate yellow floral china cups that were her favorites.

"Madeleine," Elise began as she took the cup from her friend. "I have some news to tell you and I hardly know how to begin."

"At the beginning would be nice," Madeleine said playfully.

"First, I have no way of expressing my gratitude to you and Karl for taking me in, especially these last few months when I have been anything but a cheerful companion. I do want you to know, I could never have survived my ordeal without you."

"Elise, cherie, I do not like the beginning of the little speech. It sounds like adieu," Madeleine said apprehensively.

"I'm afraid it is. Henri Brusard was here just a few moments ago. I'm surprised you didn't see him. Anyway, he has asked me to help administer medical aid to the wounded near Neuve-Chappelle," Elise said, sipping her tea.

"You didn't consent, I hope. People are being killed all around there."

"I have to. I have nothing here to hold me, and these people need me and others like me. I must go to Neuve-Chappelle. I won't be gone for long, I promise," Elise said, determined not to be dissuaded.

"I think this is wrong. I don't like this idea of yours one bit. But I will not say any more on the subject. So let's get you packed. What does one wear to the front?" Madeliene said and they both laughed in an effort not to dwell on their upcoming separation.

The rain clouds had passed over Paris during the night, and the skies were clear as morning dawned. Henri Brusard turned off the ignition on his car, jumped out, and rang Madeleine's bell. Elise answered the door, and Henri placed her light valise in the back seat of his automobile. The two women embraced each other for a long moment; then Elise ran to the car, unable to look back at Madeleines's tearful face.

Henri explained to Elise that it was well over one hundred and twenty miles to the field hospital. At Chantilly, they would ride with the caravan of new ambulances and medical personnel. Elise thought it strange that they were traveling such a distance to aid the British field hospital. However, Henri explained that this was his country and all free nations must band together and present a solid front against the Kaiser. Hers was a very small part to play in the broad scope of the war effort, she thought, but at least she was doing something for other people once again and not wallowing in the self-pity that had imprisoned her for so long. It was not in her nature to be so pessimistic and self-centered, and she was eager for the chance to atone for these months of despondency.

At Chantilly, Henri left his automobile in the care of a childhood friend who lived not far away. They went to the Allied encampment, where they met the other medical volunteers who would accompany them to the front. Henri drove the charcoal-gray ambulance, whose boxy sides were painted with a red cross on a white background. They bumped along the deep-rutted highway on their journey north. The Allied command had issued a special route, and although they were very close to the action, they were in no apparent danger of being shelled. The farther north they drove, the greater the number of wounded soldiers they saw trudging along the sides of the road. Companies of new troops marched in front of their convoy, and Elise was startled at the young faces she viewed. These were not men—some of the boys had not begun to shave. The magnitude of the situation had just begun to dawn upon her.

As she regarded the innocent-looking faces of the soldiers around her, it impressed her as mere common sense that if trench warfare tactics were exacting such incredibly high tolls in death and injury, surely some other strategy should be considered.

As they drew close to their destination, Elise was appalled at the destruction around them. She had imagined she would be working in a hospital similar to the one in Paris where she had lost her baby. However, this was an old farmhouse, and although it was quite large, it was obviously inadequate; large canvas and oilcloth tents were erected around the house's outside walls. Rows of wounded men on stretchers groaned in their pain as they awaited the healing hands that would relieve their agony.

Elise noted the confusion of the limited medical staff. She was shocked at the number of unattended men who were bleeding to death before her very eyes. She regretted deeply that she had no formal medical education with which she could treat at least some of these men. She could dress wounds and apply salves and bandages, but that was all.

As soon as Henri stopped the ambulance, they both stared in horror at the scene before them. Henri turned and looked into Elise's eyes. Each saw the dedication and determination of the other; they were here to give themselves to these men. Simultaneously, they moved from the ambulance. Henri grabbed his medical bag and sent Elise to search out the head of the hospital, a Dr. Richmond. Elise picked her way through the moaning soldiers to the interior of the improvised hospital. The stench of warm blood, rotting flesh, and sulfur permeated the stuffy air. As she walked forward, a tall, sandy-haired man in a bloodstained surgical gown approached her. She could tell he was exhausted. He had no color in his face, and his sad eyes were ringed with dark circles and lines. He looked in wonder at her. Then his face brightened ever so slightly and he said, "Are you from the convoy?"

"Yes. We just arrived under the direction of Dr. Brusard. He's outside tending one of the patients. He sent me to find Dr. Richmond. Do you know where he would be?" she said.

"You are speaking to him. I guess you can see for yourself that you and your supplies are desperately needed," he said in a British accent.

"I wish I could tell you I am a trained nurse, but I am not. I'm afraid I won't be able to help much at all," she said, doubting the wisdom of her decision.

"Nothing could be further from the truth! What you need to know, we will teach you. Right now, let's get to those drugs. We used the last of our morphine this morning. If you will manage the unloading of supplies, my nurses and doctors can remain in surgery. Now, where is Dr. Brusard?" he asked, coming closer and leading her back outside.

"Over there, Dr. Richmond," she said, pointing to Henri, who knelt briefly over the body of a boy he was too late to save.

303

"Miss . . . I'm sorry, I don't know your name," Dr. Richmond said.

"Elise, just call me Elise. Where do you want the drugs and bandages? I'll see to those supplies first."

"Bring them inside. There's a small room to the rear on the first floor where we store them. We're using the room next to it for surgery. And, Elise, thank you. I probably won't have another chance to say anything like that to you for the next few days. Never doubt that we need you. Now, get to that morphine, there's a man inside who needs it," he said as he turned and went to Henri. The two men shook hands and quickly ran inside.

By this time all the ambulances had come to a halt and the drivers were busily unloading the crates of medicine, surgical instruments, bandages and sanitary linens, blankets and extra stretchers. The crates were stacked just outside the farmhouse, and the ambulances were sent to the front to bring back more wounded. Four ambulances had been hit by mortar shells the day before; two drivers had been killed and the other two were badly burned and wounded.

During the ensuing hours that Elise labored, organizing the drugs in the little storeroom, she learned more about the war, medicine, and the plight of them all than she had in the last six months in Paris. She and a Red Cross nurse, Ann, worked ceaselessly unpacking supplies. Ann recounted their last hectic days and nights. Without interjecting a word, Elise listened to the horrors that the battle of Neuve-Chappelle had created. As quickly as they unpacked the boxes, they received calls from the surgery rooms for this or that instrument, drug, or linen. Late into the night, Elise ran back and forth with the necessary items.

The upstairs of the farmhouse had been partitioned into treatment rooms. There were four teams of doctors performing both major and minor surgeries. The few nurses present were needed inside the hospital. There were no volunteers other than Elise to do these errands. Ann gave her instructions and informed Elise that soon she would have to relieve the nurse who was assisting Dr. Brusard and Dr. Richmond. Each nurse was allowed one hour's sleep because that one hour could mean the difference between life and death to a soldier. The doctors

304

worked until they almost collapsed from fatigue, but no one ever complained. Only when the waves of wounded subsided would anyone in this field hospital even want to stop.

Elise thought that a noble statement, but she felt she would never be able to function that long without rest or food. But after forty-eight hours of ministering to the needs of the staff alone, she realized that when the task was so awesome, it was possible to draw on hidden strength.

Elise carried the bloody linens to the iron kettles in the back of the farmhouse and stoked the fires beneath them. She had long since unpacked all the new blankets, and already she could see the need for more supplies. They seemed to use medicine and bandages faster than she could put them on the shelves. Two young volunteers returned the blankets from the bodies of the British soldiers they had buried that afternoon.

The pile of blankets looked like a mountain of dark green wool, and she pictured a vast number of soldiers who were now buried in the French mud or were being shipped back to England in crates. Many of the bodies had been so badly mutilated they were unrecognizable. As she stirred the boiling cauldron of linens, she felt the bile rise to her throat. She turned and ran to the side of one of the gray ambulances and vomited.

God! This was only the beginning of this nightmare. She was so sick and weary, but she couldn't stop—too many depended on her menial tasks—and she felt proud and even glad that she could accomplish something for her fellow man.

She went back to the laundry. She took the long stick in her hand and transferred the sheets to the next kettle, and then she retrieved the rinsed linens and wrung them out. When she finished this task, she was to relieve Ann in the storeroom. Then she would be able to rest. Although she thought she could sleep for the next hundred years, she knew she would happily give up her rest if one more boy could be spared. As she labored over the kettles, she thought of the laundresses her mother had employed in Mobile. Even as a child she had marveled at their ability to accomplish so much in such a short time. Now she wished she had paid more attention to them and learned the secret of their efficiency. She took much too long to accomplish so little, she thought.

She was carrying an armload of clean gowns and surgical linens back to the storeroom when the ambulances rolled in filled with more wounded. Always more—the numbers of new arrivals never seemed to lessen. The drivers dashed around to the back of the trucks and quickly carried the stretchers to the tent area. She stood off to the side while they rushed past her. She watched as the ambulances were emptied, and then she carefully stepped around the men. One man asked for a drink of water, and another clutched her ankle and begged her for something for the pain. She ran inside, tears filling her eyes. She filled a tin cup with water and went back to the man who requested it. She held his head in her arm and raised the cool liquid to his lips. He smiled at her and thanked her.

It was the first time she had even noticed the faces of any of the men, so intent had she been upon her duties. It was then that she saw the light, curly hair of the young boy beside her. His British private's uniform was streaked with blood. His eyes were closed, and she couldn't tell if he was alive. Then he moaned, and his head rolled to the side slightly. Elise's eyes widened in shock and pain when she realized she was staring into the face of her childhood friend Andrew.

Thirty-five

ELISE thought he was still alive as she crawled toward him. She lifted the blanket and saw that he had been shot in the abdomen. His hand covered the wound, and the blood oozed through his fingers onto his uniform. Elise thought she was going to faint, her head was spinning so. Her heart rose to her throat as she felt his weak pulse and noted the shallowness of his breathing. He was so very pale, and his skin was cold when she touched his cheek. She jumped up and raced inside, returning with a clean, wet cloth and a mug of water. She bathed the dried mud from his face and lifted his hand in her arms. "Andrew," she whispered, "Andrew. Please don't die! Please God, let my friend live," she prayed.

His lips sipped at the water, and he opened his eyes. They were cloudy with pain and disorientation. He stared at her and blinked several times in an effort to focus his gaze. Only after several moments did he recognize her.

"Elise? Is that you?" he asked. "How did I get home?" Then he looked about him and said: "I'm not in Mobile, am I?"

"No, Andrew. We're both at a field hospital near Neuve-Chappelle. You've been badly hit. But I'll get you some help, Andrew. You're going to be just fine. I promise, Drew. I do. Nothing bad will happen to you. I'll take care of you. Please, Drew, hold on. I'll be back in a few minutes," she said, smiling bravely. She gently kissed his cold lips and laid his head back on the stretcher as she stood up and rushed inside.

Henri had just finished amputating the arm of a young

307

officer, and was desolate as he walked from the operating room. He had lit a cigarette and was staring at the smoke as she came running toward him, her face panic stricken.

"Elise?" he said with dread apprehension.

"Henri, please. You must help me. There . . . there is a boy outside who is gravely wounded. He's a friend of mine from home. Oh, Henri, I don't think he'll make it if he has to wait. Please, come. Please, help him," she said, pulling on his arm as she became hysterical.

"Elise, don't worry. I'll do what I can," he said, crushing his cigarette with his heel. As Henri raced outside and knelt next to Drew, she noticed how weary he was. She wondered if he had rested at all since their arrival. If he had, it hadn't been for long. None of them had been able to eat or rest much in the last two days.

Henri ordered the stretcher-bearers to carry the boy inside. As he stood up, Elise knew that the look in Henri's eyes was one of helplessness. Tears streamed down her face as she watched Henri's form disappear into the farmhouse. She felt her knees tremble and her hands shake. She screamed as she crumbled to the ground, "No! God! No! Not my Drew!" She beat her fists against the earth at her knees. All the agony, frustration, and horror of the war and her empty life rose to the surface, and although she fought to control herself, she felt her heart sink in her breast.

For the next hour she mechanically tended her duties, but her heart and mind were inside that operating room. He was still alive, she kept telling herself. But she knew God would fail her once again. He had abandoned her months ago; no longer did He hear her pleas for mercy. Perhaps through her own strength of will, she could pull Andrew away from death.

She carried a tray of clean instruments upstairs, and as she returned, she hesitated before the operating room. He was still inside. She felt utterly helpless. Suddenly, the door opened and Henri stood before her. She looked at him with pleading eyes. He put his hands on her shoulders and sighed.

"It's bad, Elise. But I do have hope. If no infection sets in and if he wants to live, he may make it. It won't be easy. The rest is up to him and God," he said as he kissed her on the forehead and ordered the next patient brought in.

Elise followed the stretcher-bearer who took Andrew to a room where they placed surgical patients. She covered Andrew with an extra blanket and knelt beside him. As she took his hand and stared into his pallid face, her mind wandered to the warm summer days of their childhood in Mobile, so far from this cold and deadly world of France.

For the next twenty-four hours, Elise tended her duties, and every hour she checked on Andrew, applying cool compresses and fetching him water or some warm broth. He was very sleepy, but he always managed to waken when she was near. The bleeding had abated, and his color had returned. She changed his dressings as Henri administered his medications. She bathed the last vestiges of French mud from his body.

During the next few days the number of incoming wounded lessened. The wounds now were not as severe as before, and the nurses and doctors were finally able to rest. The ambulance drivers took over the laundry duties, and Elise found herself tending the patients. She bathed, fed, and read to the men. She was becoming expert at changing dressings, and soldiers under her care commented on her delicate touch. Hospital activity had settled into a routine, and many of the wounded were rapidly healing. Even though it didn't seem possible, spirits had begun to lighten, and some of the soldiers who were healing faster than others would follow the nurses around on their rounds and help cheer the less fortunate. In the low light of the evening, groups of men would sit and sing melodies to the accompaniment of a harmonica that one of the British soldiers carried. Elise and Ann had discovered a box of writing paper, and at night they would help the men with letters home.

It was past midnight when a very tired Elise had finished her chores and come to check on Andrew before she retired for the night. He had been in good spirits that morning, but she had not seen him all day because she had been inordinately busy. She sat down next to him, and he stirred and opened his eyes.

"Elise, you are such a treat for my eyes. I look forward to your visits all day."

"I'm sorry I didn't see you more often today, but I've been terribly busy," she said apologetically.

"You do look tired. Are you taking care of yourself?" he asked.

"Of course I am, silly," she said, and then laughed aloud. "Andrew, there was a time when I would never have let you or anyone else see me in such a disheveled condition," she said.

"I know!" he laughed. "I'll bet this is the longest you've gone without a bath."

"Drew, I can't remember the last time I washed my hair or luxuriated in a tub of bath salts. It seems like some other world."

"It was another world, Elise. A world we'll never be able to recapture. It's all gone forever, isn't it?" he said as tears stung his eyes.

"I can't believe that! I won't let myself believe it. We can't be children again, but this war can't last forever," she said with determination.

"It can't? I'm not so sure. I'd give anything to be in Mobile at one of your mama's elegant parties. And I'd like to see you there, Elise, dressed in a blue gown and smelling of your lavender. I'd take you in my arms and swirl you around the dance floor to some beautiful waltz music."

"Oh, Andrew, let's not think of such things. You need to concentrate on getting better," she said as she took his hand and held it to her cheek. As she did so, a sense of alarm filled her, and her hand darted to his forehead. For the first time she noticed the cold beads of sweat on his upper lip and forehead. He was burning up with fever! But Henri had said he was mending quite well. She looked closer into his eyes and realized that they were cloudy and had lost their focus.

Slowly she lifted the blanket and inspected the wound. She couldn't be sure; there was not enough light and she was not trained well enough to know just what she was looking for.

She covered him up with the blanket and said, "Drew, I'm going to get you something to drink. You rest quietly and I'll be back in a minute."

She rose from her friend's bedside, hoping not to alarm him. Her suspicions grew as she walked away quietly. Her hands trembled as her heart iced over with fear. As she walked toward the door, her eyes saw a vision of death resting over her Drew's body. Death reached out and touched her friend, and she saw his body turn white and then become to a skeleton. She closed the door, then leaned against the frame. A moment later she collapsed in an unconscious heap on the cold floor.

It was to Henri's soothing voice that she awoke.

"Elise, wake up! Are you all right?"

"I . . . I guess I fainted, didn't I?" she asked in an effort to orient herself.

"Yes, you did. Do you know how long you've been here? I was just coming back from one of my patients."

"What time is it?" she asked.

"Almost one o'clock."

"It couldn't have been too long. Henri! I was on my way to find you. It's Drew. He . . . he had a fever and cold sweat. And chills, too. I couldn't see his wound, I didn't have a lantern with me. Please let's hurry. I had a terrible premonition about him. I've had these before and they always come true. I'm scared, really, I am! We've got to hurry!"

"It's all right, Elise. It was probably just a bad dream while you were unconscious. There's no such thing as a premonition. He'll be fine, but let's go look in on him," Henri said, hoping to comfort the frightened girl.

Carrying a lantern, they went together to Andrew. Elise held the lantern high as Henri removed the bandages. Andrew stared at Elise's face. She fought to smile pleasantly, knowing he would be trying to read her expression.

Henri removed the bandages and immediately saw the infected area. It was red and swollen; he would need to drain it and then apply new dressings. He knew the boy was not strong enough to fight infection. He had lost a great deal of blood, and his fever was quite high. Henri gave Elise some instructions, and she quickly left the room and returned with the necessary instruments, medication, and bandages. Elise held Andrew's hand while Henri ministered to him. She saw the pain cross his young face when Henri lanced the wound. She wished she could do something more to alleviate his agony. After Henri finished, Elise spent the remainder of the night at Andrew's side.

311

He developed cold chills despite his fever, and she tried to keep him covered and apply cold compresses. At one point he convulsed so violently that the wound broke open and he began to hemorrhage profusely. His body quaked and jerked, and his teeth chattered incessantly. It took every ounce of Elise's strength to hold him down until Henri could arrive.

When the doctor saw Andrew's condition, he found it impossible to keep the truth from her. When he looked into her pleading blue eyes, they both knew that there was not much more to be done. Henri rushed Andrew into the operating room to stop the bleeding and suture the wound. Elise paced outside the door for what seemed to her like hours. When Henri came out of the operating room, he was visibly exhausted.

"He's not dead. He's extremely weak. I've done all I can do. You know that, don't you?"

"Yes. Henri, I know. You've done more than anyone could ask. He would have died long ago if it had not been for you," she said.

"No, you are the person keeping him alive now. I don't know how he has had the strength to fight this long. The fever is dangerously high. You may sit with him for a while, but I want you to get some rest. You will do that for me?"

"Yes, but not until I know if he is going to be well again. I must stay with him. He's all I have. He's my friend, Henri," she replied.

"Elise, you have many friends. But right now, he does need you. I must get some rest, but if you do need me, you know where I'll be."

Quietly she entered the room. She sat next to her friend and held his feverish hand in hers, beginning what she knew was a death watch. He grew more pale as the hours passed.

Just before dawn his eyelids opened, and he said, "Elise, my angel of mercy, you are still with me, aren't you?"

"Yes. Drew. I'll always be here for you. You can count on me, you know that."

"Will you go back home with me, Elise? Say you'll return to Mobile with me," he mumbled in low, breathy tones.

"You get well, Drew, and I'll go anywhere you want. I promise, and you know I always keep my promises," she said, trying to be strong.

"Oh, Elise, you took a bath and I can smell your lavender cologne! It's lovely, and I can see the green leaves of the elm trees along Saint Ann Street. It's such a hot day today, it feels so good to stand in the cool shade. Take my hand, Elise, and let's walk to Saint Ann Street. Maybe we'll even see Jesse. . . . Elise . . . could you hold me?" His voice fell to less than a whisper as he spoke.

Elise lifted his head in her arms and sat next to him. She smoothed his golden curls from his sweaty brow and fevered face. She gently stroked his cheek. His breathing became quite shallow, and she felt his muscles relax.

"Saint Ann Street is lovely this time of year, isn't it, Drew? We could play lawn tennis at Jesse's. You would like that, wouldn't you, Drew?"

No answer came. His eyes were closed, and his hand slipped from hers and fell onto the bed. She watched as the blood seeped through the blanket and formed a red blotch. She rocked him back and forth, slowly at first; then she clutched his head tighter to her breast and rocked faster and faster as her tears streamed down her cheeks and fell into his curly hair. She hummed a lullaby and held him tighter, and finally all the tension escaped her.

"No, God, no, I won't let you die, Drew. Not my Drew! Come back to me, my Drew! Don't go away. Don't go to Saint Ann Street without me. I want to go with you. I . . ."

The warm rays of the early spring dawn streamed through the tiny dirty panes of glass in the farmhouse window and fell upon the boy and girl who looked like a pair of lovers bidding each other farewell.

Thirty-six

ELISE had collapsed into a state of numb exhaustion after Andrew's death. She had slept for over twenty-four hours while Henri arranged for the boy's body to be sent back to the United States. The colonel was set against it, stating that he should be buried in France the same as all the other noncommissioned officers lost in battle. However, the colonel knew that Dr. Brusard was not without political influence, and he had the boy sent to Paris. Brusard's friends would handle the arrangements from there. It was a small concession, he decided, and he didn't want to lose the valuable help of Dr. Brusard or any of his staff.

Some new hospital facilities had been erected near the old farmhouse, making it possible for more injured soldiers to be treated. More Red Cross and American Field Service volunteers poured into France every week, and the extra help was greatly needed. The number of patients never seemed to be diminished. Even in relatively quiet times, they were besieged by influenza, dysentery, pneumonia, and various other hazards of the godforsaken trench life these men were forced to live.

Elise thought that life here in the midst of the battle was deplorable for all concerned. The waiting and the daily drudgery took its toll on everyone. She wondered which was worse, to lose a limb or to lose one's sanity. She thought she would rather lose an arm, but then, running away to an inner world did have its advantages. Once a person retreated from life so completely, all the world's pain would be denied entrance. As she gazed at the lost souls about her, she almost envied the victims of shell shock. Perhaps, she thought, she was just such a victim herself.

She went about her daily routine in the hospital as if in a fog. She felt nothing. She cared nothing about her appearance or her future, and seldom did she dare to let her mind wander to thoughts of her family or friends. Somewhere in her past had been a husband, but she wouldn't allow herself to remember even his face, much less their hours together. That was a time in a long-ago world that no longer existed. She believed there was nothing left for her. Surely God had ceased to visit his wrath upon her. Hadn't she endured all the torture one human could bear? She was lost in her personal hell, and no one could free her.

She entered the storeroom and began the inventory of the new drugs and supplies that were arriving with the latest Red Cross convoy. She numbered the items and marked them off on her checklist. The need for these supplies was great and she only wished they had sent more bandages and surgical linens. Elise was bent over a crate filled with bottles of antiseptic and disinfectant when a soldier entered the small storeroom. She heard the voice of the enlisted man as he spoke to her. She slowly straightened her back and pushed her dirty hair off her face.

"Were you talking to me?"

"Yes, I was," he said. "This letter came for you today."

"A . . . a letter?" She asked dazedly. "Only Madeleine knows I'm here."

"It must be for you. It's addressed to Mrs. Christopher Mann." He looked at her quizzically. "You know, this was the first time I knew that you were married. I knew your name was Mann, but I never thought . . ."

Elise snatched the envelope from his hand.

"Well, in a way I am and in a way I'm not," she snapped.

"Look . . . Elise . . . I didn't mean to . . ." he stammered and blushed.

"Yes, I'm sorry, too. If you'll excuse me . . . I'd like to read my letter."

"Sure." He exited the storeroom as fast as possible.

Elise glared at him, then shook her head. It wasn't his

315

fault. No one knew about Christopher. She looked down at the crumpled envelope. It bore many postmarks and was at least a month old. She recognized Madeleine's script on the envelope where she had written in Elise's address in Neuve-Chappelle. Then she realized that the letter was from Sadie.

"Sadie, of all people!" she exclaimed.

She withdrew the letter slowly, savoring her first letter from home.

Dearest Elise,

As I write this letter, I wonder if and when you will ever receive it. I know that you are in Paris now, and so I have sent this to General Delivery. For some reason, I felt the need to write to you and tell you about my life. So many things have changed for me, as they have for you, too. But as you sit in comfortable security in Paris, enjoying scrumptious meals and lovely surroundings, I am based near the Western Front. Since you probably do not know much about the intricacies of warfare, I won't go into all the details other than to tell you that I am an ambulance driver for the American Field Service.

Elise, I know all this must come as a shock, especially since you probably have been under the assumption that I was still in Mobile. Obviously, dear sister, I'm not!

I was able to save some money of my own, and Violet helped me when I got to New York. I have been fortunate enough to take control of my own destiny. Imagine! What exciting times we live in, Elise! In what other period of history could a woman strike out on her own as I have? And not only that, but I am very good at my work, or at least that is what my superiors have told me. Even though this war is abominable, I feel I'm doing my part for my country and I'm able to save lives. Sometimes, I feel that what I am doing now was the reason I was put on this earth. I've always known that I was different from everyone in the family. I was set apart. And now, for the first time in my life, I feel special, and not some oddity as Papa so often believed I was.

If you should actually receive this letter, know

316

that my prayers for your happiness are with you. Know also that I am fine and very happy. I have found my purpose in life and it is such a worthwhile one.

Your loving sister,
Sadie

Elise stared at the letter and watched as tiny blotches from her falling tears spread on the paper. It was so good to hear from Sadie. And it was just the kind of letter she needed to read at this time. She needed *something* . . . a belief in someone's strength besides her own to keep going. Sadie was right: Everyone needed a purpose.

She looked at her dirty fingernails. She couldn't let herself go like this anymore. She must keep going. She could do it, she had to. Not for anyone else, but just for Elise. Just as Sadie had done for herself.

Elise stood and carefully folded the letter and placed it inside her pocket. She smoothed back her oily hair, bent over the cases of supplies, and began her work once more. One more day. She must work today. Tomorrow would come, and she would worry about her tomorrows when they became todays.

April moved into May, and the field hospital at Neuve-Chappelle continued to minister to the war victims efficiently and effectively. Elise had managed to survive just as her colleagues had these past weeks. There was always more work than could be accomplished in a given day. Each night, she fell exhausted into bed. But she never complained about the lack of rest or proper meals. Someday soon, the war would end. It couldn't go on forever. Until then . . .

The warm spring sun rose in the east and cast a golden aura over the field hospital. Larks circled overhead and sang sweet melodies to the dawn on the ninth day of May. Elise carried two buckets of water into the ward and began her morning task of bathing her assigned patients. They would need shipments of soap quite soon, she mused as she lathered up the washcloth.

Suddenly the air was filled with the thunder of heavy guns. Elise stood stock-still as the explosions assaulted her

317

ears. The British guns continued to boom and rain shell-fire on the German trenches. She had heard that preparations were being made for an offensive at Aubers Ridge, which was a small hill perhaps a mile and a half behind the German lines opposite Neuve-Chappelle. They couldn't be any closer to the fighting unless they were in the trenches themselves, Elise thought. All she could think of at this moment was the number of men who would meet their death this day. She dropped her washcloth and ran to the storeroom. She knew she had to prepare surgical trays. When the wounded began to come in, there would never be enough time to do all that was necessary. She had witnessed this type of action once before. She prayed that this time there would not be so many injured as in previous battles. Elise heard the voices of Dr. Brusard and Dr. Richmond issuing orders to ready the operating rooms, and so she went directly to work.

For the next three days, Elise and all the personnel at the Neuve-Chappelle field hospital toiled endlessly. Never had Elise seen so many bodies. The dead were stacked in heaps, and the wounded never stopped coming. The ambulances barely halted their rounds long enough to unload their bloody passengers before they were off again. Elise thought it was like a tidal wave of human suffering washing over them. Many died before the nurses or doctors could even see them. Soldiers hit by shrapnel were left for hours as the more critically wounded were administered to.

Elise had lost track of all time, so busy was she. Her legs ached as she pushed the cart of sterilized surgical instruments to the operating room. She thought that perhaps this time this assault would be worth the cost, for two days ago the Allies had broken through the enemy lines and had advanced more than three miles. Perhaps now they would receive more encouraging news.

She finished her rounds and decided that if she did not rest at least for a short while, she would surely collapse. She thought a breath of fresh air might rejuvenate her body and her spirits. When she walked to the door of the hospital, she was surprised to see rain. She peered out at the torrential downpour and heard both thunder and gunfire in the distance. It was difficult to tell which was which, but the black clouds cast an ominous feeling over her. Once again, her childhood dread of thunderstorms engulfed her.

The shelling had slowed, and Elise sighed her relief. She leaned against the doorjamb and felt the last bit of stamina leave her body. Her knees buckled and her chilled, numb body sank to the floor. As her eyes rolled back in her head; the thought escaped her lips: "I can't stop . . . not now . . . it's too . . . soon."

Dr. Brusard had been watching Elise as she gazed out at the storm. He started walking toward her, and when he realized she was about to faint, he raced down the corridor and caught her just in time to keep her head from hitting the floor. He cradled her in his arms and held her close to his warm chest.

"Oh, yes, Elise. It is time for you to stop. Yes, little one. It's time for you to think of yourself . . . for once. Time for you to rest."

Thirty-seven

HENRI administered a strong sedative to Elise before he let her return to Paris. He had sent word to Madeleine that she would be leaving Neuve-Chappelle at the earliest possible date. For the first time, he was concerned about Elise's recuperative powers. She had been witness to the war's desolation and had endured the deaths of her own child and a boy from her past. Her apparently limitless energies would surely fail her if she did not get some rest, and soon.

Elise gazed out the window of the ambulance with heavy eyelids. Weary soldiers marched in columns through the mud. She wondered if they knew where they were going. She knew. They were all going to Saint Ann Street. That's where all the brave people went. She wondered why she was not going to Saint Ann Street. She must not be one of the brave ones. She was not a good soldier. Yes, that was it. She had been sent away from the front. Even Henri was displeased with her. She should have told him she never pleased anyone. She failed Papa and he had booted her out of the house. Mama had always scolded her about her manners and decorum. Christopher had been greatly disappointed in her.

She slumped back against the seat. She was beginning to be aware that the sedatives she had been given were clouding her mind. As their effect began to dissipate, she realized that the events of the past months had presented her with some curious revelations. She wondered if she had simply been blind in her youthful naiveté or if it were merely that she had not previously delved deep enough into herself to discover what qualities she possessed. She had never thought of herself as a strong woman. She had always tried to cope with difficult situations to the best of her ability, but if someone had referred to her "great inner strength," Elise would have believed the comment to be absurd. She had never believed herself to be special. She knew she was different from most of her acquaintances. And she had been physically different too; she was not a classic southern beauty like Violet or Jesse.

Now, with her growth, she realized that at least some of her differences were positive ones. She was unique. Why she had not searched herself before now to puzzle together all the pieces that made her what and who she was, she didn't know. Perhaps she had not experienced enough of life to differentiate between reality and fantasy. No longer would she berate herself for the things she was not and could never be. Who was to say that the "ideal" woman was the ideal for *her* to pursue, Without wondering why, she had always balked at any restraints put upon her.

More than anything, she wanted her choices and decisions to be her own. Not only had she already made monumental decisions, though at times impulsive ones, she knew now that her reasons for those decisions were right. She was strong enough to bear the consequences and move forward with confidence in herself and her destiny. She would not live her life for others and their predetermined ideas of what she should be. She was Elise. No one could live her life for her. She was her own woman and had accepted herself, strengths and weaknesses alike.

Elise vowed not to agonize over her dilemma. What had passed before was untouchable and unchangeable. She had found herself, and she would determine what she wanted, for herself and her future. She knew she could pursue her goal without fear. It was up to her to shape her future. She had spent so many nights trying to banish Christopher from her mind and soul. What a fool she had been to think she could! He was in her blood. He was not the source of her happiness—only she could provide that—but he was its enhancement. He was what she wanted. She had come full circle from infatuation to hating him and finally, now, to committed love.

Oh, Christopher, I long for you so. I've needed you so

desperately these past months. Even though you don't want me, I want you. I will not exile you from my heart any longer. I don't want to exist in this void. If all I am to have is my memory of you and my dreams, then I will content myself with that.

Christopher, know that I love you no matter where you are. I want to fill my eyes with the sight of you. Even now, I can feel your arms around me. Will I ever feel your lips upon mine, and your hands. . . . She tried not to think about her need for him as she felt the heat rise in her loins and the very pit of her stomach fall away. The moan of longing that escaped her lips was almost lost in the air as her mind wandered into that quiet sphere of unconsciousness.

Elise tried to clear her brain of the last vestiges of Dr. Brusard's sedative as she rode through the streets of Paris to Madeleine's house. She gave the driver directions as best she could considering that her eyes would not focus properly. She was frightened by her loss of control due to the drugs. She must remember to tell Madeleine not to allow the doctor to prescribe such medication for her. She knew Henri had seen to it that she be under a physician's care until she fully recovered, and she was grateful for his concern, but she was determined not to rely upon sedatives for her cure. She shook her head from side to side and forced her eyes open and shut a few times. It was then that they entered rue du Faubourg-St. Honoré.

"There it is! This is the address," she said as she pointed to Madeleine's house.

The driver pulled to the curb and turned off the ignition. Elise got out of the cab. She took her valise from him, shook his hand, and thanked him.

"When you get back to Neuve-Chappelle, tell Dr. Brusard that I will write to him soon. And assure him that I will be fine. I may not look well, but I am going to get better," she said with determination.

"I'm sure you will. I'd better get going now," he said as he got back into the ambulance.

Elise stood on the step, turning the bell and pounding the brass knocker against the ornate door in her anticipation to see Madeleine once again. She thought she would break down the door if necessary. Suddenly it flew open.

"Madeleine! I'm back! Oh, how I've missed you," Elise

said excitedly as she hugged her friend and smiled a broad smile of happiness.

"Ma cherie! How I have missed *you!* You do not look ill to me! Henri said you were in a state of shock. Elise, what is happening?"

"Let's talk of pleasant things today, I don't want to dwell on tragedy now. Oh, you look so good to my eyes! I feel so much better just being in Paris. You have no idea!"

"Let's make some tea," Madeleine said as they went to the kitchen and prepared a light repast. Elise took out two white linen napkins bordered in delicate lace and laid them on the silver tray. She went to the huge cherry armoire where Madeleine stored her china and withdrew two yellow floral plates and teacups to match. She gazed out the window and noted the yellow roses that were blooming.

"Madeleine, roses in May? How did you do that?"

"The southern exposure is ideal for them, and I have experimented with these all winter. They bud out quickly, but alas, their blossoms also fade much too quickly. Go cut a bouquet for us to enjoy."

"Oh, no! I just couldn't. Let's leave them on the vines and let them grow. They are so lovely in their natural state. When there are more blooms, we'll fill the house with bouquets," Elise said.

"Now, let's go to the salon," Madeleine replied as Elise followed her to the beautifully appointed room.

They sat at opposite ends of the yellow silk settee. Madeleine noticed that Elise looked confused. "What is the matter, Elise? Is something wrong? Are you feeling ill?"

"No. It just seems so peculiar to be in this beautiful room, surrounded by this luxury that I always took for granted. I've grown so used to living amid such terrible conditions and having ugliness surround me that this . . . well, it sounds strange, Madeleine, but it almost hurts my eyes." Seeing the look of concern on her friend's face, Elise quickly smiled. "But I'm sure I'll become reaccustomed to it with no problems at all. Please don't worry," she added gently.

Still regarding her strangely, Madeleine spoke again.

323

"What plans have you made? Or have you even had the time to think of such things?"

"Not really. Oh, I do want to catch up on some correspondence. And once again I want to paint. But all I can think about today is the hottest, deepest, most highly scented bath I can take. I want to wash all the past weeks away. As if that were possible!" Elise said as her eyes grew sad.

"You need much more than a luxurious tub. You need rest and nourishment. It will take some time to restore you to your former lovely self," Madeleine said, and then hoped she had not hurt Elise's feelings.

"I know I look terrible! You needn't soften the blow. And you're right. It's been a long time since I had a decent meal. I think after all that has happened, I do need to think of myself.

"And I must write home about Andrew. It's something I've got to do. Not yet, though, because I don't think I could find the words. I just need some time to collect my thoughts and make some decisions about my future. Just believing I have a future at all has been a major accomplishment for me."

"I have a special dinner planned for just the two of us this evening," Madeleine said. "You take your bath. Oh! I have some homecoming gifts for you. They're upstairs on your bed. I think they will help lift your spirits. When you're ready, I'll order some fine writing paper for you. We'll make everything special and we'll both pretend the war doesn't exist."

"You didn't need to buy gifts for me! I'm happy just to be here with you. You know that," Elise said. Then she giggled with delight and said, "But I'm glad you did. Isn't that selfish? It's been so long since anyone gave me anything, it almost seems like Christmas! Isn't it wonderful?"

"Yes. Now you go upstairs and bathe and rest while I prepare our dinner. Nothing but the best food tonight!" Madeleine said.

Elise entered the bathroom and immediately spied the large glass container of bath salts with a huge yellow bow around it. Elise pulled the stopper out and took a deep whiff.

"Lavender! She remembered!" she exclaimed as she filled the tub with water and almost half the salts. She gathered the hard-milled bar of soap, some shampoo, and a sponge. She laid a large fluffy towel on the small cane chair near the tub. She stripped the stained dress from her body along with her undergarments and stockings. She threw them all into a pile and said, "Those I'll burn myself!" As she stepped into the soothing, silky water, she thought that a bath had never felt so marvelous. She found it impossible to believe that she had not bathed like this for over two months. There had been time and water enough only for sponge baths at the field hospital. The thought of life at the front made her stomach churn.

"Not today, dammit!" She was in Paris! There had been times during the past weeks when she believed that she would never see the lights of the city again. She lathered her body with the soap and scrubbed her skin vigorously. After shampooing, she stepped from the tub, wrapped her body in the towel, and went to the mirror.

Her skin was very pale, and she realized that all her freckles had faded completely. Her eyes had a piercing look she had not seen before, and they appeared much larger than normal, for her face was noticeably thinner. Hollows rested in her cheeks, and she knew it would take more than a bath in lavender to restore her rosy glow.

The face that gazed at her was the face of a woman. Deep sorrow, loss, and love, too, filled her eyes. The ordeals she had faced could be read in her expression.

But she knew there were many whose lives were far more difficult than hers. And she knew that she was still recovering from the deaths of Andrew and her baby.

With a strong effort of will, she forced the hurtful memories from her brain. She donned one of Madeleine's crimson silk and organza peignoirs. Over her shoulder she glanced at herself in the mirror and was surprised at how the deep red brought out the blue of her eyes and enhanced the highlights of her hair.

She bent down and brushed her hair till it was completely dry. She laid the tortoiseshell brush on the vanity and left the bathroom. As she went into her room, she noted the prettily wrapped boxes on the bed. With delight she pulled the white piqué ribbon from the huge dress box. She lifted the lid, pulled away the tissue paper, and discovered a tailored white linen skirt and a pale blue and white striped cotton blouse. The next box contained a complete set of hand-embroidered lingerie. The remaining gift was a pair of white kid pumps to complete the ensemble. Elise took her new clothes and laid them on the bed. It did seem like Christmas! She sat on the edge of the bed and remembered those happy holiday times of her childhood. When she thought of the candles, mistletoe, holly, and, of course, the tree, a vision of Jesse's face filled her mind's eye.

Jesse! I have called for you in my dreams and in my pain many times. I know that you can help me. You are all that remains of my past, of those innocent, carefree days, she thought as she concentrated on the image of her friend.

Elise crossed to the small French writing desk and rifled the drawers searching for stationery. She couldn't wait for Madeleine to place that order; she had to write to Jesse immediately. It was only right that she be informed of Andrew's passing. Most of all, she wanted Jesse to know that she was greatly missed and loved; and she thought it would relieve Jesse's mind to know that Elise was not in any danger. She found a small stack of paper, and as she sat before the open French doors, and warm spring breezes washed over the room, she wrote her best friend about her deepest feelings and her personal tragedies.

Almost two hours had elapsed when Elise finished the letter to Jesse and laid her pen down. Madeleine knocked at the door and entered upon Elise's response.

"Elise? Have you rested at all? Oh, I see you have been busy writing. And you look much better after your bath," Madeleine chuckled.

"Thank you for the beautiful clothes, Madeleine. You should not have been so extravagant," Elise said, "but I needed them very much, and I love them."

"I had so much fun choosing them. Come now and enjoy supper. Bring your letter and we'll post it in the morning," Madeleine said.

"How long will it take for it to reach Zurich?" Elise asked as they left the bedroom and walked down the stairs.

"It could take some time. However, I have some friends who have established a private underground. Among other things, they have a marvelous courier service. If I should contact my friend, your letter could be there in just a few days."

"Intrigue, Madeleine? How did you meet these people? Was it through Karl?"

"No, Elise. Not through the baron. These people were my friends long before the war began. Out of necessity, many in my station in life found it imperative they discover a new vocation. You must understand what I am trying to say. No, they are my dear and trusted friends. I most definitely did not meet them through Karl."

Elise detected a strained note in Madeleine's speech. Something had changed. Had they had a lover's quarrel? Was that it? No, she thought, it was more significant than just a lover's spat. There was a stiffness in Madeleine's voice and demeanor. And there was something else. This reference to espionage puzzled Elise, but she did know better than to question her further. Perhaps later Madeleine might want to confide in her, but not just now.

They entered the breakfast room, and Elise gazed wide-eyed at the beautiful table before her. It was covered with a full-length black moiré taffeta skirt that was, in turn, topped with a square of snowy linen. A silver bowl filled with yellow roses rested in the center of the table. It was flanked with a pair of sterling candlesticks with flickering white tapers. The pure-white china was banded in a scroll of black design on the wide lip, and a circle of gold edged the rim. Crystal flutes were filled with bubbling champagne. Elise marveled at the scene and thought the twinkling stars in the cloudless black sky created the perfect backdrop. She hugged Madeleine tightly.

"Thank you, my dear friend. I have needed this night. You have done so much and I haven't given you anything."

Madeleine's lips spread in a smile, but her eyes were sad. "You have given me a reason to celebrate life once more when I thought there was nothing worthwhile left for me. But enough of this, sit down! I hope you'll approve of my culinary efforts!"

Elise lifted her fork to spear the red snapper, and as she tasted the delicate fish, she pondered Madeleine's words.

Thirty-eight

THE blossoms of Madeleine's small gardens filled the late-May morning air with fragrance. Elise clipped a dew-kissed rose from the leafy cane and laid the bloom in her flat straw basket. The cool air was slightly damp with that silky feeling she had not enjoyed for over a year. Elise sat upon a white wrought iron chair and toyed with the lavender grosgrain ribbon that held her hair away from her face. She lifted her face to meet the warm pink dawn rays of light that filtered through the emerald leaves of the chestnut trees. The apple trees had lost the last of their pink and white blossoms, and the ground beneath them was blanketed in the aromatic petals.

Her eyes scanned the loveliness about her and her mind wandered back to Mobile, for it had been a year ago that she had met Christopher. And soon, too, she would be celebrating her twenty-first birthday. She remembered her birthday last year with Christopher and the bracelet of blue diamonds she'd been forced to sell.

As she gazed at the blue heavens, she remembered that his eyes were the same sky blue. As if it were yesterday, she felt herself drown in his eyes and fall under his spell. At the thought of his ability to play the chords and strings of her body, she felt her breath quicken; she moaned low in her throat.

"Oh, God! Why do I torture myself so? And how could so much have happened to me in just one year?"

It was more than just the war. All her experiences had changed her so much that many times she wondered just who she was. She believed she was still giving and loving, but she had discovered a great strength that had enabled her to deal with the loss and sorrow of these past months.

She was still very vulnerable, perhaps even more so than before, but she was not naive, and she knew more clearly what she wanted out of life. And what she wanted was Christopher.

She wondered if he were here in Paris. It had been six months since she had seen him in that taxicab. When she thought of the events that occurred after that meeting, she winced at the pain that shot through her. She banished the feeling and gazed back at the trees overhead.

Madeleine walked up behind her and dropped the thick white envelope into her lap.

"Voilà! You see my friends are quite capable. Not as efficient as I had hoped, but I was informed that they remained in Zurich until your friend could send this reply to you. And I can see by the look on your face that this makes you happy! I will bring you some hot coffee while you read your letter," she said as she disappeared into the house.

"Thank you," Elise replied as she tore open the letter.

My Dearest Elise,

I was so thrilled to receive your letter. You have no idea how I have missed you. I should scold you, for I have done nothing but worry about you every minute of every day. I was so afraid you might have left Europe. I had no idea how to reach you. Elise, never do that again. Always let me know where you are.

Elise, words cannot express my deep sorrow at Andrew's death. It must have been dreadful for you. In a way, I'm glad you were there. Sometimes, I think it best that one of us was with him. All I can do is remember the days when we meant so much to each other. We were such happy children, then, weren't we? My only regret is that I was not with him at the last.

My poor Elise! To have watched him die in your arms. I wish I could be there to comfort you. There is no way that I can come to you. However, I have spoken at great length with Wil about the situation. We both feel that you have remained in Paris much too long and that now, more than ever before, you need someone. Elise, I want you to come to Zurich. Not just for a visit but to live with us. We have enough room, and you know you are welcome. Actually, all the details have been planned and by the time you receive this (from the strange-looking courier you sent) all preparations will be under way.

Wil has spoken with friends who are much involved in the French underground. After many hours of discussion and planning, they have devised what I hope will be a successful escape route. It will be difficult and could be dangerous, but it's imperative you come to Zurich.

Whether you want to hear this or not (but I feel you do), we have received news of Christopher's whereabouts. I can't tell you much in this letter, but he does need our help, for he is in great danger. Even if you want nothing to do with Christopher, Wil and I are committed to him and his safety. We still want you to be here in Zurich with us where you will be safe and with those who love you. I do miss you so, Elise. I can't wait to see you once again. I think I probably won't be able to keep my mouth shut for at least twenty-four hours after you arrive. I have so much to tell you. Au revoir for now, my friend, and I will see you soon.

> All my thoughts and love,
> Your Jesse

P.S. Enclosed are Wil's instructions for your trip to Zurich.

Elise's heart was pounding as she turned over the page. In a masculine scrawl, Wilhelm had sketched out a map. Certain towns were designated with arrows and stars. The list of instructions was quite detailed, and Elise was impressed that he had been able to confirm all these arrangements in such a short period of time.

At dawn on Wednesday, she was to meet with Jacques Arnaud at a house just south of the city. Elise referred to the map, noting the point indicated for the meeting. They were to assume the guise of a farmer and his wife and travel southeast by horseback past Belfort, France, to Château-de-Fonds, which lay across the Swiss border. This forested area would conceal them in their crossing into Swiss territory should they encounter any unfriendly forces. Upon their arrival Elise would then board the train bound for Basel, and from there she would travel by rail to Zurich. According to Wilhelm's directions, the journey would not take more than four days. It was approximately two hundred and twenty-five miles from Paris to Belfort, and the train trip was less than four hours, including stops en route.

Inside the envelope Elise found a rail schedule that Wilhelm had included. The expected date of departure had been marked with an asterisk, and he had attached her ticket to the form.

While traveling through France, two of their overnight stops would be at the homes of fellow underground activists. The very first night they would be expected in Joigny, which was situated on the river Yonne. From here they would travel to Montbard, then to Dijon, and finally to Château-de-Fonds.

Elise stared at the letter and then took up the map. She could not believe it! It was all arranged, and she would be with Jesse soon. Now she must pack and say her good-byes to Madeleine. She was saddened at the impending departure from this very special person who had been through such sad times with her, but Elise knew she would see Madeleine again. They would always be a part of each other's lives, of that much she was certain.

But she was confused about this reference to Christopher and the danger he was in. At the thought of him, she felt a thrill—and then apprehension. If she went to Zurich, how could she possibly see him or help him? A thousand questions perplexed her, and now she felt the need to find the answers. She *must* go to Zurich.

She rose from the garden chair and went back into the house. She found Madeleine pouring coffee in the breakfast room. Elise searched her brain for the proper way to tell Madeleine of her trip.

She looked into her face, and before she could say anything, Madeleine said, "This letter you received has changed things somehow, has it not?" she asked.

"How did you know?" Elise asked in surprise.

"I can tell from the look on your face. Don't be so sad. Now tell me what you wish to say."

"Jesse has arranged for me to go to Zurich. Her friend has gone to great lengths to arrange everything for me."

"Is there any danger? You won't be too close to enemy lines, will you?" Madeleine querried anxiously.

"No, we'll be far from the fighting. We cross the Swiss border at a point where I will be quite safe, I'm sure. Please don't worry about me. I don't think Jesse would press me to make this journey unless she believed that all would go well. She knows the events of my past weeks. No, I'm sure that everything will be just fine," Elise replied.

"Well, if that is the way things must be . . ." Madeleine said with a despondent sigh. "I suppose it's best we concentrate on the matters at hand. We have much work to do before you leave."

"Oh, Madeleine! I'll miss you so very much. You have been so kind to me, always giving your time and yourself. It seems that all I ever do is say thank you."

"Please! Don't thank me. Even with all the sorrow you have had in your life, you have brought so much happiness to me. Never forget that, will you? That is what friendship means. It is easy to be companions during the good times, but to have shared the difficult days and remain close, that is the basis of the relationship we have," Madeleine said.

"You are so wise, Madeleine."

As they finished their coffee, Elise wondered if she would ever gain such keen insight as Madeleine possessed.

Elise paid the cab driver with crisp new francs, then watched the vehicle speed down the dusty country road on its return to Paris. After a few moments, she turned her head to survey the dilapidated structure behind her. The foundation sagged under the weight of the weathered gray boards that formed the walls. The four posts that supported the porch roof appeared ready to split. Elise doubted that it would be safe to enter. She had retreated a a few steps when a man appeared in the open doorway.

He was young, she thought, not quite thirty years old. His body was lean and muscular with wide square shoulders and very narrow hips. From beneath a short mustache, perfect white teeth flashed a roguish smile at her. He walked toward her with a swagger, and she was leery of his abundant self-confidence until she saw the warmth in his eyes. He extended his hand to her.

"Hello! I am Jacques. You are Mrs. Mann?"

Elise nodded uncertainly.

She was confused, because he was nothing like she had expected. She had conjured of a picture of a short, balding man who would, in fatherly fashion, assist her on her journey. The reality of Jacques Arnaud had little in common with her notion of a member of the French underground.

"It appears that I have somehow disappointed you, Mrs. Mann?"

"Oh, no. It's not that at all. It's just that, well, I had expected someone slightly older."

"I'm afraid that for a mission such as this, a younger person will prove to be more valuable, Mrs. Mann," he laughed.

"Please, call me Elise. Since we are to be traveling together, I think we might drop the formalities," she said responding to his smile.

"I think you are right. Actually, we will refer to you as Elise Arnaud should we encounter any others upon our travels. I have packed the saddlebags with the necessary provisions."

"I assume, then, that we are ready to depart?"

"Most definitely! The horses are tied in back of the house here," he answered, nodding in the direction of the building. He eyed her suitcase skeptically and then looked back at her.

"Is that bag necessary? I didn't bring a pack horse, I thought it best to travel as light as possible in hopes of keeping to the schedule."

"Well," she mused, looking at the suitcase, "I suppose I could take out the things that I'll need and put them in the saddlebags. Is that all right?"

"Of course! I'll get the horses."

Elise unstrapped the leather bindings and flipped through her belongings.

"Now what on earth do I really need? And what should I leave behind?" She withdrew a white cotton shirt, a hairbrush, and a riding skirt. She rolled them together and as Jacques steadied the horse, she placed the articles in the saddlebag.

Moments later they were on their way south. Much of the area was covered in low shrubs and was only sparsely dotted by an occasional tree. They kept close to the river as much as possible, for it ran directly along their route. They kept a steady pace as the morning passed, and each was lost in his thought. It was not until Elise's stomach began to growl that she realized how late it was.

"Jacques . . . do you think we could stop soon for something to eat?" she asked as he slowed his horse in order to hear what she was saying.

"I hadn't planned on it. Let's see how much farther we can go before we need to rest," he replied as he urged his horse on.

A frustrated frown creased Elise's brow; she was somewhat annoyed at his indifference to her request. But she couldn't blame him for wanting to keep to Wilhelm's schedule. He undoubtedly had only their safety in mind, but she was tired and hungry all the same.

The afternoon stretched into long weary hours for Elise, and she wondered from what source this man drew his stamina. Just then he signaled to her and headed his horse toward the river's edge. She followed, and they sat in silence while the horses drank the clear water.

Elise let her eyes wander to the cloudless blue sky above and then rolled her head about her stiff neck.

"I know you are not used to such travel, but I wouldn't be pushing us so hard and so fast if it weren't necessary. We have only another four hours' ride until we can rest for the night," he said watching her shift in the saddle to ease the soreness in her back.

"Four hours? That sounds an eternity to me!" she exclaimed as she peered into his face.

"Don't forget, this is only the first day of our journey. We have a long way to go." He noticed that she rubbed her neck with her hand.

"Don't worry," he said "When we stop tonight, I'll help you get rid of that stiff neck. I've been told I give an excellent massage," he said playfully.

Elise flicked at the reins and turned her mare away from the river as she replied stiffly, "I doubt I'll need your services." She galloped away, leaving him startled and confused. He spurred his horse until he caught up with her. He leaned out of his saddle and pulled at her horse's reins until she came to a halt.

"I think we had better straighten out this misunderstanding right here and now! I was not making any advances toward you, Elise. You are uncomfortable and I just thought I could help. That's all. I'm sorry if I upset you, and I apologize." His eyes held such an honest and concerned look that Elise believed him and nodded her head.

"All right, Jacques. It's my fault. I'm afraid of so many things these days. All I can think about is getting to Zurich and finding my husband," she said sadly.

A strange look passed over Jacques' eyes, but he quickly answered her with a broad grin.

"Then that's what we shall do," he said as he sped away like the wind. Elise dug her heels into the mare's flanks, and within minutes she was riding beside Jacques once again.

The Daumiers' farm loomed in the distance. It was much larger than Elise had imagined it would be. There were three structures, and she had difficulty discerning just which was the house. As they drew closer, the sun set, and within the structure that sat off to the left of the other building, lights burned. One of the inhabitants stood in the open doorway, silhouetted by the interior light. Jacques rode ahead of Elise and gave the man a signal, which the latter acknowledged.

Jacques dismounted. He approached the man and shook his hand, and they conversed quickly while Elise sat expectantly.

Soon he returned to her. "Everything is in order. They are expecting us. So we shall be the guests of the Daumier family this evening, Madame Arnaud."

"Jacques! They don't think I am your wife, do they?" Elise asked in shock.

"No, no. You are my sister-in-law. We certainly are having a problem guarding your honor, aren't we?" Jacques replied tersely. "I do wish you felt a bit more secure in my presence," he said, gazing into her eyes. Then he took her hand and led her into the house.

Elise thought that every muscle, nerve ending, bone, and joint in her body had been taxed to its limit. Never had she ached so much. She had not been able to rest that night, for when her body was not causing her pain, concern about her safety and Christopher's made sleep an impossibility.

She eased her legs over the edge of the bed and let her feet rest upon the rough-hewn planking of the floor. The Daumiers had been kind and thoughtful, and when they offered her their own bedroom, she had declined, but they insisted. Too tired to argue about anything, she had relented. Now she could smell the welcome aroma of breakfast sausages and hot breads. She clutched her stomach as it growled loudly. She had been so exhausted upon their arrival the previous night that she had accepted only some fruit and cheese before retiring.

She rose cautiously from the bed. With pained difficulty, she straightened her back as she crossed to the washbasin. She splashed cool water on her face and arms, then dried off with a course linen towel. She donned a clean shirt, but stepped into the same skirt she had worn yesterday and opened the door to the large keeping room.

"I must be the last to wake up!" she said, surprised to find Jacques conversing with Monsieur and Madame Daumier over mugs of hot coffee.

Jacques looked up and smiled warmly at her. "If you had not come out soon, I was about to send Madame Daumier after you. We must get started, but come and have something to eat."

"Thank you. I think I could eat everything in sight, I'm so ravenous," she laughed as she accepted a heaping plate. She ate quickly and drank a large mug of coffee.

"It is time we left. The horses have been readied and we have another day of hard riding ahead of us."

Elise turned to the two Daumiers and said: "Thank you for all you have done. It means a great deal to me that you would be so kind to someone you don't even know." She smiled at them as she rose and went out the door.

Jacques followed her out after thanking the couple himself, and within minutes they were on their way. Elise had believed that since her muscles were sore, she would never be able to endure another day of horseback riding. However, before noon she rode quite easily. She was as determined as Jacques to reach their destination. She knew no hunger, and only at his insistence did they stop to water the horses or rest.

They traveled through or around the towns of Migennes and Tonnerre to Montbard. They crossed over the Yonne River, and after nightfall found a wooded area just north of Montbard in which to bed down for the night. Their evening meal consisted of leftover breads from Madame Daumier's kitchen, some cheeses, and cold chicken. Once again Elise found she was too exhausted to eat much, and she almost fell asleep while nibbling on a piece of bread.

"I think it's time for me to get the bedrolls out, don't you, Mrs. Mann?" Jacques asked with a yawn.

Elise nodded an assent as her eyelids threatened to close for the last time that night.

Jacques unrolled the blankets for her and eased her back into a supine position. Before he could speak another word, she was sound asleep. He put the remains of their supper away and stretched out upon the soft earth, cradling his head upon his saddle blanket. He raised his arms and crossed them underneath his head, and just before he fell asleep his last thoughts were of the brilliant stars above them and the beautiful woman who slept next to him.

Before the rays of dawn revealed themselves, Elise and Jacques were mounted and on their way to Dijon. And this was not the last day of this torturous journey, Elise thought as the sound of the horses' hooves beat against the earth beneath them. Each moment and each jarring movement would well be worth it if she could once again be with Christopher; she could endure anything for him. At least now she could do something constructive toward bringing about a reunion. This was so much better than filling endless hours waiting for something to happen.

She felt so very much alive. She was taking charge of the events in her life, and the thought helped to bolster her courage. She pressed her knees into the mare's sides and urged her to a greater speed. How she wished this horse were winged like Pegasus, so that she could fly to the one man in the world who could make her truly happy.

As she sped along, she saw Christopher's face in her mind, and the miles and hours rushed into the past.

Jacques and Elise reached Dijon well ahead of schedule. They went to the inn where they were to meet Monsieur Frouard, the underground member who would shelter them for the night. The inn was quite rustic. There was an enormous stone fireplace on the far eastern wall. The ceilings were beamed, and a railed balcony overlooked the large open dining area. The guest rooms were off the balcony on the second floor, she guessed. Huge antique brass and wood chandeliers hung at three different locations down the center of the room.

Jacques gestured toward a table, and Elise preceded him to the one nearest the window. She stared outside while Jacques ordered wine and dinner for them both.

"Why such a sad look, Elise?" he asked with concern.

"Is it sad? I wasn't thinking about anything sad. At least I don't think so. Except for the fact that I'm very much in love with a man who does not love me."

"That is the greatest of all tragedies, I would think," he responded.

"There are other tragedies," she said quickly, remembering the past.

"And you have known some of these sorrows, haven't you?" he asked, peering deep into her eyes.

Elise shrugged her shoulders, not wanting to discuss the experiences that had left their mark upon her spirit and her life. "I've known a few. I'm sure there are many others who have endured more than I." She sighed, and hoped the tears that threatened to fill her eyes would abate.

"Tomorrow I'll put you on that train bound for Zurich and soon you will be with those who love you. That's as it should be. Whether you know it or not, you are even now with someone who has fallen a little bit in love with you."

Elise, incredulous, stared at him. "You can't mean that. You don't even know me."

"There is something about you. Your genuineness, honesty, and your . . . vulnerability. I am sure I am not the only one who loves you. There are probably many you don't even know of. But I know that after tomorrow I shall never see you again. So I thought I should tell you. I don't want you to act any differently toward me, because of this knowledge. I just hope someday I'll meet someone else who will remind me of you and that I will be able to feel this way again."

"Please, Jacques . . ."

"I know. But there was nothing you could do about it. You were just being yourself and that's why I fell in love with you. Don't you see that? Ah! Look! Here comes our dinner. Now, dry your eyes and be happy, because I am very happy."

"You are a very special man, Jacques Arnaud, and I will never forget you. You have risked your life for me. But even more, you have risked your heart and that takes a great deal of courage," she said gazing into his emerald eyes.

Jacques looked embarrassed, but he smiled. "Now eat! Monsieur Frouard will be here soon to interrupt us, I am sure!"

Elise began to eat her omelet. She had almost finished when they were approached by the innkeeper, a man of about sixty years, who wore a white apron over his trousers and shirt.

"I see that you like our simple country fare," he said.

"Why, yes," Jacques replied. "It's very good, Monsieur . . ."

"Frouard. And you are Jacques Arnaud. You will take rooms eight and ten." He said the words flatly, tossed two keys on the table, and left.

"Did you know that our contact is the owner?" Elise asked.

"No," he answered. "One never knows where help will come from."

Elise suddenly felt exhausted. "If you don't mind, I'd like to take my key and go upstairs. I could use some rest. In a real bed."

"I understand. I'll finish my wine. Go ahead. See you in the morning."

"Thank you, Jacques." She rose and crossed the room to the staircase.

Elise had rested well, and just knowing she would soon be on a train bound for Zurich caused her heart to swell with anticipation. Jacques had informed her that La Château-de-Fonds was at least a day and a half away from Dijon. They adhered to the route that Wilhelm had marked. As long as they remained deep in the country-side, they would not encounter any troops or warfare. With this route they would be able to bypass the trenches, and any potential danger from the enemy.

They had been most fortunate in not encountering bad weather. Each day had been glorious, and Elise felt free, riding in the sunshine with the wind blowing through her hair. No longer did her muscles ache; her requests for rest periods had become nonexistent.

At the day's outset she had thought their being so close to the border and yet so far from it would cause the hours to drag, but such was not the case. Now she was surprised to discover the sun was going down, and in only an hour or so they would find it necessary to search for a camp. They were nearing Besançon when Jacques mentioned the possibility of renting a hotel room for the night, know-ing Elise would prefer that to sleeping under the stars. But she remembered that Wilhelm had warned Jacques not to take chances.

"I don't mind sleeping outdoors, Jacques. It's a beauti-ful night. All I want is to get to that train."

"Then there will be that much less ground to cover to-morrow, and you'll be on that train wtih time to spare," he said.

Night covered the countryside in indigo tints, cool tem-peratures, and soft breezes. They were nearing the Jura mountains, and Jacques found a small clearing just be-yond a clump of tall evergreen trees for their camp. He unsaddled and tended the horses while Elise unwrapped the remnants of their provisions.

"There certainly isn't much here," Elise told Jacques as he approached her and laughed at the look of dismay upon her face.

"What's so funny? This is all we have!" she exclaimed, holding up some stale bread and a half bottle of wine.

"Oh, come now, it's not all that bad. Look at the brighter side."

"You mean there is one?"

"Sure. We could have nothing at all!"

"I suppose you're right. I'm so exhausted that it doesn't matter anyway." She took the bedroll from his outstretched hands and curled up on the blanket. Before she could finish a small piece of bread, she fell fast asleep.

Jacques watched her for quite some time before he took the bread from her hand and covered her. He brushed her forehead with his lips. He finished what remained of the wine, and then he too slipped away into sleep.

Jacques was wakened by an anxious Elise as she nudged his shoulder and shook his arm.

"Jacques . . . for heaven's sake, wake up! Today is the day! Jacques . . ."

He rubbed his eyes and tried to focus on her face.

"I've already saddled my horse. I thought the commotion I made would wake you. You must have been more tired than you thought. We need to get started if I am to meet that train. And we have yet to pass through the mountains."

He yawned and stretched his arms over his head.

"Don't worry about the mountains. There is a narrow pass we will use. It isn't that far, anyway. Now do you feel better?"

Elise playfully grasped the edge of the blanket and pulled it out from under him as he rolled off to one side.

"I'll feel better only when we're on our way," she said as she bundled up the blanket and handed it back to him. "Since it isn't that far, we can have a very large lunch before I board the train. I'm starving already."

He laughed. "Very well, Madame, we'll depart."

Still, it was well past two o'clock when they reached town. Jacques handed Elise her tickets and the papers necessary to cross the border to Basel. The train stop was located just south of town, and they found they did not have time to make stops of any kind. Elise dismounted and gathered her belongings as they awaited the approach of the train.

In the distance they heard the whistle blow, and Elise stood on the wooden riser. There were no other passengers in sight. Just as the train scratched its iron wheels against the rails, creating silver sparks through clouds of steam vapor, she turned to Jacques and placed her hand against his cheek.

"Thank you for all you have done for me."

"You are very special, Elise. Never forget that. Goodbye." He smiled tenderly.

"Good-bye, Jacques." Quickly, she stepped onto the iron steps. Clutching the saddlebag against her chest, she grasped the metal hand bar with her free hand.

"Good luck, Elise!" he called as she disappeared into the train.

The train pulled into the Zurich terminal just before nightfall, just slightly behind schedule. Elise thanked the conductor as he aided her down the steps and onto the landing, where Wilhelm was waiting for her. He took her bag and led her toward the carriage he had hired.

"You look wonderful, Elise. And I know that the journey you had was not any easy one," he said.

"It wasn't all that bad. All I could think about was seeing Jesse again. And of course, Christopher."

"As soon as we arrive at the chalet, Jesse and I will tell you about Christopher. There is a great deal you do not know, and it's time you discovered the truth about many things."

Elise took his arm. "Tell me, is Jesse all right?"

"Jesse is perfect!" he said, flashing his white teeth and allowing his happiness to fill his eyes and face.

At that moment Elise realized for the first time just what Jesse had meant when she had described their relationship as a "great love." Elise was truly happy for her friend. And now she was filled with hope—hope for the future for all of them.

Elise felt anticipation mount within her. Night had fallen quite rapidly, and she barely noticed the beautiful landscape around her as they journeyed down the country road. She toyed with the ring on her finger, and as she glanced down at it, she noticed how it glistened even in the faint light of the moon. This was Christopher's ring. For the first time in almost a year, she realized she had never removed it. She was bound to him by law just as she was bound to him by love.

When she looked up she realized they were almost to the chalet. Elise sat upright and grabbed the edge of the seat. The driver reined in the horses and they halted before the house. Elise fumbled with the latch, trying to get out as fast as she could. She started running toward the house, where Jesse stood on the balcony.

"Elise, Elise! Here I am up here! Hurry up!" she cried.

Jesse hurried inside, and she and Elise reached the middle of the spacious room almost simultaneously. They hugged each other tightly. Elise stood back and looked at Jesse.

"How is it possible for you to be even more beautiful than you were when I saw you last?" Elise asked her, feeling complete joy in her heart.

"It must be all the love Wil gives me," Jesse laughed.

"Jesse! You never change, do you?"

"No, she never does," Wilhelm said as he entered the room. "And I wouldn't have it any other way, believe me!"

"Isn't he gorgeous, Elise?" Jesse giggled as she stared after his vanishing form.

"Oh, Elise. I feel so wonderful now that we are all together. I've made a special supper for us tonight. It'll be just like a holiday."

"It *is* a holiday for me, and it's been so long since I've had a special day," Elise said with a deep sigh.

"I know. You have had enough heartache to last a lifetime. But no more, Elise. We have so much to discuss and so much news to tell you," Jesse said in a mysterious tone.

Elise flashed Jesse a puzzled look as her friend motioned for her to sit on the leather sofa and then disappeared into the kitchen.

Elise heard their laughter coming from the kitchen. Then Wilhelm was saying something to Jesse. Elise heard Jesse's muffled response, and now there was dead silence. Elise smiled to herself.

Her eyes clouded when she remembered that he had been a participant in the assassination. She wondered just how much Jesse knew about this man and his past.

Did she know that her lover was indirectly responsible for a double murder? Surely she must not, or she could never feel for him the things that she did. But then, she thought, she possessed full knowledge of Christopher's role in that great tragedy, and she knew deep in her heart that if Christopher were here at this moment, she would fall into his arms. She would not question him first; she would accept him and do everything in her power to make him love her.

Her mind wandered back to Jesse; she thought that perhaps Wilhelm didn't truly love Jesse that much, since he had not married her. Why wouldn't he give her his name?

What more could any man want than Jesse? She was totally devoted to him. Jesse was a freethinker and loved romance and life, but she was not quite this bohemian. She could only make permanent commitments. There must be some reason . . .

Wilhelm stood over the dark-haired girl, and to gain her attention, he clinked the wineglasses together.

"You were miles away just then," he said with a warm grin.

Elise jumped slightly as her reverie was broken. "Nothing important, I guess," she said, taking the glass from his hand.

He put the other two glasses on the table beside the sofa and popped the cork off the champagne bottle with his fingertips. The cork almost hit Jesse, who was approaching with a tray of canapés.

"What's this? Machine-gun fire from the German High Command? Need I dig a trench now, Wil?" she laughed.

Elise lifted her glass toward her friends. "To our eternal friendship," she said, tears glistening in her eyes.

Jesse and Wilhelm lifted their glasses to her. "To you, dearest Elise," Jesse murmured.

They were all silent for a moment. Then Wilhelm looked at Jesse, and she at him.

"Elise, we have a lot to discuss with you," Wilhelm said. "We brought you here under false pretenses. It's true that Jesse has missed you tremendously, but there is another reason we wanted you to be here in Zurich. I have to leave soon for a dangerous mission, and I thought it would be best if Jesse had you here with her. That's a rather selfish reason for bringing you all the way from Paris. Nevertheless, it is the truth," he said.

"I don't care what reasons you had. I'm very happy to be here. I can't think of any place I'd rather be, except for maybe . . ." Her voice trailed into a sigh.

"With Christopher? Is that what you were going to say?" Jesse asked as she saw Elise's woeful face.

"Yes I suppose I was," Elise said, choking back her tears.

"Elise, that is precisely what we wish to explain to you. Since late last November, I have spent most of my time trying to locate Christopher," Wilhelm replied.

"Oh, I could have told you where he was. He was in

Paris with his mistress. I . . . I happened to see them together in a taxicab one day," she said as she recalled those horrid memories.

"No, Elise, You did not see him with his mistress, because he does *not* have one!" Wilhelm stated firmly.

"He most certainly does! I've seen her numerous times. Once on the ship when we crossed the Atlantic. I saw her in Sarajevo, and then in Paris. She is very beautiful. I can see why he loves her," Elise lamented.

"I'm telling you, she is not his mistress. She had red hair, didn't she, Elise?" he demanded.

"Yes! How did you know that?"

"Because I know her too. Her name is Liza Garrett. She is a business associate, and she is part of an explanation both Jesse and I feel you are greatly entitled to."

"What are you trying to tell me?"

"All this time Christopher has kept the truth from you, because he was greatly concerned about your safety. I told him he was making a mistake, but he wouldn't listen to me. I know that the reason you fled Sarajevo was because you overheard a conversation he and I had at the Embassy Ball the night before the assassination. That's the way it happened, wasn't it, Elise?" he asked her.

"Yes, but how . . . ?"

"It wasn't difficult to figure it all out. I want to explain what was actually happening. You have a lot of misconceptions about your husband. Firstly, I suppose I should tell you that Christopher and I are not the villains you believe us to be. Actually, we are both employed by the United States Government.

"The details probably don't matter so much as the fact that the American government was very well aware of the assassination plot. We were not the precipitators of that foul deed. We merely were there to ensure that no one else would be involved. There was a great conspiracy to instigate this war. But no one, to my knowledge, ever believed it would become anything more than a localized war. In fact, Christopher and I were hoping, through our efforts, to stop such a catastrophe as we're seeing from actually coming to pass. Although our actions appeared on the surface to be those of the conspirators, we endeavored as best we could to save lives."

Wilhelm took a sip of wine and continued.

"Then, in the midst of all the confusion of our assignment and Christopher's own personal turmoil over the morality of his duties, you disappeared. Elise, he spent weeks trying to find you. He would have searched the face of Europe if the war had not progressed so rapidly. After we flew here and he realized he had just missed you, he was instructed to go to Paris to open our offices. I don't know how you managed to evade him, but I do know he never gave up looking for you. He had detectives combing half of France. He knew you had departed the train in Paris, but at that point he lost you. On November twenty-eighth I received my last communiqué from him. Liza Garrett, who is also an American agent, had relayed his final orders, and they were discussing his last rendezvous with an enemy contact when you saw them in that cab. The next morning both he and Liza were captured by an important German agent," he said. He paused to give Elise some time to digest all what he had said.

"She . . . she is an agent? She isn't his mistress?" she asked. "Oh, my God. If only I hadn't run away. If I hadn't fallen . . ." Her voice fell off. She was engulfed by despair as she realized the deadly impact of her foolishness.

"No!" Jesse pleaded. "Don't even think it, Elise! It wasn't your fault! What happened with your child was God's will. Whatever happened was meant to be. Remember that! You cannot change the past. Please, Elise. Don't dwell on it. You must think of the future now, and Christopher is your future. You must see that!" Jesse put her arm around the trembling shoulders of her friend, hoping to shield her from her guilt.

"Elise," said Wilhelm as he moved toward her and took her icy hands in his own strong ones. "Just as you feel you bear the guilt for the death of your child, so does Christopher feel guilt for the assassination—and for your misfortunes. Perhaps if you look at it that way, you might be better able to understand his remorse. Do you think you can do that?" he asked.

She raised her tear-streaked face to gaze into Wilhelm's eyes, and she could see the concern he felt for his friend. It was the same expression she saw in Jesse's face. Elise realized that Christopher had been as blessed in his relationship with Wilhelm as she had been in hers with Jesse. She felt comforted once again and begged Wilhelm to continue.

"Where is he now? What has happened to him?"

"We don't know all the details, but we do know that for the next forty-eight hours, perhaps seventy-two at the outside, he is imprisoned in a farmhouse in Germany near Neustadt. I have my men watching the area for even a slight change in routine that might indicate they intend to transfer him to some outpost or a prison camp. Because he is a spy, I am assuming they will not allow him to see other prisoners. Someone has some personal vendetta against him, and I have no idea why. I've been trying to puzzle that one out for weeks," he mused.

"Do you have any idea who this person is?" Elise asked.

"I know who. I just don't know why. The man who trapped Christopher is a very talented man. And quite efficient in his assignments," Wilhelm responded with venom in his voice.

"Who is it?" she asked.

"A Baron Karl von Gotlieb, I'm told."

"What!" she exclaimed in shock. "You can't possibly be serious!"

"Elise! You know this man?" a startled Wilhelm asked.

"I lived in his house in Paris for months," she said as Jesse's mouth dropped open.

"Jesse! Not like that! My friend, Madeleine, Madame Renaud's cousin, is his mistress. It sounds awful when I say it aloud, because I never thought of her like that. She was my friend. She nursed me back to health when I first arrived in Paris, and then after the baby died, she took me in and I've been at her home, or rather Karl's house, for the past few weeks. I just find this all quite hard to believe. He was so kind to me."

"I don't doubt it. He knew who you were all along, Elise. He probably hoped he could uncover some information about Christopher through you. I am surprised he let you slip through his fingers. He could have used you to apply pressure to Christopher."

"How?" she asked.

"He could have tortured you and told Christopher he would continue to hurt you unless he gave in. That's what

347

Christopher feared most. That's why he never told you any of this. And to think you were under Gotlieb's own roof! Damn! I still can't believe it. I wonder why he didn't take advantage of the situation?"

"When I left for the field hospital, I'd been depressed, and perhaps he never dreamed I would make such a quick decision. And again, when I received Jesse's letter, I left on less than twenty-four hours' notice. And Madeleine acted quite strangely the past few weeks. In fact she mentioned he was away on business, and I never did see him. I did come and go quite quickly, when I think about it now. That still doesn't explain her attitude. They had been so much in love when I first met them, and then something happened. But I don't have the slightest notion what it was," Elise said.

"Elise, think about it. Didn't she mention anything about her friends? Did she explain to you how she sent your letter to us?"

"She mentioned a courier and that her friends had certain connections. I guess I didn't pay much attention," she said as she tried to remember Madeleine's words.

"Her friends are part of an underground network of French, Swiss, and British spies. She discovered at some point while you were in Neuve-Chappelle just who Karl was and what his purpose in Paris was."

"Now I remember! All those inquiries at the onset of the war. He was constantly being scrutinized by the French authorities. Is this what that was about?"

"Yes. He's been under suspicion for a long time. But no one could prove anything. At any rate, Madeleine's friends sought her out, and it was through her efforts that we were able to free Liza, who is now back in the United States. It's very strange. We had so much information on Madeleine, but not once was it ever mentioned that she had a guest, much less that the visitor was you! How could we have missed something so important?" he said, dismayed at the enormous oversight.

"Obviously, most of this took place during the months I was at the field hospital. So naturally, there was no mention of a house guest in your reports; at that point, Madeleine didn't have one," Elise replied.

"That could very well be the case. Anyway, we haven't had news on the baron for weeks. He seems to have disappeared. He is not in Paris. We also have sworn to protect Madeleine. We aren't certain whether he discovered that she had turned against him. We were very cautious with all our transactions regarding her. She could find herself in grave danger if he does return and try to get revenge against her for what she has done," Wilhelm said.

"What made Madeleine decide to become involved in all this?" Elise asked him.

"Up until now, I just assumed it was because her friends needed her. They told her about the baron's true allegiance. She has a deep love for her country. A real patriot. But now that you've told me you were her guest, perhaps it was because she made the connection between you and Christopher. She would have realized that Liza was also an ally who needed her aid, and she would have known that Liza wasn't Christopher's mistress, as you had believed. Or maybe she simply wanted to help you. I'm not sure. I am more than a little thankful that she was in a position to do so much."

"Now I will worry about her. She was so good to me, and now I have brought her trouble." Elise said sadly.

"Don't you think such a thing!" Jesse said. "She found out that Karl was an enemy agent. That was what motivated her; there was more than one reason for her involvement. Don't take all this upon yourself."

"You're right. Madeleine is much too wise and wordly to make a hasty decision."

"Oh! There is something I've been keeping for you, Elise. Do you suppose this is the right moment, Wil?" Jesse asked.

"It could have waited, but this is as good a time as any," he replied. Jesse left the room and went down the hallway. She returned a moment later with a small black leather case. She handed it to Elise and said, "I've kept this here for you. After Christopher was captured, Wil arranged through friends to have all his personal belongings sent here. This was among the articles in the shipment."

Elise opened the box and sat in stunned surprise as she regarded the sparkling diamond bracelet that Christopher had given her. It was the one she had sold in Belgrade to the jeweler. She looked at Wilhelm, her blue eyes wide with confusion.

349

"How . . . how did you ever get this?" she said haltingly. "I sold it in Belgrade!"

"I know you did! That is undoubtedly the most expensive bracelet you will ever own! We tracked you to Belgade, and Christopher deduced that you had planned to sell some of your jewels when he discovered they were missing from your hotel room in Sarajevo. He scoured Belgrade until he found them. He bought the bracelet back for more than he originally paid for it. We were both rather surprised you didn't sell the blue diamonds your father had given you," Wilhelm said, blatantly trying to discover the answer to a question that had plagued him.

"The bracelet was more valuable. It gave me enough money to get to Paris and to live for months. I thought it would be easier to sell the other pieces later."

"Elise, you didn't have to sell the rest of your blue diamonds, did you?" Jesse inquired.

"No, I still have them. Madeleine hid them for me while I was at the field hospital." She gazed at the bracelet and wondered why Christopher had paid such an exorbitant price for it. After all, he must have been unbelievably angry with her at the time. She touched the brilliant stones with her fingertips and felt all the loneliness of the past months rush over her.

Jesse looked at Elise and knew what she was thinking.

"You do want to be with him, don't you, Elise?" she whispered.

"More than anything in the world. I don't think I can make it another day without him. And now, knowing that he is in a German prison . . . I'm so scared! What if they've hurt him? God! Jesse! I don't want anything to happen to him. Even if I can't be with him, I've got to know he is safe!"

"Don't worry. Wil has been planning Christopher's escape for days. He'll be back with all of us very soon. Won't he, Wil?"

"Of course he will. However, we won't be able to wait much longer. In fact we must act immediately."

"I have told Wil that although I want Christopher to be safe and here in Zurich for you, Elise, I don't relish the idea of Wil's going to Neustadt alone." Jesse said.

"I can't ask you to do this! It's too dangerous. Isn't

350

there some other way?" Elise asked as her eyes darted anxiously from Jesse to Wilhelm.

Elise watched her friend draw a determined breath.

"Wil," Jesse said, "I won't have you go to Germany without me. I have never before questioned a decision you made, but this time I draw the line." She jumped up from the sofa and stood tall before him.

"You're crazy! I'm not going to take you with me! It's out of the question."

"You're just making excuses," she said petulantly.

Wilhelm grabbed Jesse by the shoulders and peered intently into her eyes. "Don't be foolish, Jesse. We are not playacting now. We must be very candid about what is happening. Christopher is in great danger. I believe that I can rescue him and bring him safely home. But this is not a lark, and any small mistake could bring death to Christopher and to me.

"Elise, you must understand this, and you must make Jesse understand. War is not a game."

Jesse stared at the floor, trying to hide the tears in her eyes. "Oh, Wil," she stammered. "I'm so scared that something will happen to you . . ."

"Don't be afraid, my little Jesse. I would risk hell to come back to you. Never fear that I shall return." He pulled her close to him.

"Wilhelm is right, Jesse," Elise said after a moment. "It would be dangerous to everyone."

"It was a ridiculous idea," Jesse said softly. "I see that now. Isn't there some way we can help?" she asked.

"Just wait here for Christopher and me. That is the hardest thing to do, I know . . . In the meantime, Elise, why don't you get some rest?" he said.

"I am tired, but I would like something to eat before I retire." Elise was about to go when Jesse interrupted her.

"My God! My dinner! I forgot all about it!" she exclaimed as she flew from the room to the kitchen.

"I think I'll help Jesse," Elise said, laying her hand on Wilhelm's shoulder. "I trust you to do what is right for us all. But be very careful. Please?"

"Of course," he replied.

Elise entered the kitchen as Jesse was ladling cold consommé into three soup lugs. She looked up at Elise.

"I don't understand how I can even think of food at a

time like this, but I'm absolutely famished!" Jesse exclaimed.

Elise noted that Jesse had consumed most of the canapés herself. And she wondered at her strange behavior. Elise knew Jesse well enough to know that this was a sign of nervousness or that she was hiding something from Elise. She intended to find out. "Do you always think so much about food?"

"Not as much as I used to, believe it or not. At least not since Wil and I have been married."

"Married! When? I thought . . ."

"I know. That was also part of Christopher's plan. Everyone was to believe I was Wil's mistress. That way, supposedly, I would be safe from all those horrid enemy agents who were lurking around in the shadows," Jesse laughed.

At this point, Wilhelm walked into the room. "It was a good idea, Jesse. And it has served its purpose. Besides, you have loved every minute of playing the role of the fallen woman, haven't you, dear?"

"Isn't he just awful, Elise?" Jesse said as she took the soup into the dining area.

Elise looked perplexed.

"I guess it is difficult for you to understand all this at once, isn't it?" Wilhelm asked as he downed the last of the wine.

"At this point, I am angry and confused. Why did everyone—even Jesse—keep the truth from me for so long? I feel like all of you believe I'm some kind of child."

"Many times I felt the same. But Christopher had other ideas. All Jesse and I could do was to comply. We'll never know if his decision was the best or not. Who knows what might have happened if he had arranged things differently. If you had known the truth, perhaps you would have been in danger. I can see his point of view. I would do everything in my power to protect Jesse in a similar situation."

Wilhelm watched Jesse as she continued to prepare their meal, and Elise wondered if Christopher would ever gaze on her with so much love.

Thirty-nine

PREPARING for his departure Wilhelm had been gone most of the night.

As he came up the steps, he breathed heavily, not so much from exertion as from the weight of his impending task. Not much time remained, and he needed to finalize his plans. He flung the bundle he was carrying onto the sofa as Jesse and Elise looked up from their breakfast coffee.

"What's that parcel?" Jesse asked.

Wilhelm studied her concerned expression, wondering just how much he should tell the two women.

"This, dear heart, is my uniform I will be wearing. I also have one for Christopher."

"I see," Jesse replied, holding her trembling hands behind her back. "You shouldn't have any trouble disguising yourself as a German." Jesse's eyes scanned his face, and she realized her efforts to lighten the mood had been vain.

"It's all right Jess," he said as he held her in his arms. "I'll make it across the border without any problems. I've done it before. This time it won't be any different."

"But it is different," Elise's voice cracked with emotion, as she placed her coffee cup on the saucer and stared into space. "This time Christopher's life *and* your own lie in the balance. You've been such close friends . . . you . . . you will be careful?" She raised her eyes to meet Wilhelm's and he saw that she was fighting tears.

"Of course I will. Even though it will be difficult, I don't want to worry. I've done everything in my power

353

to prepare for this. I do not anticipate any problems, and I've been on escape missions far more complex than this. I'm not minimizing the danger, but it could be worse. The most important thing is for me to leave as soon as possible. Now, if you ladies will excuse me, I must go change."

Wilhelm picked up the bundle and disappeared down the hall, as Elise and Jesse sat in pregnant silence, each contemplating the fate of the man she loved.

Wilhelm unrolled the uniforms he had procured. Beneath the officer's uniform he would wear enlisted men's clothing. This was meant for Christopher. He could not take an extra pair of boots, he knew. They would just have to make do. Inside his own boot he placed a map of the border area around the Black Forest. There would be someone to assist them should the need arise. He strapped an extra knife to his calf and pulled on the black leather boot. He filled the pockets of the extra shirt with ammunition and then stuck a small revolver into a shoulder holster. He shoved his arms into the officer's jacket and fastened the shiny buttons. He buckled the black leather holster around his waist and rammed his loaded pistol into it. He placed a small square kit containing a file, lock pick, and skeleton key into his left inside jacket pocket. He adjusted the black leather strap that fit diagonally across his chest. Placing his officer's cap securely on his head, he picked up his traveling papers and passport. As he left the room, he glanced at his watch. There was no time to waste.

Wilhelm appeared quite imposing and authoritarian as he advanced toward Jesse and Elise.

"You look very much the German commandant, Wilhelm," Elise stammered, as she felt a dread of the enemy uniform pervade her spirit.

"Jesse, it's time. No long good-byes. We'll be on the noon train tomorrow. You meet us at the station. All right?" He hugged her tightly to his body and kissed her forehead.

"Hurry home, darling."

"I will. I promise."

"Jesse and I will have a homecoming dinner waiting for you both. Won't we, Jesse?" Elise said, trying to raise all their spirits.

"Yes, we will." Jesse replied, and looked back at Wilhelm.

"Go now, so that you can return even sooner."

Wilhelm walked over to Elise and kissed her cheek. "Don't worry. By tomorrow he'll be with you once again." He cast a loving glance at Jesse and rapidly descended the spiral stairs.

As his departing footsteps echoed through the still house, Elise held her head in her hands and wondered just how she and Jesse would survive the next twenty-four hours.

The train rested heavily upon the iron rails, exhaling great amounts of steam into the noonday air. The passengers and conductors scurried about the great locomotive and its trailing cars, tending business and bidding their families and friends adieu. Porters hustled about carrying luggage, and men in uniform were everywhere. Wilhelm bounded up the iron steps and entered the narrow passageway that led to his compartment. He slid the door closed behind him and locked it. He pulled the shade down over the window and fell heavily upon the seat. Taking off his cap, he ran the palm of his hand across his damp brow and felt the train jerk as it pulled out of the station. Wilhelm pondered the array of information that he had been given the previous night. Only two men guarded Christopher. Wilhelm prayed that the report was correct. He could handle two men, but if there were more, the consequences could be serious.

His concentration was broken by the knock at the door. Wilhelm unlocked it and greeted the conductor cheerily in perfect German. He presented his ticket, and the man informed him it was fifty miles to Rheinfelden, then only twelve miles or so to Basel. At Basel his papers would be checked when he boarded the train bound for Germany. Wilhelm thanked the man and then settled back to rest for the next hour.

According to his calculations, he would travel by train approximately twenty miles to Freiburg. There he would procure two horses, one for himself and one for Christopher. From that point, it was a mere ten miles or less to the farmhouse. Neustadt was nestled in the midst of the Black Forest, and no train ran directly to it.

The Germans were taking no chances with Christopher. There was no easy access to the farmhouse, and even the roads in the area were mere ruts in the ground. After he freed Christopher, they would ride back to Freiburg, board the train to the border at Basel, make their rail connections, and be back in Zurich by noon. He smiled to himself at the plan's simplicity. Yet he could not rid himself of an ominous sensation. He and Christopher had executed many missions that were far more intricate. Why should he have this feeling? He lifted the shade to let the June sun stream into his compartment.

Christopher licked his parched lips and peered through the slightly swollen lid of his left eye at the barren room about him. He tasted the dried blood at the corner of his mouth, and as his mind tore its way through the haze of unconsciousness he had dwelt in for the past day, he realized that they had moved him once again. He wondered where he was now. There seemed to be only this large room. No, there was a hallway to the right.

A massive stone fireplace filled the wall to the left, but there were no cooking utensils in sight. No firewood filled the opening of the hearth. A crudely made narrow table sat in the center of the room with two long benches. The two small windows on either side of the rough-hewn plank door were dirty and grease-smeared. There were no curtains to block the small amount of light that filtered through the tall, dense trees outside the structure. He looked down and realized there was no flooring at all, just hard packed dirt strewn with moldy straw.

Every muscle in his body ached, but it was the area around his rib cage and near his kidneys, where they had beaten him with rifle butts, that caused the searing pains that shot through him with each breath. His arms were locked over his head. He moved his neck to look up at the iron rails of the bed and discovered that he was handcuffed to the bed, which was bolted to the wall.

His legs were tied together with a rope that cut into his ankles. His clothes were filthy and smelled of sweat and blood. Not much remained of his shirt, it had been ripped and torn in so many places. His only solace was knowing that summer was almost here and he would no longer be a victim of frostbite. He wondered how he had made it through the long winter at all. He had been treated like an animal for months.

The only time he had bathed was when he was pushed into a stream by the perverted sergeant who taunted him incessantly, or when one of the guards complained about his foul stench and doused him with a pail of water. Such had been the case just yesterday. They had even seen fit to shave off the week-old stubble of beard he had acquired.

He wondered why they kept him alive. He possessed no valuable knowledge. The baron must have believed he knew more than he actually did. Christopher knew that the baron issued the directives, for he had heard the guards discussing their orders from him.

He was able to handle the physical abuse they heaped him, but the waiting, the endless days and nights of limbo, tortured him.

He felt tears trickle down his cheeks, and their saltiness stung the cut on his lip. When would all this end? He had tried to escape, but had been captured and beaten for the effort. He almost believed there was no hope for him. His strength, both physical and mental, had been taxed beyond endurance, and he found he could not formulate a new plan of escape. His brain was fuzzy with pain and exhaustion.

Perhaps tomorrow he would think of escape. But not today. Today he thought it sufficient that he should just exist. If he could just live one more day, perhaps . . .

Wilhelm had just seated himself on the train destined for Freiburg when the German commandant, wearing a condescending smile, approached him. He stopped and conversed with Wilhelm regarding his travel plans. Wilhelm tried to appear nonchalant as he explained that he was on furlow.

Presently they finished their conversation and the commandant went on his way. Wilhelm turned his eyes toward the window and sucked in a deep breath while watching the trees stream past his window. This leg of the journey was a short one, and he had little time before their arrival in Freiburg. He wondered if the German officer had been suspicious of him. There was no reason for him to have struck up a conversation with him; there were so many other soldiers on board. When he left the train, he must be cautious, for he could not risk being followed.

It was not long before the train slowed and he saw the white sign printed with large black letters: FREIBURG.

Wilhelm adjusted his cap and proceeded down the aisle to the door. He was surprised at the number of soldiers disembarking at this station. He glanced around and spied the face of the commandant.

"Damn!" he cursed under his breath. He could not go directly to the livery from here. A diversionary plan was needed. Wilhelm strolled down to the main street and casually window-shopped as he continued toward the white stucco, black-timbered Tudor hotel. He entered the small lobby, which was filled with people. He went straight to the desk and addressed the harried clerk in German. He signed the register and accepted the key from the gray-haired man. He ascended a dark staircase to the second floor, walked up to the door marked with a brass numeral four, and unlocked it. He quickly locked the door behind him, crossed to the window and pulled back the lace curtain from the window.

"He did follow me!" Wilhelm exclaimed aloud as he viewed the German commandant when the latter exited the hotel and stopped to light a cigarette. The man looked up and down the street and then turned to the left and vanished.

Wilhelm spun on his heel and unlocked the door. As quietly as possible, he slipped down the hall and through a back door to a set of stairs that led to an alley below. He raced through a maze of dirt back streets until he reached the livery stable.

A man not much younger than Wilhelm hammered forcefully on a red-hot horseshoe, and the muscles in his arms bulged with each movement. Sweat poured from his brow, and his skin glistened in the crimson light from the forge fire. He picked up the horseshoe with long black tongs and plunged it into a bucket full of water. The sizzling sound muffled Wilhelm's footfalls as he entered the livery. The man looked up through the silvery vapors of steam and smiled.

"Wilhelm!" he exclaimed. He threw out his enormous arms. "It's so good to see you, my friend."

"Shh! Not so loud," Wilhelm replied, checking the doorway once again.

"What's wrong? Do you think you were followed?"

"I'm not sure." Wilhelm breathed out deeply. "I wonder what it's like not to constantly be looking over my shoulder." He turned back to the man. "How are you, Ludwig?"

"Fine, but you aren't. You're in trouble again, aren't you?" he asked, continuing with his task.

"No, I'm not. But a friend of mine is, and both he and I need your help. I'd like two horses with the necessary gear. Have you any to spare?"

"Of course I do. You know I'd be most willing to help you in any way. You are not in a position to give me any of the details, are you, Wilhelm?"

"No, Ludwig, I'm afraid not. The less you know about any of this, the better for you. I'm doing you a disservice by coming here. It's not my intent to place you in any danger, and I'm afraid I've done that already. So, the less said, the better for all of us."

"I understand. I'll saddle the horses," Ludwig replied as he wiped his sweaty hands on his dirty cotton trousers.

Wilhelm went to the livery doors and peered out. There was no one in sight; he was reasonably sure that his presence had not been detected. He pulled out his pocket watch. He had not lost any time. He heard the horses whinny behind him, and he turned and took the reins from the outstretched hand of his friend. Ludwig smiled at him as he mounted the black steed.

"Godspeed, Wilhelm."

"I'll get the horses back to you late tonight, if all goes well."

"Don't worry about it. They are old friends and know their way back. Be careful. I hope to see you soon."

Wilhelm leaned down and grasped Ludwig's strong forearm in a friendly hold. "When all this is over we will sit down over steins of beer and reminisce about the days when we were children."

"That is a world long past for us now. But the war will not last forever, and there will be better days in the future. I do believe that."

"I think we must all place our hope in tomorrow. Now,

I've got to leave. Another friend needs my help. Good-bye, Ludwig. And many thanks," Wilhelm said.

Wilhelm ducked his head down low to avoid collision with the pine tree as he rode through the thickly forested area. The path that he followed was so overgrown that it was barely visible. His heart beat laboriously, and he thought this was the longest ten miles he had ever ridden. Through the thick foliage Wilhelm noted that the sun had begun to set, and he still had another three or four miles to cover. He pulled out his map with his right hand while his left hand held the reins and guided the horse. He used his teeth to open the map, and in the filtered rays of the setting sun he studied the terrain and calculated his approach.

Embedding the details in his mind, he folded the map against his chest and replaced it in his inside jacket pocket. Luckily, the sun would be setting just as he was to arrive at the farmhouse. The cover of nightfall would aid him tremendously in rescuing Christopher, he thought.

Wilhelm rode for another mile when he realized that something was greatly amiss. The rutted road had ended abruptly and he was lost in thick undergrowth. He knew he should have found cleared farmland just over a hill at approximately this point. Nowhere on his map was this forest indicated. He dismounted and, leading the horses, set out on foot over a deep layer of dried pine needles. He worked his way through the trees as best he could. Wilhelm surmised that he should continue in a northerly direction. Even though the terrain was not what he expected, he was banking on the hope that his instructions had at least provided him with the proper location of the structure itself.

"Damn it all!" he mumbled as he pressed on. "It's going to take much longer than I had anticipated. And we've got to make that train. . . ."

For over two hours he watched the stars, his only compass, and prayed that he was headed in the right direction. Presently he smelled smoke. It was not enough to cause him to fear a forest fire. As he rode on, the trees began to thin, and over their tops he spied a thin stream of smoke.

My God! he thought. A chimney! That must be the farmhouse! Jesus! Let's hope it's the right farmhouse.

Wilhelm tethered the horses far enough away from the house so that no one would hear him. He crept up to the last row of trees and peered at the structure that sat in a small clearing. He could see a light burning through the two tiny windows.

A large, muscular man was leaning against the door-jamb and smoking a pipe. He appeared quite content as he gazed at the moon and the starlit night. Wilhelm saw another man through the window. He was motioning with his arm as he walked about the room; now his back blocked the light from the interior.

Two guards, Wilhelm thought. He was about to circle around to the back when he heard footsteps off to his right. Quickly he squatted behind the tree trunk. The man on the porch waved and spoke to the third man, who approached him out of the shadows. The men spoke for a moment; then the third, carrying his armload of kindling, entered the house. Both men wore military boots, despite their lack of official German uniform.

Damn it all! Three guards, not two! Now how am I going to handle this? Wilhelm said to himself. "One by one . . . that's how," he whispered in reply.

Wilhelm made his way through the trees of the back of the house. He ran up to the stone wall and noted the back door. Slowly and with great care, he turned the knob. It was locked! He couldn't go in through the back. He must take care of the man on the front porch. Wilhelm stole around the corner of the house. He pulled the knife from his boot. As he came toward the front, he crouched in order to pass unnoticed under the windows.

Stealthily, he pounced upon his victim and plunged his knife into his back as he covered the man's mouth with his hand so that there would be no sounds. The muscles in the man's back constricted around the knife, and Wilhelm had to twist and turn the knife to pull it out. He sheathed it in his boot once more. Then he pulled the body off to the side. He crouched once again as he passed under the window, and then stood upright with his back against the wall of the farmhouse. He pulled out his revolver, then used his boot to tap at the door. The voices he had heard earlier from within fell silent. He could hear one man giving directions to the other. Then Wilhelm heard one of them come to the door and open it.

Wilhelm swung into the doorway, took quick aim, and shot the man between the eyes. He stumbled backward into the house and landed face first up on the floor.

The third man was quick to act and fired three shots at Wilhelm as he dove for the cover of the table. The third bullet met its mark, and Wilhelm clutched his shoulder. In those split seconds the German fired again, but his pistol had run out of ammunition. He flung his gun down and, noting that Wilhelm had been hit, ran across the room and pounced on him, trying to wrest the gun from his hands.

The German knocked the gun out of Wilhelm's hand, and it skidded across the floor underneath the bed where Christopher was tied.

The pain from his wounded shoulder blurred Wilhelm's vision. The German was on top of him now and was pounding Wilhelm's head against the floor. Though he struggled to free himself, Wilhelm was pinned to the ground, and he could not get a firm hold on the man's neck. Wilhelm gathered his strength to push with his powerful thighs and hips. He unbalanced his assailant and the man rolled onto the floor. Wilhelm rammed his knee into the guard's groin and battered his face with his fists. The man screamed and clutched his face. Wilhelm's hand flew to his boot as his fingers felt for his knife. He sank his weapon into the man's throat and watched as the body sank to the floor.

Wilhelm fell back on his knees, trembling. He rubbed his eyes in an effort to correct his blurred vision. He was dizzy and disoriented from the beating he had taken. Finally he focused on Christopher's motionless figure. He feared his friend was not alive, so still was the body.

"No! It can't be!" Wilhelm exclaimed as he rushed to him and felt for a pulse. It was very faint. He pulled back one of Christopher's eyelids and realized that he was unconscious. He drew out the small black kit and, using one of the narrow picks, opened the handcuffs. He peeled Christopher's filthy shirt from his body.

Laboriously, he unbuttoned his own uniform jacket, unbuckled his holster and let it fall. Favoring his wounded shoulder, he worked his arms out of the garment. Inspecting his wound, he saw that he had been grazed; most of the bleeding had already stopped.

Christopher groaned aloud. His eyelids opened, then closed again. Wilhelm lightly slapped Christopher's cheeks and managed to revive him. "Wake up, old man, wake up," he pleaded.

Christopher blinked away the fog that hampered his vision. He was so spent that all he wanted was to fade back into merciful oblivion. Only pain, guilt, and loneliness awaited him in the world of consciouness. Someone was shaking his shoulders.

"No! Please, leave me alone! Not again," he moaned. He could not focus properly, and he wondered how many there were to torment him this time. Would they beat him again, or flog his mind with questions? His eyes opened fully and he focused upon Wilhelm.

"Hallucinations . . . just . . . just a dream," he mumbled as he closed his eyes.

"No! No! Christopher. It's me—Wilhelm! Wake up. We don't have much time."

Christopher rolled his head on the bed, squinted his eyes, and then was thunderstruck at the reality of Wil's presence. His mouth flew open.

"Is it really you? Where did you . . . How . . . how did you get here?" Christopher asked in a raspy voice.

"Time enough for questions later. We've got to get out of here. Unfortunately, you are in worse shape than I am. God! Christopher! What have they done to you?" Wilhelm absorbed the sight of Christopher's beaten anatomy.

He had lost a great deal of weight. He was a mass of bruises and welts. His face was swollen about one eye; luckily, most of the cuts were almost healed. It was the familiar flash of his blue eyes that gave Wilhelm the feeling of relief. As Christopher fought for self-mastery, they became clear and intent once again.

Christopher eased himself onto his elbows as he noted Wilhelm's wound. "Are you all right, Wil? You've been shot."

"It's not bad. But you'll have to dress yourself. I have a German uniform for you to wear. Here," he said, handing him the shirt. "Put this on."

Christopher slowly placed his arms in the sleeves and, with numb fingers, buttoned the shirt.

"What about trousers?" he asked.

"Those are underneath the ones I am wearing."

Christopher smiled wanly while Wilhelm sat on the edge of the cot and took off both pair of trousers. He handed one to Christopher. They both dressed quickly. Wilhelm picked up his holster, and with Christopher's aid adjusted it across his chest.

"Very official looking, Wilhelm. What do we do about him?" he said, nodding at the body of the dead guard.

"Leave him. We'll need all our strength to get out of here and make that train at Freiburg."

"Right." Christopher stood slowly. He almost passed out, but managed to steady his wobbly legs and still the spinning within his brain.

Just then, Wilhelm heard a voice issuing orders in German. He raced to the window and squinted. It was the commandant from the train! And there were two other men with him. They had dismounted their horses and were headed straight for the farmhouse!

"What is it?" Christopher asked.

"Trouble . . . and lots of it! Come on, we'll have to go out the back door."

Wilhelm unlocked the door. Just as he was closing it behind them, the Germans entered the farmhouse through the front door. The last sight of them Wilhelm had as the two fled the house was of the reflection of the moonlight off the barrels of their bayoneted rifles.

Christopher and Wilhelm ran toward the trees in the distance; Wilhelm noted with alarm that Christopher was out of breath. They could never outrun the enemy. He had to think fast! Just beyond the first row of trees, Christopher stumbled and fell into a newly dug trench.

"What the hell?" Christopher cursed as he struggled to his feet once more.

"New latrines . . . they haven't been here long," Wilhelm said. "Get in, Christopher."

"What?"

"You heard me. We can't escape them. We'll have to hide. Get in. I'll cover you up."

Christopher lay prone in the hole as Wilhelm quickly filled it with dirt and the dried pine needles and leaves that blanketed the area. Then he smoothed the surface with his foot and hand until it appeared natural and un-disturbed.

A second long latrine hole had been started, but not completed. It was not as deep as the one in which Christopher lay. Wilhelm made two big piles of needles and leaves on either side of the trench. He stretched out and then pulled the debris over his body to cover himself. He held his breath and listened.

In a matter of seconds he heard footsteps and the commander whispering to his men.

The Germans were taking no chances. They went over the area step by step. Suddenly Wilhelm felt the same chill that had engulfed him while he had been on the train. One of the men was just above him.

He stared open-eyed at the canopy of leaves above his face.

Quite suddenly the tip of a silver bayonet pierced the foliage and nicked his cheek. He heard the men thrusting their bayonets through the thick cover of pine needles into the ground all about him. Every muscle in his body tensed. He held his breath. His eyelids refused to close. If he were to die, he would do so with his eyes open. The bayonet plunged into his shelter three more times. Once it fell between his legs near his ankles, once just past his ear. The third time it fell just short of his hand.

Wilhelm remained as still as death until he heard the Germans continue into the forest. They moved slowly, and he waited for what he surmised was close to thirty minutes before uncovering himself and rising from his premature coffin. For the first time, he thought of Christopher. What if he had escaped death and his friend had not!

He sat bolt upright at the precise moment that Christopher did. The sensation both men felt at that moment was eerie, as though they were rising from the dead.

They spoke not a word, but each covered the latrine holes, carefully leaving no trace of their presence. Wilhelm checked to see that they left no footprints. He motioned to Christopher, indicating the position of the horses. Together they made their way around the farmhouse and out into the woods where the horses were hidden.

As Christopher was about to mount his steed, Wilhelm remembered that the Germans also had ridden into the camp on horseback. He doubled back and found the Germans' horses. He untied their reins, then slapped their flanks, sending them off into the woods to the north. He hoped that the Germans would believe he and Christopher had stolen their horses, and would search for them to the north. Since they were headed west, that should keep the pursuers off their trail for a few hours. They would need that time. He brushed over his footprints with a tree branch and went to join Christopher.

When he reached his horse, Christopher was leaning against the neck of the brown steed, breathing deeply.

"Are you going to make it?" Welhelm inquired, frowning worriedly.

"Yes. I have to. I'll make it," he responded with determination. He took the reins in his hands. Then he steadied the horse and planted his worn shoe in the stirrup. He closed his eyes as he strained the underused muscles in his thighs and mounted the horse. Finally sitting astride, he breathed in relief. His shoulders slumped, and his head swam as he waited for Wilhelm.

"You lead the way, Wil."

As the land cleared and they gathered their bearings, their pace quickened and they rode through the forest.

Christopher's thoughts were only about freedom! He could breathe again. And he could hope again. He wasn't sure where he was. The past weeks were only a blur of faces and places of captivity. As he fastened his eyes on Wilhelm's back, he knew he would be wise to place himself in his friend's hands.

The ride that night was taxing, and Christopher was relieved when Wilhelm informed him that it was only ten miles to Freiburg. They were able to retrace the route with a fair amount of ease.

They approached the livery stable. Ludwig was nowhere in sight, but had left the doors unlatched. The two men dismounted and led the horses to the interior. They had just finished tethering the horses when Christopher noted the sausages and bread on a small corner table. His eyes flew to Wilhelm's face.

"You don't suppose we should be so bold as to indulge ourselves, do you?"

"Knowing Ludwig, I'd say that was left for us." Before

366

Wilhelm had the words out of his mouth, Christopher had ripped off a hunk of the bread and devoured it.

Wilhelm turned and cautiously checked the alleyway. There was little activity this late at night. They would be able to catch a few hours' sleep before the town awakened. He glanced over his shoulder to see Christopher approaching. He handed Wilhelm a hunk of the dark bread.

"What do you think?"

"Looks clear to me. We'll leave in a couple hours, and then we'll board immediately. I don't want to be standing around in that station. It's too risky."

"What time does the train leave?"

"Seven-thirty. So we are right on schedule."

Christopher nodded and wearily crossed to a pile of hay. He sank down into its fresh softness and promptly fell asleep. Wilhelm followed him and lay down with an arm propped underneath his head. Sleep would not come easily for him tonight. Although he was tired, he was the master of the mission and it was imperative they meet the morning train. Christopher's absence would not be reported until morning, because the Germans had no communications to the city. They would be forced to patrol the forests on foot or horseback at best. By that time they would be almost to Zurich and home free, he thought. Yes. He could rest, but not sleep. Not tonight.

Forty

CHRISTOPHER and Wilhelm filed onto the train alone with the other passengers and lost themselves in the confusion. Since the train had no compartments, the two men sat in the front row of the first passenger car. Christopher sat next to the grimy window. He found it difficult to clearly view the commotion outside the boarding area, but he was able to discern the blurred images of uniforms as they moved past his window.

When the inspection officer passed their row, Wilhelm held out their papers for the man to examine. When he inquired about their destination, Wilhelm said "Müllheim." Christopher watched solemnly as the man went about his duties, then got up and sat on the seat facing Wilhelm and stretched out his legs.

"One of us should keep an eye on the rear of this car, don't you think?"

Wilhelm's eyebrow raised. "Yes." He studied Christopher for a few moments longer. "I can see a glimmer of your former self."

Christopher shook his head. "If you knew how rotten I feel physically . . . but, God! To be free again! I don't want to take any chances. We've got to get across the border. We *have* to . . . that's all," he whispered.

Wilhelm nodded in assent and absentmindedly touched his shoulder. There was no pain or bleeding whatsoever. He had been lucky. His uniform had not been stained at all. He did worry over Christopher's appearance. His hair was quite long and dirty. Apparently the same thought had occurred to Christopher, for just then he ran his fingers through his hair and then tried to smoothe it.

Reaching inside his jacket, Wilhelm pulled out a folded cap and tossed it onto Christopher's lap.

"Here, this might help."

Christopher pulled the cap down over his forehead and crossed his arms over his aching chest so that he would appear nonchalant to those who passed by.

The train jerked as it began its forward motion. Slowly they pulled away from the station, and within minutes the rails beneath the massive black iron wheels clicked away the passing German countryside. Christopher had great difficulty distinguishing among the blurs of green color that seemed to smash against the greasy windows. The train tracks ran very close to the dense forest, and many times he could see that entire sections of tree limbs had been broken off by the trains.

Just as they were nearing Müllheim, Christopher recognized two of the three German officers approaching from the back of the passenger car. The slight twitch in Christopher's face told Wilhelm that trouble was near. Christopher looked at Wilhelm, who nodded his head toward the exit door at the front of the car, directly behind Christopher's back. Only when one of the men obviously recognized Christopher as a former "special prisoner" did the officer ease his hand toward his revolver. Christopher noted the action, and at that same moment Wilhelm bolted for the exit door. In a split second Christopher followed, as the three officers raced toward them, pistols unholstered and ready to fire. Wilhelm jumped off the slow-moving train and rolled down the embankment as Christopher followed. Wilhelm clutched his shoulder as a pain shot through his arm; then he straightened and raced toward a dense thicket of trees that stood beyond the grassy meadow in which they found themselves. He could hear the rapid thud of Christopher's feet behind him.

Panting and out of breath, they crouched behind a large rock.

"Do you see anyone?" Christopher asked.

"Not yet, but they surely had to follow us. Take this revolver," he said, pulling the extra gun from his shoulder holster. "And take my knife. You may need that too. Now hurry up. They can't be too far behind."

Christopher paused.

"Will you go?" Wilhelm demanded tersely.

"All right!" Christopher hated being the recipient of orders, but there was too much at stake. He darted into the trees. Wilhelm fired and the man in the center sank not twenty yards away. His fingers held the gun firmly as he watched the three Germans running toward Wilhelm's hiding place.

One man left the group and circled to his right through the trees. Wilhelm fired and the man in the center sank to his knees. With blood oozing through the left side of his shirt, he fell face down into the grass. The remaining soldiers fired at Wilhelm. The bullet ricocheted off the edge of the rock, just missing Wilhelm's face. He steadied his hand and fired off two shots at the man's forehead. The second bullet found its mark and the man sprawled backward.

Christopher saw the third soldier raise his revolver and aim at Wilhelm's back. Christopher took three steps away from the tree, steadied his hand, and fired quickly at the center of the man's back. The German dropped his gun as his hands flew around to his back, seemingly searching out the source of his pain. He stumbled a few paces before he died.

Wilhelm spun around on his knee in time to see his attacker collapse. As he looked up, he saw Christopher running toward him.

"Wil! Are you all right!"

"Yes. Let's get out of here."

They worked their way through the forest in a southwesterly direction, making slow but steady progress through the dense foliage.

"We aren't out of danger yet, Wilhelm."

"I know. We're much too close to Müllheim."

"When that train reaches town, this forest could be swarming with Germans."

"That is . . . if, and only if, those three had enough time to wire their suspicions ahead."

"I don't think they did. Judging from how quickly they were upon us, I'm inclined to believe we are pretty safe. For the time being, at least."

"We'll make our way to the Rhine and work our way down to the border near Basel. That's about twenty miles.

We can cross there at a place I know. But we have no time to waste." Wilhelm felt his pocket to reassure himself that he still possessed his map.

Jesse and Elise watched intently as the passengers disembarked the noon train. Their eyes scanned every face and each car.

"They aren't here, Jesse!" Even on this hot day, Elise felt the terror chill her bones.

"Of course they are! They have to be. Perhaps they're waiting for the crowd to thin."

"Yes, that must be what they are doing." Elise hoped Jesse was right.

They waited and searched. After another thirty minutes, Christopher and Wilhelm were still not to be seen.

"Jesse," Elise said, "go to the window and ask the stationmaster when the next train from Basel is expected."

Jesse nodded and scurried over to the white-haired man with the friendly face. They conversed a few moments, and Jesse came back to Elise and stared intensely into her face.

"Elise! Not until eight o'clock tonight!"

"Oh, God! How will we live through the hours, Jesse?" Elise felt a wave of depression suffocate her spirit.

"Let's go home. We can't just sit here until eight o'clock," Jesse reasoned.

"What can we do there? The waiting will still be just as horrid." Elise wrung her hands and thought she must control herself. She wanted to scream the anger and frustration from her body.

Jesse sensed Elise's torment.

"I don't know what we'll do," Jesse said. "Something constructive. They *are* coming back. Just keep telling yourself that. We'll do something special," Jesse said, grasping for a plausible project that would keep them both occupied. "Remember that homecoming dinner we promised to Wil?"

Elise looked wide-eyed at Jesse. "You can't be serious! This is no time to plan a party!"

"And what better time? I refuse to play a funeral dirge, Elise. Wilhelm's coming home to me. He must!" she cried as her small amount of courage began to wash away with her sudden tears.

Elise had been hurt and disappointed so many times by fate that she wondered if those short-lived moments of hope were worth the effort. She looked at Jesse once again and realized that her terrified friend was only searching for survival through the afternoon.

"I'm sorry, Jesse. You're right. They will be on the train tonight—and probably will be very pleased to have a special meal."

"Let's get a carriage, Elise. I can't stay here much longer."

"Yes, I agree." Elise mumbled as they made their way through the crowded main terminal and out onto the street. Elise asked the porter to hire a cab for them, and he acted promptly.

Within moments they were on their way toward the chalet. Elise nervously smoothed the skirt of her green cotton lawn dress while Jesse stared at the white gloves she carried. Elise felt the perspiration trickle down her back as the sun grew more intense, but she knew the heat she felt was more the result of nerves than of temperature. Her jaws were clenched so tightly that her head pounded. She closed her eyes, thinking it was the brilliance of the sunlight that caused the pain.

"It's no use," she sighed.

"What? Did you say something, Elise?"

"No. Nothing important."

The driver halted the horses and climbed down from his seat. He opened the door for the two women. Elise paid the man and followed Jesse up the hill in silence.

As they entered the living room, Elise untied the grosgrain ribbons of her summer hat and sank down onto the leather sofa. Jesse discarded her gloves and purse onto the dining table as she passed it on her way into the kitchen. Elise was faintly aware of Jesse's movements and heard her light footsteps as she descended the stairs.

Moments later Jesse returned and placed a large wooden bowl, full of apples from the storage cellar, in Elise's lap.

"What's this?" Elise looked quizzically at Jesse's troubled face.

"Here's a knife. Peel the apples and slice them thin.

372

They must be paper-thin for the strudel. I'll start the pastry." She turned away from Elise, who blinked and mechanically began to do as Jesse had instructed her. As she worked diligently, the monotonous ticking sound of the clock appeared to increase in volume until Elise thought she would scream. The seconds thundered in her head, and yet the hours had frozen.

Regardless of their involvement in their tasks, time was relentless. Its passage refused to ease their torment. Elise spread a thick coating of fresh butter over the tissue-thin pastry layer. Jesse folded the dough over itself until she once again had a perfect rectangle in front of her. She rolled the wooden pin over the pastry for the sixth time, until the muscles in her arms ached. She straightened and, with a flour-covered palm, pushed away a long blond lock from her sweaty forehead. Elise spread another coating of butter upon the strudel and then stood in passive silence as Jesse repeated the process.

They worked throughout the afternoon, never conversing, each lost in prayer. It was all Elise could do to keep her tears locked away. Her nerves were taxed to their limit. She realized she could not remain inside these walls much longer.

"Jesse . . ." she began slowly. "Let's walk to the train station tonight."

"That is a ridiculous idea. Although it will still be light at that time, it's miles to the terminal. Why don't you go outside on the balcony and get some fresh air, I just have the chickens to dress and we'll be finished."

"No, I'll help you first, and then we'll both take some fresh air before we change to leave for the train," Elise replied.

Jesse tied the legs of the stuffed fowl together and smeared the skins with seasonings.

Jesse was numbly immersed in her preparations and was not aware of Elise's distraction.

The isolation Elise experienced from time to time was all-encompassing, and she often felt she could not possibly function physically or mentally when bound within it. It would press upon her spirits to such a degree that the only thing she truly wanted was to pull the bed linens over her head and wish away the whole world.

Christopher and Wilhelm stayed in the Black Forest and avoided any contact with the residents of Müllheim. Evening fell early among the tall trees. Because they were not able to travel as fast as he had hoped, Christopher judged that after four hours they had covered only eight miles. The forest at night was virtually impenetrable. Both men were tired and weak from the ordeal. Finally, they came to a small grassy area, free from underbrush, where they could rest for the night. It had been a hot day, and Christopher welcomed the cool evening breeze as he stretched his weary body upon the warm earth. He placed his arms under his head and gazed at the black canopy of branches above him.

"I know it's too dark now to look at your map, but what are our chances of making that early train tomorrow, Wil?"

"None. The train leaves Basel at ten, and the next train is not until six in the evening. We could possibly make that one."

"As long as our strength holds up. I feel so drained and exhausted," Christopher said, closing his eyelids.

"The worst is behind us. I don't think we are being followed. We would have seen some signs by this time. It's only twelve miles to the border. And we should be able to cover that in six hours." Wilhelm turned his head toward Christopher, whose rhythmic breathing told him he was asleep.

"Good night," Wilhelm whispered, and for the first time in two nights, he allowed himself to rest.

Once again Jesse and Elise returned from the train station tense and frightened. This time it was Elise whose strength bolstered her friend. Jesse had sealed her emotions all day, and this second disappointment caused her to panic.

"My God, Elise! Do you think they are dead?" Jesse's voice cracked over the final word.

"No! More than ever, I believe they are both alive. The timing was not right for them to be on this train tonight. Jesse? You don't suppose we misunderstood Wilhelm, do you?"

"What are you saying?"

"I mean, what if . . . in all the confusion he really meant

374

to say that they would be on tomorrow's noon train? Maybe that's what went wrong!"

"Of course! We didn't get the facts straight, that's all."

"Yes. Or perhaps we did not hear him correctly. Either way, I'm convinced that's what happened. Just a lack of communication. It's the only answer that makes any sense," Elise stated, and added silently to herself, At least it's the only explanation I can accept and deal with for now.

She hugged Jesse and said good night, walked to her bedroom, and closed the door behind her.

The pink rays of early dawn wove through the tall trees of the Black Forest and hit the rising fog. The haze it created resembled a huge spiderweb studded with gleaming dewdrops. Christopher slowly opened his eyes. His stomach growled loudly at him, and he sat up and clutched at his abdomen.

"Wilhelm, wake up."

The blond man flinched and sat bolt upright, his hand on his revolver.

"Anything wrong?" he asked quietly as his eyes darted about the area.

"No. We're safe. But we need to leave. Where is your map?"

Wilhelm pulled the folded paper from his jacket and handed it to Christopher.

"I just want to see what the quickest route will be. Judging from this, I suppose we should just follow the river, since it leads directly into Basel."

"Right," Wilhelm replied. "My only concern is entering the city midday and perhaps not meeting our contact at the border."

"Where is he located?"

"Just north of the city, near the riverbank. He owns a house in the woods. He's a carpenter who will take us to the station in his delivery wagon."

"What is his name?" Christopher asked as he rose and brushed the pine needles from his trousers and shirt.

"Rolf Zwingli. He knows of the possibility of a visit from us."

"Good. If we had been able to remain on the train, none of this would have been necessary."

"Well, we can't do anything about it now," Wilhelm said as he stood and stretched his stiff arm out to his side. He picked up his cap and, flinging the holster and leather strap over his shoulder, followed Christopher out of the clearing.

Traveling west with the morning sun at their backs, they approached the Rhine. The forest thinned somewhat along the banks. Christopher scanned the grassy areas for wild berries.

"I think the first thing I'll do when we get back to civilization is go to the best restaurant I can find and gorge myself."

"Ah! Sweet self-indulgence!" Wilhelm replied, rubbing his empty abdomen.

"I haven't seen any nuts or mushrooms under the trees. I thought I would."

"Wishful thinking. It won't be long till we reach Basel, and Rolf will surely have something for us to eat."

As they walked, the pine needles and dry leaves crunched under their feet. The sun rose to its zenith, and as they passed out of the woods and the river widened, the heat of the sun intensified. Christopher unbuttoned the top two buttons of his shirt and rolled up his sleeves. He gazed at the churning river water. It was still crystal clear, but no longer shallow enough for him to see the water-smoothed stones below the surface as he had while deep in the forest.

Approximately two miles north of Basel, they changed direction. There were narrow dirt roads through the countryside that radiated from the main road that led to Basel. They followed the narrow side road until they reached a small stone country house that sat nestled in a cluster of tall trees off to the right. The exact size of the structure was obscured, for it was virtually encased in vines and surrounded by thick shrubs. The ornately carved front door testified to the owner's expertise in his craft. However, the door looked curiously out of place, as the remainder of the dwelling was in need of repair. There was no sign of life, and the windows were shut; for such a warm day, Christopher thought it odd. He felt a chill as they approached the door. Obviously, Wilhelm sensed something was amiss, for he quickly ran to the side of the house, slammed his back against the wall, and drew out his revolver. With his pistol he motioned to Christopher to continue on. Christopher nodded. He went to the door and knocked twice. No answer came. He cautiously lifted the latch and then pushed the door, letting it swing open as he quickly stepped to the side.

"Rolf! Rolf Zwingli!" he called. Again there was no response. He edged his leg around the portal, then sprang into the house. Wilhelm was immediately at his back.

"There's no one here," Christopher said as his eyes scoured the small room for the owner.

Wilhelm noted the cheese and milk on the table and said, "Perhaps he's in the back. Looks like he was halfway through lunch." He nodded toward the table.

"I see what you mean. You check the other rooms while I look in the yard."

Christopher circled the house to the rear, but found nothing of any consequence. He was coming through the front door when he heard Wilhelm call from the bedroom.

"Christopher! I'm in here!"

He raced to the opened door and stopped on the balls of his feet.

"What . . . Oh, God!" he exclaimed under his breath as Wilhelm stood up and moved away from the body.

"He's been strangled," Wilhelm informed him.

"How long ago?" Christopher asked.

"Not long. The body is still warm."

"I wonder if the Germans killed him or if it was something else. It seems to me that they would have taken him prisoner."

"He hasn't been beaten, either. Whoever it was either got the information he sought or . . ." Wilhelm's voice trailed.

"Or . . . the murderer had no questions to ask. Maybe they have known our whereabouts all along. And now they plan to watch us flounder into their trap," Christopher responded.

"Maybe they believe we will panic now."

"Exactly. So now all we have to do is not panic." Christopher assumed the composure that had set him apart from less competent agents for the past few years. Wilhelm thought he could almost hear his friend's analytical mind click through a roster of optional courses of action.

"Actually, Wilhelm, do we need Rolf's presence to cross the border, or merely his knowledge and directions?"

"The latter. Ah! I see what you are saying." Wilhelm smiled.

"If Rolf was the man you seem to think he was, then somewhere in the house he has hidden what information we'll need to return to Switzerland." Christopher looked past Wilhelm into the main room. "I just hope the Germans didn't find it first."

"Rolf was an exacting man and prided himself on his ingenuity and creativity, if that could help you any."

"Let's look around. And we haven't much time to spare. Surely, they must be watching us. Unless—"

"Unless," Wilhelm broke in, "they did not discover anything to connect us to Rolf and left empty-handed. Perhaps now they believe that this was merely another blind alley."

"Let's hope so."

Wilhelm rose from his crouched position and began to search the bedroom while Christopher investigated the main room. After fifteen minutes they had meticulously explored every piece of furnishing in the house. Wilhelm tapped walls and mantels for secret panels. Christopher inspected the floorboards, all in vain. Frustrated, he collapsed into a wooden rocker over which the owner had flung a small patchwork quilt. He threw his head back against the hand-rubbed wood and ran his fingers through his black hair as his eyes focused upon the carved panels of the front door. He immediately bolted out of the chair, raced to the door, and frantically ran his hands over the wood.

"Wilhelm! Here, I think I've found it!" he exclaimed as his fingers probed the thumb-sized indenture in the bottom panel. He tapped it with his knuckles. A hollow sound met his ears.

"You're right, Christopher! How does it come off? Can you pry it free?" Wilhelm watched anxiously as Christopher pulled the panel off and a small cache of yellowed papers tumbled out. Christopher unfolded them and quickly scanned their contents.

"It's all here, Wilhelm. Maps, directions, names of various German officials. . . . Look at this. A list of the ones who can be bribed. And this note from Rolf states we can find his German marks hidden inside that quilt over there." Christopher pointed toward the rocker, and Wilhelm quickly grabbed the quilt and felt the various sunburst patterns for evidence of the secret treasure. Within seconds his fingers sensed an odd stiffness in the yellow scalloped border. He popped open the seam and withdrew one paper mark after another.

"I've got it, Christopher! Anything else?"

"I'd like to think we had the time to give our friend a proper burial. But I don't think it would be wise."

"Agreed. Do you think the Germans found those papers and then put them back for our benefit?" Wilhelm asked.

"No. I think we are safe. We shouldn't let our guard down, though. There could still be a trap when we do reach the border."

"Which is how far from here?"

"Only a couple miles. We'll be there in less than an hour. I'll let you read this note on our way, and you can do all the talking. After all, we'll be on foot. Then we board the train in Basel."

Christopher handed the map and note to Wilhelm as they entered the yard once again, reverently closing the door to Rolf Zwingli's home behind them. They walked with a quick pace, following the back roads Rolf had indicated. Wilhelm straightened his cap and smoothed the lapels of his jacket as they approached the two guards at the border. A small enclosed structure stood off to the right, and there were two wooden barricades across the road.

Rolf had instructed them to enter Basel at this point, for the guards were easily bribed and this was the most obscure of the three border areas. The woods and river were highly patrolled, and if one had the ill luck to be caught, no questions were ever asked. One met death easily under such circumstances. Wilhelm took a deep breath and formulated his course of action.

Christopher assumed the role of the intimidated enlisted man who had no mind of his own. Wilhelm walked a few paces ahead, tall and erect. The guards were obviously not bright; physically, both were pudgy, middle-aged, and quite slovenly in their unpressed uniforms.

Wilhelm did not return their smiles, and he barked at them regarding their shortcomings. Both guards were taken aback. Wilhelm saw no reason to resort to a bribe. He flashed passports in their faces and rattled off something in German. Christopher watched as one man waddled into the interior of the enclosure. He made a telephone call and returned to Wilhelm, meekly mumbling something as he cast an apologetic eye at Wilhelm.

Wilhelm never faltered. Impatiently, he slapped his thigh with his palm.

In minutes a black open sedan rolled up from the south and halted at the gate. Wilhelm spouted what Christopher assumed were orders to the guards, one of whom opened the car door for him. Wilhelm entered the sedan and sat ramrod straight. Christopher followed him and shut the door.

The sedan shot forward as a dusty fog rose under the tires and curled across the road in their wake. Christopher and Wilhelm rode in stony silence to the train station.

When they arrived, the nervous driver slammed the brakes with a greater pressure than was his intent, jolting all three of them forward. While Christopher alighted from the sedan, Wilhelm berated the young man in harsh tones, then spun on his heel and led the way up the steps to the passageway inside the train.

Wilhelm slid open the doors to their compartment, and after Christopher was inside, he closed the doors and locked them. Wilhelm slumped onto the upholstered bench seat opposite his friend.

"Christ, Wilhelm! What the hell did you say to them back there? Here I was expecting the subtle bribe, and then you start bellowing at those idiots at the border . . ."

"Suffice it to say that the guards were merely trying to right a wrong."

"Cover their asses, you mean. What did you convince them that they had done?"

"Merely that we were to have suitable escort from Müllheim and the automobile had broken down and I as commander refused to walk any farther. I simply told them if they could requisition a car immediately, I would personally write a formal recommendation for promotion for them both. If not, the contents of the letter would contain certain facts that would most assuredly lead to demotions." Wilhelm smiled to himself as he pulled off his cap and flipped it across to the seat next to Christopher.

"A genius! That's what you are."

"As soon as we are out of Basel, I'll breathe easier. We can still be yanked off this train, you know. And we have half an hour before departure. Plenty—"

"Oh, God!" Christopher saw the German lieutenant just outside the window. He was instructing a group of four enlisted men. He pointed in different directions, and the four men dispersed, leaving the officer standing alone.

Christopher jerked his head away from the window and slammed his back against the seat.

"They know we are here. They are looking for two men in German uniform. Think fast. We need a disguise and have no change of clothes." Christopher's thoughts swarmed across his brain. His face brightened, and he bolted for the door.

"Where are you going?"

"I'm famished. We are going to the dining car," Christopher laughed.

"You must be crazy. They aren't serving yet. Not all the passengers have boarded. No one will be there," Wilhelm replied exasperatedly.

"Wilhelm! I'm surprised at you! There are always a few, uh, shall we say 'customers' in the dining car before departure."

Wilhelm saw the look in Christopher's eye and knew exactly what Christopher was planning. He followed him to the first-class dining car.

They entered the car quietly. Christopher looked at Wilhelm and winked.

"What luck, old man, three of them to choose from!" Wilhelm said. He strolled up to the expensively dressed woman in her midthirties and flashed her a friendly smile. The heavily rouged woman let her eyes travel the expanse of his muscular frame, and after pausing an inordinate length of time on his pelvic area, she smiled back at him. She nodded, but spoke not a word as she picked up her reticule. Wilhelm extended his hand; she placed her gloved hand in his and rose from her table. She led the way in the direction opposite the one from which Wilhelm had entered the car.

Christopher shook his head, cleared his throat, and looked out the window. One of the officers was running alongside the train. He was most certain to enter this car soon, Christopher thought.

He spun around and accidentally bumped the arm of the blond woman, who was sipping a glass of water. She wore a tailored suit of summer linen in a light blue. Her jacket was unbuttoned, and she wore nothing underneath her cream eyelet blouse. She placed her hand on her waist and opened the jacket so that he could see her dark nipple and full breast through the fabric. He smiled at her and immediately helped her up. He took her hand and led her toward his compartment. She babbled in French, needing no response to her conversation. He hustled her inside, and she lowered the shade and seated herself. Christopher leaned his ear against the door. He could hear scuffling in the passageway. First he heard a knock; then the compartment doors next to his slid open and then shut. They were coming closer.

He turned around and smiled at the woman. He sat and kissed her, and in another moment had divested her of her jacket and had unbuttoned the eyelet blouse, exposing her breasts to the warm air.

There was a knock at the door. The woman frowned. Christopher merely smiled. The knocking continued, and finally the doors were unlocked and flung open. The young German soldier was so shocked by the scene that met his eyes that he stood immobile and could only blink at them. Christopher rose and opened his mouth as if to say something. The young soldier mechanically shot out his arm, grasped the door, and slammed it shut.

The blond woman could not take her eyes from him, and when he turned to regard her once more, he knew exactly what she wanted from him. He reached in his pocket and withdrew some of the German money, and handed her the bills.

She stared at them incredulously. Then she looked up at him with great disappointment, shrugged her shoulders, and began to dress herself once more. She shoved the notes into her reticule and exited, still baffled, as Christopher held the door for her. After she left, he surveyed the scene outside the window and then checked the companionway.

The soldiers were conversing with their lieutenant. Each man shook his head. Although displeased with the negative reports he received, the lieutenant obviously sought no other action. He turned and marched off, with the four soldiers taking up the rear.

Presently, Wilhelm returned.

"Excellent idea of yours, old man," he chuckled. Christopher eyed him skeptically as the train jerked forward. The engine built momentum, and soon Basel was but a maze of swirled colors that passed outside the window.

Elise was lost in her depression. Although she could see Jesse's lips move, her ears heard nothing. For two days they had met every train from the west. The pain of Christopher's absence plunged her into a world of emptiness. It was that familiar sphere she had grown to know well in the past months. Though she was not a stranger to the hurtful surroundings, the agony was tenfold this time. Christopher was all that remained for her, and she was losing the last vestiges of hope that had kept her heart open. It was not until Jesse physically shook her by the shoulders that she made any effort to acknowledge her friend's presence.

"Elise! Are you listening to me!" Jesse scolded her.

"I didn't hear what you said," Elise replied, and blinked her eyes, hoping to clear away the haze of desolation that filled her soul.

"Are you all right? You're as white as a sheet!" Jesse's eyes were wide with concern as she stared at the vacant expression on Elise's face.

"No. I'm not . . ." Elise mumbled.

"Oh, Elise. Please don't give up now. You are stronger than I am. I've never been able to cope with things like this. I need you to help *me!* Christopher wasn't alone, you know. God! Elise! Wilhelm was, I mean, *is* with him. We've got to keep believing . . . don't we, Elise?" Jesse's determination crumbled and she gave in to the flood of tears that had threatened her all afternoon.

Elise numbly watched Jesse collapse onto the sofa beside her. The sound of her friend's sobs crept into her brain. She placed an arm around Jesse's shoulders and felt her trembling with the same fear Elise was experiencing. From the well of her inner being came the strength that had seen her through so many crises. Elise's back straightened as Jesse leaned against her shoulder.

"Jesse, listen to me. Crying won't help anything. It's not time for tears. But we have to be realistic at the same time. You know that, don't you?"

"Yes . . . yes," Jesse said uncertainly.

"If something has happened to them, it may take quite some time before we receive word. Until then, we have to hope. You said that yourself. Have faith in your own words, Jesse."

Jesse wiped away her tears with her fingertips, sat upright, and looked into Elise's eyes.

"Do you believe they are still alive, Elise?"

"Yes, I do," she replied firmly. "Wilhelm will come back to you, Jesse. I know it."

"But I see such fear in your eyes, Elise. What is it? You aren't lying, just to make me feel better, are you?"

"No, Jesse. My fears are greater. I do believe Christopher is alive. He is capable of finding his way back, no matter what the obstacles."

"Then what is it?"

"I'm afraid he won't come back to *me*." Elise felt every long buried insecurity about herself rise again.

Jesse looked at her and realized all too well that Elise's doubts were well founded. A wide chasm of noncommunication existed between Christopher and Elise, and even she wondered if they would ever be able to build the bridge necessary to rejoin their lives.

Elise looked over at the clock. It was almost an hour and a half before the last train was due in from Basel.

"I don't think I can stand going to that station this time, Jesse. Perhaps you should go alone."

"But you just said we should believe."

"I know—and I do. I want you to go alone. That way, when Wilhelm gets off the train you'll have a few private moments together, at least."

"What are you going to do in the meantime?" Jesse asked as Elise stood up, squared her shoulders, and stared out the opened French doors.

"I am going to do something constructive. Just look around here, Jesse. This does not look like a homecoming.

There are no flowers. And the table needs to be set . . ."

"Just where are you going to get flowers now? The markets are all closed." Jesse watched as a wistful look came into Elise's eyes.

"Come here, Jesse." Elise led the way to the balcony. She stood at the railing and pointed at the meadow beyond the chalet, near the foothills. "Back there are some wild flowers that should add some color to the table. We want everything to be perfect, don't we?"

"Yes . . . perfect. . . ." Jesse's thoughts were with Wilhelm.

"You get dressed and go to the station. I know they'll return tonight." She wanted to reassure Jesse even though she had difficulty believing her own words. Jesse smiled back at Elise with renewed confidence and squeezed Elise's hand.

"If I want to look my best, I'd better get started, hadn't I?"

"Yes. You really should, Jesse," Elise laughed lightly.

"Goodness! Do I look so awful? Are my eyes puffy? Are they red?" Jesse pressed her hands to her face.

"Jesse! You always look beautiful. Honestly, you can be so silly at times. And this is not the time to worry about swollen eyes. Wilhelm won't care. He'll be thrilled to see you."

Jesse tittered softly. "He will, won't he?"

"Yes." Elise sighed as Jesse turned and flitted away to her bedroom.

Elise's shoulders slumped as soon as Jesse was out of sight. She trudged across the room to the kitchen and assembled the dinnerware and linens she hoped they would need. She numbly went about her task, her mind a blank.

Not much later, Jesse entered the room attired in a fitted summer suit of Alice blue linen. Beneath the short jacket, she wore a sheer white blouse with a double-ruffled neckline. Her kid shoes matched the blue linen, and as she pulled on her lace gloves, she spoke.

"I'm leaving now." Jesse looked expectantly at Elise.

"I know. I heard the carriage outside."

"I called Johann, my neighbor. Sometimes he takes me to town . . ." Her voice fell.

"Go, Jesse. Now," Elise ordered.

385

"We'll be back soon." Jesse's eyes never left Elise's face.

"Everything will be ready when the three of you return."

"Yes," Jesse replied, almost whispering. Then she pivoted and raced down the stairs and out of sight.

Elise watched her disappear. She stood immobile for quite some time. Her eyes traveled the expanse of the room as they filled with tears. She crossed to the hearth and picked up a large flat wicker basket, then descended the stairs to the outdoors.

Wilhelm opened the window and leaned out as the train pulled into the Zurich terminal. An unusually large crowd had gathered to meet the inbound locomotive. People were waving and shouting to the passengers, many of whom were half falling out their compartments, so anxious were they to be reunited with their loved ones. Wilhelm's eyes darted from face to face, but he could not find Jesse.

"Do you see her?" Christopher asked as he leaned over Wilhelm's shoulders to peer out the window.

"No, there are too many people. . . ."

The iron wheels sparked as the train braked and then stood still. Expelling a voluminous cloud of steam, the locomotive awaited the emptying of its interior. The passengers streamed out and onto the landing in an excited rush.

Christopher turned around and unlocked the compartment door.

"Let's go. We'll never find Jesse by standing here." Christopher entered the vacant companionway as Wilhelm snatched up his cap from the seat and followed him.

Jesse pushed her way through the crowd of passengers, greeters, and porters, almost stumbling over a misplaced suitcase. Her eyes were glued to the train, and she was oblivious of those around her. Her heart pounded thunderously; she thought she could not withstand the pain should Wilhelm fail to appear. Most of the passenger cars were empty now, and she saw no trace of him. She quickened her pace. There were only two cars remaining before she would reach the engine.

She stopped abruptly when Christopher stepped off the

train. Her eyes widened as his locked on her face. There was question and disappointment in his expression, and she knew he was hoping to see Elise. Just as he opened his mouth to speak, Wilhelm appeared at the top of the steps.

Jesse's face sparkled with happiness and relief as she flew into Wilhelm's outstretched arms. He held her so tightly that for a moment she could not speak.

"I had almost given up hope! I was afraid that something had happened," Jesse said as Wilhelm released her.

"Sweetheart, you should have known I would come back to you. I always do."

"I know. And if it hadn't been for Elise, I doubt I could have endured the long hours of waiting. Every time we came here and you weren't on the train . . ."

Christopher grabbed Jesse's arm and stared intently into her face.

"What did you say about Elise?" he asked as a lump caught in his throat.

Jesse looked to Wilhelm, and then back to Christopher.

"You mean Wil didn't tell you?"

"Tell me what?"

"That she is here, Christopher. She's at the chalet now. I don't think she believes that you want to see her, Christopher."

"That's crazy! But I don't understand—how did she get to Zurich? I thought she was in Paris. How long has she been here? Is she all right? Why is she here?"

"Slow down, old man," Wilhelm laughed. "There's plenty of time for explanations." He squeezed Jesse's waist. "Let's get out of here and get you home, Mrs. Schmidt."

Wilhelm began to raise his arm and place the cap upon his head when a pain shot through his shoulder.

"Oh, God!" He grimaced and let the arm dangle.

"What is it? Wil? What's wrong with your arm?"

"Just a hazard of the job. I'll be fine. Jesse, take that worried look off your face. It's just a graze. I had completely forgotten about it. I guess I just moved too quickly."

"We'll get a doctor right away—"

"Jesse!" he exclaimed as he put his good arm around

387

her and led her out of the terminal. "I love you!" He laughed as she smiled back at him.

Christopher followed them out into the street. A legion of thoughts and emotions tumbled across one another at the knowledge of Elise's presence in Zurich.

As Elise strolled through the meadow, a cool evening breeze rustled the leaves overhead and ran itself over the tall green grass, softly manipulating each blade. She thought the change of color from green to silver-blue was much like the shimmering waves of the gulf as they crawled onto the sand at Mobile Bay. She bent down, plucked a fragile pink wild flower and held it to her nose, then placed it in the basket. Walking toward the clusters of tall pines, she filled her basket with nature's floral assortment.

Elise lost track of direction and time as she ambled through the foliage and gathered various sizes of cones and squirrel-eaten nutshells. She raised her eyes to the vivid blue sky above. The setting sun smeared crimson across the airy canvas, creating a marbled effect.

As the sun continued its descent, the trees formed a screen that filtered the light. Elise pushed deeper into the forested area, harvesting wild daisies. Soon she found herself in an open clearing, where a pool of clear water glistened in the diffused light. It was fed by a shallow brook that cut its course through the hills from the mountains.

Mesmerized by the play of sunbeams upon the ripples, Elise advanced to the water's edge. The wind gusted and lifted her hair off her shoulders. With her laden basket still in hand, she picked up the sheer blue voile fabric of her skirt. She kicked off her shoes and stood barefooted on the cool ground. She stepped onto a water-smoothed rock, and, balancing upon her left foot, immersed the right foot in the icy mountain water. Goose bumps rose on her flesh; she shivered. She involuntarily jerked her toes out of the water, and lost her footing. Her outstretched arms failed to stop her fall, and she landed face-first in the frigid water. Her basket spun away in the wake her body had created. The pond was not deep, and she pushed herself up with her hands. She rolled over in the ripples and sat upright, facing the almost spent sun.

The streams of light fell upon her wet face and blinded

her to his presence. Christopher stood tall with his arms crossed over his chest. Her collection of wild flowers whirled about her thoroughly drenched body. Her wet hair was like a veil of black silk as it fell down her back. The droplets on her eyelashes and face caught the rays of light and twinkled like diamonds. She was still not aware of him, he knew.

"Elise," he called to her.

She stiffened and tilted her head to one side, avoiding the direct light. It was then that she saw him. She blinked her eyelids, testing the reality of the apparition. The mirage did not vanish. It spoke to her once again.

"Elise . . . you aren't hurt, are you?" he asked as he dropped his arms to his side and strode over to her.

Her gaze was fastened upon his intent face. Slowly she stood, and his breath caught deep within his chest. She had never appeared more beautiful or womanly to him. The voile of her summer dress was matted against her bare skin. The water had rendered the gauzy fabric transparent. Her sensuality invaded his being, and his hands trembled under the impact.

Elise looked down at herself, blushed slightly, and raised her head. She made love to him with her velvet blue eyes, her senses reeling with pleasure of his presence.

Christopher moved close to her and placed his foot upon the slick rock. He extended his hand to her. Their fingertips touched cautiously, and Elise tingled at his touch. Her heart raced as the echoes of his voice rolled over her body and massaged it. She lifted one slender leg and was about to leave the water when her wet hand slipped from his. As he jerked forward to catch her arm, he fell off the rock and tumbled into the water beside her. He began to laugh as they both stood knee deep in the icy pool. His black hair dripped tiny rivulets onto his bruised face.

She lifted her hand and explored the cuts on his cheeks. His face was much thinner, and it pained her to behold the scars of his torment.

He stood hypnotized by her eyes, and his nerves thrilled at her feather-light touch. Even in the cold water, her hands were warm. He kissed the palm of her hand and placed his arms about her waist. He pressed her body into his own. Her lips skimmed his ear, and he felt as if he would melt in her arms.

"Oh, Christopher, I want to heal all your hurts. I love you so. I want to hold you forever and cradle your body within mine," she whispered in his ear.

"I love you, Elise. It seems like a thousand years since I held you. I feel so warm in your arms." He kissed her throat and moved his lips over her cheeks, her eyelids; finally they returned to her lips. He devoured her mouth and held her tight.

"I adore you, Elise. I don't know quite how to put it into words, but we are very fortunate. Most people just exist all their lives and never know the kind of love we have."

She buried her lips in his throat and let her hands roam the expanse of his back.

"I never want to be away from you, Christopher. Loving you is like coming home. I've found all that I'll ever want or need here with you."

"Just love me, Elise. Always love me. Promise me that."

"I will, forever and ever," she said.

The sun extinguished its light. Elise's shoulders shook with cold shivers. Christopher put his arm around her waist and they helped each other onto dry land. As they walked back through the trees, Elise put her arm around Christopher. Peace and contentment settled over their hearts. No longer would they be separated. Together they would combine their strengths and grow within the sphere of their special love.

Bestselling Historical Novels from
Lois Swann

THE MISTS OF MANITTOO   57380 ... $2.95

When her father betrothed her to a Puritan minister
she despised, Elizabeth Dowland ran into the forest
to escape her fate. Overcome by fear and exhaustion,
she almost gave herself up to the relentless pursuers
sent by her fiancé. But suddenly Wakwa, the tall Indian prince, stood before her. Together, they would
boldly defy Puritan and Indian opposition—and turn
a forbidden passion into a resplendent and ennobling
love!

"A magnificent tapestry, a glowing, gleaming pano-
rama of life in early America . . . written in a lovely,
lucid style that frequently touches on the poetic. . . .
An experience few will forget." Tom E. Huff (Jen-
nifer Wilde)

TORN COVENANTS   56523 ... $2.95

Surrounded by a nation at war, the love of Elizabeth
and her Indian prince is tested against all odds: Beth
must accept sharing Wakwa with his Indian first wife;
the minister whom Beth once refused in marriage
seeks revenge. But the bond between them is deep,
and Beth and Wakwa are determined to somehow
hold fast to their love.

"Moving. . . . Rich and subtle. . . . Pulsates with a
poignancy that summons tears . . "

Publishers Weekly

AV⊙N Paperbacks

PASTORA

JOANNA BARNES

AVON Paperback   56184 • $3.50

Available wherever paperbacks are sold, or directly from the
publisher. Include 50¢ per copy for postage and handling; allow
6-8 weeks for delivery. Avon Books, Mail Order Dept., 224 West
57th St., N.Y., N.Y. 10019.

Pastora 12-81

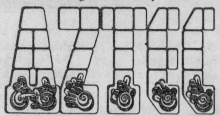